topping
from below

topping
from below
laura reese

HODDER

First published in Great Britain in 1995 by Hodder & Stoughton
A division of Hodder Headline PLC

This edition published in 2012 by Hodder & Stoughton
An Hachette UK Company

1

A CIP catalogue record for this title is available from
the British Library.

ISBN 978 1 444 76576 2

Typeset in Plantin Light by Palimpsest Book Production Limited,
Falkirk, Stirlingshire

Printed and bound by Clays Ltd, St Ives plc

Hodder & Stoughton policy is to use papers that are natural,
renewable and recyclable products and made from wood grown
in sustainable forests. The logging and manufacturing processes
are expected to conform to the environmental regulations of the
country of origin.

Hodder & Stoughton Ltd
338 Euston Road
London NW1 3BH

www.hodder.co.uk

*Because nurture makes a difference, this is
for my parents, Howard and Jane; and all
my brothers and sisters,
Howie, Ben, Mary, and Janet.*

ACKNOWLEDGMENTS

My thanks to the following people for their help, encouragement, and frequent forbearance: my editor, Charles Spicer, who worked closely with me on the final manuscript, turning my best efforts into something even better; my agent, Barbara Lowenstein, who accepted my work, flaws and all, then forced me to walk through heuristic doors, making wonderful things happen; her assistant, Nancy Yost, who gave me advice and suggestions on the original manuscript, steering me in the right direction; Mary Mackey, who believed in my writing and influenced me in ways she is unaware; Mary Koornpin-Williams, the Yolo County Coroner, and J. L., who both tirelessly answered my many questions; C. Michael Curtis, who gave me hope and advice when I needed them the most; and my very special friends Gail McGovern, Charles Smith, and, in memoriam, Bob Stovall – catalysts each, in their own unique way, whose unstinting support conferred faith in times of doubt.

It is his extremity that I seem to have lived through. True, he had made that last stride, he had stepped over the edge, while I had been permitted to draw back my hesitating foot. And perhaps in this is the whole difference; perhaps all the wisdom, and all truth, and all sincerity, are just compressed into that inappreciable moment of time in which we step over the threshold of the invisible.

– Joseph Conrad,
Heart of Darkness

And this also . . . has been one of the dark places of the earth.

– Joseph Conrad,
Heart of Darkness

Before I Begin . . .

This is not an easy story to tell. I dedicate it, in memoriam, to my sister, who, only ten months ago, was found in her Davis apartment in the spring of last year, on a lazy day of squawking scrub jays and warm sunshine and tender, budding trees in first bloom. It was a glorious day, the kind of spring day that holds out a promise of pure innocence and new beginnings, the kind of day in which the sunlight, like a thousand popping flashbulbs, brightens the town; and on that day, while spring was making itself known, inside the apartment, with duct tape across her mouth and wound around her bare ankles and wrists, lay my dear sister, brutalized and tortured, her body – unnoticed for two weeks – rotting in the heat of a room in which the thermostat had been set at seventy-two. This is her story, and the story of Michael M., a music professor at the university, still living in the city of Davis, whom I believe to be her murderer.

My name is Nora Tibbs, and my sister, Frances, was twenty-four when she died. We grew up in Davis, a small college town just fifteen miles west of Sacramento. Death is not new to me. I had a younger brother, Billy, who died in a hiking accident when he was only twelve. It was a difficult time for us all, Billy's absence so painful, his memory still present in every room of the house. My mother and father took Franny and moved to Montana, desperate for a change. I was ten years older than my sister, and I stayed behind, moved to Sacramento, where I'd just begun a new job as a journalist. But within a year, my parents had been killed in a car crash and Franny, only fourteen, came to Sacramento to live with me.

She and I were not at all similar. Like my father, I'm athletic, tall, assertive when the occasion demands it. Franny was soft and plump and pale, her skin as delicate as a baby's, and there was a lived-in, rumpled look about her: her clothes always big and loose, her long brown hair a jumbled mass of curls. Inordinately shy, she was easy to overlook. Her voice would dwindle away if people listened too intently to what she said, and at parties – those few I could drag her to – she tended to fade into the background, chameleonlike, merging into the furniture. If someone attempted to draw her out a little, to press too close to her, she would take on a brittle, furtive quality, as if she'd spent her entire life nervously dreading the moment some teacher would single her out and call on her for an answer she didn't know: an uneasiness would appear in her eyes, she would look away, and then duck her head; she'd fold her arms across her chest, hugging herself, scrunching inward.

Franny was a hemodialysis nurse in Sacramento, which meant she spent most of her working days with people who had kidney problems, hooking them up to machines that filtered the wastes from their blood to keep them alive. It was not by chance that Franny became a hemodialysis nurse. Six months before his accident, our brother got an infection, glomerulonephritis, that left him with renal failure. He had to have dialysis, and was on a waiting list for a kidney transplant. After Billy died, Franny was determined to become a dialysis nurse. I could understand her motivation – she and Billy, only a year apart, had been very close – but she seemed obsessive in her determination, as if she were driven by guilt more so than love.

But the work seemed to suit her. She was – and this surprised me – competent. All shyness and uncertainty disappeared. She bustled around the office, passing out medications, hooking up a patient, taking another's blood pressure, consoling yet a third. She was in *control,* and if you knew Franny you would know that that's not a word people normally applied to her. But, after hours, like an Arran turtle, she'd retreat into her shell as soon as she felt things were about to overwhelm her.

By this time, she'd moved back to Davis. Sacramento frightened her – she never got used to it, the crowded freeways (which, really, aren't so very hectic compared with the traffic in Los Angeles or San Francisco), the reports of violence in the newspapers, the shootings, an occasional stabbing, a murder among gang members. Franny preferred to commute to work. Davis was quiet, hardly any crime except for a stolen bicycle or two. She liked the Farmers' Market in Central Park on Saturday mornings; she liked riding her bike along the Arboretum on campus and feeding the ducks at Putah Creek, which is where she met Michael M.

My sister had a Macintosh computer, and on it she kept an incomplete diary which she called 'Franny's File.' When I read it I discovered that I didn't know her at all. She wrote about her passions and yearnings and sorrows. She wrote about M., about the things he did to her, her humiliation and despair. His blackness, so subtle and insinuating, oozes out between her words; yet there was a naive, unsophisticated tone to her diary entries. She seemed unable to read between her own lines, unable to see how M.'s mind was diseased. Like a metastasizing cancer, he maneuvered himself into her life and then set about to destroy her.

The police have not yet apprehended her killer, and although they read her diary, they still let M. go. Lack of physical evidence, they said; he had no motive, nothing to tie him to the crime. The only thing the diary proves, one detective told me, not too tactfully, is that 'your sister had bad judgment in men.' They have reached an impasse, but I intend to get them the evidence they need. Just because M. hasn't been charged doesn't mean he isn't guilty of the crime. If you read her diary entries, if you read what he did to her, you would understand his culpability and why I can't – why I won't – let him go free.

I used to think men were basically good, born in a state of grace that only unfortunate surroundings could change. I used to think that evil – ingrained, innate evil – did not exist. But now I'm not so sure. I am a journalist, a science writer for *The*

Sacramento Bee, and what I have learned, over the years, is this: in the nature vs. nurture controversy, nature is coming out the winner. More and more, brain researchers are discovering that genetics plays a far greater role in human behavior than was previously thought. Scientists are even speculating that violence is genetic, and that men, the male of our species, carry a gene that urges them to act aggressively, to pursue war rather than peace. Quite simply, men behave and act differently than women, and these differences, some scientists believe, are rooted in biology. At this point – just so there's no misunderstanding – I should tell you I like men, and always have. Male-bashing is not my metier, and my aim is not to malign the entire gender for my own ulterior motive. I've had good relationships with men.

But if it's true that men are genetically predisposed to violence and aggression, is evilness, also, a matter of biology? Does evil exist as an aberration – a genetic error perhaps, heredity gone awry? Does it exist so profoundly in some men that it is inherent to their being? I do not know the answers. What I do know is that some men, by nature or nurture, are evil, and this story, Franny's story, is about the suffering one man has caused.

The evil are not dressed in black, nor do they cast a penumbra of malignant illumination; they are indistinguishable from the people next door. M. still teaches at UCD, the University of California in Davis. I see him in the company of other women, young and old; he says something, they smile and laugh. He looks harmless, he looks incapable of murder. Yet when I read my sister's diary, I come away with the impression that he is a vile man, a man without conscience or soul. He destroyed Franny, and he did it deliberately, methodically, and without remorse. She had been bound and tortured, yet the Yolo County coroner could not determine the cause of her death. To this day, it remains a mystery.

I begin this story not knowing how it will end. I'll try to remain faithful to her diary, recording the events as she entered them. But there are big gaps, specifics she left out, details that will entrap her killer. For this, I will have to go to Michael M. I've seen him, of course, observed the man from afar. And before I finish my story I will meet him and know him quite well.

After my sister's death, I returned to Davis. Having saved some money in the bank, I was able to take a leave of absence from the newspaper, although occasionally I still freelance an article for them. I'm renting a house on the south side of town, on Torrey Street, in a subdivision known as Willowbank. M. also lives here, in Willowbank, in the older part where the homes are large and spread out, where the trees canopy the streets and offer shaded relief in our hot, dry summers, where there are no sidewalks and where the fences, those few that do exist, are wooden and low and friendly, built for aesthetic reasons rather than for protection. I moved here to be closer to M., to see him firsthand.

I read and reread Franny's diary. It starts out hopeful, with a subtle sense of irony I didn't know she possessed:

I feel I'm about to take a journey. Something wonderful and exciting is happening to me. I feel re-created, and it's all due to Michael. He sees things in me no one has seen before; he makes me feel things I've never felt before. I am changing, this much I know. I want, desperately, to step out of my tired, safe life, and confront my dreams, unleash my passions. I want to turn myself over to Michael, give him full rein. Last night, he promised to take me places I've never been before. I said to him, 'The Galápagos? Hawaii?' but I knew he wasn't referring to geography. Oh, Michael! I've never dared to dream of someone like you. I thought you would be beyond my reach, but now I find your fingertips touching mine.

Such an innocent beginning, full of naked hope and joy. Her journey was not to be so innocent. It began as a dream, Franny's descriptions of her earlier sexual encounters with M. tinged with a romanticism that has an almost dreamy, storybook quaintness, and it ended a nightmare, a slow descent into the black heart of an evil, sadistic man, a one-way journey into hell.

And so I dedicate this story to Franny, in her memory. I write it because I must. I feel I have no choice: she has become my obsession. Like Conrad's Marlow, like Coleridge's Ancient Mariner, I am compelled to tell this story. Writers, I am learning, do not choose their obsessions; their obsessions choose them. I tell Franny's story because she is unable; I tell her story to reveal the truth and expose M., to do what the police were incapable of doing. We live in a society where people are held accountable for their actions, and M. must take responsibility for his. He took Franny on a dark journey from which she never returned. I shall take the same journey, but I've lived longer than my sister, and even if I'm not wiser than she, I am more experienced. The journey will have a different ending this time, I'm positive – for M. and for me.

PART ONE

Franny

I

On the last day of October, while riding her bicycle across the UCD campus, Frances Tibbs realized that she, for the very first time, was in love.

Or rather, she thought she was in love. She hadn't said it out loud yet, hadn't tested the words on her tongue, but it felt like love: everything seemed fresh and new and exciting.

Then a man stepped in front of Franny and scared the living daylights out of her. She slammed on the brakes of her bicycle and swerved, barely missing him. He was wearing a nylon stocking, one half of a panty hose, over his head. In his right hand he carried a huge gun, or perhaps it was a rifle or a shotgun. Franny did not know the difference, but, staring at it, she could see that it didn't look quite real. It was smaller than she imagined a rifle would be, and it seemed to be made of plastic.

Plastic.

A toy gun. It was Halloween, she remembered. The man – she could now see he was only a college student – leered, pleased with the effect he had scared out of her, and plodded on by, toting his rifle.

Feeling foolish, she got back on her bicycle and pedaled down the path along the north fork of Putah Creek. The water here, in the dammed-up northern end of the creek, was low and stagnant and a sickly green, giving off a stale, rotten smell that she was glad to leave behind. Once she got past the uppermost end of the creek, the path was pleasant, lined with trees and dense dark green vegetation, the air scented with the earthy, woody smells of a forest. She was riding out here in the hopes of running into her new friend, Michael. She couldn't explain, exactly, why she was drawn to him. She only knew that she thought of him constantly, and that her life, somehow, seemed a little brighter, more full of possibilities, since she'd met him. In a way, he reminded her of her father, a patient man whom she had known would protect her. It had been such a long time since her mother and father died and, even though she had a sister, she felt alone in the world. But Michael had an empathic way of looking at her, as if he could take in her whole history in a glance. It was a nice feeling.

She hit a downward slope and picked up speed. Bicycling was part of her new regimen to lose weight. She had several favorite routes: through the solar homes in west Davis; the Howard Reese bike path along Russell Boulevard out to Cactus Corners; and the route she was on today, the one she took most frequently, the path following Putah Creek on the southern edge of the university campus. The path was narrow and wound through the campus's Arboretum, a woodsy enclave of shrubs and trees, redwoods and conifers and eucalyptus. Franny loved it here; there were picnic tables hidden beneath the trees, wood chips on the ground, fallen leaves decomposing in the dirt, and the smell in the air was an ancient one, reminding her of earlier times. It was the dank, humus-heavy smell of places long forgotten, of ancient civilizations buried beneath layers of detritus and decay.

She rode across an arched wooden bridge to get to an open, grassy mound on the other side of the creek. Here, the water expanded into a wide, murky pool, a good spot for duck watching. At this time of day, late afternoon, the campus was quiet, and she had the area much to herself. She got off her bike and sat on the grass and daydreamed, hoping Michael would pass by. The air was cool – not as cold as it would be in several weeks, when the tule fog settled and crept into your bones – and the sky a sort of dingy dishwater color, flat and gray. Lightly, the breeze rippled the surface of the water and rustled through the treetops. Reddish-brown leaves flitted about, carried by the sudden gusts of wind.

Franny wrapped her arms around her knees to keep warm. The lawn had been mown recently, and it had that fresh, moist green smell of newly cut grass. Years before, her father had brought her and Billy, her brother, here when they were children. Nora, her older sister, had been a teenager then, and couldn't be persuaded to accompany them. But Franny and Billy loved the Arboretum, and sometimes they'd just sit, trancelike, eyes closed, and absorb the sounds around them. They would listen as their father, an environmental scientist, told them of man's connection with nature. There's an evolutionary bond, he'd explained to them more than once, developed over millions of years that tie people, inextricably, to their surroundings, the earth, the sun, the sky. And here, outside, with little noise but the wind breezing through the trees, the sporadic squawks of the ducks, the squishy sound of rubber every now and then as a bicyclist rode by – here she felt somehow calm, rooted. Whether it was the pull of nature that calmed her, or the protective pull of her father's sweet memory, she did not know. By now, the two had become inseparable.

Two college students, a boy and girl, arms linked, walked across the bridge and stopped halfway, looking at the water beneath them. Wistfully, Franny watched them, their dreamy smiles and untroubled faces. They were obviously in love, and this made her smile. She could hear them talking, but couldn't make out the words; sounds of their laughter lifted up into the treetops.

Farther on, toward the campus, she looked for Michael. She'd met him here three weeks ago. She had brought a bag of stale bread and was feeding it to the ducks when someone behind her had said, 'You're not a student.'

Startled, she'd turned around. It was the first time she'd seen Michael. He was tall and olive-skinned, with dark hair graying at the temples. She'd guessed, by the lines in his face, that he was in his late forties. There was a knowing look about him, almost cynical, as if he'd seen and done it all. Both his hands were in his pants pockets, and he stared at her without blinking, his face inscrutable. Franny lowered her head. When she looked up again he was still watching her, his eyes cold and unfeeling, she'd thought, but then a slow smile emerged from his lips. She was uncomfortable being the cynosure of all his attention, and felt as though he was sizing her up for something, coming to some sort of decision about her.

'No,' she had said, 'I'm not a student,' and she blushed, as if she had been caught doing something wrong, even though she knew she hadn't. She turned away. She tore off a piece of bread and threw it to a duck. There were five of them in front of her, all glossy green-headed mallards, and they scrambled for the bread. She threw the rest of it and reached in her bag for more. The man hadn't moved and she felt him watching her, making her feel self-conscious.

'You don't look like a student,' he finally said, and Franny wondered why she didn't. She hadn't been out of school herself that long.

'I've seen you out here, lying on the grass, feeding the ducks. You always come around this time, always by yourself.'

Franny gave him a quick, oblique glance, but didn't say anything. It was a bit unnerving, discovering someone had been watching her the past few weeks. She glanced at him again. All his features were sharp and definite: a square jaw, a straight, precise nose, a lean but sturdy body. He wasn't what you would call a handsome man, she thought, but he was impressive. Too impressive. She wished there was something amorphous about him, something to make him a little less intimidating, a thickening waistline, maybe, or sagging jowls.

'May I?' he said, and without waiting for an answer he lifted her arm by the wrist, took the slice of bread from her hand. Franny, taken aback by the intimacy of his gesture, said nothing. She watched as he fed the ducks with her bread.

He said, 'I've begun looking out here around this time of day, expecting to find you here. When you're not, I feel as though my day is somehow incomplete, that something is missing.' He turned his face slightly and looked at her, a sparkle of amusement in his eyes. 'It seems I've come to rely on you, like my morning cup of coffee.'

Franny had smiled at this; she'd never been compared to caffeine before. Then he'd introduced himself, and for three weeks now she'd been meeting him here. He didn't always come. Sometimes he'd miss several days, and she'd get an anxious knot in her stomach, wondering if she'd ever see him again. But then he'd appear and just start talking, without any explanation for his absence. He had a smooth, relaxed manner that made it easy to talk to him although, in truth, she let him do most of the talking. He didn't seem to mind, though, as some people did, and he didn't put her on the spot, trying to get her to open up. He seemed to know, intuitively, that she would come around when she was ready. She was grateful for this – most people gave up on her before she felt at ease around them – and it wasn't long before she found herself riding to Putah Creek not for the exercise but for the express purpose of meeting him, always being disappointed when he didn't show.

Michael was a professor in the music department; he was sophisticated and intelligent, not the type whom she thought would ever be interested in her. Not that she had a type. She'd dated a few men, but nothing ever seemed to work out. Just last month, Nora dragged her to an office party at the *Bee*, and she'd met a man there. He was a reporter, like Nora, and had blond hair and such a frank, wholesome look about him, such a boyish innocence, that she trusted him instinctively. He seemed sincere, but the next morning – after she'd slept with him – he sheepishly told her he'd had too much to drink the night before. Franny could blame no one but herself. She'd never acted so impulsively before, sleeping with a man she'd just met. She'd been too eager, too desperate, hoping the sex – which wasn't very good – would lead to further intimacy. It didn't. He took her out to breakfast at the Food for Thought Café on K Street, but his discomfort was evident all during the meal. He was too polite, too solicitous: he'd made a mistake and was trying graciously to extricate himself. She could see the misgivings in his eyes, the pity, the uneasiness. If she hadn't felt so bad herself, she would've felt sorry for him. After that, she waited several days for him to call, and when he didn't she phoned him. It was awkward and humiliating. Maybe they could be friends, he said kindly. She'd hung up, declining his well-intentioned but spurious offer.

Michael would never behave like that, she thought now. Michael. He was twice her age, forty-eight, she'd learned – only six years younger than her father would have been – but she felt comfortable around him as she never had with anyone else. Sometimes, at home, she'd fantasize about Michael, putting him in her life, making him her boyfriend. She had no idea what he thought of her, or if he even thought of her at all. Even though he was friendly and appeared to genuinely like her, he seemed out of reach.

She heard rustling footsteps in the grass behind her and she smiled, knowing it was Michael.

'Hello, Franny.'

She turned around at the sound of his voice. He always seemed to appear out of nowhere, catching her while she was daydreaming. She smiled at his appearance. There was a sensuality about him that she didn't understand, something powerful, pulling her along like an undertow, yet something remote – in his dark, cool eyes, in the controlled tone of his voice – that made her want to reach out and draw him near, although she knew she never would.

He sat down on the grass beside her, then leaned back on his elbows, unaware of the chill in the air. He was dressed casually, brown slacks, a jacket with the sleeves pushed up to his elbows, but there was always something formal about him no matter what he wore. He seemed so well put together, always comfortable with himself, while Franny, feeling frumpy and cold, was a shapeless bundle of bulky clothes: oversized coat, black jeans, cable-knit sweater, wool scarf and mittens.

Silently, he watched the young couple on the bridge. They turned and walked, hand in hand, off into the distance.

'Young love,' he said, with just a trace of sarcasm. Franny looked at him, waiting for something more. But he said nothing.

'I think it's kind of sweet,' she said finally, softly.

Michael looked at her, considering. His gaze was penetrating, as if he could read her mind. Discomfited, she bowed her head. A sudden gust of wind tossed her hair. Then, ever so lightly, she felt him brush her cheek with the back of his hand – the first time he'd touched her.

'You're right, Franny,' he said. 'It can be sweet.' He added, 'It's never been like that for you, has it?'

Was she that transparent? she wondered, and she felt her cheeks redden, embarrassed that he knew, that at the age of twenty-four, she'd never before been in love, had never even come close to being in love. She started to say no, that love had never been sweet for her, but just then a woman, a petite lady with wavy black hair, smiled and called out to Michael as she walked by, flirting with him. Obviously, they were friends. She was very pretty, with arched plucked eyebrows and painted lips, and wore a snug, wine-colored linen suit that only a small woman could attractively wear.

Franny played with the grass. She pulled a weed out by its root. 'She's pretty,' she finally said. Then added, 'I think she likes you.'

Michael gave her a half smile and she blushed, knowing he had guessed she was jealous.

'It doesn't matter,' he said. 'I'm not interested in her. Would you like to know the kind of woman who does interest me?'

'Oh,' Franny said. 'Well . . .' And her voice trailed off. She didn't know if she wanted to hear him talk about other women.

Michael laughed, deep and kind. He said, 'Let's go to my house. I think it's time I made love to you.'

Franny blinked. In her fantasies, it didn't happen like this. Never once did he say, 'I think it's time I made love to you.' She was expecting something different, something a little more romantic.

When she didn't reply, he stood up. 'Come on,' he said. 'Take a chance.'

Franny felt she had never done anything really daring in her life, nothing adventuresome, never taken a chance is what it came down to. Nora, her older sister, was always taking chances. She went to Nicaragua during all the fighting down there. She went backpacking by herself. And for one vacation, she went white-water rafting down the Urubamba River in Peru. Franny could not imagine herself trekking around the world, putting her life at risk for sheer amusement. Perhaps, she thought, it was her time to take a chance, and so she looked up at him and said the only thing she could think of: 'Okay.'

Michael put Franny's bike in the trunk of his car and they drove out to his home in Willowbank in south Davis. All the homes were large and old, most of them well kept, with ivy-covered entrances and sweeping lawns and mature trees everywhere. Michael's home was set far back from the road, a sprawling ranch-style house, the front shrouded in wisteria. Inside, the house looked newly remodeled: polished solid oak hardwood floors, skylights in the kitchen and foyer, ceramic-tiled counters, a floor-to-ceiling wall of windows in the living room. It looked precise yet comfortable, Franny thought, much as Michael looked.

Nervously, she walked around his house. Most of the colors were warm and rich, earthy brown tones. It should have put her at ease, but it didn't. She felt strangely out of place, awkward, like a duck in a dress shop: she didn't belong here.

Michael watched her as she surveyed his house. One by one, he took off her coat, then scarf, then mittens. Franny had the feeling he was peeling her away, layer by layer. He fixed her a drink without asking if she wanted one, and handed it to her, saying, 'Drink this. I think you need to relax a little.'

Normally, she didn't drink liquor – she didn't like the taste – but, like a child, she did as she was told. He led her to the couch and they sat down. He talked to her as he had on campus, soothingly, quietly, caressing her with his words. She thought of her father's words, also soothing, and finally she relaxed, not sure if it was Michael's voice that calmed her, her father's silent words, or the liquor she was drinking. And finally, when Michael did kiss her, it was tender, not boozy and sloppy like the kisses of the last man she'd been with, the reporter from the *Bee*. Gentle and warm and utterly erotic, it was all she had hoped for.

He took her into his bedroom and hung his jacket over a chair. The high, arched-ceiling room was spacious and had a light, airy feel to it, the walls papered in pale shades of blue and gray, the furniture blond and modern and comfortable, with a king-sized, four-poster bed. The drapes were open, and through the bay window she could see his backyard, in the middle of which was a huge black dog lumbering across the lawn.

Michael watched Franny, who was standing stiffly by the doorway. 'Don't look so grim,' he said. 'You're going to like this.'

'Sorry,' Franny said, and she essayed a brief smile. She turned off the light. It wasn't yet dark outside, and everything in the room, even with the light off, was visible. She wondered how she could get in the bed, under the covers, without him seeing her. She wasn't fat, exactly – she was what some people called pleasingly plump. Rubenesque. Whatever you called it, she didn't want to expose it. Michael was broad-shouldered and of average build. No fat on him. She eyed the bed again, trying to figure out how she could negotiate it, biting her lower lip.

Michael came up and put his arms around her. 'Franny, you look positively morbid. Tell me what's the matter.'

'I haven't had much experience at this sort of thing,' she said.

He smiled at her. 'I realize that.'

He lifted her sweater over her head, and she felt she ought to apologize. 'I guess I need to lose a few pounds,' she said.

Michael laughed softly. He kissed her on the neck, then whispered, 'I'm going to give you what you want, Franny,' and she wondered what that was. What *did* she want, anyway?

And then he was taking off the rest of her clothes, rubbing her ample body with his hands, kneading it like bread dough, soft and warm. This embarrassed her at first – he wouldn't let her hide under the covers – but then she got lost in the feel of his capable hands. He seemed, truly, not to mind her plumpness at all. He turned her this way and that, rearranged her limbs as if she were a mannequin, sucking and pulling on her heavy breasts, inserting fingers in every orifice, probing, massaging, until she felt a deep stirring inside her, like the pull to nature she'd felt earlier at Putah Creek, only this was stronger, more urgent, and he forced her to open up to him, dipped his tongue into the very core of her, fed on her until she surrendered, for the very first time, to the primeval stirrings inside her, a wondrous release that was both awesome and grand. And at some point, on some inexpressible level, she came to understand what it was that she really wanted: a parent, a boyfriend; a father, a lover.

2

Sue Deever, an adult-onset diabetic, was sitting in a mauve upholstered recliner next to a dialysis machine, waiting for Franny to hook her up. She was a pudgy woman, in her early fifties, and missing both legs. Franny had worked at the University Dialysis Clinic for almost two years now, and she had witnessed the slow decline of Mrs Deever. She was the mother of one of Franny's childhood friends, and, until Franny began working at the clinic, she hadn't seen her for years. She had been shocked at her appearance. Her right leg had been amputated four years ago, and her left shortly after Franny joined the clinic. Her vision was blurry, her nerves damaged, her liver malfunctioning from many years of alcohol consumption. And she had kidney failure, requiring regular dialysis. She lived in a nursing home in Davis and came to the clinic three times a week for treatment. She was a sweet woman and it saddened Franny to see her in this condition.

The clinic was in Sacramento, in a medical complex on the corner of Alhambra and Stockton. The waiting room of the clinic looked much like any other waiting room in a doctor's office, a row of low chairs, a fan of magazines on the end tables, but to get beyond the waiting room, patients had to be buzzed through a locked door. A narrow hall and another door led to the anteroom – several chairs, a sink, a standing scale flush with the floor to accommodate wheelchairs – which finally opened into the main treatment room, a large and pleasant room, painted in a soft, soothing pastel. Two nurses' stations were in the center of the linoleum-floored room, and eighteen large recliners – similar to comfortable La-Z-Boys – lined the four walls, a dialysis unit next to each chair. It was early morning, just after seven, and the staff was busy. Each recliner was occupied, with people already connected to their artificial kidneys or waiting to be connected, most of the patients old and worn out, their bodies damaged beyond natural repair. Most of the patient work was done by the technicians, but today they were short a tech and Franny had to take three patients, one of whom was Mrs Deever.

Mrs Deever had already been weighed in, had her temperature taken and her arm scrubbed with betadine, a form of iodine to kill bacteria. Franny finished taking her blood pressure, then listened to her lungs and heart, periodically making notes on the flow sheet attached to her clipboard. She looked up, over Mrs Deever's chair. Blackout screens shaded a row of windows on the far wall. Outside, a fierce northern wind cleared the sky of clouds. When Franny had driven to work this morning, the wind shouldering her car as she'd crossed the Yolo Causeway, she had seen, rising in the distance, the snow-covered mountaintops of the Sierra Nevada. Maybe she could get Michael to take her there this weekend, she thought.

'Cold today, isn't it?' Mrs Deever said, watching Franny. 'I'll bet you're daydreaming about that new boyfriend of yours.'

Franny looked down at her and smiled. Mrs Deever had shoulder-length, straw-colored hair, which she curled, even though it was thinning and brittle on the ends. And she was wearing makeup, she always did: bright red lipstick, face powder to cover her blotched skin, carefully applied mascara and eye shadow. She was a woman trying to hold herself together, even if her body wouldn't cooperate. Her face, although puffy-cheeked and heavy with a double chin, was open and friendly. Franny had gotten close to her over the last two years, and she saw her not only here, but also visited her regularly at the convalescent hospital. Mrs Deever, with her own two children out of state, was almost motherly in her concern over Franny. She was sympathetic and listened whenever Franny had a problem, doling out advice whether she asked for it or not.

Franny knew their close relationship was based on loneliness, but it didn't matter. Mrs Deever's presence reminded her of how much she missed her own mother; and Mrs Deever, she knew, missed her children.

'Well, yes,' Franny said, smiling. 'I was thinking of him.' Over her blue scrubs she was wearing a plastic apron. She also was covered with a clear face shield and rubber gloves, standard procedure for the techs and RNs during the hook-up process to protect themselves from blood splatters. Franny accessed the graft, a permanent shunt that tied an artery and vein together, on Mrs Deever's forearm. Most of the patients had grafts located on their arms, although several patients, none of them here now, were unable to use a normal shunt and had Quinton catheters installed in the subclavian vein below their necks. Franny inserted two needles in the graft, then connected the tubing from the needles to the dialysis machine, which would pump out the arterial blood, filter it, and give it back through the vein.

'Did he take you someplace nice last weekend?' Mrs Deever asked.

'Yes,' Franny said. 'We went to Napa Valley and stayed there overnight.'

'Napa? Did you go wine tasting?'

Franny nodded. 'We went to a bunch of wineries. I can't remember them all. And he took me to a really nice French restaurant for dinner. The food was terrific.' She took another blood pressure reading as she spoke; every half hour during treatment she would take additional readings. She told Mrs Deever all about the trip, adding as many details as she could, the charming bed-and-breakfast they stayed at Saturday night, the souvenir wineglasses he bought for her, the yeasty smell of fermenting wine in the air.

In fact, it was all a lie. Franny was embarrassed to admit that Michael didn't take her anywhere at all. They had been seeing each other for almost a month now, and he'd never taken her out. He was busy at UCD with his classes and students, and then he had his own music to work on and papers he was writing. With all this, he just never seemed to have much time to spend with her. Franny understood that he was a busy man, and she didn't like to complain, but she wished that he would take her out occasionally, to a movie, perhaps, or out to dinner. Whenever they did meet it was almost always at his house, when he called her and told her to come over, usually later in the evening, as if she were an afterthought.

'He sounds like a good catch,' Mrs Deever said. 'You better hold on to this one.' She said it as if Franny had many men to choose from, many to hang on to. Franny glanced at her other patients to see how they were doing.

Sighing, Mrs Deever slowly rolled her head from side to side, working out the kinks, then closed her eyes. She raised her hand to the hollow of her neck, fingering it lightly. Franny started to walk away, but Mrs Deever opened her eyes and began talking again, tiredly.

'My Frank wasn't such a good catch. He always gave me a hard time. I don't know why some men are like that. He spoilt me against other men. After him, I didn't want to take a chance on another one.' She closed her eyes again and within a minute had dozed off.

Franny remembered going to Mrs Deever's house after school with Jenny, Mrs Deever's daughter, when they were in grade school together. Jenny's father was always going on mysterious trips, during which Mrs Deever kept herself happy with a bottle of booze. While she and Jenny were playing in her room, Mrs Deever would burst through the door with a plate of cookies or brownies, or sometimes with nothing at all. She'd just wanted an excuse to be with them. She'd waltz in the room, smiling too hard, and interrupt their play. She was beautiful back then, a curvy, busty woman with long painted nails and golden hair and jewelry that clinked and glittered as she moved, enthralling the ten-year-old girls. With her legs crossed at the knees, her foot swinging absently, she'd sit on the end of Jenny's bed, smoking a cigarette and sipping her amber-colored drink – she always seemed to have a drink in her hand, ice cubes tinkling, that both girls knew came from the liquor cabinet – and she'd chatter mindlessly and laugh too loud about something that wasn't really funny. Franny thought it was sad, the way Jenny's mother acted, and Jenny must have thought so, too, because she preferred to play at Franny's house. By the time the girls were in junior high school, Mrs Deever was divorced. She was sick most of the time, and Jenny had stopped inviting Franny to her home. She and Jenny were still best friends, but Jenny always came to her house, and she seemed to adopt Franny's mother as her own, seeking her out, hugging her for no reason at all, effectively replacing her own mother as if she were a defective piece of merchandise, something that could be returned and exchanged for a better model. It was strange the way things turned out, Franny thought now. Jenny needed Franny's mother when they were kids, but now it was Franny who needed Jenny's.

Franny checked on her two other patients. She took their blood pressure, asked how they were feeling, scribbled notations on their flow sheets. Then she walked around the room, supervising the technicians. The room had settled into a quiet buzz of routine, everyone hooked up, their machines whirring softly beside them, the techs, dressed in pastel scrubs or whites, calmly monitoring their patients. Everyone was doing fine, so she decided to take a break while it was slow. She used the bathroom, and then went into the employees' lounge and got a candy bar out of the vending machine. Her diet wasn't going anywhere, but Michael didn't seem to mind. She still went on her bike rides in the afternoons, trying to keep up a pretense of losing weight, but they weren't as much fun as they had been. Michael was busy and no longer had time to meet her at Putah Creek. She missed their long discussions and strolls around the Arboretum. They still talked, of course, but somehow it was different.

Franny nibbled on her candy bar, crumpling the wrapper when she finished it. She decided she was imagining things, creating a problem where none existed. It wasn't as if they jumped into bed the minute she arrived at his house. They did talk, they talked a lot, and he had cooked her dinner several times, and they watched TV together, and she always spent the night when she went over there. Michael was sweet and attentive when they were together, and just because he didn't meet her at Putah Creek or take her anywhere – well, she shouldn't fault him just because he had to work long hours. She decided to call him at his office at school to see if she could come over this evening. When she dialed, he picked up on the first ring.

'Yes,' he said sharply, sounding annoyed.

Franny wished now that she hadn't phoned him. 'It's me,' she said. 'Did I call at a bad time?'

'As a matter of fact, yes. I'm going to be late for a class.'

'I'm sorry. I'll call you later.'

He gave an impatient sigh. 'Franny,' he said, and then he caught himself. He sighed again and didn't say anything for a moment. Then he began again, his voice not so harsh. 'You caught me at a bad time,' he said. 'Why did you call?'

'I thought maybe we could spend the evening together. Maybe have dinner out someplace.' She heard him drumming his fingers on the desk.

'I have to work late,' he said. There was a pause. The drumming stopped. 'Come over at nine o'clock. And Franny?'

'Yes?'

'Wear your nurse's uniform tonight. Not your scrubs. The uniform. The white dress, white shoes and white nylons, the hat, stethoscope, the complete outfit. I've got a surprise for you,' and, abruptly, he hung up.

Franny replaced the receiver and smiled. Michael was always pulling surprises on her. The past month had been an eye-opener. She wished she had a close girlfriend she could confide in. The person she was closest with was Mrs Deever, and she couldn't imagine talking to her about sex. She thought of her sister: Nora would know about these things. She picked up the phone again and dialed *The Sacramento Bee*. Then she hung up, without leaving a message. She decided, after all, that she didn't want to talk to Nora about this. It was much too personal.

Later that night, in bed, Franny snuggled up close to Michael. She was wide awake, but he was breathing deeply, almost asleep, lying on his back. Earlier, they'd played out a variation of his doctor-nurse fantasy on the dining room table, which doubled as an examining table. He'd told her that if she wanted to keep her job she'd have to minister to his needs as well as to his patients'. He wore a white lab coat and latex surgical gloves, and he'd made her call him Doctor. He'd unfurled a red velvet cloth containing an array of gleaming stainless-steel instruments, some of them medical, most of them not. This was new to Franny. Until she'd met Michael, she didn't know that people actually played out their fantasies. He'd led her along, examining her with his instruments, poking and prodding carefully, coaxing her to play along. And then he gave her her reward: he touched her the way she liked it, and played with her until she was ready to come. He made her close her eyes and give in to his fantasy, turning it into her own, and all during this he spoke to her in a firm, persuasive tone, urging her further, pulling her along with his words, and she had the uneasy feeling, even while she came, that he was preparing her, tutoring her, for something more.

She listened to Michael's deep, easy breathing, watching his chest rise and fall. Moonlight filtered through the gauzy curtains. A tree swaying in the wind, its branches upswept and reaching like beggars' arms, cast pale, ghostly shadows through the window of the darkened room. She toyed with the black hair on his chest until, annoyed, he placed his hand on hers, stopping her. She wanted to tell him something but wasn't sure how to begin. Propping herself up on one elbow, she looked at him in profile, his jaw square and resolute even in rest. She was in love with that jaw.

'I'm not sure if you want to hear this,' she began uncertainly. 'You probably don't. I know you don't feel the way I do, but

I just wanted you to know how I feel about you.' She could hear herself stumbling over the words. 'The thing is, I think I'm falling in love with you.'

She chewed on a fingernail, waiting for him to respond. She knew he had heard her because his breathing had changed. He didn't say anything.

'Does that upset you?' she asked him finally. 'Do you wish I hadn't said that?'

Slowly, he reached for the bedside lamp and switched it on. It glowed, bright and harsh. In the stark realities of a lighted room, her proclamation of love seemed naked and vulnerable, like a tiny spider caught out in the open. She wanted to crawl under the covers.

'Oh, Franny,' he said, and he rolled over on his side, facing her. He pushed the blankets down to her knees, exposing her to the harsh light even though he knew this made her uncomfortable. She tensed, then made an effort to relax. With his eyes he took in the milky-white fullness of her, her fleshy thighs and hips, her ample belly, her big drooping breasts, plump and squishy soft. He put his hand on her cheek, stroking it, smiling, then let it drop to her breast. He rubbed the rosy nipple, as pink as a dusty damask rose, between his fingers, getting it hard, then took the heft of her breast in the palm of his hand, circling it with his thumb and fingers, holding on to it as if it were a doorknob. It was a funny way to hold her breast, she thought.

'Dear, sweet Franny,' he said. 'It's been a long, long time since I've been in love. And of course I'm glad you told me how you feel. It pleases me that you're in love with me.' He spoke quietly, still gripping her breast. 'I don't fall in love easily, but I'm glad I'm the recipient of yours.' He paused, then said, 'You know what this means, don't you?'

Franny shook her head.

'It means' – he squeezed her breast, giving it a little painful twist, smiling – 'that officially you're now my girlfriend, and that gives me territorial rights over your body. It gives me a proprietary interest in you. You belong to me now.' He smiled again, playfully, and jiggled her breast. 'This tit belongs to me. Your body belongs to me, and I can do whatever I want with it.'

Franny laughed. His girlfriend, *his* girlfriend: she loved the sound of it. She didn't think she'd ever been this happy. He wasn't in love with her yet, but that would come. What mattered was that he cared for her . . . he really cared. And he said he thought of her body in a territorial way; he would protect her as her father once had.

She snuggled closer to him, a content smile settling across her face. Teasingly, she asked, 'And what do you plan to do with my body?'

He licked her nipple, looked at her, and winked. 'All in good time,' he said.

3

The sky was dark with huge, slow-moving, black-bottomed clouds. Big drops of rain, falling dolefully in spread-out intervals like long, sad regrets, splashed on the windshield of Franny's car. She hated driving in bad weather. Just as she flipped on the windshield wipers, the rain came down faster, harder, instantly turning the highway into a Postimpressionist blurry landscape of smeared divider lines and wet concrete and seal-slick passing automobiles. She was meeting Nora for dinner at the Radisson Hotel off Highway 160. They tried to get together at least once a month, and usually they ended up at the Radisson for their chin-chin salad, the best Chinese chicken salad, they both agreed, in Sacramento.

Franny pulled into the parking lot of the hotel, a dun-colored stucco building that looked, from the outside, like a modern-day monastery. She drove around to the front, but all the empty spaces near the hotel's entrance were tiny, made for compact cars. Franny owned an old, black, fin-tailed Cadillac, an antique, her most prized possession. It was a gas-guzzler, behemoth in size, made back in the fifties, but she loved it. She had a special relationship with the car, as if it were a dear old friend; and, like a good friend, she lovingly took care of its needs, washing and waxing it, polishing the chrome, checking the white-wall tires for air, vacuuming its insides. She'd had it since high school, when she lived with Nora, and when she first brought the car home, her sister had called it a monstrosity, an eyesore, a blight to the environment. But Franny, usually so docile, refused to sell it. She wasn't sure why, but she loved this car.

The Cadillac glided around the parking lot, sleek and silent, like a shark circling in the water. She found a large, empty parking space in the rear. She parked, the car clunking to a stop as she switched off the ignition, then checked the backseat for her umbrella; it wasn't there. She pulled on her coat, jerked it up over her head in a makeshift tent, then made a dash for the long breezeway leading up to the hotel's main building. When she reached the double-doored entrance, she stopped and adjusted her coat, shaking off the rain like a wet animal shaking off water. She looked up to see the doorman, a skinny man with heavy, plastic-framed glasses, give her a look she couldn't interpret. He hesitated, then opened the glass door for her.

'Thanks,' Franny said in a breathless whisper, and she rushed past, not meeting his gaze. She walked through the carpeted hotel, decorated in a palette of muted shades, past the registration desk, past the potted plants and gift shop and hanging artwork, up a few steps to the raised dining room. She had just got off work, and before she'd left the clinic she'd changed into a long black skirt and sweater. Her hair, frizzled by the rain, was damp. She tried to comb her fingers through it, but it was a long, tangled mess. Giving up, she searched in her purse for a barrette. Next to her wallet was Billy's silver medical bracelet, with the words 'dialysis patient' etched on one side. She kept it with her always. After her parents died, she wore it on her wrist until, one day, Nora insisted she put it away. Nora believed the past belonged to history, and that Franny was being morbid, wearing Billy's medical bracelet as though it were an amulet, a good-luck charm. But she never thought of it as an amulet; it was more like a stigma, weighing heavily on her wrist. Now she kept it in her purse, or wore it on a chain around her neck, under her blouse so her sister wouldn't see it.

She found a barrette and was putting it on when she spotted Nora in the back of the dining room, sipping a glass of wine. She looked chic and aerobicized, wearing a tight-fitting knit dress, short and sexy, that showed off her body and long legs. Franny knew, for a fact, that Nora was almost neurotic about her weight, working out at the Capital Athletic Club six days a week to keep her body trim, always being careful about what she ate.

Nora looked in Franny's direction, smiled and waved. She was wearing red, flashy lipstick, and her black hair was cut stylishly short, falling level to her chin. Franny walked over, feeling dumpy in her sister's presence.

'Hi,' Nora said. 'What kept you? I was about to give up on you.' She had a pleasant, almost teasing face, with lips that turned up just slightly at the corners, as if she was about to smile.

Franny took off her coat and hung it on the back of her chair. She sat down, saying, 'Sorry. We had an emergency at work.'

'Oh?' Nora raised her eyebrows, a faint lift of inquiry.

'A patient's blood pressure got too low and he went into a seizure. I had to stop his pull and the dialysis.' She put the folded napkin on her lap. 'I think the tech should have watched him more closely. I've never had a patient seize on me before. I gave him some saline, then called the doctor.' She could tell that Nora was only half listening, her eyes distant-looking, nodding her head slightly in agreement to what she was saying. Franny finished the story off quickly. 'Anyway, we sent him to the hospital.'

Nora took a sip of wine. Her eyes were a deep blue, like drops of melted sapphires, that matched the color of her dress. They were fake, Franny knew, color contact lenses, because Nora's eyes actually were a light, dusty blue. Still, the dark color suited her. The waiter came over to take Franny's drink order, and she asked for some hot tea, herbal. After he brought it, they ordered their salads.

'Do you like these?' Nora asked. She leaned forward and brushed her hair back so Franny could see her earrings, cylindrical cones of silver with tear-shaped jade insets.

'They're nice,' Franny said, dipping her tea bag in a pot of hot water. The waiter brought them a basket of assorted breads. Franny reached for a piece of sourdough and buttered it.

'I was in Berkeley last Thursday, doing a story on a zoologist studying the mechanics of motion. He uses insects – centipedes, spiders, ghost crabs, cockroaches. Really interesting. It'll be in the paper next week. I was about to get on the freeway, coming home, when I saw this cute jewelry store. They had great stuff. That's where I bought these.'

Nora took a piece of dry flat bread out of the basket and nibbled on it, unbuttered. She looked around the room, surveying the other diners, the waiters and waitresses, the man playing the piano in the corner. Nora had always been especially observant, probably due to her journalistic background. Her eyes never relaxed; subtly, she would shift her gaze around the room, taking in everything as she spoke, or as others were speaking to her. Some people found this annoying – they thought she wasn't paying attention – but Franny knew that Nora never missed a word of conversation, remembering it long after the speaker had forgotten it.

'Cockroaches?' Franny said, looking skeptical.

'Uh-huh,' Nora said, and she flashed the waiter a smile as he set down their salads. She asked for another glass of white wine, then broke apart her chopsticks and turned back to Franny. 'He puts them on mini treadmills and videotapes them. Then he watches the tapes in slow motion. He's postulated that all animals and insects are similar in their walk, that they all share the same bouncing motion because their leg muscles move the same way.'

She went on, talking about the insects' energy consumption while in motion, and their push against gravity, the force of generation. Wielding her chopsticks, she told Franny the implications this could have in the fields of human physiology and robotics and medicine. Franny was proud of Nora, even if she didn't completely understand what she was saying. Sometimes she wished she were more like Nora, was even envious of her, but then she reminded herself of the foolishness of such thinking. It didn't serve any purpose to wish for something you couldn't have. She might as well wish for the lottery.

When they'd finished their salads, Nora was still talking about cockroaches and centipedes. Franny wanted to bring up the topic of sex, but she didn't know how to go about it. They had talked about sex before, in a general, joking manner, but had never got into the details. Franny hadn't even told her about Michael yet. She'd meant to, she hadn't planned to keep him a secret, but the time just never seemed right. Nora was always so busy. Whenever Franny called her, it seemed she was on her way to a meeting or busy writing against a deadline or about to go out on a date. She didn't want to tell her about Michael unless she had time to explain what he was like. The last several weeks had been strange. She was beginning to wonder what was normal, sexually, and what wasn't. She didn't have any experience in this area, but she thought Nora could enlighten her. Some of the things Michael wanted to do seemed downright weird. She'd hesitated a few times, telling him she didn't want to do something, but he always coaxed her into it, and, to her surprise, she enjoyed it – most of the time. Still, it seemed a little weird, his collection of nipple clamps and labia clips, the ankle and wrist tethers, and the way, lately, he always wanted to dominate her, each week becoming more and more demanding.

'Are you going out tonight?' she asked. 'You look dressed for it.'

Nora nodded. 'I'm going dancing at The Rage. You want to come?'

Franny shook her head. They both knew Nora's invitation was only a formality. Franny didn't like bars, and she hated dancing even more.

Nora put her elbows on the table and leaned forward. Even in the dusky lighting of the room, her hair shined. She grinned. 'I met this really neat guy there last week. He's a great dancer and super good-looking – big chest, at least six feet tall, tight butt. *Real* tight butt.'

Franny looked around to see if anyone had heard her sister, relieved that no one was paying attention to them. 'Do you like him?'

Nora shrugged. 'He's a lineman for the phone company. He's funny and nice, but I just don't think he's bright enough for me. I know I'd get bored with him after a while.' She picked up her glass of wine. 'Too bad,' she said regretfully. 'He's got a great body.'

Franny was used to her sister's cavalier attitude toward men. Nora always had plenty of boyfriends, but she was never really serious with any of them, even with the two men she'd lived with. Several men had asked her sister to marry them, but she'd told them right from the beginning that marriage was not in her plans. Franny, on the other hand, liked the idea of married life, of having someone there for you, knowing there would be a person who always cared for you and who would look out for your best interests. She would give just about anything to be married, whereas Nora casually discarded her marriage proposals and her men. She threw them away when she was finished with them as if they were something disposable that could be easily replaced, like a Bic pen or a used tampon.

'Did you sleep with him?' she asked, then blushed for being so straightforward. Although Nora was frank about her boyfriends, telling her whom she'd slept with, Franny had always merely listened in these conversations, never commenting, never having any stories of her own to relate.

Nora laughed, a distinctively cheery sound that tumbled out of her mouth. 'Since when did you start asking me questions like that?'

Franny smiled sheepishly.

'Actually,' Nora said, 'I didn't. I thought about it, but it just seemed like too much trouble.'

Franny must have looked puzzled because Nora twisted her mouth a little, in an expression of exasperation, and went on to explain.

'Oh, you know. All the precautions. Asking their sexual

history, dragging out the condoms and spermicide, making sure the condom is latex and the lubricant is water-based, et cetera, et cetera. Who needs it? Especially for someone who isn't going to be in your life very long. It seemed easier just to go home alone. Sometimes, the sex isn't worth it.'

Franny thought this would be a good time to bring up Michael, to mention, casually, the things they did. She started to say something, but Nora was pulling on her coat, getting ready to leave. She wanted to go dancing.

Standing up, Nora looked at the bill, then put some money on the table. 'What is it?' she said, seeing that Franny had hesitated.

Franny gave her a small smile, shaking her head. 'Nothing,' she said. She decided not to tell her she had a boyfriend. She wasn't willing to submit him to her scrutiny yet. Nora only dated men her age or, preferably, younger, and had often said she could see no advantages to dating a much older man. She would think it odd that Michael was twice Franny's age. And what would she think if she found out they didn't go anywhere or do anything together? Nora tended to be cynical about men, and she probably wouldn't understand. She would want to meet him, and what if he wouldn't agree to that? Franny decided to wait. The time was not yet right. She also decided, on her way home, to stop off at the Baker's Square in West Sacramento for a hot-fudge brownie pie.

The green light on Franny's answering machine was blinking when she got home that night. It was a message from Michael, telling her to come to his house. She smiled to herself, delighted by his message. Walking through her apartment, still shivering from the cold weather outside, she began taking off her wet clothes, the rain-soaked coat dripping water on the floor, the long black skirt, which was damp around the hem, clinging to her legs. She draped the skirt and coat over the back of a chair to dry. Her apartment was small, a one-bedroom unit on the first floor of a complex filled almost entirely with university students, and it was completely ordinary. Bland beige walls blended into an equally bland wall-to-wall carpet. The rent was cheap, though, and she'd tried to liven it up with colorful pillows, hanging plants, and bright prints on all the walls.

She entered the bedroom and took off the rest of her clothes, piling them on the bed, then went into the bathroom. Standing under the shower, she let the warm water take the chill out of her body. She was glad Michael had called. She'd never realized how lonely she was until she met him. She'd become inured to the loneliness, like a minor wound that never heals: you get used to it, you forget it's even there. But not anymore. Now her empty apartment was unbearable. Whenever she went to Michael's house for the evening, she felt as though she were escaping, breaking out of her solitary life.

Her body was pink from the hot shower, the room steamy and warm. She turned off the water and grabbed a large towel from the rack. As she toweled off, she remembered her shower last week with Michael, how he'd lathered her up, rubbed his hands all over her body, pushing her flesh around as if he were a sculptor, the look in his eyes greedy and determined. Then he'd turned her around and pressed his body into hers, plastered his groin against her buttocks, absorbing her, and she'd felt slender and desirable and graceful in the strong embrace of his powerful arms, and she'd wanted to stay like that forever, her body melded to his, secure in her love, but then he'd doubled her over and spread her buttocks, plunged into her roughly, his penis soapy and slick and hard, moving her as he wanted, telling her to take it even as she was groaning in pain, gripping her then even more firmly, continuing, ordering her to relax. Confused and sore, she'd wondered how she'd got there, bent and wedged between the tiled shower walls, and when he was finished, finally, when he'd wrapped his arms around her, holding her tight, still inside her, when he was kissing the back of her neck, sweetly soft and loving, saying, 'Sometimes it's going to be like that, baby. Sometimes I like it hard, and you're just going to have to learn to take it' – when he was doing all this, she'd wondered if that was the way love was supposed to be.

She brushed her teeth, put on fresh clothes, and drove to Michael's house. When he answered the door, he was holding a cordless telephone, talking to someone. He was dressed in corduroy slacks and a burgundy lamb's wool sweater, and he looked tired, greeting her with a worn-out smile, his dark hair slightly tousled, spilling over the top of his forehead. He waved her in and she followed him into the den, a large, long room with elegantly overstuffed furniture and tall bookcases. A black piano, a five-foot baby grand, was at one end of the room, and a couch and desk at the other. He sat on the couch, continuing with his conversation. Franny shrugged out of her coat and drifted around the room, glancing at the book titles as he spoke on the phone. His desk was next to the bookcases, and mounted on the wall, above a framed picture of his parents, was his father's sword, a steel cutlass almost three feet long, with a solid brass decorative hilt and a wooden handle, which he'd used in World War II. His father had been in the Navy, Michael had explained, and in 1944 he had captured and boarded a German submarine – the last time the Navy officially used the cutlass. Framed photographs of his relatives, aunts, uncles, grandparents surrounded the sword. Franny was envious of his family history; she'd never known her own grandparents, all of them dead before she was even born.

Michael lay back on the couch, putting his feet up on the cushions. Apparently, he was talking to a friend in San Francisco. They were arranging a time to meet at Fisherman's Wharf this Friday night. Franny didn't think he would invite her to go along. She sat at his desk, which was scattered with papers. He taught a musical literature and theory class, and he'd been grading some student essays. She picked up the one on top and read: 'Dvořák's *New World* Symphony is a combination of American and Bohemian thematic material. It was written in the musical language indigenous to Bohemia, permeated with the musical temperament characteristic of Dvořák, and infused with the spirit of America.' Franny put the paper down. Since they'd been sleeping together, Michael never talked about his students *or* his work *or* his music. Whenever she asked, he brushed her off. He, on the other hand, knew everything about her. No longer was he content to let her be silent. He pried intimate details out of her, about her parents and Billy and how they'd died, about Nora, about her one-night stand with some nameless reporter from the *Bee*. He wanted to know how he kissed her, how he made love to her, what she did for him. He wanted specifics. The nitty-gritty. But when it came to his life and his relationships, he was closemouthed.

Franny waited for him to finish his call. When he hung up, he stretched his arms and yawned. He put another pillow under his head and looked over at her, considering.

'I've had a tiring day,' he said. 'Come over here.' It sounded like a command.

Franny stayed at the desk. 'Michael, I think we should talk.'

He cocked his head to one side and raised an eyebrow, not saying a word. His level gaze was daunting. She bowed her head, looked at the carpet, and nervously began playing with her hands, rubbing one with the other.

'You don't tell me anything about yourself,' she said. 'I don't know anything about your work . . . or your life . . . or your friends.'

'We've been over this, Franny,' he said, his voice firm. 'I'm not in the mood to rehash it again.'

She was silent for a minute. Quietly, she said, still looking at the carpet, 'I'm not happy with the way things are. We never do anything together. You find time to spend with your other friends – why can't you spend more time with me? Why don't you take me to Fisherman's Wharf?' Slowly, she shook her head. 'I don't know. At times, you seem so distant.'

'Franny, look at me.'

She folded her hands on her lap and raised her head. Michael was watching her, reclining on the couch, his hands clasped behind his head, looking patient, as if she were his student.

'I don't have a lot of free time, Franny. You knew this about me all along.'

'I thought, eventually, you'd make time for me, that you would change. I—'

He held up his hand, indicating he hadn't finished. 'You knew what I was like when you first met me. I never promised you I would change. It's unreasonable of you to expect me to act differently just because you want me to.'

Franny looked at the wall above his head. His words sounded so matter-of-fact, so calm, as if he were tolerating her. She didn't say anything.

'You have a choice, Franny. If you're unhappy, you can stop seeing me. Is that what you want?'

She looked at him and shook her head. 'No,' she said. 'That's not what I want. I wasn't even thinking of that. I love you.' She looked over at the piano, not really seeing it, just thinking. 'I was hoping that maybe, with time, you'd feel the same way.'

Sitting up, he swung his feet to the floor. 'Come here, Franny.' His voice was low and patient, and she thought she heard a hint of empathy in it.

She went over to him and he pulled her gently down to her knees between his legs. She rested her head on his knee, feeling defeated, and he stroked her hair, rubbed her shoulder.

'I am fond of you, you know that,' he said, still caressing her, speaking softly in a deep voice as smooth as grosgrain. 'I won't make you any promises, but perhaps one day I will fall in love with you. Will you settle for that?' He lifted her chin up so she had to look at him. A single tear rolled down her cheek.

She nodded, then kissed the palm of his hand. 'Yes,' she said. 'I can wait. No matter how long it takes,' and she wrapped her arms around him, burying her head in his lap. He continued to hold her, stroking her head, neither of them speaking. In the silence she could hear the clock on the wall ticking, a dog in the distance howling, the rhythmic sound of their breathing. She thought of how wonderful it felt just to be close to Michael, to have him hold her, to feel the warmth of his body, the comforting touch of his hand.

Softly, he asked, 'Are you okay now?' and she nodded, pleased with his tenderness.

'Good girl,' he said. He pulled her head up and gave her the barest flicker of a smile. 'I've had an exhausting day,' he said. 'I'm really tense and I need you to relieve me. I want you to give me a good suck.'

Franny stared at him, wondering if she'd heard him correctly. But he was pulling down the zipper of his pants, taking out his penis.

'Michael, can't we do this later? I'm not—'

'Shhh,' he said, putting his fingers over her mouth. 'I really need you to take care of me. Now do as I say,' and he pushed her head into his lap. 'Suck me off good, baby,' he said, holding her head down.

Franny did as he asked, tears forming in her eyes.

'Oh, my sweet baby,' he said, sliding down an inch, making himself comfortable. 'You're going to have to do better than that. You're not getting me very hard.' He brushed the hair back from her face, gently, and said, 'I'll give you five minutes to make me come. If you don't, then I'll have to punish you.'

4

Franny's days at the clinic passed uneventfully. She had to work late tonight, and by the time she was driving home, around six-thirty, fog was settling in. It wasn't too bad crossing the causeway, just wispy films of it floating along like gossamer, but as she got close to Davis it turned into a ground-hugging, heavy fog: tule fog. The sharp beam of her headlights dissipated into a gray illumination, dreamlike and hazy, the fog so dense it soundproofed the world. Oleander bushes lining the freeway median materialized a few feet in front of her car, then were swallowed in the dark haze as she drove on.

She got off at the Mace exit, turned left over the overpass, then slowed down and deliberated. She had three choices: McDonald's, Taco Bell, or Burger King. She went straight and headed for the Burger King, ordered her dinner at the drive-through, then got back on the street, driving carefully in the tule fog. She turned onto the old frontage road paralleling the railroad tracks, a dreary and forlorn road even without the smothering fog, then turned right on Pole Line and headed out to Driftwood Convalescent Hospital. Franny used to visit Mrs Deever only on weekends or on her days off, but lately, since she gave up her bike rides, she visited her three or four times a week, stopping by when she got off work, bringing her dinner along.

As soon as Franny opened the door to Driftwood, the faint, underlying ammonia smell of urine hit her, as enveloping as the fog. Driftwood was clean, the floors always scrubbed, but under the disinfectant and cleanser and the fragrant smells of flowers left as gifts were the indelible sour odors of decay, the urine and feces and vomit from dozens of incontinent patients, from soiled bedclothes and adult-sized diapers, sad reminders of what these old people, who could no longer care for themselves, had come to. It was hard to find cheer in a place where most of the patients were left to die.

She walked down the long corridors. Festive Christmas pictures were hung on the walls: Santa Claus and his reindeer, bulbed and tinseled trees, peaceful Nativity scenes. In wheel-chairs, old men and women rolled slowly in the hallways, going nowhere in particular. Some of the patients were ambulatory but senile, talking to themselves as they wandered throughout the rooms, setting off alarms with their Wonder-Guard anklets when they crossed the boundaries of the building, like prisoners on the lam.

Franny entered Mrs Deever's room, paused just inside the doorway for a moment. The walls were white, with two patients to a room. Beige draperies were pushed back against the walls, but they hung from the ceiling on rails so they could be pulled around each bed, enclosing it for privacy. Mrs Deever's room-mate was a tiny, gray-haired woman in her eighties who slept most of the day. Rarely was she awake when Franny came to visit, and she was sleeping now, the blue bedspread pulled up to her chin, her slight body a mere ripple under the covers. A urine bag was attached to the side of the bed rail, and the clear tubing from her catheter drained into it, displaying an unhealthy, orangish urine. Neither she nor Mrs Deever had many visitors, although old get-well cards were taped on the walls by their beds.

Mrs Deever had been staring out the glass sliding door to the courtyard. It was dark outside, with nothing to see, but still she stared. Her stocky body was slumped down in the bed, and her face was drawn with fatigue. Around her neck she wore a white terry-cloth bib. When she saw Franny, she brightened, widened her heavy-lidded eyes. 'Hi, sweetie,' she said. 'It's so good to see you. Crank me up so we can talk better.'

Franny set her purse and bag of food on the counter. She

bent down and used the handle at the bottom of the bed to raise it. Mrs Deever's dinner, turkey and peas and a fruit compote, was on the bed tray in front of her, uneaten.

'Weren't you hungry?' Franny asked.

Mrs Deever made a face at the food. 'My stomach was upset earlier. I'll try to eat it now.' She picked up a fork and took a bite of the turkey, poked at her peas. Franny pulled a chair to the bed and opened her bag. She had a Whopper, a large order of fries, and a chocolate shake.

Putting her fork down, Mrs Deever pushed her tray away. 'I better not eat anymore,' she said, her voice shaky. 'I feel like I might throw up.' She put the white bib up to her lips. Her chest and shoulders heaved, but she didn't vomit.

Franny got a beige plastic container out of the drawer by her bed and placed it next to Mrs Deever in case she needed it. She patted her on the arm.

'You're a good girl,' Mrs Deever said, looking up at her. 'Your mother and father would be so proud. You know that, don't you?'

Franny smiled.

'They were nice people. Family oriented. Always taking you and Nora and Billy somewhere – camping, museums, picnics. I wish my Frank had been more like your father, taking more of an interest in the family.' She paused a moment, then said, 'It was a real blow to them when your brother died. They never got over it. But what parent would, losing a child like that? It changed them.' She squeezed Franny's hand. 'It changed you too, didn't it? It must've been hard, finding your brother right after he died. You were too little to see something like that.'

Franny listened quietly, not saying a word.

Abruptly, Mrs Deever lurched for the plastic container. She held it below her mouth and spewed out a phlegm-colored lumpy liquid. When she finished, Franny took the tray into the bathroom and washed it, then replaced it on the bed by Mrs Deever's side.

'You're not having a good day, are you?' Franny said, standing next to the bed.

Mrs Deever shook her head, then sighed heavily. 'Whatever happened to me, Franny? How did I get like this?' She stared down at the covers, at the place where her legs had once been, where now only two thick thighs ended abruptly in stumps. Sighing again, she placed her hand on Franny's.

Franny looked down. She had a small stump of her own, where she'd accidentally cut off her little finger with a paper cutter. That was a long time ago, shortly after Billy died, when she'd moved to Montana with her parents.

Mrs Deever caught her gazing at the space of the missing finger. 'It's better than losing a leg,' she said. 'No one minds a nine-fingered woman. You shouldn't worry about it – it's hardly noticeable.' After a minute, she added, 'I used to be pretty, do you remember? Young and pretty, full of hope and good intentions.' There was a wistful tone to her voice.

Franny nodded and sat back down. Mrs Deever stared out the dark window again, remembering her better days. Franny picked up her Whopper. Those were better days for her, too, before her parents died. It had been ten years, but still she remembered, vividly, the day she was told her parents had been in a car accident. Her sense of security had been ripped out from under her. And then she was whisked off to Nora's. Just like that, everything changed: never again to feel that someone would love her, unconditionally, no matter what; never again to feel truly secure. Her sister tried, of course. She did the best she could. But Nora was young herself at the time, just Franny's age now, recently out of college and trying to get her career started. She was too involved with her own life to see that Franny needed more than room and board to get through those difficult years. And now, after hoping to find in Michael the security and love she'd sought for so long, their relationship was not turning out as she had expected.

Franny reached for a handful of fries.

'Ha!' Mrs Deever said suddenly, getting worked up. She

snorted. 'Hope and good intentions, my foot! Frank took all those away. I should've known better than to marry him.'

Franny didn't comment. This was an old refrain.

'He's just like the Kennedy men. If you want to know who you're marrying, check out the father. Like father, like son.' She tugged on the white bib around her neck. 'Frank's father was no good, cheated on his wife just like Frank cheated on me. He's a Kennedy man, through and through. I should've known he'd be trouble.' Bitterly, she threw the bib on her food tray. 'The sons watch; they learn how to act from their fathers, even if they act no good. Jack and Bobby and Ted – they're spitting images of Joe Senior. And just you wait – it'll be the same for John-John and the newer Kennedy men. It runs in families, goes down the generations.'

Franny didn't know what to say. She finished her hamburger and fries.

'I don't want to talk about him anymore,' Mrs Deever said. 'It's depressing enough just being here. Let's talk about something more cheerful.'

Franny picked up her milk shake, and as she drank it she spun a wishful tale of Michael, who was not, and never had been, a Kennedy man. He took her to the symphony at the Sacramento Community Center for an all-Beethoven present-ation. Then she mentioned a new restaurant in Davis they had tried last night – too trendy, they both agreed – and a movie they rented for his VCR. They ate popcorn and made a fire in the fireplace. In her stories, he was the perfect boyfriend.

5

Franny, naked and wiggling her toes in the carpet, stood in the middle of Michael's bathroom. Everything was color-coordinated and neat and tidy, with all the towels folded precisely, as if a maid had recently cleaned. The room, suffused with a warm, bluish tinge, was larger than her kitchen and much more elegant: sapphire-blue and silver wallpaper, a sunken tub, double onyx vanities, a full-length wall-sized mirror. She half expected a gorgeous, tan showgirl, with a blue feathered head-dress and tassels and pasties, to emerge from the tub. Instead, she had only herself.

She slipped a red satin-and-lace halter bustier over her head and pulled it down below her shoulders, twisting and stretching the garment to accommodate her body. She hated red. It made her pale skin appear even more washed-out than it actually was. Turning around, she looked at herself in the full-length mirror: a ridiculous sight. The bustier hugged her body much too tightly, and white folds of skin extruded from the edges of the bodice. It was a crotchless piece of lingerie Michael had bought for her, too skimpy, too revealing, and designed for a body much slimmer than hers, a showgirl's body. Her breasts, squeezed and lifted from the underwire cups, jutted out and spilled over. She tried smashing them in, then pulling the bustier up, but the higher she tugged it, the more she revealed of her crotch. There was not enough material to cover all of her. She gave up, yanked on the bottom edges and pulled it back down. It was a four-piece set: bustier, G-string, thigh-high nylons, and a short satin robe, all in bright fire-engine red. Michael, who was waiting for her in the living room, had given her strict orders not to wear the G-string or the robe.

Leaning against the sink counter, Franny slipped on the red nylons and attached them to the garters. She forced her feet into five-inch spiked high heels, also red, then wobbled over to the mirror. Turning so she could see herself from behind, she groaned. She didn't like what she saw. Her buttocks were dimpled and meaty, her thighs unsightly massive slabs. She turned again. The bustier ended just below her stomach, revealing her pubic area, shaven clean per Michael's instructions, a delta of raw skin. Instinctively, she reached for her crotch and palmed it with her hand. Without hair, it looked vulgar, obscene, and it made her feel totally exposed. She wanted to grow it back so she could hide behind it, but Michael wouldn't let her.

When she removed her hand, she looked in the mirror again, still embarrassed by what she saw. She picked up the satin robe and slipped it on. Even without tying the belt, it made her look slimmer; it covered her thighs and buttocks. She decided to wear the robe, even though Michael expressly forbade it. When he saw that she looked better this way, certainly more sensual, perhaps he would let her keep it on. She drew back the curtains and looked out the window. The sky was dark and bleak, and rain came down at a harsh slant; the backyard grass took on a grayish color, and water pooled wherever there was hollow ground.

She started to leave the bathroom, but stopped suddenly when she remembered the lipstick. He wanted her to wear lipstick; red, garish lipstick. She applied it carefully, blotted her lips with a tissue, then giggled. She sucked in her cheeks and rolled her eyes upward. She looked so silly. Shrugging her shoulders, she wondered what it was about red lipstick that turned men on. It looked so unnatural, so fake. And very, very silly.

Slowly, uncertainly, she walked through the house, tottering on her spiked heels, trying not to feel like a prostitute in the red crotchless bustier. She found Michael in the living room, sitting on the couch, reading a magazine. She stood back, watching him. He was wearing gray slacks and a black shirt, something soft and silky, something sexy, opened at the collar. She felt the heavy heat of desire, the ache of a passion too many years denied. Whenever she saw him – dark, handsome, trim – a surge of pride coursed through her. Even now, after all this time, she couldn't believe he had chosen her, and she felt blessed in his presence, as if he were an undeserved gift.

He turned the page of the magazine. His fingers were long and tapered, the hands of a pianist, narrowing exquisitely to the fingertips. When she entered the room, he looked up, a trace of annoyance crossing his face. She thought she'd done something wrong, but then he smiled and set aside his magazine. Relieved, Franny smiled also.

'Walk around the room,' he told her. 'I want to watch you.'

She smiled again, shyly, and walked across the room, trying not to hobble. When she got to the front window, she peeked through the draperies. Low black clouds roiled overhead; a zigzag of lightning flashed across the sky, and then she heard the loud crack of thunder. She turned around and went back to Michael, stopping in front of him.

'Do it again,' he said. 'But slower this time.'

Franny did as he asked. She was becoming accustomed to the heels. They were still tight and uncomfortable, but she didn't feel as though she would topple over at any minute. She tried to walk gracefully, imagining she was a model on a runway. She imagined all the fat away, and saw a young, beautiful woman. Feeling more confident, she circled the room again. She tried to put a little flourish in her walk, tried to act a little sexy, swinging her hips, continuing her promenade around the room. Michael didn't care that she was overweight. He wanted her to dress in lingerie; he liked the way she looked. She imagined herself an earth goddess: round, plump, the flesh symbolizing fertility and good health.

'That's enough,' he said abruptly. His voice pulled Franny out of her reverie. 'Come here.'

She went over to the couch and started to sit.

'No,' he said. 'Stand in front of me so I can see you.'

Clasping her hands in front of her shaved crotch, trying casually to cover her genitals, she stood before him, wondering what would come next. Music played softly from the den. Earlier, she'd been too nervous to notice it. The volume was turned down very low. Something by Brahms, she thought, but she wasn't sure.

'Your hands are obstructing my view,' Michael said. 'Put them at your sides.'

She removed her hands and bowed her head, trying to act natural in the crotchless bustier, as if she always wore sexy lingerie. The music ended, and the room became quiet. Too quiet. She could hear herself breathing softly.

'You look like a slut,' she heard him say, his harsh words cutting into the silence.

Franny grimaced. Nervously, she chewed on her lip. She hated it when he called her that, but knew better than to protest.

He stood up and walked behind her. Pushing her hair to one side, he leaned down and kissed her gently on the neck. Franny started to turn around so she could return his kiss, but he held her in place.

'Don't move,' he said, and he kissed her again, sliding his tongue along the nape of her neck. She leaned back against him, felt his body against hers, then saw him reach into his pants pocket. He pulled out a black scarf and slid it up her arm, along the front of her neck, across her face. It was silky and soft against her skin. He reached around with his other arm and took the opposite end of the scarf, stretching it tight, and placed it over her eyes. He tied the ends behind her head.

'Michael—' she began.

But he put his finger to her lips and very quietly said, 'Shhh.'

It was dark behind the scarf. And scary. He took her arm and slowly pulled her forward. She had no choice but to follow, stumbling awkwardly along the way. She clung to him as they walked through the house, seeing nothing, the blackness disorienting her. She thought they were in the hallway, but then she heard her high heels clicking on the tile. A sense of vertigo overcame her, and she wanted desperately to remove the scarf. She took a deep breath to calm herself. Suddenly, Michael was pushing her down. She struggled, a reflexive reaction, but he forced her down, and with an ungainly thud she fell into a chair. When she realized it was only a chair, Franny gave out a short, nervous laugh of embarrassment. She'd thought he was attempting to trip her, and now she felt foolish. She ran her fingers along the edges of the chair. Wood, smooth, cool to the touch. It was a dining room chair. Feeling grounded and more secure now that she was seated, Franny began to relax. She felt Michael's hands, rubbing her shoulders and neck, then he took her arms and gently drew them back behind the chair.

'Cross your wrists,' he said, 'and hold them still.'

A second later she felt him lashing her wrists together. Her apprehension returned.

'Michael,' she said again, but once more he put his fingers to her lips.

'I don't want you to speak,' he said, then removed his fingers. She heard him walk away, and felt panicked at his desertion. She wanted to call out, but knew that would displease him. She pulled her wrists. The lashing was secure. She could not untie the rope. What if he left her here for a long time? What if he left the house and there was a fire and she couldn't escape? She told herself to calm down – her imagination was working overtime. He was probably still in the room, watching her. She sat up straighter, feeling spied upon. Then another thought occurred to her: what if someone else was watching her? She fidgeted in the chair, worrying, wanting to call out. How long had she been here? The low rumble of thunder reached her ears, and she was comforted by the sound. Earlier, the clap of thunder had seemed threatening, ominous even, but now its familiar noise steadied her.

After a while – she wasn't sure how long – she heard footsteps. Turning her head to the left, she listened intently, and when something brushed against her thigh, she jerked her leg, swallowing a scream.

'Spread your legs,' she heard a voice. It was Michael's voice, and she wanted to cry or laugh – she wasn't sure which – with relief. She had the feeling he was kneeling in front of her.

'Spread your legs,' he repeated, sternly now.

She opened them a little. He placed his hands on the insides of her knees and he spread them further. She knew, even with a blindfold on, what she looked like without pubic hair: completely open and vulnerable, her labia pulled apart, as gaping as any wound.

He took her right ankle and placed it on the outside of the chair leg. She felt him lashing her leg to the chair, the rope tight against her flesh. Then he tied her left leg. Her heart beat faster, she could feel the pounding in her chest, and her breathing came in short, anxious gasps. She tried to close her legs, just a little, but couldn't. He had tied her too securely.

Michael put his hand on the inside of her thigh, gripping her flesh firmly, making her wince. 'You're very naughty,' he said. 'I told you not to wear the robe.'

Franny got a sinking feeling low in her stomach. She had forgotten about the robe.

'Someday you'll learn to pay more attention to my requests,' he told her. 'I'm going to discipline you. You need to learn to follow my orders.'

Franny felt the ropes around her legs, holding her open. A wave of panic rushed through her.

'Please, Michael,' she said. 'Don't—' but then he stuffed a gag in her mouth, and her words came out as a muffled slur.

PART TWO

Nora

Before I Continue . . .

At this point, I feel I must meet M. I've learned all I can from Franny's diary, and now it's time to deal directly with the man himself. I wish I could quit now, but an indefinable force pushes me forward. Franny wrote of an instinctive pull toward her natural surroundings. I also feel drawn, not to nature but to her – her secret life, her death, the mystery surrounding her death. I have a tropism for revelations, it turns out. Like people chasing down fire trucks, like passersby craning to see the accident victim, I have a powerful need to know. It's involuntary, it's inexorable. I must find out what happens next; I must, at any cost, know how and why Franny died, and bring her killer – whoever he is – to justice.

Yes, my trepidations are great, but still, deep down, I feel I will prevail. I am not the shy, timid girl that Franny was, and in me M. will find his equal. Surrendering meekly is not my style: I do not, nor shall I ever, give in without a fight.

I have been watching M. for months now. I follow him around town, I know his routine. He shops at Nugget Market, usually on Saturday afternoons, he eats out frequently, spends a lot of time at home, jogs three days a week in the early morning with his dog, a full-grown Great Dane. This quarter he's teaching classes four days a week, and before he drives on campus he stops at Fluffy Do-nuts in the University Mall. Occasionally, he'll have a glazed doughnut, but normally he only has coffee, two cups, black, and sits at a booth to read the newspaper. He subscribes to two papers, *The Sacramento Bee* and *The Davis Enterprise*. He reads the *Bee* at Fluffy's in the mornings and the *Enterprise*, presumably, at home.

I've seen him on campus many times, and Franny was right – he is a popular teacher. I've followed him around, overheard his conversations, and both the faculty and students seem to like him. He has several friends, men, whom he sees regularly. They play golf on the municipal course, eighteen holes, once a week; occasionally they drive up to Tahoe to gamble. M. plays only blackjack. His relationship with women is more difficult to describe. As far as I can tell, he stays away from female students, which I'm sure has more to do with practical concerns than moral ones. He's been with various women since I've been observing him – some middle-aged, some young, all of them attractive – but he never stays with any of them for very long. Whether he ends the relationship or they, I have no idea. And, unlike his treatment of Franny, he does see them socially: dinner, theater, weekend trips. He doesn't know it yet, but I shall be the next woman in his life.

A few words of clarification and regret:

In all honesty, I must say I dismissed Franny's sexuality. It never occurred to me that she had a boyfriend. I thought of her as a neuter, without sensual feelings, as asexual as a piece of furniture. How could she have gotten involved with a man like M.? How could I have not noticed the changes in her? Was I so self-absorbed, as she hinted, that I saw nothing? I think back, I rack my brain, I try to remember: when we met for dinner, were there ever any bruises on her arms or wrists? I'm ashamed to say, I never noticed.

I was also unaware of Franny's close ties to Mrs Deever. They had formed a symbiotic relationship that had served them both, and yet Franny failed to mention her to me except in the most casual of terms. Not once did she say she was coming to think of Sue Deever as a maternal figure, as a sort of ersatz mother. Or did she? She may have dropped subtle hints of their symbiosis that passed me by. Perhaps *symbiosis* is too clinical a term to describe their connection. I admit I have a tendency to view the world in an empirical manner, filtering my observations through the objective lenses of scientific methodology. I am infinitely more comfortable with detached observation than subjectivity. But perhaps I need to step out from behind the magnifying lenses so I can see more clearly the extent of her intimate ties with others, binding ties, apparently – a subject with which I have little personal experience.

But the diary reveals how I have failed her. I had no idea Franny was still suffering from the loss of our parents, desperate to have someone take their place, still longing for, still needing, unconditional parental love. When she came to live with me, she was so quiet and well-behaved, always doing well in school and never causing any trouble, that I thought she had adjusted to our parents' death. I thought she was okay. Several months before he died, my father had called me and said Franny was misbehaving. She was acting like a tomboy, he said, and he hinted about an incident involving stolen bicycles. But when she came to Sacramento, Franny was docile, quiet, timid. There was no misbehavior, no tomboyish activities. She stayed close to home, did her schoolwork, and watched TV. Other than gain weight, each month putting on a few pounds, she seemed relatively normal. How was I to know she was so unhappy? I tried my best to take care of her, but my best wasn't good enough. I can see that now.

6

I'm meeting M. at Fluffy Do-nuts this morning, located in the University Mall across the street from the UCD campus. Fluffy's is almost a landmark in Davis. It's long and narrow, with plate-glass windows facing the Safeway grocery store, and, in the mornings, it's probably the busiest place in town. I don't know why. There's a plastic look to it – functional, hard-backed Formica booths, laminated tabletops, overhead lighting that glares, a worn linoleum floor – but the doughnuts and coffee are good, and over the years it's become a sort of unofficial gathering place for Davis residents.

I don't jog – I prefer low-impact, high-intensity aerobics – but I'm wearing a pink-and-gray jogging suit so it will appear that I do. I want to attract M., I want him to assume we have activities in common. Attracting men has never been a problem for me, but this morning, as I dressed in the jogging suit – a recent acquisition from Macy's – and white Reeboks, I was worried. I needed to impress M. I took special care with my makeup, and was pleased with the result. I have a pleasant face, attractive but not beautiful, just beginning to show the wear and tear of thirty-five years – a few lines around the eyes, skin not quite as elastic as it once was. But I still wear a size eight, even if I have to work out at the gym six days a week to do so. My hair is jet black – no gray, yet – muscles toned, ass firm, and my breasts still bounce rather than sag. All in all, I look pretty good, and when I finished dressing for M. this morning, I looked in the full-length mirror and was pleased with what I saw – an attractive woman in her mid-thirties, tall, athletic-looking in a sexy way. I

admonished myself for worrying; I shouldn't have any
problem with M.

Through the plate-glass windows I see him near the back
of Fluffy's, reading the paper and drinking coffee. I enter
the building and stand in line. The place is noisy. Around me,
people are talking loudly, the two girls behind the counter are
ringing up doughnut orders, people are shuffling in and out
the door. After I pay for my coffee, I look around, feign
annoyance that there isn't an empty booth, then head for M.
I don't know why Franny found his appearance so intimidating.
He seems deep in thought as he reads the newspaper, his
posture erect, his face serious. He is swarthy, good-looking,
if you like that type, slimly muscled and dark-complected,
with an angular face that could have been sculpted – strong
chin, high cheekbones, a long, straight nose. But he's close to
fifty, and it shows in the deeply lined forehead and in the
permanent wrinkles set around his eyes. He's distinguished-
looking, in a professorial way, and, for Davis, he's overdressed.
Davis is a casual town; people ride bicycles, they vote
Democratic, they wear Birkenstocks or tennis shoes. Everyone
in Fluffy's is dressed informally, in jeans, sweatpants, and
rumpled jackets. Even the older people are dressed in everyday
wear they'd lounge around in at home. But M., he looks . . .
English. He's wearing a brown sports coat and tan slacks –
common enough – but on him they appear tailored and a bit
formal. He has the well-groomed appearance of a country
gentleman, and is, as Franny said, well put together.

When I approach his booth, I see he is reading the business
section of the *Bee*. The other sections are scattered across the
table, and his coffee cup is almost empty. I discover I'm
nervous.

'If I refill your coffee, can I share your booth?' I ask him.
He looks up at me, tilts his head to one side, smiles slightly.
'There aren't any empty tables,' I say, by way of explanation.
'Of course,' he says, clearing off one side of the table. 'Have
a seat.'

I put my coffee down, then go back up to the front counter where two coffeepots and one pot of hot water are warming on a three-plate burner. I get the coffeepot, return to his table, and fill his cup. Then, on the way back to the counter, I fill several other patrons' cups. Fluffy's is that kind of place: you help yourself, you help others. I slide into his booth.

'Nice morning, isn't it?' I say. The air outside is cool and crisp, perfect weather for jogging – if I jogged.

Behind me, a man coughs hoarsely and rustles his newspaper. M. drinks his coffee, regards me over the rim of his cup.

'Yes,' he says finally. 'It is a nice morning.' He sets down his cup, a calculated move, then leans back in the booth, waiting, it seems, for me to say something. I introduce myself. I tell him my name is Colleen, which happens to be my middle name. I don't give him my last.

'Colleen,' he says, an amused glimmer in his eyes. We talk about the weather, our mutual enjoyment of jogging, the news on the front page. He tells me he's a music professor at UCD; I tell him I'm a physical chemist, working on a project to separate the length and charge effects that occur with DNA undergoing electrophoresis.

'By itself,' I tell him, 'the project doesn't amount to much; however, it's another piece in the puzzle. Its main interest will be to the people who are designing fluorescent molecules for the next generation of sequencing technology being used in the Human Genome Project. Also, from the basic science point of view, this work will be of interest to the theoreticians working on electrophoresis.'

M. looks mildly interested; he nods as if he knows what I'm speaking about, a faint, droll smile appearing and disappearing quickly. I wonder if I imagined it.

'To my knowledge I'm the only person who has ever systematically modified the charge on DNA and looked at its effects on DNA mobility in agarose gels.' This is accurate, of course, but a lie. I am appropriating the life of a scientist

I interviewed several years ago, adopting his work as my own. I hope M. won't question me further, and he doesn't. He finishes the last of his coffee.

'I'm glad all the tables were full this morning,' he says. 'I enjoyed talking to you.' He gathers his paper, stacks the sections together and folds the bundle in half. 'I'd like to finish our conversation,' he continues, 'but I must leave. I have a class at nine.' He pauses, looking at me from across the table. 'Would you like to go out to dinner sometime this week?'

Inwardly, I sigh with relief. I thought it might be difficult to get to M., but he's proving to be less complicated than I imagined. 'Sure,' I say. 'I'd like that.'

He stands up and I join him. We walk out the front door and stop on the pebbled sidewalk. Patchy clouds mottle the sky in a pearly-gray tessellated pattern. This early, there are few cars in the parking lot and the mall, normally busy, is deserted except for Fluffy's. Two bicyclists, both college students with black backpacks strapped on their shoulders, ride up and park their bikes. They lock them to a metal bike rack, and enter the doughnut shop. A cold late-winter wind suddenly starts up and tosses my hair.

'The day after tomorrow?' he asks. Then he frowns. 'No, that won't work for me. How about tomorrow night? Will that be a good time for you?'

With my hand, I brush the hair out of my face. 'Tomorrow would be fine.'

He pulls out a pocket notebook from inside his coat. 'Great. If you'll give me your address, I'll pick you up at seven.'

I don't want him to know where I live, that I rented a house only a few blocks from his. 'I have a better idea,' I say. 'Why don't you give me your address. I'll meet you there at seven and you can cook me dinner.'

He laughs. 'You want me to cook you dinner? On a first date?'

I shrug and smile. 'I love a man who cooks. You *can* cook, can't you?'

He writes his address on the paper and tears it out of his notebook. He hands it to me, saying, 'Sure. I enjoy cooking occasionally.'

So far, I think, this is easy.

Ian McCarthy is my boyfriend. He works at *The Sacramento Bee* also, a staff reporter who covers the capitol news. I've known him for years, but I didn't start dating him until ten months ago, shortly after Franny died. If I didn't believe in serendipitous events before, I do now: when I needed someone like Ian, he appeared – almost miraculously – by my side. We were barely acquaintances at the *Bee,* the most superficial of friends, and I considered him an annoyance at first – the importunate way he seemed to edge himself into my life immediately after Franny died – but I quickly warmed to his heartfelt manner. 'I know what it's like to lose someone you love,' he'd said simply, trying to console me.

I knew what he was referring to. Several years ago a man stalked and killed his girlfriend. She had been a TV reporter for the Channel 3 news, and the *Bee* – along with every other local paper and news station – had covered the story extensively. The man had made threatening phone calls to her home, sent her photos he'd taken of her surreptitiously, then finally cornered her in the television station parking lot and stabbed her repeatedly. Now he's in San Quentin.

'At least you know who killed Cheryl,' I said, thinking that must be of some satisfaction.

But Ian just shook his head, a look of pain on his face. 'It doesn't help to know who murdered her,' he said, and he put his arms around me.

From that common element – violent death – Ian and I established a rapport. He understood me as no one else could; he comforted me, even helped with the funeral arrangements and memorial service.

When Franny was murdered, something inside me closed up. Her death, so senseless and violent, affected me more profoundly than even my brother's or parents' deaths. Even now, I find it unbearable. Ian – gentle, staid, levelheaded Ian – has been a great help to me, and the progression of our relationship has been slow and steady. When I was considering a leave of absence from the Bee, he agreed it might be a good idea. He didn't want me to move to Davis, but when I did he was supportive. He helped me move, and he never complains about the distance between our homes. We see each other several times a week, and being with Ian is comfortable. He's compassionate and bright and even-tempered. I find, since Franny died, my attitude toward men has changed. I know she thought I was frivolous with my boyfriends, and maybe I was. But with Ian, it's different. I really care about him, and maybe it will lead to something more.

He stayed over last night, and he's in the bathroom now, shaving. I'm reading the newspaper, clipping articles that depict violent acts in Sacramento. Two teenagers were wounded in Land Park in a drive-by shooting. In Franklin Villa a man was pulled from his home and beaten with a baseball bat. A woman, shot three times, was found dead on 14th Avenue, a pile of clothes near her nude body. I've begun a collection of articles about violence, death, destruction. I'm not sure what I'm going to do with them – write an article perhaps, on the growing tide of violence, and submit it to the *Bee*.

Ian comes up behind me and puts his arms around my neck. He leans down and kisses me on the cheek. He smells good, of shaving lotion and Old Spice, and his lips are as soft and smooth as blossoming petals. Looking at him, with his square face and crooked nose that had once been broken, you wouldn't think his lips would be so soft. He's a few inches taller, and a few years younger, than I, and even now while he's dressed in a dark suit to meet with a legislator, he has an unsophisticated, farm-boyish look about him, his body beefy and strong, his fingers blunt. Even his blond hair is the flaxen color of silky tassels on an ear of corn. He's a good-hearted man, frank and simple. I used to think he was a trifle dull, but, since Franny died, I've come to admire his steadfast manner.

The only area in which he is not supportive is where it concerns M. Several months ago, when I told him I was following M., Ian blew up at me in a rare display of anger.

'Why are you doing this?' he said, pacing the room, agitated, his face flushed. 'Why can't you just leave the man alone?'

'Because he killed my sister.'

Ian was clenching his fists, his knuckles white. 'Then let the police do their job. Stay away from him.'

I couldn't understand why he was saying this – he should be helping me to find Franny's killer, not deterring me. 'I can't,' I said.

He left the house, slamming the door behind him. I don't know why he reacted so vehemently, but I suspect he was jealous of the time I was devoting to M. Since then, I don't mention his name. Ian has no idea what he looks like, and has no inclination to find out. He doesn't know I still follow M. around town, or that I'm writing Franny's story. He doesn't know I met M. yesterday at Fluffy's, and he definitely doesn't know about my date with him tonight.

I'm jittery all afternoon. I don't like deceiving Ian, but I know he wouldn't approve of my plan for M. I think of how M. committed the perfect murder. As soon as the police read Franny's diary, they took him into custody. He freely admitted his interest in bondage and punishment, but denied he killed my sister. With no prior arrests, no history of violent behavior, no physical evidence to place him at Franny's apartment, they had to release him. I obtained a copy of the coroner's report and made my own conclusions. I don't know how he did it yet, but M. is responsible for her death.

I take a shower, then wonder how to dress. I want M. to be distracted this evening. I squeeze into my siren's outfit, guaranteed to seduce, then lure a man to his destruction – a form-hugging red knit dress, thigh high, with the back cut down to my waist. I put on red lipstick the color of a maraschino cherry, slip on high heels, then grab a coat.

When it's close to seven, I drive over to his house and sit out front in my car, a maroon Honda Accord, for several minutes. The darkness of the night is blue-black, the sky as glossy as ink, and the shrubs and trees, devoid of sunlight, have lost their color. There is a gathered, closed-in feeling to Willowbank after nightfall; a crepuscular claustrophobia sets in. Overhead branches and vines intertwine in a shadowy bower; walls of hedges, dense and impenetrable, form a verdant screen that surrounds and encloses. I think of what I am about to do. I could go home and let the police handle him as Ian has told me so many times. But even as I'm thinking this, I'm opening the door to my car and getting out. I head up the long cobbled walkway to the front porch and ring the doorbell. Light from inside seeps through the drawn curtains, setting the picture window all aglow. Above the door, a bug light shines down on me and makes my hands look yellow and jaundiced. I wait under the light, the night air cold on my skin.

M. answers. He greets me with a warm smile and ushers me into his home. I feel a nervous flutter in the pit of my stomach. This is the man who most likely killed my sister. He is tall, with thick, dark hair that falls voluptuously over his high forehead, and he's dressed in black: black leather shoes, black slacks, a black cashmere sweater. He looks elegant in an understated way, with a simple gold watch clasped to his wrist.

In the foyer, I get an uncomfortable feeling of déjà vu. His house is exactly as Franny described it in her diary. He takes my coat, then shows me around – but I already know what to expect: earthy tones, hardwood floors, spacious rooms, comfortable furniture. It is the home of an organized man living alone, without mess or clutter. I look out the glass doors at his backyard and see his black Great Dane hunkering in the shadows. M. tells me his name is Rameau, after a French composer of the late-Baroque era. We go into the kitchen, which is well stocked and orderly, with modern appliances and fixtures that obviously did not come with the original home. While he prepares dinner, I chat with him, mentally recording each word he says. Gravid with expectation, my senses are heightened, sharply attuned to his every nuance. Perhaps I am mistaken, but regardless of his casual manner, each word he speaks and each gesture he makes seem fraught with special significance and hidden meanings.

This man is a killer, I think, and I try to keep the nervousness out of my voice. M. moves around the room gracefully, perfectly at ease. He pours both of us a glass of white wine, then goes back to the stove, checks under the lids of several pots. His geniality flusters me a little; he seems almost likable. I hadn't expected that. I ask him what he's cooking.

'Salmon steaks,' he tells me. 'I'll broil them in a few minutes.' He lifts the lids. 'A dill sauce for the fish, asparagus with cashew butter, gingered carrots.' He looks over at me. 'I didn't make dessert. Franny told me you didn't eat sweets.'

I freeze at the sound of my sister's name, then slowly swallow what's left in my wineglass and set it on the tiled counter. Instinctively, I gauge the distance to the door.

'How did you know?' I ask him, my voice barely a whisper.

He picks up a wooden spoon and stirs the sauce. 'You're not a very good detective. I've seen you around, following me, showing up a few too many times for it to be a mere coincidence. Besides, Franny showed me your picture.'

Watching me, he tastes the sauce, furrows his eyebrows, adds a pinch of spice. He replaces the lid and turns to me. Leaning against the counter, he folds his arms and cocks his head, smiling just a little. 'As a matter of fact, she told me a lot about you. More, I'm sure, than you want me to know.'

I'm shocked into silence. I can't believe he knew, all along, my identity. We stare at each other without speaking. I'm still stunned; he's only amused. He looks down at my wineglass and sees that it's empty. He gets the bottle of wine, uncorks it, and takes a step toward me. Reflexively, I tense. He sees my fear and smiles, then pours me another glass of wine.

'What were you planning to do?' he asks me, saying it as if he were inquiring about the time of day. 'Why are you here?'

I tell him the truth. 'I want to find out more about you. I think you killed my sister.'

I expect M. to act insulted or outraged, but he only raises one eyebrow, mildly intrigued. 'You know, of course, the police don't share your opinion.'

'They don't have any evidence – that's all I know.'

He nods thoughtfully. 'So you came here to . . . what? Collect evidence? Disclose the murderer?' He is making fun of me.

'Yes,' I say, trying to hold in my anger.

'What if I told you I didn't kill her. Would you believe me?'

'No.'

'Ah,' he says, thinking. 'I suppose not.' He crosses over to the refrigerator and pulls out a head of romaine, scallions, tomatoes, and marinated mushrooms. He washes the tomatoes and begins to slice them into small wedges. His insouciance infuriates me. I want a reaction from him.

'She kept a diary,' I say. 'She wrote about you. I know what you did to her.'

'"Franny's File,"' he says, still slicing. 'The police mentioned it, of course, but I already knew about it. From Franny.' He looks up at me. 'And I doubt if you knew what I did to her. You wouldn't be here if you did.'

'I intend to find out.'

'Really?' The word sounds like a challenge. He gets a wooden bowl for the salad and dumps in the tomatoes and mushrooms. He slices the scallions. 'How do you plan to do that?'

I don't know anymore. My plan was to put myself in Franny's place. Find out everything I could about M., get him, somehow, to betray himself. Now I don't know what to do. He is still making the salad, tearing apart lettuce leaves as if this were a friendly dinner date.

'If you really believe I killed Franny, you should stay away from me.' He takes a sip of wine and regards me with an unworried casualness. 'What's to stop me from killing you?'

I've already thought of this. He's a clever man, and that's what is protecting me. The police know of my consuming passion to put him behind bars, and if anything happens to me, now or later, they would zero in on him. It would be too much of a coincidence: two sisters, the same man. I tell him so, and he nods.

'Yes, if you die I better have a good alibi this time, hadn't I?'

When I hear this, my body stiffens. Even though Franny's body was decomposing when she was found, the Yolo County coroner, using a sodium chloride test on her eyes, analyzing the vitreous humor, the clear gel behind the lens, and also evaluating the degree of insect infestation and rate of bodily decomposition, and processing the scene markers – the dated store receipt on the counter, the mail in her mailbox, the time recorded on the unretrieved message on her answering machine, an open newspaper on the table – using all of these, the coroner was able to establish a time of death, give or take a few hours. M. was home alone during that time, he claimed, with no alibi.

I'm suddenly impatient with him and his indifference. I despise this man more than I fear him. 'Why did you invite me to dinner?' I ask him. 'If you knew who I was, why didn't you say so?'

'You're the one who began this charade. I was just playing along.' He adds salad dressing and mixes the salad. After a few moments, he says, 'I did it for my amusement, I suppose. The same reason I started with Franny' – he looks over at me and gives an apologetic shrug – 'for amusement.'

When he mentions her name, I cringe. He speaks of her as if she was insignificant. He sees the look on my face.

'Would you rather I lied?' he asks. 'Do you want me to tell you she meant more to me than she really did?'

I say nothing.

He sighs patiently. 'It's been almost a year since she died. Do you expect me to mourn her still? Life does go on.'

'If you killed her,' I say, 'I'll find out.'

'How?' he asks. 'Did you think you could simply come over here and trip me up? Do you actually think you're a match for me?' He shakes his head. 'I have nothing to fear from you.'

I don't say anything, so he puts down the salad tongs and continues.

'Your sister's death was tragic, but I'm not responsible. I had nothing to do with it.'

'I'm not convinced of that.'

He is silent. The steam from the asparagus hisses beneath a slit in the lid. He reaches over and turns the heat down.

'Let me tell you what I think,' he says finally. 'You want someone to blame. You want to avenge Franny. That's understandable – that's human nature. But I think you want something else, something only I can give you: answers. That's why you're really here. I knew more about your sister in the five months we were together than you knew about her in a lifetime. You treated her like a casual acquaintance. You didn't know her at all, and now you feel guilty, you feel remorse. You're here to make amends.'

'That's not true,' I say. 'You don't know what you're talking about.'

'Don't I? Then tell me – why are you here?'

For a moment, I'm confused. Then I shake my head in disgust. 'You're twisting things around,' I say. 'I have nothing to feel guilty about. I'm not the one who mistreated her. I'm not the one who turned "Franny's File" into a diary that reads as if it came out of a book on sadism.' I look down at my hands and see that I'm clenching them. I relax. 'But you're right – I am here for answers. I came here to fill in the blanks, to learn more about you, to find out if you killed Franny.'

M. is silent for a minute, then he says, 'You don't know what you're getting involved in.'

'I'll take my chances.'

He gives me a steady look, his eyes level and unblinking. 'All right,' he says. 'We'll play your game if that's what you want. But first let me do you a favor and issue another warning: you're not going to like the answers I'll give you. You'd be better off to go home, resume your life, forget all about me.'

I say nothing.

He waits, giving me time to change my mind. I choose to ignore his warning.

'Very well,' he says finally. 'I didn't kill Franny, but I can fill in the blanks for you. I can reveal your sister.' He hesitates, then says, 'You want information, you want to know what really happened between Franny and me – I'll tell you. But your curiosity is going to cost you.'

I look at him with distrust and this makes him smile.

'What do you mean?' I ask. 'Cost me what?'

'Time,' he says. 'A portion of your life.'

His reply mystifies me.

'You want information about Franny – I'll give it to you. But don't think you'll get all the answers during dinner. This will take time. Months, perhaps. And you may not get any answers tonight. Think of our . . . what shall we call it? An alliance? Think of our alliance as an ongoing process of discovery.'

This seems too easy. 'What's in it for you?' I ask. 'Why are you willing to do this?'

He places the salmon steaks under the broiler. 'To amuse myself,' he says finally. 'For no other reason.'

'This is just a game to you, isn't it?'

'Precisely.' He picks up my glass of wine and puts it in my hand. 'Well, how badly do you want to know?'

I pause, then take a sip of wine. I could – and should – walk away. But our lives were thrown together, an unholy alliance to be sure, the day Franny died. I know he won't intentionally incriminate himself, but even clever people make mistakes. Let him play his game, let him have his fun – it'll only help me tighten the noose around his neck.

'Bad enough,' I say.

He picks up the salad bowl and starts to take it into the dining room. 'You may be a challenge, after all,' he says as he passes me. 'Franny, although dear, was no challenge whatsoever.'

And I may be more than you bargained for, I think, following him into the dining room.

7

I have been to too many funerals, Billy's, my father and mother's, and then Franny's. They are all buried at the Davis Cemetery, lined up in a row. I wouldn't have made it through Franny's funeral if it hadn't been for Ian. We weren't lovers then, or even friends really, but he came over early that morning to see if I needed help – which I did. Desperately. Maisie, my best friend who also works at the *Bee*, had offered to stay with me, but I'd turned her down, wanting to be alone with my grief. I'd got through my parents' and Billy's funerals without assistance, and I thought I could manage Franny's as well. But on the day of her funeral, I started to unravel.

I lived in Sacramento then, in a small house near McKinley Park, and when Ian rang my doorbell that morning, arriving unannounced, I was in a slip and dark nylons, still not dressed, my nerves frazzled. He'd worn a black suit and his body filled the doorway, blocking out the morning sun. His blond hair was slicked back, and despite his six-foot-plus height he looked like a young boy who was worried he'd done the wrong thing, worried he shouldn't be here and that I'd send him away. He waited in the living room while I went back to finish dressing. The bedroom closet was much too small, only half the length of the wall, and it was recessed behind white louvered folding doors that opened and closed like an accordion. Suddenly, I began throwing my clothes on the floor. Then I emptied out my dresser drawers, and when Ian heard them crashing to the floor, he came running into the room.

'I don't know what to wear,' I told him.

He put his arms around me, trying to give comfort, but I

pushed him away. 'Leave me alone,' I said, suddenly feeling angry. 'I don't want you here.'

A pained expression crossed his face. He sat on my bed and began folding the sweaters and slips and bras I had carelessly flung onto the floor.

'You don't know what it's like,' I said. 'She shouldn't have died like that.' My voice was dismal and frayed, unraveling at the ends of my sentences.

Ian stood. Tentatively, he reached out again, but this time I didn't push him away. He pressed me to his chest and stroked my hair, saying, 'Shhh, shhh,' even though I wasn't making any noise.

I stood there and let him comfort me, this man dressed for a funeral, almost a stranger to me until recently, and kept my head pressed to his chest. With his palm, he rubbed the top of my head, messing my hair even worse, his hand so large it seemed to belong to a Titan.

'I do know what it's like,' he said softly. 'It took a long time for me to get over Cheryl's murder. I'm still not over it. We got in an argument the day she was killed. I was so angry with her. So—' Ian shook his head, remembering. 'I know this won't help,' he added, 'but it does get easier with time.'

'No,' I said. 'It won't get easier. I won't let it. Not until I find out who killed her.'

Abruptly, Ian shoved me away. I looked up at him, surprised. In his eyes, I saw something strange – anger, maybe, but something more than that.

Sharply, his jaw clenched, he said, 'You're not going to do anything about Franny. The police will handle it. Do you understand?'

Stunned by his outburst, I didn't say a word.

'Do you?' he said, raising his voice, the words whipping out.

I backed away from him, hurt that he was yelling at me now, at a time like this, not understanding.

Immediately, Ian was contrite. 'I'm sorry,' he said. 'I didn't mean to get angry. It's just—' He hesitated, then began again.

'Cheryl meant so much to me. Dying the way she did, it was hard. And now, with you, the last few days . . .' His voice trailed off. 'Maybe I'm being overprotective, but I just don't want anything to happen to you. It could be dangerous to look for her murderer. You have to let the police take care of this. Do you understand?'

I nodded, still confused at his outburst. Then I looked around the room, at my scattered clothes, feeling at a loss. I needed to get ready for Franny's funeral, but I couldn't seem to move. Thinking of how Franny was killed, I bit down on my lip.

'Don't do that,' Ian said firmly. 'You're bleeding.' He massaged my lip out from between my teeth, wiped my mouth with his handkerchief. I swallowed my memories of Franny, all the pain; it disappeared when I heard the scolding in his voice: *Don't do that.* The pain was buried in me somewhere, safely out of reach. I felt nothing then. I surrendered to him, let him take over completely. I stood before him, numb, while he finished dressing me, talking to me in a very calm, reassuring voice, as if I were his child.

During the funeral, Ian held my hand. I was in a stunned, numb state, and didn't pay much attention to the minister at the church, although my eyes had been glued to his face. And at the cemetery, I still clung to Ian, fearing that if I lost his hand, I might lose myself. At some point, I remembered thinking how odd it was that I was holding on to him instead of a close friend, instead of Maisie. But then I recalled Cheryl Mansfield, and thought how fitting it was that death brought me and Ian together. Except for Ian, no one at the funeral could really understand how I felt. Losing someone from a brutal murder, as I lost Franny and Ian lost Cheryl, is different than losing someone from an illness or accident or old age.

I walked around in a dreamlike state, waiting for the funeral to end. I'd expected a simple ceremony, with Franny's friends and a few of my own. But hundreds of people had shown up, most of whom I didn't even know. My friends and coworkers from the Bee were all there, and all the neighbors had come, and the few friends I'd seen with Franny over the years. But who were all those other people? Store clerks where she went shopping? The boy who delivered her newspaper? Curiosity seekers? Or had Franny formed a network of acquaintances all over Sacramento and Davis that I hadn't been aware of? There was a distinguished-looking man in a very expensive suit; a group of little girls, in brown Brownie uniforms, huddled together; an extremely fat lady who had trouble walking; two men in wheelchairs – who were all those people? I felt cheated, that I had missed out on part of her life – most of her life – just as I felt cheated because of her death.

After the service, a few friends came back to my house. The entire time, I sat mutely on the sofa next to Ian. He held my hand in his lap, clasped in both of his. Maisie had taken care of all the food and drinks, and she was busy arranging platters of sandwiches and cakes on the dining room table. She's a few years older than I, and at least fifty pounds heavier, with thick calves and deeply tanned skin. She brought Ian and me a plate of food, patted me on the arm, then went back to the kitchen. People milled about, speaking in hushed tones. They would come up to me and say something nice about Franny; I would smile politely, not saying a word. Ian had to thank them for me. If I was to say anything, I was afraid I would cry, which I hated to do.

At last, I started to come out of my daze, and a weariness set in. Everyone was still talking about Franny, and I wished they would all go home. I sighed, but it stuck in my throat and came out as a ragged sob. I leaned my head against Ian. I didn't want to hear another word about Franny.

Ian, as if he sensed this, had leaned over and said quietly, 'Did you want to go outside now? We could take a walk.'

I nodded and, with my hand in his, I followed him out the door. The air was warm and breezy, a perfect spring day. It felt good to be outside. I was feeling claustrophobic in the house, although I didn't know it at the time. Closing my eyes, I listened to the birds singing in the treetops, to a car pulling out of the driveway, to the sad bleat of a broken truck horn. Ian put his hand on my shoulder.

'Why don't we go to my house?' he'd said. 'You can spend the night with me. I'll sleep on the couch.'

I shook my head. 'No,' I said. 'I can't.'

'People will be leaving soon. You don't have to stay – Maisie will take care of everything.'

'I want to stay here tonight. In my own home.'

Ian didn't say anything; he rubbed my shoulders, the back of my neck. Finally, he said, 'I'd feel better if you came home with me. I don't think you should be alone tonight.'

'No,' I said. 'I don't want to. I'm going to stay here.'

'All right. I'll stay with you, then.'

Later that night, when Ian was asleep on the couch, I snuck over to Franny's apartment. The police had sealed it off, and I was unable to enter. I stood outside the door, the night air cool, the sky black, waiting, just waiting – for what, I have no idea.

Three weeks later the police released the apartment. Franny had paid the rent until the end of the month, and I convinced the apartment manager to give me a key. That night, I drove over there. I went into her living room but didn't turn on any of the lights. A dizzying sense of helplessness washed over me. I went around to the couch and curled up on it. The apartment had been professionally cleaned and painted, and I could still smell the odor of fresh paint. But underneath that, embedded in my memory, was the foul stench of a dead body. No amount of paint can remove that smell from my mind. When Franny was found, the police removed her body before I arrived – but the odor had lingered. It had permeated everything in the apartment: the curtains, the furniture, the carpet. And, as I sat on her couch that night, I could feel Franny's presence, lingering, like the odor from her body. The smell was in my imagination, but in the darkness of the room it came back to me and made me want to take small, shallow breaths. It saddened me to think I associated Franny with a smell so foul.

A tear rolled down my cheek. She didn't deserve to die the way she had. And at that moment, still sitting on her couch, I swore to her that if the police couldn't find her killer, one way or another, I would.

8

I live in a small custom-built house on the corner of Torrey and Rosario. Actually, it's a duplex, but it's on a corner lot and from the road it looks like a single-unit home. My landlord, a man who lives in the older part of Willowbank – just a few blocks from M. – is retired, but he used to own a small construction firm in Davis, and he built this duplex himself, adding personal touches that one doesn't normally find in a rental: a floor-to-ceiling stone fireplace, wood paneling in the living room, built-in oak bookcases, parquet floors in the entryway and dining area, and walls decorated with textured wallpaper in patterns of autumn leaves and blades of grass. His tastes are reflected throughout the duplex, and he did a good job with the area in which he had to work. But the house is long and narrow and small, and the living room doesn't get much light. Even in the summer, with the drapes opened, the room is dim and gloomy. Furniture that wouldn't fit in the house is stored in the garage, and every inch inside is crammed with my possessions. The walls seem to be pressing in on me, and sometimes I feel squeezed in; I feel that I have to hold my breath just to make everything fit, like stuffing yourself in clothes one size too small. And even though I've been living here for eight months now, I have trouble calling this my home. I feel like a sojourner, passing through, killing time, waiting for my real life to start up again.

The only part of my life that does seem real to me is the part with Ian. Despite his occasional outbursts, he seems perfect for me. There's a natural ease to our relationship that's out of proportion to the time we've been together. Some people might call us boring, but I find a peacefulness in our simple lives, and it pleases me enormously. Our routines are predictable and extremely prosaic, but since Franny's death I've come to cherish the ordinary. I feel secure with Ian, grounded, and that, for now, is enough.

I'm in the living room tonight, sitting in an armchair reading *The New Yorker,* and occasionally I'll look over at Ian. Just the sight of him makes me smile with pleasure. Men, by my choice, have always been a temporary presence in my life, like a car you drive until you decide to trade it in for a new model. But with Ian, my vocabulary – along with my preference for the transient – is changing. Words pop up in my mind I've never seriously thought about before: *permanence, long-term, commitment, marriage*.

He's sitting on the edge of the couch, hunched over the coffee table, a knife and a small block of holly in hand, whittling. Wood carving is a hobby of his since childhood, and for several years he has concentrated primarily on miniature sculptures. It is meticulous, painstaking work, and for hours he'll sit with a piece of wood in one hand, a knife or gouge or chisel in the other, and make minute cuts that will transform a block of holly or basswood or ebony or boxwood into a small figurine, usually no larger than three inches: birds, animals, insects, caricatures. Tonight, he's carving a snake hatching from an egg. A tuft of his blond hair has fallen forward over his eye, but I doubt that he has noticed; his concentration is total, his cuts in the wood precise.

I set down *The New Yorker* and go over to him, rest my hand gently on his shoulder. He looks up, quizzical, his knife suspended in the air. I can't help but smile at the odd picture he creates: a husky man who looks as if he could plow fields without assistance, working on a miniature carving so delicate it appears lost in his fist. Unconsciously and very lightly, he rubs the wood with his thumb.

'I feel like making popcorn,' I say. 'Would you like some?' and, distractedly, he nods, smiles, and returns to his carving.

'I have to go to the store,' I say. 'I'll be back in a few minutes,' but Ian is already working on the snake sculpture, and I doubt that he has heard me. I grab my keys and purse, and back my Honda out of the garage. Around the house, high-pressure sodium streetlamps give off an eerie orangish glow that barely lights up the neighborhood, and once I turn onto Mace Boulevard the lamps are spaced far apart, and the street is dark and quiet, deserted, the adjacent fields tenebrous with moon shadows. I drive farther, where fields give way to subdivisions, past El Macero Country Club on the right, the lower-priced homes on the left, then pull into the shopping center. Inside the store, I locate the popcorn and spend a few minutes deciding what to buy: natural, butter flavored, herb and garlic flavored, salt free, light buttered, cheddar cheese flavored. I decide on a box of the light buttered and walk to the front of the grocery store. Just a few people are shopping this late at night, and the store seems oddly quiet, the silence broken only by the sporadic sobs of a small girl following her mother down the cereal aisle.

I hand the cashier five dollars, wait for my change, then go outside into the cool, night air. The sky is black and clear, and I absently take in the images around me – up ahead, an old man fumbling with his car keys; a heavyset blond woman yelling at her boy to stop running between the parked cars; a bag boy rolling a queue of shopping carts across the asphalt and into the store.

'Hey! You!'

I look up and see the old man waving at me, frantic.

'Watch out!' he yells, and at the same time I hear an engine, the motor loud and too close, and I turn slightly and see a dark car speeding in my direction, fishtailing as if it's out of control. I jump back and slam into a parked truck, watching the other car – its windows blackened, the driver invisible – miss me by inches. The car accelerates and screeches around the corner, disappearing. I stay down, heart pounding, unable to move.

'Damn teenagers,' the old man mutters when he reaches me,

and he pulls me up by the elbow. 'They drive too damned fast. Never watch where they're going. They could've killed you.'

I rise to my feet, still shaken.

'You okay?' he asks.

I nod, thinking not of teenagers but of M., getting angry. The blond woman I saw earlier comes running across the parking lot, dragging her boy by the arm.

'Did you see what kind of car it was?' I ask the old man.

'Black,' he said. 'A black car. That's all I saw.'

'Are you all right?' the woman asks, breathless from her jog across the parking lot. The boy pulls on her arm, trying to get loose. She grips him tighter. 'I thought for sure you were going to get hit.'

'What kind of car was it?' I ask her. 'Did you see the model? The license?'

She shakes her head. 'It all happened so fast. It's a miracle he didn't hit you.'

I rub my elbow where it banged against the truck, berating myself for not thinking fast enough, for not getting the license number.

'It's them damn teenagers,' the old man repeats, but I have some doubts about that. I see my popcorn lying on the asphalt, the box squashed from the car's tires.

When I return home, Ian is still in the living room, working on his block of holly.

'I'm going to take a bath,' I say, and he looks up briefly.

'Weren't you going to make popcorn?' he asks.

'I changed my mind. I'd rather soak in the tub.'

He says, 'I'll join you in a bit,' and makes a cut in the wood.

The tub is in the guest bathroom in the hallway. I turn on the bath water, adjust it to the temperature I want, and let it run as I go into the bedroom. Stepping out of my clothes, I grab a robe and return to the bathroom, shutting the door behind me so the steam will not escape. I set my robe on the counter, then test the temperature with my big toe. The water is hot, too hot, almost scalding – just the way I like it – and I have to inch myself in. Hot water gurgles out of the spigot; beads of moisture drip down the yellow-tiled walls. My skin prickles and reddens under the water, and it takes me minutes just to get both feet in the tub. I see bruises already forming on my right thigh and shoulder where I slammed into the truck. Could M. have been driving that car?

I slide down slowly and watch the water as it covers my body. When the tub is almost full, I lean forward and turn off the spigot, then settle back again, closing my eyes, thinking of the black car. I vow to be more cautious in the future.

After twenty minutes or so, the water becomes tepid. I drain out a few inches, then add more hot water, swirling it around with my arms. I hear the doorknob turn, and Ian walks in. He kneels down by the tub. Frowning, he says, 'How did you get this?' He points at my thigh, where the skin is red and slightly swollen. 'And this?' he asks, moving his finger up to my shoulder.

'I fell on the porch step,' I lie. 'It's nothing.'

Ian kisses the wound softly. With the washcloth, he begins rubbing my arms and shoulders, being careful to avoid the damaged skin. Neither of us speaks, but the pleasure he takes in washing my body shows in his face. I close my eyes and lie still, content, feeling the tenderness in his touch, so loving. Languid and sodden, I yield completely under his hands. He slides soap and washcloth over my flesh, stopping to massage the muscles in my neck, calves, the unbruised thigh. Now is the moment to tell him of my dinner last night with M., I think. In fairness to Ian, I must make a complete disclosure – that I saw M. and will continue to see him until I learn everything he knows, and everything he did, to Franny. Ian is part of my life now, and I owe him the truth. But when I open my eyes and look at him, I know I will tell him nothing. He would argue, he would say I was being foolish – especially if I told him what happened tonight at the store – and he would insist I never see M. I fear I might lose Ian over this, and that fact keeps me from telling the truth.

Smiling, he takes off his clothes, then, as I lean forward, he steps in behind me. The water rises, almost spilling over the rim. He's a big man, and the two of us don't fit easily in my small tub. One of his legs is resting on the edge, the other bent at the knee. I'm wedged back against him, between his legs, my knees drawn up to my chest. It's cramped, uncomfortable, awkward, but somehow strangely soothing. His physical presence calms me, and as he snakes his arms around my body, holding me, I tell myself that it is better, for Ian's sake, to keep M. a secret. Still, this rationalization does not work. I feel my deception acutely; it's as tangible as the two large hands resting on my belly.

9

Although my home on Torrey Street is within the city limits, on the southernmost tip, the subdivision is separated from Davis proper by Interstate 80, and if you continue southward from my home, the area becomes distinctly rural, miles of flat agricultural land, open and cultivated fields broken only by farm equipment and an occasional old home or a small one-building business – a seed company, a wholesale nursery, the Sierra Sod building. M. jogs out here regularly, Rameau trotting at his side.

Dressed in a black sweatsuit and tennis shoes, I surprised him earlier this morning on the corner of Montgomery and Rosario, up the street from my house. He seemed amused when he saw me; he invited me along. The sun is not yet up, but streaks of purplish-gray light, emerging from the east, seep across the horizon like trickling water oozing from a sluice gate. We jog south on County Road 104, past open fields – dewy, mist-covered monochromatic landscapes, shadowy in the sunless sky. In the cool air, our breaths come out in white clouds, mine more labored than his. I haven't jogged for ages, and although I work out regularly at the athletic club, I'm not prepared for a three-mile run, which is M.'s routine on Mondays, Wednesdays, and Fridays.

I glance over at him. I admit he's an attractive man. Lean and in good shape, he has the placid, slightly bored expression of a runner who's nowhere close to pushing his limits. I'm sure he's jogging slower than normal just to accommodate me. He's wearing a navy blue jogging suit with a white stripe down the outside of each leg. And mittens. I wish I'd remembered to wear mittens. My fingers feel numb in the chilly early morning air.

'Where were you the night before last?' I ask him.

He gives me a quick, sidelong glance. 'The night before last?' he asks.

'Yes. Around eight-thirty.'

He thinks for a moment, then says, 'Home.'

'Alone, I suppose.'

'That's right.'

'How convenient. And you don't know anything about a dark car with blackened windows that nearly ran me down?'

M. stops jogging. 'Are you serious?' he says, a look of concern spreading across his face. I keep on going. He catches up to me.

'I'm not about to run you over with a car,' he says. 'Obviously, it was an accident.'

'Obviously.'

He looks over at me with a droll smile. 'If I decide to come after you, Nora, you'll know it. I won't hide behind blackened windows.'

'And it'll take more than a near-miss to scare me away. I intend to find out the truth about Franny. And you.'

We jog without speaking. To the right, a lone tractor slowly trundles across a patch of brown land, and in the distance I see a man rambling through a field in some sort of three-wheeled vehicle, stopping every now and then to check on the irrigation pipes.

Breathing heavily, I run along, my feet pounding the asphalt, feeling ungainly next to M. with his light-footed, easy pace. 'I usually work out in the gym,' I tell him, trying to breathe normally. 'Swimming, weights, aerobic classes, Jazzercise. I haven't jogged for years.'

'I can tell,' he says, and I hear the condescension in his voice. I pick up my speed, even though it makes my lungs ache.

'You said you knew about Franny's diary,' I begin.

'Yes, I even read it.'

'Then you know how sketchy it was. And that she stopped making entries toward the end. The last part of her life is missing.'

I stop speaking to catch my breath, and we jog in silence. A backhoe, like a defunct dinosaur, is poised on the edge of the road with its clawed scoop turned in on itself, as if it were digging its own grave.

'You didn't tell me anything about Franny the other night,' I continue. 'I want to know what happened in the weeks right before she died.'

'Not so fast,' M. says. 'Time to back up; we're going to do this chronologically. I'm saving that for last.' He hesitates, then adds, 'And I can only give you information up to a certain point. I didn't kill Franny; you'll have to search elsewhere for that piece of information. Even so, there's plenty I can tell you.'

We jog on. I am irritated but try not to show it. This is, after all, his game, and I have to play by his rules – or so he thinks. My shoes thud rhythmically on the road. I thought my reservoir of energy was near depletion, but I feel a renewal, a determination to continue, despite the pain in my calves and lungs.

'Okay,' I say finally. 'We'll do it your way. Tell me something about Franny – something I don't know.'

In thought, he gazes across an immense field of sod, the grass gathering color in the lightening sky, flocked like velvet in the early morning dew, seemingly endless. M. does not vary his pace; it is steady, even, and, for him, leisurely.

He says, 'There were two things Franny was very good at: communicating – which I know comes as a surprise to you – and oral sex.' He pauses. 'On second thought, I suppose both will surprise you.'

Oral sex? I say nothing. After reading Franny's diary I realized she had, like everyone else, sexual desires. Still, I have trouble imagining her sucking this man's cock – and being good at it. Or even liking it.

He continues, 'At the beginning, she was horrible at both. She was very shy when we first met and had a difficult time speaking about you, or your parents or brother, or what she was feeling inside, but once she trusted me she opened right up. Or perhaps it would be more accurate to say I forced her to open up. I gave her no choice: I questioned her relentlessly, probing deeper into her psyche each time. She was timid and apprehensive until the end, and she never stood up to me, but at least she got to the point where she could articulate her feelings quite well – to me, if not to anyone else. I know a lot about you, Nora, from Franny's point of view – I know what she thought of you, and what she needed and couldn't get from you.'

I ignore his attempt to make me feel guilty. I was not much more than a kid myself when Franny came to live with me, and I did the best I could to take care of her. My parental skills were lacking – I know that; I was not perfect, but I did my best. I jog on, not taking his bait.

'As for the oral sex,' he says, 'she was truly dreadful when we first met. Clumsy, ineffectual, artless – not to mention downright dangerous. I had to endure the agony of her sharp, scraping teeth more than a few times.' He laughs softly. 'But she was extremely willing to please, and a fast learner. Once I taught her what to do, she was excellent. I'd even go so far as to say she had quite a knack for it. Of course, the inducement I offered her probably had something to do with her willingness; she quickly learned that the consequences of not pleasing me far outweighed any reluctance she might have had. As a result, she became quite adept.'

I withhold my anger, keeping his cold words at a distance. He wants to reduce me to tears or anger or guilt. His machinations are transparent, and I am glad we're jogging; the physical exertion diverts some of the anger I feel. He is unable to see the effect his words have on me.

'What consequences were those?' I ask.

'Not as harsh as you're imagining. Remember, she was in love with me. She wanted to please me.'

Instead, I remember her diary, how he tied her to the

dining-room chair, legs spread, to punish her for a minor transgression, for wearing a red satin robe.

'What consequences?' I repeat, but he ignores me. We reach an old, concrete bridge and circle back. A blue farm truck with a wooden slat railing in the back rattles by. It is the first automobile on the road to pass us this morning.

'That's enough for today,' he says. 'Why don't you tell me something about yourself?'

With exasperation, I sigh. The pounding of my Reeboks, as rhythmic as a beating heart, accentuates the silence. We jog down the road, neither of us speaking. Broken asphalt and small clods of dirt crunch and crumble beneath my shoes. Rameau trots along at M.'s heels, never veering from his side.

'What do you want to know?' I say finally.

'Everyone has a secret, Nora. Everyone has unresolved issues, problems they don't, or can't, deal with. Franny seemed to think you didn't have any; I believe differently. I want to know yours.'

I shrug, unwilling to share anything with this man. I find his question intrusive, and his manner irritating. Over dinner a few nights ago, he quizzed me on the details of my life since Franny died – a leave of absence from the Bee, moving to Davis, a new boyfriend, occasional freelance work – and my sister, according to M., had filled him in on my life previous to her death. What more can he want? A long, white sedan with dried mud splattered on the side speeds by.

'Talk to me,' he says.

I am silent again, uncomfortable with the direction the conversation is taking. We jog past a row of trees lining the road – old country trees, some asymmetrical from a previous disease or infestation, or perhaps from a natural force, the limbs wind-torn or lightning struck. In the gray dawn, they appear ghostly and skeletal, the trunks weathered and tough-looking.

'Tell me about the men in your life,' he says, trying to encourage me. 'Franny said you're aloof with them, that you had numerous boyfriends but were never serious about any of them. She didn't find it strange, though – she thought you were strong, courageous, much too independent to rely on a man for anything. She envied you your many boyfriends – she wanted one of her own – and even though she didn't agree with your easy-come-easy-go philosophy regarding men, she didn't find it strange.' He turns to me and smirks. 'You were a feminist, a trailblazer, an independent soul,' he says mockingly. 'She admired you for that.'

He jogs a few yards without speaking, then says, 'Franny was not an exceptionally insightful woman. I think her admiration was misplaced. I think there's another reason for your self-imposed unapproachability, something of which she was totally unaware. Tell me.'

'There is no reason. And I'm not aloof with my current boyfriend. I'm very close to him.'

'A natural response – and only temporary. You lose your sister, you turn to someone else for comfort. It won't last.'

I feel the anger rise in my cheeks. 'You know nothing about me,' I say. 'Or my boyfriend.'

'Forget about him. He's of no interest to me. I want to know why you've never been in love.'

I shake my head. 'I've had lots of boyfriends,' I tell him, looking at the ground.

'But never been in love.' His voice is insistent.

'I'm in love now.'

He throws me a cold glance. 'Okay,' he says, but I can tell he doesn't believe me. 'You're in love now – for the first time, at thirty-five. Rather odd, don't you think?'

'No, not odd. I just never found the right man.'

'You're lying. There's more to it than that.'

'I was busy with my career,' I say. 'And before that, with college. I didn't have time for an intense relationship, or the inclination. I didn't want to get seriously involved with anyone.'

M. is silent for a moment. Then he looks at me. 'Now tell me the real reason,' he says.

I am quiet. I know the answer to that question – I've had

years to think about it – but he's the last person in whom I'd confide. We jog past the Sierra Sod building, our run nearly over, and turn left onto Montgomery.

He waits for me to respond. When I don't, he says, 'Franny wanted desperately to be loved, but until I came along, she had no one. You had numerous boyfriends, but refused to allow yourself to get close to any of them. You don't see it now, but the two of you are flip sides of the same coin. You're more alike than you can imagine.'

This makes me smile to myself: he may have guessed correctly that I have a few hidden problems, as do all people, but there are no two women more different than Franny and me. He's way off base, and he doesn't even know it; he's grappling, trying to get a hook in me and coming up short.

'Maybe I didn't get close to any of my boyfriends because I just wanted to have fun – no serious involvement, no commitment, just fun and games.'

'Maybe,' he says, 'but I doubt it. You're holding back on me, Nora.'

A bicyclist in blue bike shorts and a white top rides by, nodding to us beneath his bike helmet. We are back where we started, on the corner of Montgomery and Rosario. M. stops, and so does Rameau. Panting, the dog's tongue lolls on one side of his mouth.

I put my hands on my hips and face M., looking him in the eye. 'You don't need to know anything about me,' I say. Then I shrug. 'There's nothing to know.'

My sweatshirt is soaked at the neck, and drops of perspiration dribble down my forehead, which I wipe with my sleeve. M., neither sweating nor breathing heavily, looks as if he's about to begin a jog, not end it.

I look down the road. From here, I can see the front of my house, and parked at the curb is Franny's black fin-tailed Cadillac. It's been there since she died, and now the battery is dead and it doesn't run. I could never bring myself to drive it, but I couldn't sell it, either. At first, the neighbors complained about its unsightly presence, its sheer enormity, its ugliness, but when they realized it belonged to Franny, the complaints stopped. Now we – everyone in the neighborhood – pretend it doesn't exist. The car just sits there, day in, day out, like a bad memory that won't go away.

'You haven't told me anything about Franny,' I say. 'She could talk to you and give good head – so what? I want to know what she left out of her diary.'

'You shall,' M. says, 'you'll learn more than you want to.'

He turns to leave, but I grab him by the arm. 'Now,' I say. 'I want to know something now.'

M. removes my hand. Curtly, he says, 'Curiosity didn't kill the cat – obstinacy did. Something Franny never learned. Something you'd better learn before it's too late.'

My breath catches. Was that why he killed her? Her stubbornness over something? But what? A ripple of fear, chillingly cold, goes through my body. 'What's that supposed to mean?' I say.

M. just smiles, then he and Rameau jog up Montgomery, leaving me behind.

10

On the northeast corner of Eighth Street and Pole Line Road, secluded behind a tall, dense wall of dark green shrubbery, lies the Davis Cemetery. It is hidden away, as if it were a family secret, something not to be exposed.

I drive through the Eighth Street entrance and follow the curved, asphalt road to Franny's plot. The road was recently paved, the surface a bituminous black. This is not one of those old, run-down cemeteries with cracked headstones and bare, stippled walkways and dirty tombs cramped together like row houses in a high-density, low-rent neighborhood. Here, neatly trimmed lawn, stretching out like a gently waving blanket in the wind, completely covers the sloped land, and shade trees are scattered about, interspersed among the grave sites.

I park along the edge of the road close to Franny's plot, in the newer section of the cemetery, and get out of my car. I just attended a Saturday-morning Jazzercise class, and I'm still wearing my workout clothes – a red leotard, black Capri tights, and a zip-up hooded sweatshirt. The sky is blue and flawless, one of those late-winter, crisp morning skies, with an icy coldness in the air that seeps through your pores and tightens your skin. I walk across the lawn, past granite and marble headstones, blades of newly cut grass sticking to my tennis shoes. A half-dozen birds, magpies, with shiny black feathers and snowy-white bellies, hop on the lawn, searching for insects, not bothered by my presence. I am the only person here this morning.

I stop in front of Franny's gravestone, a simple marker flush to the ground. My mother and father and Billy are to her right, and an empty space is on her left. When my parents died, I was surprised to learn my father had purchased a family plot, five spaces. What had motivated him to secure sites for my brother, Franny, and me? Didn't it cross his mind that we would marry and move away and choose to be buried next to our spouses, most likely in a different city, a different state, even? Sometimes, I make light of his decision – perhaps there was a sale, two plots for the price of one. Other times, his prescience gives me pause. I see the empty grave site, and I wonder if I shall lie there, like Franny and Billy, without a future, our family eternally intact but without heirs to guarantee perpetuity.

I close my eyes. The smell of winter is still in the air – the green smell of wet grass from yesterday's rain; the lingering, ashy odor of an extinguished blaze in a nearby fireplace. I think of what M. said. *Obstinacy killed the cat – something Franny never learned.* What did she do that was so obstinate that he would kill her over it? Since then, he's refused to elaborate on his statement. I told the police what he said, that he practically admitted to killing her, but they said it was only hearsay, that they needed physical evidence to go after M.

Opening my eyes, looking at Franny's grave, I realize I came here for strength and guidance. I've not made much progress with M. I jog with him three days a week – when Ian has not stayed overnight at my house – and I no longer have trouble keeping up with him, but the information he gives me about Franny is inconsequential. Instead, he wastes my time, quizzing me on *my* life, *my* beliefs, *my* feelings – of which I tell him nothing. I'm an intensely private person, and I don't share my life easily with other people. And I see the way he looks at me; I know what's on his mind. He wants to fuck me – a terrible prospect, but it would be less intimidating than giving him bits and pieces of my soul. I could use his desire to my advantage.

Suddenly, I know what I'm going to do. I suppose I knew all along. Kneeling down, I run my fingers lightly across Franny's gravestone. My fingertips read the etched inscription as if it were braille; the cold letters – which render a premature, chiseled finality to her life – exude an unsettling chill that travels the length of my spine. I promise her, once more, that I shall find her killer.

In his den, M. has one of those large sectional sofas in a reddish-brown color, chestnut, that wrap around a wall. The lights are dim, the mood ersatz romantic, and he sits opposite me in an easy chair.

I dressed carefully for this evening, and I look good in an eggplant-purple dress that clings to my body. A zipper starts at the V-neck and runs all the way to the hem. Underneath, when M. gets past the zipper, he'll find a lace push-up bra and thong bikini panties, a garter belt and nylons, all in black. Tonight, I am here to seduce.

I slip off my high heels and lean back on the sofa, putting my legs up on the cushions. If M. thinks he can string me along for months, doling out inconsequential facts about Franny, he is wrong. And if he thinks he can emotionally overwhelm me the way he did my sister, he is wrong again. Men are not that difficult to understand. I've controlled all the men in my life, and I can control M. By the time I'm through with him, he'll tell me everything I need to know.

'You want to fuck me,' I say.

M. does not reply, but I see one eyebrow lift. He has a drink in his hand, a martini, and he raises it to his lips. The light is behind him and a shadow covers his face, filling in the contours, hiding his eyes. He's wearing a dark shirt, something soft and silky, and, sitting in the shadow, he looks vaguely mysterious. I see an image of him with a knife in his hand, carving my sister's torso. Feeling a sharp tingle of misgiving, I bring a hand to my stomach.

'Playing the seductress, Nora? That's rather transparent, don't you think? I expected more from you, something not so obvious.'

'Sorry to disappoint,' I say, taking a sip of my drink, scotch and water, to wash the image of Franny away, to bolster my courage. 'But I've always found sex to be the most direct route to a man's . . .' I hesitate.

'A man's what?'

I shrug. 'Mind, heart, soul, pocketbook. Whatever.'

He leans forward and sets his drink on the table beside him. 'And what would your new boyfriend think about this philosophy of yours?'

'He doesn't have anything to do with this.'

M. gets up and walks toward me. Abruptly, he grabs my hair and yanks my head back. 'I don't think you're nearly as cynical as you'd like me to believe,' he says. He leans down so his face is in mine. I see every threatening pore on his skin, every dark lash curling on his eyelids. He stares at me, unblinking, and cups my chin with his free hand. 'And you're definitely not as cautious as you should be. I killed your sister, remember? Or so you think. You shouldn't be here.'

I stare back at him, trying not to show fear. But I do. This is the first time he's touched me, and his hand burns on my chin as though it were a brand. 'I'm not scared of you,' I tell him.

'You should be,' he says. He looks me long in the eye, then adds, 'And you are.' He releases me and stands back, smiling, a snide, self-satisfied grin. I sit up but resist the temptation to rub my scalp where he pulled my hair.

He goes back to his chair and sits down. 'Seduce me,' he says. 'Show me what you can do.'

I ignore him, then take another drink, stalling for time. He's turned things around, and I need time to turn them back again, to gain control. I stretch out on the couch once more, affecting a nonchalance that I don't really feel. 'Don't ever pull my hair like that again,' I tell him.

M. says nothing, drinking his martini.

Slowly, I rub one leg with the other. Then I shift around on the sofa, languidly, as if I have all the time in the world. I wait for M. to come to me, for him to make the first move. The clock ticks off the minutes. He sets his drink down.

'Take off your dress,' he orders.

I smile; I didn't have to wait very long. I stand up and pull the zipper all the way down. The dress falls off my shoulders. 'Do you like what you see?' I ask. I turn around slowly, letting him see my ass, then turn back again and face him. I reach behind to unhook my bra, but M. raises his hand.

'Not yet,' he says. 'Sit.'

I remain standing. M. watches me, an annoyed look crossing his face.

'There's something you might as well learn right now,' he says. 'If we're going to fuck, we're going to do it my way. If I tell you to get on your knees and suck my cock, you better head for the floor. If I give you an order, I expect you to obey. Now sit down.'

His chauvinism makes me want to laugh. Never before have I taken orders from a man, in bed or otherwise. But I'll play along, if that's what it takes. I smile sweetly and sit, crossing my legs.

'That's better,' M. says. 'I don't like the sarcasm of your smile, but we'll work on that later.'

He gets up and goes over to the desk, then rummages around in the top drawer, puts something in his shirt pocket, and walks back to me. All his movements are unhurried, deliberate, as if calculated for effect. Gracefully, he kneels in front of me, then puts one hand on my face. He traces my lips with his finger, saying, 'I'm going to break you, Nora. It may take a month, it may take only a week – but you'll learn to obey. And you know what? It's going to be easy, and you're going to like it.'

His voice has a sinister timbre, low and soft yet still conveying a threat. His dark eyes look into mine. They are cold and confident, the eyes of a predator certain of its prey. My breathing quickens. He says, 'Now spread your legs.'

Again, his voice is quiet, as smooth as soft, silky fabric, but I hear the weight of his words. I uncross my legs and open them.

He puts his hands on my thighs, says, 'Wider,' and pulls them open. 'That's better,' he says. He takes my hands and arranges them on my thighs, palms up. 'Now close your eyes.'

I hesitate. My heart beats faster at this uncommon ritual. Nervously, I glance at his shirt pocket. What is inside it?

'Close them,' he repeats, and he rakes his hand gently down my face, closing my eyes, then takes away his hand.

Legs spread, eyes closed – I am completely vulnerable. My body is taut, my chest tight. I want to open my eyes, but I don't. I sense that M. is conducting some sort of test, a trial of nerves, a test of my nerve. Pinpoints of anxiety prickle my skin. I think of his shirt pocket and what he could've slipped inside it.

'Stay like this,' he says, and I jerk when I feel the touch of his hand. His fingers trace my jawline. 'Relax,' he says, removing his hand. 'But don't move. And keep your eyes shut.'

I hear him walking away, or at least I think he is walking away – the room is carpeted, and I'm not sure. I let my eyelids slide open just a crack, an almost imperceptible slit so M. will not notice if he's watching. A filament of dim light seeps through my lashes. My range of vision is narrow, and all I see are the palms of my hands and the tops of my feet. I think of Franny in her red bustier, tied to the dining room chair, legs spread, ready for M.'s punishment, the nature of which I can only imagine. I clench my fists, fearing M. may have something similar planned for me. But then, from across the room, I hear music. I open my eyes. M. is at the piano. What a strange man he is. I'm sitting here, in black lace bikini underwear, legs spread wide, and he's playing the piano on the other side of the room.

The irony makes me smile. With M. at a distance, I can relax. A halo of light shines down on him, and he looks almost angelic – his expression tranquil, his fingers graceful on the keys, the lines on his face softened in the flattering light. The piano is a baby grand, five feet long, probably, and shiny black, with the lid propped open. The music seems to float lightly in the air, soft, romantic, lyrical – a piece by Chopin, I'd guess, although I'm not positive.

I close my eyes and listen. The melody dances slowly, lightly, and goes on and on, like a free-flowing, fresh water stream, and I let it carry me along to some idyll of years past, picking wildflowers and chasing after yellow butterflies. It is a beautiful melody, hypnotic in its simplicity. But then, just as the last bit of tension leaves my body, the tempo changes.

I watch M. He doesn't look so angelic now, bent over the keyboard, concentration furrowing his brows. He pounds out the music, loud, rhythmic, sexual. It laps out like a violent body of water, lapping, overlapping, growing larger and larger. In undulating chords, it fills the room, every corner, from the ceiling to the floor, and then fills me. My pulse quickens. I feel M., I feel his intensity, his heat, from across the room. The melody draws me toward him, although I haven't moved an inch. He seems oblivious of me, of everything, as the music speeds to an end, and then, abruptly, concludes. He sits for a moment, composing himself. The room is silent; deadly, passionately silent. He rises and walks back to me.

'That was . . . wonderful,' I say, and I mean it. Franny never wrote in her diary how gifted he was. I still feel the music, its unsettling melody, but M. seems completely recovered.

He stands above me, one hand in his pants pocket, thinking. A tuft of black hair has fallen over his forehead, but he doesn't brush it back. 'Music,' he says, 'is my passion. It's the one aspect of life that's enduring, lasting.'

'Not everyone would agree with that,' I say. 'What about other forms of art? Sculpture, painting, literature? And what about people? Some people marry, and have children, to form a union that will endure.'

Pulling me up to my feet, he says, 'Art is enduring, yes, but not people. People are the least permanent of all, and the most disposable, the most interchangeable. You'll be with me for a certain period of time, and then, when your shelf life has expired, you'll be replaced with someone new.' He smiles, and I wonder if he's teasing or being sincere.

He sits on the couch and motions me to put a leg up on his knee. He caresses my calf, my thigh, letting his hand linger. It is a simple gesture, yet it catches my breath – and it shouldn't.

I've slept with a lot of men. It must be the aftermath of the music.

He unsnaps the garter and rolls down the stocking, his gentle hands moving leisurely on my leg, expertly, as if he's done this many times before. He kisses the inside of my bare ankle, and I feel it up to my groin. With his lips still touching my skin, he looks up at me, and I see the undisguised smile in his eyes. He knows he pleases. He places my leg on the floor, motions for the next leg, and proceeds to remove the other stocking. My body feels fluid, pliant, still filled with the music. M. is a dangerous man, yet the thought of sleeping with him – the danger, the fear – excites me. And he knows it. I despise this man with all my heart, but still his touch titillates me. I've never experienced anything like this before.

He peels off my bikini panties, but leaves the black bra and garter belt on, then pulls me down on his lap so I'm straddling his legs. He kisses me. His hands on my hips pull me closer, and I feel the fabric of his pants against my exposed crotch. His tongue is warm, searching, and I know I shouldn't be here. He reaches in his shirt pocket. A frisson of fear shoots through me. But all he pulls out is a set of chrome nipple clamps. This is what he'd gotten from his desk earlier, what I had been so worried about – tit clamps.

'First time with these?' M. asks.

I don't say anything, feeling a bit nervous.

'They're tweezer clamps,' he says. 'Not too intense – good for beginners.' He takes off my bra and attaches the clamps to my nipples, watching me for a reaction. There is pain at first – which I refuse to show – and more pain as he tightens them, then a gradual numbing as the blood circulation is cut off. He smiles. His tongue goes back in my mouth, his hand goes between my legs, and the fingers that played the piano now play me.

He pulls his head back. 'You're already wet,' he says, and he places me on the couch, then kneels on the floor, and licks my clitoris until I come.

He looks up at me, between my legs. 'That was easy,' he says, a note of smugness in his voice. He stands and kicks off his shoes.

'I'm not through yet,' I say.

He unbuttons his shirt, and I sit up to watch him undress. He slips it off, hangs it over the back of a chair, then takes off his slacks and folds them neatly. He looks as I imagined him: slimly built yet muscular, sexy for a man close to fifty, no paunch, no sagging skin. He's wearing black briefs, and he has an erection. His penis pushes the material out, bulging erotically. I wait for him to strip off his underwear, but instead he takes off a sock. Then the other sock. Then his watch. Finally, he slips the underwear down and stands in front of me. 'Suck me,' he says. It comes out as an order.

I hesitate briefly, stopping to gaze at a fine specimen for a forty-nine-year-old man. I've never been one to dwell on the size of a man's cock. Big, small, thick, thin – I have no preference. They're all pretty much the same to me. But there's something about the sight of an erect penis that stirs me profoundly. I think the feeling must be innate, going back thousands of years, to an ancient world, to a time before consciousness when fucking had to do with survival more than sport, because I felt that hoary stir upon sight of my very first penis, an immediate lust-felt response.

I take his cock inside my mouth, and then, licking and sucking, I traverse that ancient, throbbing universe with the new. But now, here, with M., there is a new dimension to cocksucking. And it's all about power, that unharnessed force reigning in this small piece of turgid flesh. I suck for his power, wanting to drain him of every drop. I feel his hands on my shoulders, knowing he could wrap them around my neck and squeeze. I realize I am playing a dangerous game. I renew my efforts. I want to – I must – milk him until he comes.

But he stops me.

'I'm going to fuck you,' he says, and he shoves me back on the couch. The abruptness of his movements, and his force, startles me. Instinctively, I push myself up. M. shoves me back down. With a snap of his wrist, he flicks off a clamp. A sharp pain shoots to the tip of my nipple as the blood rushes back. He flicks the other one off, then climbs on top of me and fucks me roughly. Gradually, while he's fucking, I relax. I maneuver into a position that is good for me, but he yanks me back. He moves me as he wishes, allowing no freedom of choice. I watch him fuck me, objectively at first – hovering over me, lifting my legs, turning me on my stomach and twisting my body, flipping me on my back again – then something happens and I lose my objectivity and some of my fear. I'm pulled into his world. He is on his knees, sitting up, fucking me fast and hard, his arms straight out, gripping my breasts as if they were round handles or knobs, grinding my shoulders into the couch. His face is changed, dark, mysterious, twisted with pleasure. I think of cavemen, of early man with his hairy body and low, threatening forehead. More animal than man. I am home, wherever that might be, and I think I must be crazy to stay here. He grabs my hair and pulls my head to the left, hard. I start to object, but then close my eyes and see the wild man. I hear his voice in my ear. 'You like this, don't you? You'll do whatever I say. You like being my whore.'

And the truth is, I do. I can't explain my reaction. My feelings are paradoxical: I hate him, fear him, yet at the same time his dominion over me, however brief, is intoxicating. I come, and then minutes later I come again.

11

I wake with a start. Jerking myself up, I look around the room. My heartbeats are rapid and frantic. I'm in M.'s bedroom, in his bed. Particles of light from the morning sun seep through the draperies, giving just enough illumination to bring out the colors of the room, soft shades of gray and blue, etiolated from the stingy early light. The room seems almost cavernous: huge, hollow, hazy. I hear the steady streams of water coming from the shower in the bathroom. I hadn't heard M. get up this morning, and this alarms me.

I have no idea when I finally, unintentionally, dozed off last night. M. took a sleeping pill, which he said he does occasionally, and fell asleep immediately. I lay awake for several hours, positive I was in bed with a killer. The thought of M. waking and watching me while I slept makes me shudder. I was at his mercy, exposed, unprotected. I mustn't be so stupid in the future. I lie back down, hugging a pillow, gripping it tightly, and listen to him in the shower. My head feels light and groggy, my mouth dry – too much scotch, too little sleep. I think of Ian, my trusting Ian, and immediately feel guilty about last night. But I know I had no choice. I want information about Franny, and if I have to sleep with M. to get it, then so be it. The sex was impersonal, I rationalize, and had nothing to do with me and Ian. Still, I feel a deep, bruising knot of remorse. My rationalizations do not provide the palliative effect I desire. I'll deal with my feelings later; I don't have the emotional wherewithal to deal with both Ian and M. now. I need to stay focused so I can handle M.

The water in the bathroom is still running. I think of what

M. said to me last night. I was wary of him, expected something violent; I expected, at the very least, a modicum of pain. He laughed at me and said, 'You imagine me a monster, don't you? What do you think I did to Franny? Use force to get her to submit to me? Everything we did, she agreed to do. She could have said no, but she never did. Oh, it's true she balked at times. She was unwilling to engage in certain . . . activities. Nevertheless, she acquiesced. She could have said no, but she didn't. She could have walked out any time she chose.' Bitterly, I remember his words.

I sit up in bed and lean against the headboard. I'm not wearing anything, so I pull the blankets up to my armpits. This is Monday morning; M. has a class at nine. If he lets me stay here when he leaves, I scheme, it'll give me a chance to go through his house, a chance to find the physical evidence the police need.

The shower water stops. After a few minutes, he comes out of the bathroom. He's naked, one blue towel slung casually over his shoulder. He looks at me, says nothing, then goes to the bay window and opens the drapes, revealing an immense silvery sky. The room brightens. I see a vast expanse of lawn, two nectarine trees, a redwood, three Brewer blackbirds roosting on an overhead telephone line. The entire yard is enclosed with an ivy-studded fence. M. walks over to me, confident, at ease, arrogant. In the morning light, without the softening effects of booze and dim bulbs, I view him with a critical eye. At forty-nine, he still has an athlete's body, but the smooth slimness of youth has been replaced with a hard-edged solidity. There's nothing soft or vulnerable about him. Placing a hand on my bare shoulder, he leans down to kiss me, but I turn my head so all he gets is a cold cheek. I fold my arms across my chest. I have no intention of having sex with him this morning. He tilts his head, looks amused by my small show of defiance, then straightens, willing to let it go.

He crosses over to the bureau and takes out a pair of socks and underwear. Then he tosses his towel in the bathroom and comes back to the bed, sitting on the edge of it. His penis is flaccid and it lolls over to one side like a lazy dog's tongue, like Rameau's tongue. He begins dressing and talking at the same time.

'Your sister had magnificent breasts,' he says. 'They were wonderful, simply wonderful. She talked about going to a plastic surgeon to have them reduced. They were so large they hurt her back and shoulders. She said it was quite uncomfortable. You didn't know this, did you? That she'd considered breast-reduction surgery?'

I didn't, but I don't say this to him. He smiles.

'I didn't think so. Anyway, I told her as long as she was with me she'd leave them alone. I love big-breasted women, and Franny had the largest I'd ever seen. They were spectacular. I loved to touch them. I loved to just look at them.' He smiles thoughtfully, as if he's deciding how much he can tell me.

'Sometimes, when we were eating, I would make her take her top off so I could look at them during dinner. I'd reach over the table and fondle one while I ate. I never got tired of her breasts.' He pulls up his socks. 'Or maybe it was the way she reacted. She hated to expose herself like that. I don't think it was modesty so much as self-consciousness about her weight. It made her uncomfortable to walk around with her clothes off – and that's why I made her do it. I found her discomfort . . . erotic. When I felt like it, I would make her parade around in high heels and a garter belt and nylons, no panties. I have clamps that are attached to the ends of a small twelve-inch chain. I'd put the clamps on her nipples to keep them standing erect, then all I had to do was give the chain a pull and watch it tug on her nipples. I'd make her stay dressed like that all evening: while she ate, watched TV, read a magazine. She never got used to it. Sometimes I'd make her shake her shoulders so I could see her breasts swing back and forth, two great gobbets of shimmying fat. Other times, I'd give them a little slap so they'd jiggle for me.'

He gives me a sidelong glance to see how I'm taking this. I'm furious, my jaw clenched tight. I want to say something, I want to rage at him, but I'm afraid if I do he'll stop talking. At the same time, I'm afraid he'll continue. I don't want to hear any more, and silently I plead with him to stop. Hearing him talk about Franny like this, his cruel treatment of her, is almost unbearable. But I am silent. My need to know the truth is overpowering.

He goes over to the walk-in closet, comes out with a striped button-down shirt and a pair of gray slacks. Walking over to the bay window, he slips on his shirt but doesn't button it. The window is recessed, goes down to within two feet of the floor, and has a long seat running lengthwise across the bottom. He puts one foot on the seat and looks out the window, setting his pants down neatly next to his foot.

'One day I called her at the clinic,' he begins again, still gazing out the window. 'I told her to meet me at my office that night at seven. She was' – he pauses, searching for a word – 'surprised. I'd never invited her before. So she was pleased when I asked her, and surprised. I could hear it in her voice. When she walked through my door that evening it was as if she were walking on air – she looked so happy. She waited, sitting in a chair opposite my desk, while I finished a few things. A huge grin kept creeping across her face; she'd try to stifle it, but in a few minutes it would be back again. That's all it took to elate her, an invitation to my office. That's a bit sad, isn't it?' He stops for a moment, thinking.

'Then I told her to come with me, that we were going for a little walk across campus. I took her over to the hog barn.' He turns to look at me. 'Do you know where that is? It's the building south of the Crocker nuclear lab. Franny had never been there before. It's one of the oldest buildings on campus, and it houses about two hundred swine. There's one section they call the maternity ward – rows of pens with sows and their newborn piglets. She thought they were adorable, their little squeals, their miniature snouts and hooves. We walked around the barn, breathing in the musky odor, looking at all the different pigs. She held a few of the young ones.'

I wonder where this is heading. I've been to most of the science and agriculture buildings at the university for articles I've done for the *Bee*. He buttons his shirt, then picks up his pants, brushing off a piece of lint.

'I've been there,' I tell him impatiently. 'I know what it looks like. They keep it locked at night. How did you get in?'

He turns and gives me an indulgent smile. 'I know my way around the campus,' he says. 'I've been there almost twenty years now. Getting into the hog barn is not a difficult task.' He slips on his pants, tucks in his shirt before he zips them up. His movements are fluid, almost sensual, a striptease in reverse. He sits in the embrasure of the bay window to put on his shoes.

'She was strolling around the barn, looking at the animals, enjoying herself. I came up behind her and kissed her on the neck. I told her I was going to put a pig at her breast. She laughed, a sort of nervous laugh. She was hoping I was kidding, but by this time she knew me well enough to know that I probably wasn't. I took off her coat and unbuttoned her blouse. I was still standing behind her; I could feel the tension in her shoulders, the stiffness in her body. She whimpered, barely audible, then she said my name. "Michael." It sounded like a plea, as if she was begging me to stop. But she didn't resist; she knew better than that. I unhooked her bra and slipped it off. Taking off her brassiere was always a great pleasure for me: watching her breasts bounce free, rid of their restraints. I cupped her breasts in my hands, squeezed them gently as I held her to me. Her breathing was heavy with apprehension. I actually felt a little sorry for her, but, more than that, her fear excited me. Her timidity, her trepidation of the unknown, her sheer panic – it was stimulating. I told her not to worry. "This is such a minor request," I whispered in her ear. "Try to relax; it'll be like having a baby at your breast." I leaned over the pen and scooped up a piglet and put it in her arms. I took her left breast and rubbed the nipple across its mouth. He seemed tentative at first, but then he took it. He sucked on her, wanting milk. I stroked her other breast and watched the pig on her tit. "You see," I told her, "there's nothing to it." She smiled a little, relaxing. I thanked her for pleasing me, then kissed her, long and deep. "Does it feel good to have him suck on you?" I asked her, nuzzling her cheek. "You like it, don't you?" She leaned in closer to me. I told her I was getting turned on. She said she was also – which is what I wanted.'

He gazes out the window, remembering. Then he leans back and crosses one foot over the other and continues his story, his voice distant with memories, not really looking at me.

'I returned the pig back to its mother and led Franny to an empty pen. I made her get down on the ground, on all fours, then I went to the railing of the adjacent pen and lifted out six piglets, one by one, and set them, oinking and squirming, in the pen with Franny. She was looking nervous again. She started biting her lower lip the way she always did when she wasn't sure of something. The pigs started sniffing around the pen, acclimating themselves, and Franny was in the middle of it, on her hands and knees, bare from the waist up, her huge breasts hanging down, pendulous, heavy, swaying just a little as she shifted her weight. One pig trotted right up to her tit and put his mouth on it as if it belonged to him. Franny flinched; she jerked up, popping the nipple out of the pig's mouth, and started to rise. The piglet squealed in frustration. I ordered her to get back down and stay down. The pig went back to her, reached up and started sucking. The others weren't going to her, so I grabbed one and pushed it up to her breast. I squeezed the nipple, rubbed it on his mouth until he took it. Then I backed up and watched. I had an erection by now, but I was content just standing against the railing, watching the two pigs suck and pull on her breasts. The others began nosing their way in, curious. Franny was still biting her lower lip, trying not to cry, I think. Her sense of erotic play had vanished. The second pig had given up by now and walked away; another butted right in to take his place. Then he left and another came.

This continued for some time on her right breast, the pigs sucking until they realized she was dry, another scrambling for its place. The pig on her left breast, though – he wasn't about to release her tit. He kept at it, greedily, and wouldn't let the others nudge their way in. I had brought a small camera with me and I took it out of my pocket and snapped a few pictures. Franny kept looking over her shoulder at the barn door. I think she was afraid someone would come in. I don't know what bothered her most: the pigs on her breasts or someone walking in and seeing her like that. After a while, she started to groan. "He's hurting me," she said. "He's sucking too hard." I told her it was because he wanted milk. She wanted to stop; she begged me to let her get up. I told her no, to let the pigs pull on her nipples. I told her I liked watching her suckle the pigs. I told her I was going to put other animals on her breasts, a goat, a foal, a lamb, a calf. I went over to her and started pulling down her jeans, telling her she had the udders of a cow, telling her I wanted to milk her.'

He stands and gives me a short smile, shrugs his shoulders and raises his hands, palms upward, in a what-else-could-I-do gesture. 'So I knelt down behind her and fucked her while the pigs sucked on her tits.'

I'm trying to contain my anger. 'While Franny was crying,' I say tensely, my throat tight.

He goes to the bureau and picks up a watch, clasps it on his wrist. He pockets the change on the bureau top. 'No, she wasn't crying. She didn't like it, but she wasn't crying.'

'She was upset.'

'Yes, of course.'

I don't say anything for a moment. 'And you can tell me this story, calmly, without it bothering you at all.' I shake my head in disbelief. 'How can you talk about her like that?'

He comes over and sits next to me on the bed. 'I wouldn't be,' he says, 'if it wasn't for you. Don't forget – you're the one who's dredging this up. I'd just as soon let it go. Tell me you've heard enough about Franny and I'll never mention her name again.' He pauses, giving me a chance to reply. 'Well?' he says. 'What's it to be?'

'I can't let it go.' I clutch the blankets to me. My voice, I know, sounds strained. 'I won't.'

He leans toward me and strokes my cheek. Softly, he says, 'It would go better for you if you did.'

I shove his hand away. His gentleness does not fool me the way it did Franny. One thing I know for sure: he does not care what is best for me. His warnings are part of his game.

'Is that your plan for me, also?' I asked him. It comes out as a dare. 'To take me to the hog barn?'

He raises an eyebrow, turns up one corner of his mouth. 'Do you want to go?'

When I say nothing, he gets up and goes back to the bureau. He puts his wallet in his back pocket, then turns around and faces me, leaning against the bureau. 'Franny always thought of sex in romantic terms. She wanted flowers, sweet caresses, words of love, and I gave them to her at first. But then, after she trusted me, I changed the rules on her. We had sex on my terms. Whenever we fucked I called her my bitch, my cunt, and told her what I was going to do to her. I pulled her out of that romantic idyll she'd created and slammed her into my reality, into my world.' M. gives me a hint of a smile. 'Last night, when we were making love, I called you my whore, and it excited you – you can't deny that.' He hesitates just a moment to see if I'll argue the point, but I don't. I know it's the truth.

He continues, his tone matter-of-fact, as if he were lecturing his students. 'Franny, on the other hand, cringed whenever I called her my whore, my slut.' He looks over at me, his eyes level. 'She hated those words. Even when I used them in the context of sex, which is the only time I said them, even then she hated them. She wanted flowery words. When I first put the pig to her breast – while I kissed her, held her, told her it was okay – she liked it. She was uneasy at first, but she admitted it aroused her. It was only when I had her in the pen, on all fours, with me as the observer, that she complained.'

'That, plus the fact that it made her breasts sore.'

He waves his hand in a dismissive gesture, as if the pain was of no concern to him.

'She wasn't getting any enjoyment out of it,' I continue. 'It was degrading to her.'

He rubs the bridge of his nose, then crosses his arms. 'And still she did it,' he says. Then, quieter, he repeats, 'And still she did it.' The room is silent. His last sentence hangs in the air between us, a fateful nexus locking us together, the words as binding as links in a chain. He glances at his watch, then comes over to me. 'As will you.'

I look up at him and say, 'Don't count on it,' but he just ignores this. He hovers over me, regarding me, then puts his hands on my shoulders. It's a subtle show of force, a tactical move to let me know he is in control. He bends down and moves one hand to my neck, encircling it, forcing me to look up at him. His grip on me is firm, but he's not hurting me. He kisses me lightly on the lips. I don't move. I don't respond. I refuse to give him the satisfaction of a struggle.

'I wonder if it'll be degrading to you as well,' he says, looking me in the eye, then adds, 'I think not.'

He releases me and straightens up. He heads for the door, then stops and turns, waving one arm around the room in an inclusive gesture. 'Feel free to stay here as long as you like,' he says, the perfect host. 'I imagine you'll be searching my home for evidence of some sort – well, do as you must. But please try to be neat about it.' He seems amused, and his cooperation takes me by surprise. I didn't think he'd let me search his house so easily. He starts for the door again, and once more he stops.

'Those pictures I took of Franny – the ones in the hog barn and all the others – you won't find them. When I read of her death in the newspaper, I destroyed them. With no alibi, I thought it best not to have them scattered around.' He hesitates just a beat, observing my reaction, then he walks out of the room, yelling back at me to lock up when I leave, adding that he'll call me when he wants to see me again.

I hear the sound of his footsteps going through the house. The door leading to the garage opens and closes. I get up and put on M.'s bathrobe, a brown monogrammed robe. Barefoot, I walk to the living room and peek out the window. I watch until I see him backing his car out the garage and driving up the street.

I wonder where to begin. I start with the den. Looking around the room, above the desk, I see the World War II cutlass that belonged to M.'s father. I run my finger along the blade; it is still sharp, ready for use. I go through his desk and bookcases, but find nothing. Hidden in a cabinet near his VCR, I find, judging from their titles, a collection of pornographic videos and a stack of dirty magazines. I quickly flip through the magazines. Nothing I haven't seen before. The guest rooms and linen closets, likewise, are bare of incriminating evidence.

I enter his bedroom. Searching the nightstands by the bed, I turn up a collection of sex toys – vibrators, cock rings, clips, lubricants, massage oils, dildos, nipple rings and clamps, solid metal ben-wa balls in various sizes – again, nothing out of the ordinary. I search his bureau and come up empty-handed. Nothing under his bed. Nothing in the bathroom, although I do find his sleeping pills in the medicine cabinet. In the walk-in closet, I turn on the light and go through his clothes. This man is very neat: shirts in the same direction, the fronts facing west, all similar colors grouped together, shoes lined up like cadets awaiting inspection, evenly spaced and polished to a high shine. I look in all the boxes on the shelves – more shirts and sweaters and shoes, packed away. I get the folding step stool I saw earlier in the kitchen and bring it into the closet so I can inspect the top shelves. And then I see it on the top shelf, hidden behind stacks of shoeboxes and shopping bags filled with old towels: a large plastic container the size of a suitcase. I pull it down, take it to the bed, and open it. Inside, I find leather straps and tethers, a harness, bondage cuffs, various lengths of rope, a whip and a riding crop, a set of handcuffs, leg manacles, a studded leather collar, a heavy-duty Ping-Pong paddle, and several gadgets and devices, the use of which I have no idea. And, in one corner, a partially used roll of duct tape.

Suddenly, I feel sick. My head throbs from the booze I drank last night. I close my eyes and see Franny at the funeral home, five days after her body was discovered. In movies, you see a member of the bereaved family walking down a metal-gray corridor to identify the body at the morgue. Not so in real life. In a homicide, family members aren't allowed to view the body until it's been released to the funeral home.

And the details of her death, which also would have been given out freely in the movies, I didn't learn until two months later. All I knew, at the beginning, was that it was a homicide and the cause of death could not be determined. The coroner, the ID techs, the detectives, they all said it would jeopardize their investigation to divulge more information at that time. The manager of Franny's apartment, the older woman who discovered her body two weeks after she died, was of no help, either. It made her sick, she said, and she looked away; all she could remember was the horrible smell and the flies swarming around the room. I was left to my imagination, and as a science writer I knew what she would've looked like. I've been to autopsies. Her lips and tongue and fingers and toes would have been desiccated, dry and dark black. There would be some bloating and blisters, purged liquid from her mouth, dried blood on her body, maggots in the wounds and orifices, and lots of blowflies, large and fat. There is a universal scent of death, and even in a closed-up apartment, insects will catch a whiff of this, find a way to enter the building, and descend upon a corpse.

And then, two months later, when the investigation had come to a standstill, they told me the details. I can picture her in my mind as clearly as if I were there. I see her lying in her apartment, gagged, blood dripping off her torso, cut marks on her naked body like fine engravings carved in wood, duct tape across her mouth and wound around her ankles and wrists.

I shake my head to clear it. I sit down on the bed, picking up the handcuffs and duct tape. I set them on my lap. The bed is covered with the contents of the box, spread out like a proud man's tool collection on display: whips, ropes, paddles, manacles, chains. This collection convinces me I'm correct about M.; still, I'm disappointed. I find no razor blades, no utility knives, no pictures of women in bondage, their bodies displaying M.'s handiwork with a knife, no pictures of Franny. Nothing, in short, that will place M. at the scene of the crime. I'll show the tape to the police, but after nearly a year and no arrest for Franny's murder, I have little faith in them. I can almost hear them now: anyone can buy duct tape in a hardware store.

The front door slams shut.

I freeze. My hand, about to pick up and inspect the studded collar, stops in midair. I hear footsteps in the foyer, muffled but audible, and suddenly my body reacts. I move without thinking. I jump off the bed, the handcuffs and tape falling to the floor, and start throwing everything into the plastic box, the whips, the chains, all of it.

'Nora?' M. calls out. He is in the hallway.

I grab the handcuffs off the floor and throw them in the box. Where is the duct tape? I don't see it.

'Nora? Are you still here?'

I shut the lid, carry it into the walk-in closet, replace it on the shelf, rearrange the shoeboxes and shopping bags in front of it. The step stool. I fold it and put it behind a rack of clothes. I stand in the closet doorway, looking around, making sure nothing is amiss. The box is back where it belongs, the step stool is covered by M.'s coats and jackets and raincoat. I reach up to turn off the light switch and feel a hand, icy cold, on the back of my neck. I gasp.

M. says, 'Didn't you hear me call you?'

I shake my head.

He looks at me, questioning.

I fumble for words. 'I was just getting your bathrobe,' I say, thankful I had put it on earlier. 'I was cold.' I put my hands in the pockets.

'I forgot my coat,' M. says, and he walks in the closet and

takes a brown suede jacket off the hanger. The step stool is not revealed. I go back into the bedroom and glance around for the duct tape. I see it on the floor next to the bureau, and I dash over to pick it up.

'I see you found my accoutrements,' M. says, walking out of the closet, putting on his jacket.

Straightening up, I say, 'What?' With one hand, I hide the tape behind my back.

He goes over to the bed and picks up a black whip – the handle peeking out from beneath the sheets – which I'd overlooked in my rush to put everything away. He walks over to me, places the whip in my other hand.

'Put this back where you found it,' he says. 'Do you under-stand?' His voice is low and controlled, purposely devoid of emotion, a voice to be obeyed.

I nod my head, not taking my eyes off him. The air feels charged with tension, prickly.

'Good,' he says. 'I'm sure I'll have occasion to use it again,' and he leaves the room.

12

As soon as I get home, I dial the police. In my hands, I'm holding the duct tape that I've stolen from M.'s house. A man tells me that Joe Harris, the detective who's in charge of Franny's case, isn't in yet. I leave my name and say I'll call later, then hang up.

The Sacramento Bee is on the kitchen table. Opening it to the Metro section, I read about two young men arguing at a basketball court on T Street in Sacramento. One of the men went to his car, pulled out a gun, returned, and fired five shots into the other man. Argument settled. I clip out the article and add it to my folder, which I've entitled 'Death and Violence – Sacto.' Since I started it, less than a year ago, it's become thick with articles, and I'm beginning to feel overwhelmed by all the violence. I feel lucky to be out of Sacramento, but then I remind myself that living in Davis hadn't saved Franny.

Once more, I dial the police. In a flat, bored voice a woman tells me that Detective Harris won't be in for another hour. I try to keep the irritation out of my voice as I leave my name once again. To keep myself busy, and while my mind is still fresh, I jot down notes from my latest encounter with M., including his memories of Franny at the hog barn. Afterward, I take a shower, feeling tainted by M.'s touch. Even though the Ivory cleanses my body, it'll take more than soap to purge my mind. What disturbs me most is my own response last night. Knowing what I know about M., how could I have responded to him sexually? I anticipated repulsion, I had been prepared for that; but what I felt was attraction, arousal: the sex was good. I feel betrayed, defiled by my own emotions.

I dry my hair, put on some blood-red lipstick and black mascara. I decide to go for the chic-but-tough look, and dress in tight jeans, a black sequinned T-shirt, and a leather bomber jacket. I place the duct tape in a brown paper bag, and drive toward town.

The police station is on the corner of F and Third in an old cement building that, until thirteen years ago, housed the city hall. The words city hall, in inlaid dark blue tile, still adorn the arched doorway. It's a quaint Spanish-style building that had been erected in the 1930s. It is painted a pale peach color and, from the outside, looks more like someone's home – with flower beds, a curved pebbled walkway, shade trees, a well-mowed lawn, even a bench to rest on – than a place of law enforcement. On the corner stands a bronze statue of two joggers. The only real clue to the building's occupation is the small, unobtrusive sign, dwarfed by the overarching branches of a nearby tree, and, more noticeably, the row of blue-and-white police cars parked on the side.

I pull in the lot across the street, take the paper bag, and head for the police station. There's a cold bite to the air, but the sky is white-blue and free of clouds. A girl, most likely a college student, is selling flowers from a cart, and a few people are sitting in front of Café Tutti, talking, oblivious to the cool weather, sipping on coffee or cappuccino. A young policeman in his dark blue uniform cruises by on a bike, part of the city's bicycle patrol.

I cross the street and enter the building. An officer, a dark-haired short woman, is behind the front counter. Off to the left, two dispatchers are in an enclosed, glass-windowed room. I tell the woman that Joe Harris is expecting me, and she picks up the phone and calls back to confirm this. She's new and doesn't know me. I sit on the bench to wait. The reception area is small, wood paneled, carpeted, and it looks more like a place to pick up a business license or file an application. On one wall, a glass-enclosed case displays the local police officers on small cards that resemble baseball trading cards.

I wonder if they're for sale – to collect, to trade, to pass around among friends. I wonder which cops have an exchange rate of two for one.

After the officer confirms my appointment, I go down the steps that lead to the detectives' offices. I've been here so many times since Franny died, I know my way around. Most of the people know me here, or at least they know who I am. A few say hello as I walk down the corridor, some nod, but most of them, the detectives, turn and pretend they don't see me. I know what's on their minds – they think, in my obsession with finding Franny's killer, that I've gone over the edge. They wish I wouldn't come to the station anymore, and they most assuredly want me to stop my importunate demands, my harangues to keep them on Franny's case. My presence is an annoyance to them. Only Joe listens to me now.

I go back to Joe Harris's desk. He's a large man, in his fifties, who always looks as if he's overflowing – too big for his desk and chair, his clothes always snug, his curly gray hair in need of a cut. He's wearing a white shirt with buttons that strain in the buttonholes; the sleeves are rolled up, and the left collar, unbuttoned, is frayed. He doesn't look too happy to see me, and I know he considers me a pain in the neck. He's a nice man whose patience has been tested the past year by my refusal to stay out of the investigation. On the corner of his desk is a picture of his wife and three kids, his children all grown now but teenagers in the photo.

Without being invited, I sit in the chair across from him. I reach over and set the brown bag in the middle of his desk. He leans back in his chair, not touching the bag, his expression long-suffering. From the beginning, Joe has always treated me kindly. When he told me the details of Franny's death, he did it as gently as he could. And when I began calling the police station, asking more questions, he always took my calls and answered as best as he was able. But when the weeks became months and they weren't getting anywhere with Franny's case, no new suspects, no additional leads, and

when I continued to call, pushing them to do something
more, even though they told me there was little else they
could do, Joe started to lose his patience. Now he avoids my
calls occasionally and admonishes me to stop playing detective.

'Open it,' I tell him.

Joe doesn't even give the bag a glance. He looks at me, a
flat, level gaze, slightly wary, and says, 'What's in it?'

'Duct tape.' I pause. 'I got it from his house.' He knows I'm
talking about M.

'Jesus, Nora.' He sighs, a long, exasperated sigh, then opens
the bag and peers inside. 'Did you break into his home?'

'No,' I say, debating how much to tell him. 'I'm seeing him,
kind of. He invited me in.'

Joe rubs both eyes with the heels of his palms. He looks as
if he's about to lecture me, but then he decides against it and
just shakes his head. He's sitting on one of those efficient swivel
office chairs that are mounted on wheels. Skeletal in structure,
it's made of stainless steel and black vinyl, with no armrests
and a back support that looks as if it hits him squarely beneath
the shoulder blades. Because of his size, he seems not so much
to sit in the tiny chair as to pin it down.

'Even if we get a perfect match on the tape,' he says, 'there's
no way to prove it came from his house or that it even belonged
to him. If we arrested him, it's unlikely we'd get a conviction.
You removed the evidence, Nora. His lawyer would find a
million loopholes for him to crawl through.'

This, I expected. In anger, I raise my voice. 'What was I
supposed to do? Leave it there? By the time you guys went to
a judge and got a search warrant – if you could even get one
– he could've destroyed it.' I realize I'm sitting on the edge of
the chair, practically shouting at Joe. I also realize, deep down,
that he's a competent man who, legally, has done everything
he can to find Franny's killer. I'm overreacting out of frustration, and Joe knows this. I can see it in his eyes. I slide back
on the chair and lower my voice.

'Are you going to do anything with it?' I ask him.

He reaches for the bag and closes it. He says, 'We'll check it out, do a chemical analysis, see what we come up with. But don't get your hopes up. Duct tape is not an uncommon item. Hell, I've got some of it myself out in the garage.'

Flatly, I say, 'But I'll bet yours isn't in a box along with whips and chains and every other kind of S&M paraphernalia you can imagine.'

Joe Harris stares at me, not fazed by what I said. 'Stay away from him, Nora. The hair samples we found by your sister's body didn't match his. The carpet fibers we took weren't from his house. We have no physical evidence to suggest he had anything to do with her death. We checked him out. We talked to his old girlfriends. He's into light S&M – a little whipping, bondage, some domination – but nothing heavy. The women who participated said they weren't forced, that it was consensual, that it was fun, just a big game. He never used duct tape with any of them, he never used knives.'

Joe shakes his head. 'So what if he likes to tie up women? That doesn't make him a killer. And if you harass him, you're the one who'll end up in trouble. He can get a restraining order to keep you away from him.'

'Not likely – I slept with him last night.'

He shakes his head at me again – he's done a lot of that the last several months – and sighs. 'We don't have any evidence that he killed her, but that doesn't mean he didn't. He'll be a suspect as long as the case is unsolved.'

'There's something I didn't tell you,' I say. 'Several days ago a car nearly hit me while I was in a parking lot. The windows were blackened, so I couldn't see who it was, and it happened too fast to get an ID on the car, but don't you think that's kind of a coincidence? I've never been run down before – not until the day after I tell the professor I'm going to find out who killed Franny.'

'You're being stupid, fooling around with him. You're just asking for trouble – and you'll foul up our investigation. We don't need any amateur sleuths, Nora. Leave him alone.'

I stand up. 'I can't,' I say. I nod my head toward the bag. 'Let me know what you find out,' and I turn to leave.

I drive back to my house. I see one of my neighbors across the street, Ann Marie, a small woman in her forties, pruning the hedges between her and her neighbor's property. She's dressed in jeans and a flannel shirt that's much too large for her – probably her husband's shirt – and garden gloves. Branches are scattered everywhere. I wonder if it's the right season to be pruning, but I don't say anything. I know little about gardening; the landlord takes care of my yard. I get my mail and walk in the house, then check the answering machine and discover I have four messages: one from a friend living in Reno; one from Ian; one from Maisie, my friend from the *Bee*; and the last from M. I didn't give him my phone number or address, but they're listed in the directory under 'N. Tibbs.' Apparently, he found this out. His message is short and simple: 'I'll pick you up Saturday morning at nine.' He didn't leave his name, but there is no mistaking his voice.

I'm not sure what to do about Ian's call. He wants to get together this evening, but I don't think I can face him yet. My betrayal is profound. I leave a message on his answering machine. I prevaricate to stall for time. I tell him I'm sick and don't feel like company tonight. Perhaps I'll feel better in a few days, I say; I think it's just a touch of the flu. I hang up the phone, thankful I live in an age with the technology that allows people to bypass the truth. I am a coward, I know.

13

When M. rings my doorbell Saturday morning, I'm ready for him. He didn't tell me where we were going, so I'm dressed in an all-purpose black skirt, short, and a crimson pullover sweater, long. When I open the door, he walks in, uninvited, as if he belongs here.

'Aren't we going out?' I ask him.

'Yes,' he says. 'Eventually.' He adds, 'May I?' and he begins a tour of my small house. He's wearing brushed twill trousers and a very expensive-looking gray sweater, and he has the self-assured demeanor of a man used to getting his way. It shows in the manner in which he carries himself, the precision of his movements, the modulated tone of his voice, the way he made love to me Sunday night. I remember how he touched me – confident, certain he would please me – and, in spite of my enmity, a wave of desire goes through me. I know I am treading on dangerous ground.

'If we're going someplace,' I say, 'let's go.'

M. smiles. 'We're definitely going someplace. A place that'll be of great interest to you.'

But he makes no move to leave my house. I follow him through the foyer and into the narrow hallway. There are two bedrooms, one on each end, and a guest bathroom in the middle. I've converted the smaller bedroom into an office, with my desk and computer and two walls of bookshelves. He gives this room a cursory glance, then heads down the dark hall to my bedroom. He stops in the doorway, looks around. A sliding glass door leads out to the backyard patio, giving the room extra light, and closets run along the length of the opposite wall, with sliding mirror doors that make the room seem wider than it actually is. Pink and dusty-blue satin pillows are tossed on my king-sized bed. He sees Ian's picture on the dresser, then walks over to pick up the brass frame. In it, Ian is smiling down at me, one arm around my shoulder, head cocked to one side as if he's about to burst out in a laugh. Turning to me, the picture in hand, M. says, 'The boyfriend?'

Grudgingly, I nod.

He studies the picture, his face expressionless. Finally, he says, 'What's his name?'

I shrug. 'Does it make any difference?'

He looks over at me, waiting for an answer. The heater clicks on and makes a muffled, humming sound, unworldly. A rush of warm air blows out of the vent in the ceiling. It hovers over us, like a spirit settling in. M. still waits.

'Ian,' I say. I take the picture from his hand, set it back on the dresser with a sharp thud. 'His name is Ian McCarthy. Now let's go.'

We go out to his car, a new Mercedes, sleek and black. The sky is overcast, so light and thin and misty that it looks as if it's been loosely woven, like gauze. He opens the car door for me, holding it as I get in. When he gets behind the wheel, I ask him, 'Where are we going?'

'For a ride. Up to Lake Tahoe.' He backs out the driveway and heads up the street. This is not a great day for a ride. It's the end of winter, and earlier this morning it rained. He pulls onto the freeway and I settle back for the two-hour ride. His car seems to almost glide down the road, smooth and soundless.

We drive along in silence. It begins to drizzle lightly, and M. turns on the windshield wipers. Mile after mile passes. I wonder why he's taking me for a ride. I stare out the window, the sky gloomy with rain. We're in Sacramento now, where Highway 50 splits off from 80. The traffic isn't as crowded as it is on weekdays, and even though M. is driving over the speed limit, cars still shoot by us.

After a while, I say, 'In the entire time you knew Franny, you never took her out. You never took her on a date, not a real date.'

He's quiet for a moment, and I think he's not going to respond, but then he says, 'Quite frankly, she wasn't good company. Your sister was boring.'

I get angry at his callous words. But, more than that, I hear echoes of myself. In her diary, Franny had written that I said the same thing about men. 'I know I'd get bored with him after a while,' I had told her. The words haunt me now. Did I sound as callous as M. sounds now?

'If she was so boring, why did you see her?' I ask him. 'Why, of all the women you could've had, why Franny? She wasn't your type. Anyone could see that.'

'As I told you before, I saw her for my own amusement.' He gives me an oblique glance. 'I wanted to see what I could do with her.'

'What you could do with her,' I repeat stupidly.

I pause to collect my thoughts. I say nothing until I'm sure my feelings are under control. Dispassionately, as if I'm discussing a stranger, I say, 'You wanted to control her – isn't that what you really mean? She was easy prey for you. It wouldn't take much effort for you to dominate her, for you to corrupt her. Don't you think you should have picked on someone more suitable, someone more . . .' The words trail off.

'Challenging?' he says when I hesitate. 'Someone more like you?'

I ignore this remark.

He drives for a few miles, then says, 'You misunderstand. The domination, the control – that's part of it, but not all. When I first saw her at Putah Creek, before she even knew me, I sensed her loneliness. She became my project for the winter quarter. I was going to teach her to love – to love so deeply she would do anything to keep that love. I pushed her limits. I wanted to see how far she'd go.'

For a moment, I'm speechless. He talks about Franny as if she were an experiment, a culture in a petri dish. 'That doesn't strike you as manipulative?' I manage to say.

'Very much so,' M. replies. 'I never said it wasn't.'

'And that constitutes your amusement?' I realize there is an edge to my voice. I rub my right temple with two fingers. How could Franny have gotten hooked up with him? 'You used her – that's what it amounts to.'

'Yes, but don't sound so indignant. I gave her what she needed. She wanted a boyfriend, someone who'd love her despite her size and personality. Let's be clear about that – she was boring and fat. Well, I couldn't love her – but I could make love to her. And I made her feel desired. I made her feel wanted.' He pauses, then adds, 'That's more than you ever did, Nora. You ignored her, which was far more cruel.'

His words sink in, so true they hurt. I say, 'And then you split up with her. When you got tired of her, you let her go.'

'My relationship with your sister was temporary – it always was. I'm just surprised it lasted as long as it did. People are disposable, Nora. I've mentioned this before. They have a shelf life, a time span. You, of all people, should understand that. Don't forget – Franny told me everything about you. I know your likes, your dislikes, your past, and I'll bet I even know your future. I know you. Men in your life are as temporary as women are in mine. And—'

'That's not true,' I say. 'Not anymore.'

'And,' M. continues, not acknowledging my interruption, 'as you said earlier, she wasn't my type. I was fond of her, she knew that, but I didn't love her, and I never told her I did. I never promised her anything. I took what I wanted from Franny – and I gave her what I could.'

Again, I think of the men in my life. I, also, took what I wanted and gave what I could – or, more accurately, gave as little as I could. 'You broke her heart,' I say, remembering the men I had discarded so easily.

His voice softens. 'She was lucky I let her go. I would've pushed her even further.'

I think of the hog barn and the box in his closet. I think of Franny's diary entries and how she kept M. a secret, how her entries, although sketchy, became progressively anguished, how she submitted to him completely. 'How much further could she have gone?' I ask.

The question is rhetorical; I don't expect him to answer, but he does. He looks over at me and says, 'You're about to find out.'

A sense of unease creeps through me. 'What do you mean?' I ask.

He ignores me.

We're out of the valley now, in the foothills, heading into the white-capped, snowy mountains. It starts to rain harder. In giant arcs, the wipers swoosh across the windshield. M. is contemplative, his expression bemused. He says, 'I suppose I did break her heart. But she was stronger for it. She would've gone on to someone else. She would've survived a broken heart.'

'If she'd been given the chance to survive at all.'

He sighs; at once, a tiresome look covers his face. 'We're back to that, are we? Did I break her body as well as her heart? I hadn't seen her for several weeks before she was killed, Nora. I broke it off with her. Why would I go back and kill her? Why would I want her dead?'

'I saw your box in the closet. I know what you did to her. You like pain – other people's pain. I think you're a control freak who lost control. You went too far. Things got out of hand, and Franny ended up dead.'

'In the first place,' he says, his tone instructional, 'you don't know what I did to Franny, and you won't know until I decide to tell you. Second, if that's your theory – that I killed her in an uncontrolled moment of sadistic passion – aren't you afraid I'll lose control with you?'

'You can't touch me. The police would be all over you.'

'But if I lose control, I won't be thinking rationally. The consequences won't enter my mind.'

Suddenly, I feel closed in, as if his car had just gotten smaller. I say, 'If I go – you'll go, too. The police will know you're involved, and this time they'll get you. That will be of some satisfaction. You'll pay for what you did.'

He is silent for a minute. Slowly, like a parent expressing disapproval, he shakes his head. He says, 'Nora, you're extremely foolish. That kind of thinking won't bring back Franny – it'll only get you killed.'

I get that closed-in, anxious feeling again, pinched off from the world. 'Some things are worth dying for,' I say, but I know I don't sound convincing.

His eyes still on the road, M. says, 'Then the big question now is, will I put you to the test?'

'You tell me,' I say, frightened by his words.

He watches the road. Rain splashes on the windshield. 'If I were to kill someone,' he begins, then he glances over at me and adds, 'if I were to kill you, for instance, it wouldn't be in an uncontrolled frenzy. It would be very controlled, deliberate, very methodical. If I were going to commit an act so . . . final, I would want to enjoy it. I imagine one would lose out on the total experience if one was not in control.'

He hesitates for a moment, thinking, then says, 'I imagine I'd begin by tying you up, binding your arms and legs. Then I'd mummify you. Do you know what that is, Nora? It's a bondage experience. There are many ways to do it, but the basic principle is the same: to completely wrap someone up, head to toe, shutting off as much sensory input as possible, rendering them immobile. You would be helpless, unable to move, unable to fight back, unable to scream for help. It would give me pleasure to see you like that. But I'd have to go a step further, wouldn't I? – if we're talking about murder. And I wouldn't want to get caught. I'd have a wooden box ready, the size of a coffin, and I'd place you inside it, then nail down the top. I'd bury you, perhaps in my own backyard. You would hear the dirt fall against the coffin as I shoveled it in. There would be nothing you could do, just listen and panic as I buried you alive.'

I stare at M. as he says this, feeling a coldness go through my body that has nothing to do with the low temperature outside. He looks at me and smiles, that snide half smile of his that I'm coming to hate.

'But this is all hypothetical,' he adds. 'I'm not a murderer.'

Again, I feel my isolation. I should not be alone with M. I look out the window. We're in the Sierras, the mountains white and hushed, the road banked high with dirty snow. I reach for the heater and turn it up. White firs and the shorter, brown-barked incense cedars stud the mountain, covering the melting snow with a crusty mantle of scaly leaves, pointed needles, and rounded cones. The highway, slick and slushy gray-black, twists around the mountain in sharp turns and bends; M. drives slowly, carefully. The temperature outside isn't cold enough for snow, and the rain, now just a soft, muffled sprinkling on the car, seems to isolate M. and me, setting up a wet carapace between the two of us and the rest of the world.

'That stuff you had in your closet,' I ask him, 'did you use it on Franny? All of it?'

He does not answer immediately. Finally, he says, 'The relationships I enjoy most involve some form of sadomasochism, and I usually choose women who also enjoy this. Franny was different; she wanted a more traditional arrangement. However, she was in love with me, more so than any other woman I've known, and because of this she allowed me to do virtually anything I wanted with her. I demanded that she prove her love to me, and she did – over and over and over. And her pliancy, her unwillingness to say no, made me even more demanding. I was far more exacting with her than with any other woman. She had a personality that begged to be abused. She refused me nothing, therefore I took it all. So the answer to your question is yes, she had firsthand knowledge of everything in the box – plus more.'

Momentarily, I am unable to speak. I take a deep breath, then say, 'I want to know more. Tell me the specifics. Precisely what did you and Franny do?'

He glances at me, then turns back to the road. 'We've talked enough about her,' he says.

I feel my anger rising. He gives me just enough details about Franny to keep me in line. 'How long are you going to do this?' I ask him. 'Doling out information at your leisure; giving me a bit here and a piece there. Do you think you can control me the way you did my sister?'

'We'll see,' he says.

I stare out the window. Ponderosa pines, with yellowish, deeply furrowed bark, drift by as the car curves through the mountains. Both of us are silent for a while. The rain has stopped, and we're on the backside of the mountain, past the crest of Echo Summit and heading into the lower elevations of South Lake Tahoe. Here the snowfall is already starting to melt. The berm of the highway is splotched with small muddied patches of snow, and the mountainside is dotted with a white icy patchwork quilt, melting around the edges.

M. looks over at me. 'You thought of Franny as good-natured, with no problems, an even-tempered, colorless, dull person you had to see occasionally because you were sisters. You loved her, but she wasn't your type, just as she wasn't mine. She wasn't the kind of person you would have chosen for a friend, and if you weren't related you wouldn't have seen her at all. Franny knew this; she knew you found her boring and she accepted it. She never spoke badly of you, and she never reproached you for your disinterest. Perhaps she should have. You never took the time to get to know her as an adult. I did know her, however. On Christmas – you remember Christmas, don't you? The day you spend with family? The day you were too busy to celebrate with your only relative? – on Christmas Franny visited the convalescent hospital so her friend, Sue Deever, wouldn't be alone. And once a week she helped with a Brownie troop just because she liked being around kids. You never knew any of this, did you? She might as well have been a stranger. Yet she admired you; she thought the world of you and defended you relentlessly. When I said you sounded selfish, she made excuses for you. She said you were busy, you had your own life.'

I'm staring out the side window, seeing nothing. I wanted to know more about Franny, but now that he's telling me I don't like what I hear. I felt guilt before – I realize I should've made a bigger effort to include her in my life – but now it runs deeper.

He says, 'It makes you wonder, doesn't it? Why all this devotion to you when, plainly, you didn't deserve it.'

I am unable to answer him. When Franny died, people, many of whom I didn't know, came up to me and expressed their heartfelt sympathy. None of them chastised me; none was aware of my neglect. Only M. knows the truth. I pray for him to stop, but he continues.

'Earlier, you said she was easy prey – perhaps you had something to do with that. You were her sister, Nora; you should have known she needed you. You should have cared for her a little more.' He is quiet. Then his voice changes, becomes lighter, irreverent.

'Maybe that accounts, at least in part, for my fascination with you. I want to know this person who claimed such loyalty – undeservedly.'

My throat feels dry, and I know if I speak it will be with difficulty. He is correct, of course. I should've cared for Franny more. Reflexively, I strike back at him.

'You don't have any right to judge me, not after what you did to her.' My voice breaks as I speak. With effort, I regain my composure.

M. takes pity on me. Gently, he says, 'Maybe that's why I can judge you – because of what I did to her. Because—'

'Is this a confession?' I ask, rejecting his pity. 'Are you telling me you killed her?'

Slowly, with patience, he shakes his head. 'What I'm telling you is that we both hurt her.'

'But I did it unintentionally.' My voice sounds unnatural, strained with emotion and with the tears I won't allow to flow. I want forgiveness, yet realize it isn't forthcoming, not from this man. 'Maybe I wasn't a good sister, maybe I was self-absorbed, maybe I was a lot of things – but I didn't set out to hurt her.'

'No, you didn't. But the end result was the same. Deliberate or not, she got hurt. You hurt her, I hurt her – that's life. You have to share the blame.'

I look out the windshield. My alliance with M., born of necessity, is taking a new turn. I made a pact with this man, a deal with the Devil, to complete the puzzle of Franny. Now he's complicating me in the mystery, making me an accessory to her undoing. I hadn't bargained for this. I don't want to be part of the puzzle, yet I feel a tightening force uniting me with M., a bond as secure as a manacle around my neck.

I hadn't noticed the last few miles go by, and I'm amazed to see we're at the California-Nevada state line. M. drives past the casinos. He pulls onto a side road and stops in front of a two-story redwood house, the A-framed roof covered with snow.

'Why are we here?' I ask.

Opening the car door, he says, 'To learn more about Franny.' The cold air rushes in. He reaches in the backseat for his coat, a navy blue wool blazer. He gets out and walks around the car, slipping into his coat, then opens my door. I hesitate, wondering what will happen in the house.

'Come on,' he says, and he holds out his hand. I get out, ignoring the offer of his arm. We cross the driveway, our breath coming out in short, frosty-white puffs, and go up to the front door. M. rings the doorbell.

'You won't be expected to do anything,' he says. 'You're only here as an observer – unless you decide to participate. All I ask is that you remember you're a guest in this home. Refrain from making any comments or judgments while here.'

I start to say something, but just then the door opens. M. introduces me to a tall, portly man. His face is round and ruddy, friendly-looking; he's casually dressed in brown corduroy slacks, and not wearing any shoes.

'You're just in time,' the man says, and we follow him through the carpeted hallway, then up a flight of stairs. The entire home is done in redwood and glass, sparsely decorated yet elegant. 'We were about to begin.' He leads us into a large den with black leather furniture. We sit, and while we are talking a naked woman in red high heels walks in the room. She is not a beautiful woman – maybe in her late forties, ten or fifteen pounds overweight, too much makeup – but her manner is serene. She's wearing a black studded collar, like a dog's collar, and she goes directly to the man and kneels in front of him, her head bowed. He ignores her, as does M. Red welts run diagonally across her buttocks and thighs.

'I see you're admiring her marks,' our host says as he leans forward and caresses the woman's shoulders. 'I just finished punishing her when you arrived.' To the woman, he says, 'Get up. Give them a closer look.'

'Yes, Master,' she says, and rises.

'Master?' I whisper, glancing at M., but he ignores me.

She walks over to us and smiles, as if she is proud of the welts, and turns around so we can see.

'Very nice,' M. says, running his hand down her thigh.

I whisper to M., 'You brought Franny here?'

He nods.

To me, the woman says, 'I'm glad you could come today, even if you're not going to play.'

Feeling nervous, I wonder what she means by *play*.

'We'll start now,' the man says, rising from the chair. He spreads a white sheet on the floor, then beckons to the woman. She lies on her back, and her breasts, with thin stretch marks spreading to the nipples, sag to each side. Her hair is short and curly, reddish gold, just like her pubic hair. She closes her eyes and begins to breathe deeply, as if she is meditating. Sitting next to her, the man opens a small leather case. I see a row of stainless-steel needles.

M. seems surprised and oddly uneasy. He whispers to me, 'This wasn't what I expected – I thought he was just going to do a whipping and bondage scene.'

We watch as he pinches the skin above her breast and pushes a needle through a thin layer of flesh. I hear her moan.

'Breathe,' the man says to her, his voice soothing. 'Just relax,' and he pushes another needle through her skin, on the other breast, then caresses her forehead. She opens her eyes and looks up at him, smiling. Dots of blood spot her breasts.

'This is play?' I whisper to M. as she is pierced with yet another needle.

M. leans close to me. Quietly, he says, 'For some people, yes. As you can see, she is enjoying this. Just watch – I think he's going to do a design with needles on her chest.'

But he doesn't. From under a piece of fabric in the case, he picks up a gleaming knife. It looks like a surgical scalpel. I tense, drawing in my breath, knowing what he is about to do. Quickly, I look at M. He is leaning forward, just slightly, his expression wary.

Feeling sick, I walk out of the house and stand on the porch, catching my breath. In a few minutes, he joins me.

He says, 'It's called scarification. You don't have to worry about her – he won't cut her deeply. And the scars won't be permanent.'

The cold air goes through my coat, tingling my skin. 'Why did you bring me here?'

'So you could see how they interacted.'

'Is that why you brought Franny here?'

'No. Franny was never an observer – she was a participant. Not with the cutting; we never did that to her.'

'You're lying.'

M. shrugs. 'I have no reason to lie. You wanted to know what Franny and I did together – I'm telling you.'

'And?'

M. smiles. 'And what? Did I let him fuck her? Figure that out for yourself.'

We get into his car and leave for home. We drive without speaking. It's only four in the afternoon and the rain has picked up again. When we turn onto the main road, I stare at the passing shops, motels, people rushing along under umbrellas. We wind around the lower half of Lake Tahoe, the water pocked by big drops of rain. Everything around us – the tall, dripping trees, the homes planked with redwood, cars swishing by – everything takes on a sodden, grayish tinge. I can't stop thinking of Franny in that house, of what M. forced her to do.

The city falls behind. We pass the airport and head into the mountains, where the rain, quite abruptly, turns into a light shower. The droplets drizzle on the car in a languorous, misty dance. Soon it's dusky outside, nearly twilight. The trees are sparse now, and the steep mountains have given way to the rolling, grassy foothills. We reach the flat stretch of land that becomes Sacramento and continue west. When we get to Davis, he drives up to my house. He turns off the engine and looks at me, draping his arm across the seat. Without comment, he studies me. I become uneasy.

'What?' I ask defensively.

'Come over here,' he says. This is a demand, not a request. Instinctively, I stay where I am. In the silent moments that ensue, the air becomes heavy with tension.

He smiles, smug and ominous. 'Defiance,' he says, releasing his seat belt and sliding over to me. 'I like that.' In a sudden move I'm not expecting, he pins me up against the door, blocking me with his arms so I can't move. He puts one hand under my chin and lifts my head to him. 'Some of it. But don't go too far. Defy me at the wrong time, and you'll pay for it.' He pushes against me, then he kisses me. I feel the danger again, as I did the night I slept with him; I feel, against my will, the excitement.

Abruptly, he stops. He grips my chin and mouth with one hand, pushing my head back against the window. I feel the strength in his arms, in his body pressed to mine.

Quietly, with his hold on me secure, he says, 'You want to believe I killed Franny. It gives you something to hold on to. It's a better alternative than to think her killer might go free. But you're attracted to me. I can feel it in the way you kiss me, I can feel it in your body. You and I are going to become friends. In spite of yourself, you will like me. You may not know it yet, but we're more alike than you ever imagined. We're cut from the same mold, Nora. You won't be able to resist me.'

His words scare me. To think I might be similar to him is repugnant. I struggle against the hand gripping my jaw. 'Don't be too sure,' I manage to say.

He kisses me lightly on the cheek, then releases me. I go inside the house, hearing him drive away. Immediately, I call Joe Harris at his home and tell him about the scarification. Joe tells me he'll check it out.

A few minutes later, the doorbell rings. Ian is standing on the porch – blond, big, looking boyish in blue jeans and a red-and-gold 49ers jacket. His face is square and smooth, no discernible lines yet, with straw-colored eyebrows that look like paintbrush bristles. Rushing in with a loping gait, he kisses me on the same cheek that M. had kissed.

'What are you doing here?' I ask, perplexed.

'You didn't get my message? I called you earlier; I said I'd be over this evening.' He puts his arms on my shoulders and kisses me again, deeper this time. I expect him to sense my betrayal, to stand back and say, 'You've been with another man' – but he doesn't. In his kiss, I feel passion and true affection.

I rest my head against his chest and hold him tightly. He's

a thickset man, built like a wrestler – which is what he was in college – big and brawny, but his life is mostly sedentary now and in a few years, by slow degrees, the flabbiness will appear. I can feel it beginning now. I think of M.'s naked body: sleek, taut, danger running through his blood. The image makes me nervous. I reach under Ian's T-shirt and press my fingers into his cool, pale flesh. His sheer mass comforts me.

'No,' I say, 'I didn't get your message. I just got home.' I look at him, his trusting face, and know, most assuredly, I can't tell him about M. Instead, I tell him I went up to Tahoe with a girlfriend.

I follow Ian into the kitchen, where he gets a Pepsi out of the refrigerator. I don't drink sodas, and keep them only for him. Glancing at my answering machine, I see I have two messages. I press the button and, sure enough, Ian, in a loud voice amplified by the machine, is telling me he'll be over later this evening. The other message is from Maisie, wondering where I am, why I haven't returned her calls. I haven't spoken to her since I met M., unwilling to tell her about my clandestine affair. I erase both messages.

Taking off his jacket, Ian tosses it on the counter and says, 'Did you win? Up at Tahoe?'

'Not much. A few dollars.'

He flips back the tab and takes a drink out of the can, pushes his light hair out of his eyes. He looks at the answering machine and, without much energy, says, 'I had lunch with Maisie today. She doesn't understand why you're avoiding her.'

Maisie writes a human-interest column for the *Bee*, and she and Ian have become fairly good friends. 'I'm not avoiding her,' I say. I start to fabricate an excuse, but Ian seems distracted, and I don't think he heard what I said. He pulls on his lower lip.

'What's the matter?' I ask him.

He's silent for a moment, as if he's gauging the effect of

his reply. Finally, his voice irritated, he says, 'Maisie isn't the only one you seem to be avoiding.' He finishes the Pepsi in one long gulp and sets down the can. 'I've been trying to reach you all week. You don't answer the phone, and when you return my calls, you do it during the day when you know I'm not at home.'

All week I've been telling Ian I had the flu.

He continues. 'You act like you don't want to see me. As if there's someone else in your life.'

'No,' I say quickly. 'There is no one else. I've been sick; that's all.'

He looks off to the side, his face troubled, then back at me. 'Are you sure that's all?'

I nod.

He closes his eyes, sighing. When he opens them, he says, 'I shouldn't have said that, about you seeing someone else. I shouldn't have jumped to that conclusion. But I love you, Nora. You can't just disappear for a week. And you can't push me away just because you're sick. I want to take care of you when you're not feeling well. I want to be with you – good health or bad.'

'I'm sorry,' I reply. 'I'm just . . .' I shrug, not knowing what to say, not wanting to compound my lies. Lamely, I add, 'I knew you were busy last week.'

'I was – but I would've made time for you.' He relaxes, leaning against the counter. The beginning of a smile appears on his face. 'I would've brought you chicken soup.'

I go over to Ian and wrap my arms around him. I hold him to me, lean against him, then hold him even tighter. This is the man I want. He's reliable and dependable and loving. He gives me what I need.

Gently, Ian pushes me at arm's length. 'Hey,' he says, concerned. 'Are you all right?' He searches my face for an answer.

I nod. 'Yeah, I guess I'm just tired.'

'What you need is a little TLC – which I would've given

you all along if you had let me come over.' He leads me into the living room, turns on the corner lamp, and we sit on the couch. The lamp has only forty-watt bulbs in it, three of them, and they give off a mellow, amber glow that fades into a furry darkness in the far corners of the room. On the coffee table lies Ian's latest wood carving – an unfinished scorpion in holly – along with several sharp knives and chisels. I put up my feet on the couch and lie down, resting my head in his lap. I find security in the bulk of his body, and I nestle closer, wanting his solidity to anchor me.

'I mean it, Nora,' he says. 'Just because you're sick, you can't tell me to stay away. If I get the flu, are you going to say, "Call me when you're better. I don't want to see you until you're well"?'

'No.'

'Okay, then. So don't tell me to stay away. Don't shut me out like that.'

I burrow into his lap, turning away so I don't have to look him in the face. His concern for me makes me feel even guiltier about M. 'I guess I'm not very good at being a girlfriend,' I say.

He strokes my hair and his voice softens. 'You're fine as a girlfriend,' he says, and I know he means it. 'Just fine,' he whispers, and he continues stroking my hair and face, his hands so large, his fingers so thick and blunt-edged you wouldn't think they could be so gentle.

'Do you want to stay home tonight?' he asks. 'Just take it easy? We can watch TV if you like.' His touch is as smooth and silken as warm butter, and I can feel the love in it. I contrast him with M. and find there is no comparison.

I nod, then roll over so I'm looking at him. His eyes are blue and clear and gaze at me with absolute trust, his face open and honest. He palms the top of my head and rubs his thumb lightly across my forehead. His touch is purifying. 'What I'd really like,' I say, 'is for you to make love to me.'

Ian gives me a slow grin. 'I thought you were tired.'

'Not that tired,' I say. I want my thoughts of M. to be replaced
with ones of Ian, and my negligence of Franny to disappear. I
want Ian's purifying touch to take away my guilt. I want, quite
simply, complete and total absolution.

14

Since Franny's death, I've learned much about the world of sadomasochism. In an S&M relationship, the dominant partner is referred to as the top, the submissive as the bottom; and if the submissive attempts to control or manipulate the relationship, his or her behavior is negatively referred to as 'topping from the bottom.' This is an apt phrase for my relationship with M. He is unaware of it, but I'm topping him from below.

When Ian doesn't come over, I spend my evenings with M. I usually don't see him until dinnertime. When he returns from his last class on campus, he goes immediately to his piano and is loath to be interrupted. Tonight, we just finished dinner and we're taking a brief walk around the neighborhood, Rameau – like a shadow, ever present – a few feet behind us. There are no sidewalks here, so we walk along the edge of the road, kicking up pebbles now and then. In a neighbor's yard, pink-tipped yellow dahlias shimmer in a gentle flurry of wind, and a bird whistles in a tree. Through the treetops we see an orange sun hover low in the horizon. Soon it will be dark.

M. takes my hand in his. He's wearing lightweight gloves, which strikes me as odd since the air isn't very cool. Two young boys zip past us on bicycles, riding in the middle of the asphalt road.

'Do you always wear gloves?' I ask him.

'Nearly, if there's a hint of coolness in the air. My hands chap easily.' He looks over at me and adds, 'You don't want my hands to be rough, Nora. It would be distracting. Trust me. For what I have planned, you want my hands to be soft.'

I almost ask what he has planned, but decide he's only

teasing. We walk together, my hand in his, and I can't help thinking that it was by this gloved hand that Franny was murdered.

We pass a home that has a small manmade pond in front. Bluish-gray translucent insects skitter on the pond, the surface rippling slightly when a breeze, carrying the sweet smell of jasmine, comes our way.

'Tell me something about Franny,' I say.

Without hesitation, he replies, 'She was impeccably honest. She would never consider deceiving one man with another.'

I bow my head and sigh – a soft, repentant sigh – letting him think I'm overcome with guilt. But it's all I can do not to laugh out loud. He's the last person in the world who should be lecturing me on deception. A ratcheting cricket breaks the silence.

'You won't be able to keep seeing two men for very long,' he says quietly. 'It'll start to eat away at you. Drop Ian – he doesn't have what you need.'

I hear the jealousy in his voice and make a note to use it to my advantage, if possible. Again, I say nothing, just sigh a little so he'll think I'm troubled. The bottom of the sun disappears and long, red-flamed tendrils become visible, fringing the horizon like a decorative border of coiling threads. In the dusky twilight, the street takes on a closed-in, sheltered look, all the shrubs and trees and lawns grayish-green in the diffused light of the vanishing sun.

We finish our walk hand in hand, our shoulders touching occasionally. When we get back to his house, M. goes into the kitchen and puts a pot of water on the stove. With his back to me, I watch him fiddle at the counter, arranging two mugs, getting out two Bigelow tea bags, pouring in the boiling water.

'I'll be back in a second,' he says and disappears. He returns with a magazine and gives it to me, *Taste of Latex,* issue five.

'Homework,' he says, sitting me in a chair at the kitchen table. He opens it to page twenty, and I read the title of the article: 'Fisting, Part 1: The Cunt.'

I lay the magazine on the table. 'Forget it,' I say. 'There's no way you're getting your entire hand inside me.'

He places his palm on my shoulder. 'This isn't something we have to do tonight,' he says. 'Or even next week. Just read the article. Learn a little about it, and try to keep an open mind.'

I look at the pictures. 'I'm not big enough. You'd tear me apart.'

'Read it,' he says, and he brings me a mug of tea and walks away.

I shout at his back, 'That's all I'll be doing.' I sip the tea, not looking at the magazine, wondering if this is something he did with Franny. I drink more tea, almost finishing it, then finally glance at the pictures again. A woman is on all fours, another person – hard to tell if it's a man or woman – behind her, a hand inserted in her vagina. I start to read the article but find it difficult to concentrate. My gaze wavers back to the picture, back to the hand disappearing inside a vagina. I return to the opening paragraph and yawn – something about fisting not actually performed with your hand shaped in a fist. I reread the opening paragraph, not understanding, feeling drowsy. I look up and see M. at my side.

'Finished?' he asks.

I shake my head. 'I don't seem to be concentrating,' I tell him, and yawn again. 'I'm really tired.'

'Maybe you should lie down for a while,' he says, and I see him helping me to stand.

Feeling disoriented, I say, 'Yes, just for a few minutes.' My words sound slow and unreal. I lean on M. as he takes me into the den, his arm firmly around my waist. He sits me on the couch.

'Are you all right?' he asks, his dark eyes looking into mine. I nod.

'Lie back. You'll feel better in a while,' and he pushes me down gently, lifts my feet onto the couch, takes off my shoes. 'Just sleep,' he says. 'Close your eyes and sleep,' but my eyes are already closed. I think he is saying something else, but his voice sounds distant and I can't make out the words. Visions of vaginas and disappearing hands cloud my mind. I try to focus my thoughts, but everything is a sleepy blur. Giving up, I roll over onto my side and let my mind slip away.

I wake up slowly, feeling groggy, and when I open my eyes I see the ceiling, the long wooden beam along the length of it, high above. I close my eyes and open them again. This time I see M. Leisurely, he swings in and out of my vision like a doll on a string. I turn to see him better, but my neck feels stiff, restricted; the movement is minimal, and my vision peripheral. He is siting in a chair next to me, leaning forward, and he places his hand on my forehead, but I don't feel his fingers or the touch of his skin, just a gentle pressure.

'Try not to be frightened,' he says, and I close my eyes again, wondering what he's talking about.

'You were asleep for a while,' I hear him say. 'I put something in your tea. Chloral hydrate.'

I open my eyes once more, still feeling drowsy. I start to speak, but find I cannot.

'It's a sleeping pill,' he continues. 'I only gave you a tiny amount, just enough to knock you out for a short time.'

I'm not as sluggish now, and I realize something is very wrong. I feel as though my mind and body are on a time-delay system, thoughts and senses dilatory. Only now do I recognize the full meaning of M.'s previous words: *Don't be frightened. I put something in your tea. A sleeping pill.* I struggle to sit up but am unable to move. Then I feel the pressure on my body, the pressure that has been here all along – a tight, constricting sensation, squeezing in on me. Suddenly, I am aware of what has happened.

'Don't try to move,' he says softly. 'It's impossible – you'll only exert yourself unnecessarily.' He keeps his hand on my forehead, rubbing gently, as if that alone will calm me.

'Here,' he says. 'Take a peek,' and he holds a mirror up to my face. My eyes look back at me, blue and frightened. The rest of my head is wrapped in a flesh-colored elastic Ace bandage. Mouth, ears, scalp – everything is wrapped except my eyes and a small slit for nostrils. He tilts the mirror so I can see the rest of my body. It's entirely encased in rolls and rolls of Ace bandages. My legs are wrapped together, arms pinioned against thighs, torso covered, no flesh visible whatsoever. I groan, feeling dismay, my utter helplessness, and a wave of panic goes through me. I'm shrouded in bandages. Mummified. A sense of claustrophobia overcomes me, and I feel I'm not getting enough air. I breathe rapidly, shallowly, the pounding of a terror-driven heartbeat exploding in my ears.

'Just relax,' M. says, laying a hand on my shoulder. 'Try to calm down. It'll go easier for you if you're relaxed.'

I look over at him. I try to speak again, but he has stuffed something into my mouth and the words come out mumbled. I blink back tears, refusing to cry.

'Shhh,' he whispers, and he kisses me softly on each eyelid. 'You look beautiful like this. Don't be frightened. Try to enjoy the experience, if you can. I took great care in wrapping you. I wanted you to feel the total isolation, the complete loss of skin sensation. I wrapped your right leg separately before wrapping both legs together – so you wouldn't feel skin against skin. I wrapped your torso before pinning your arms to your sides, then wrapped you again, over and over, like a cocoon. You should feel no skin at all, nothing, just the tightness of the bandages.'

He puts a hand under my head and lifts it slightly. 'I wanted you to be able to see when you woke up,' he says. 'I wanted you to understand your predicament fully, but now I'm going to finish the cocoon.'

I groan again, attempting to speak. I try to shake my head.

'I know you're frightened,' he says, winding the elastic bandage around my head, cutting off my vision, 'but try to relax. There's nothing you can do at this point, so you might as well give in to the feeling, to the sense of isolation, to the knowledge that your very existence depends on me.'

Everything is black now. He has wrapped the bandage several times over my eyes, and no light at all seeps through. I wait, fearing he will wrap the bandage over my nose, suffocating me, but he lays my head back onto the couch.

'I'm going to leave you for a while,' he says. I feel his hand caress my bound breasts, then trail along my bandaged torso. Very softly, he says, 'You look wonderful, absolutely wonderful,' and then I hear him walk away, out of the room.

Under the bandages, I feel my body tremble. Blackness, all is black. I remember the description of the second half of his death scenario: the wooden coffin, the sound of dirt as he buries me alive. I breathe faster, desperate for more air. I want to cry out at the unfairness of this. I want someone to help me. The bandages feel tighter than they did a few minutes ago, pressing in on me. Is this how I will die? I begin to cry, feel my body quiver, hear muffled sobs. This isn't fair, I tell myself. *This isn't fair!* I think of all the mistakes I've made. I thought I had the upper hand; I thought controlling M. would be, if not easy, manageable. I was wrong. So wrong. My breathing is hard and fast, frantic, and I try to slow it down. In and out, in and out slowly, deeply, in to the count of ten . . . out to the count of ten . . . in . . . out.

My body feels heavy, leaden, as though I'm sinking deeper and deeper into the couch. Has an hour gone by? Two? Three? I don't think I've been lying here that long, but I'm not sure. Maybe it's been only an hour. A dog is barking outside. It's not Rameau – his bark is lower, more threatening. And a car just drove by. In . . . out . . . I listen carefully, trying to block out the thoughts and images running through my mind, grateful for any sound I hear. An airplane flying overhead. More cars. Some kind of insect that got into the house. The low rumble of a distant train . . .

How long have I been here? And why doesn't he make any noise? Is he still here? I feel the couch beneath me as pressure points supporting my body, very light under my legs, heavier beneath my torso. There's a twinge in my lower back, discomfort, and I will it to go away. With each breath, I tell myself I'm getting lighter and lighter, lighter than air. In . . . out . . .

I no longer feel my body. I'm separate, detached. There's nothing I can do. My life belongs to M. I must accept whatever he does. It's out of my hands, out of my control. There's no defense, no fighting back, no way to protect myself. Live or die, it's completely up to M. I listen to the silent words in my mind, louder than spoken ones, and frown. What am I doing? This is what he wants – fear, acceptance, complete submission. I'm reacting exactly how he'd expect me to react. He's an asshole. He had no right to do this to me. He's a fucking asshole. A fucking professorial asshole. I hear the words, shrill and clear, as if I'd screamed them out loud. I concentrate, attempt to think rationally. He's trying to scare me, that's all. He wants me to stop looking for Franny's murderer. He wants me to leave him alone. He can't kill me – the police wouldn't let him get away this time . . .

How long have I been here? I think I dozed off, but I'm not sure. I hear a mosquito, with its shrill, high-pitched whine, circling the room. Outside, an owl screeches. I breathe in and out, very slowly. My nose has taken on monumental importance, and I'm acutely aware of my nasal passages, the left nostril being slightly congested. If I can control my breathing, I tell myself, I'll be okay. I breathe deeper. Sniff. Expel rapidly. I can't clear the left nostril. I cry again, knowing I am utterly helpless.

'Hello, Nora.'

Instantly, my body tenses. I feel a knot of terror tightening in my stomach. When did he return? He slides an arm under my shoulders, another under my legs, and lifts me up. He carries me a short distance, a few feet perhaps, then lowers me onto something hard and flat. He's just trying to scare me, I tell myself, and I struggle to control my breathing, but now it doesn't work. My breath is rapid, shallow, frantic. I hear a lid closing over me. My screams come out muffled, inaudible. Then I hear a hammer pounding: nails in my coffin. Every muscle is tensed, my chest tight. The hammering stops. Silence. More silence. I wait for the sound of scraping as he drags the coffin outside, but there is no sound. Did I misjudge the distance he carried me? Am I already outside? Still, there is no noise. I wait for the sound of dirt being shoveled on the coffin. I wait, not breathing. When the dirt doesn't come, I take a short breath. Then another. My lungs ache, my jaw clenches, I feel as though each muscle is constricting upon itself. Time goes by. Minutes, tens of minutes, I don't know. I wait for the sound of dirt.

But it doesn't come. Instead, there is only silence. Dark, interminable silence. Hellish. Stygian . . . Have hours passed? Nothing seems real anymore. I dream I'm dead already, in the underworld ferried along on the River Styx, another soul transported . . . How long before the air runs out? Did he cover me with dirt? Did I miss it? . . .

Something groans metallic. I hear nails squeaking as they're pulled out of wood, then the sound of the lid being removed. I'm lifted out of the coffin, as if I'm rising from the dead, and set back onto the couch. A hand is placed under my head and I feel the bandages unwinding.

'You may want to keep your eyes shut for a while,' M. says. 'The light will seem extremely bright.'

Despite his warning, I open them as soon as the bandage is off. I blink, squint, then open them again, more slowly this time. He continues to unwind the bandages, exposing the rest of my nose, cheeks, mouth, neck.

'Open,' he says, and he pulls a foam rubber ball out of my mouth. Words of anger are on my tongue, but to my surprise instead of cursing him I begin to tremble. He cradles my head against his chest.

'Shhh,' he says. 'It's over now. I'm not going to hurt you.' He stands me up and begins unwrapping my body, layer by layer. I still do not speak, partly from emotional exhaustion, partly from good sense: I want to make sure I'm free before

I begin my assault. I sway slightly, unsteady, and lean against M. for support. Looking around the room, I see I was in his den the entire time. There is a wooden crating box in the corner of the room, a hammer and nails on the floor.

'I did this for several reasons,' he says. He finishes another bandage and begins on the next, moving downward from my shoulders, chest, midriff. 'I wanted to prove my trustworthiness. You were so convinced I killed your sister, convinced I might even harm you – this should change your mind. I had every opportunity to hurt you, even murder you, if I was so inclined, yet I didn't. Perhaps now you'll stop this nonsense of believing I killed Franny – or at least take into consideration that the murderer may have been someone else.'

There are two piles of Ace bandages on the floor. It looks as though he used three- and twelve-inch widths. When he's finished with my torso, he unwraps my hips and thighs. I still feel weak and unsteady. M. lays me back on the couch, props my head with a pillow, then elevates my legs and begins on them.

'But that was only one reason. You wanted to know Franny better – this was the perfect opportunity. You stepped into her shoes, so to speak, and experienced what she experienced. I can tell you only so much, Nora. To understand what Franny went through, to truly understand, you have to go through it yourself. If I simply told you how I mummified her, you never would've grasped the implications of the experience, the depth of feeling that surfaces. Think of tonight's episode as a tactile filling-in of Franny's diary.'

My hands are free from my thighs, although each arm is still tightly encased. I move them gently, feeling stiff. As he unwinds the outer cover from my legs, I see my right leg has been bandaged separately and that he has tied rope around my ankles and just above the knees. He unties the rope and begins unwrapping the right leg. When he's through, I stretch each leg. My body is naked and cold, stiff from lack of movement. M. covers me with a blanket then lifts one arm. He unwinds the bandage.

'The most important reason, however, is simply because it pleased me.'

I glare at him and open my mouth to say something, but he interrupts.

'Not yet,' he says, and begins with my other arm. 'Don't speak yet. I know you're angry and want to rant and rave at me for a while, but first things first. I have a reward for you; a present for your pain.' He takes off the last bandage and adds it to the pile. There must be two dozen Ace bandages on the floor. I move around under the blanket, feeling the stiffness leave my body. Surprisingly, I have no desire to get up or to see what time it is, or even to vent my anger. I feel drained, exhausted, and very withdrawn, as if I am on an inward journey, inside my head. I have been reprieved. All I want is to stay under the blanket, where it's safe and warm.

He goes over to his desk and returns with a sheaf of papers. 'Franny gave this to me shortly before she died. It's a short story, sort of. About Franny when she was fourteen, several months before your parents died, before she moved back to Sacramento to live with you. Originally, it was in her diary, but she deleted it. She wanted to destroy this copy also, but I wouldn't let her. I kept it in my office on campus.'

He hands me the papers. 'This will explain a lot about Franny,' he says. 'I think you'll find it a just reward for the ordeal you've been through,' and he leaves the room. I look at the first page and begin reading.

15

FRANNY'S LAST STAND
by Frances Tibbs

The first thing that people notice about me is this: my hair is short, really short, maybe only half an inch, sticking out straight and stubbly all over. That wouldn't be so unusual except that I'm a girl, which still wouldn't be so unusual if I was in Davis, California, a place where no one much cares who or what you look like.

But now we live in Montana, my parents and me, where a girl looking like a guy isn't too common. When I began cutting my hair – first just six inches of curls off the bottom, two weeks later another four inches up the sides, then an inch or two when I had a bad weekend, and another two when the rain came – when I started chopping it off, Mom never said anything at all. It was like she didn't even notice, as if I had been nearly bald-headed for all the fourteen years of my life. My dad noticed, though. He said I looked scruffy with nearly all my hair gone, and with me always wearing jeans and a bead-studded jacket fastened with feathers and leather cords and horse hair. He told me to let my hair grow back, and then he forgot about it until we were eating dinner, six weeks later, when he looked up from his crushed-potato-chip-tuna casserole and said, Didn't I tell you to stop cutting your hair? and then he shoved the fork in his mouth, crunching down on the potato chips, forgetting about my hair once again, while Mom just sat there, pushing carrots around on her plate, ignoring us, not hearing, not seeing, and it made me angry, her not being part of the family anymore, and I almost said, Stop playing with your food! but, me being the kid, she being the parent, I didn't.

When Dad told me we were moving to Montana, the first thing

*I thought was this: so this is how life is gonna be now: Montana.
And I pictured things you don't see in California, old-fashioned
country things, dusty roads, wooden-planked sidewalks, kids in
wide-brimmed hats and faded overalls, kids not even knowing about
acid-washed jeans or Day-Glo shoelaces or MTV or Madonna or
Joan Jett and the Blackhearts. Montana seemed as far away from
life as you could get, far away from neon-lit malls, video arcades,
chili-cheese fries at Murder Burger, and Joey Walker in his black
leather jacket and high-top Reeboks, the boy I dreamed about
constantly and almost kissed at the Davis water tower on Eighth
Street. But all that changed for me, even before we moved to Montana,
and Joey Walker wouldn't recognize me now, not with my bristly
hair.*

*This is what my mom told me before we moved here: Montana
has soft rolling plains and you can look forever and not see anything
but clear blue skies and brown hills that never end. My dad just
said that the tule fog in winter was getting to him, and it was time
for a change. But I know why we really moved, even if they didn't
say it: to forget. Maybe they thought we could start over here, that
things would get lost in the rolling hills, that things would get
absorbed in the wide open spaces in a way that they never could
in Davis, Davis with its low-hanging January fog, trapping everything, even memories, under its misty gray haze.*

*But clear blue sky doesn't help. No matter what you do, no matter
where you go, memories are still there, popping up at unexpected
times. It's like the cars in Montana. People here don't know what
to do with cars. You can drive in the country – which is pretty much
anywhere – and there's nothing but land, maybe a cow or two
grazing, and all of a sudden, out of nowhere, you see an abandoned
Chevy, rusted with a door missing, or maybe an old Ford pickup
with headlights smashed in, and it's on the side of the wad, in a
ditch, and – get this – it's upside-down. Every time we drive by
one of those cars, my parents in the front, not talking, me in the
backseat looking out the window, I think about extinct animals and
endangered species, and for the next few miles I'm wondering. This
has got to mean something, but I don't know what. It's times like*

this that make me wish Nora, my older sister, was here. She could explain the car situation to me, but with her not being here, I gotta figure it out for myself. People in California don't abandon cars on the side of the road, just turn them over and walk away. It's a Montana thing, I decide, like tule fog is a Davis thing, both of them reminding you of stuff you don't want to remember.

Right after we moved here, about a year ago, I decided to do better in school to make things easier on my parents. I study a lot more, and as my hair gets shorter, my grades get better. I'm a straight-A student now, and when I show Mom my report card, she smiles dreamily and says, That's nice, honey, and then she looks away and I can tell she already forgot about my A's, forgot about me. The thing she doesn't forget is this: Billy, my little brother, is dead.

History is what I study the most. In Mr Kendall's class, we learned about the Plains Indians. That's when I learned about Sitting Bull. He was the great leader who united all the Plains Indians, even if things didn't work out so well for him at the end. Now when Dad orders me to change my bead-studded jacket or stop chopping off my hair, I just tell him I'm working on a school project, on the Sioux Indians I say, and he grunts and goes into the living room to watch TV. For some reason that seems to make sense to him; maybe he thinks all the kids in my class are bald-headed. Well, they're not. They laugh at my stubbly head and my bead-studded jacket and my hair-fringed shirt. A Sioux warrior wannabe, is what they call me, Chief Sitting Bullshit. I'm not a guy and I'm not an Indian, I know that, and I never said that I was. But I like to do things the way Sitting Bull did them, like wearing feathers and horse hair and leather leggings. He was a determined man, Sitting Bull, and just by looking at a picture of him, you can tell that he was strong. If he wanted to hold on to his enemies, they wouldn't be able to get away. He would wrap his fingers around their arms, fingers that were like the talons of an eagle, and clamp down, sink into the skin and flesh and even the bones if necessary, and hold on as long as he had to. Sitting Bull wouldn't let anyone down.

I figure I can learn a lot from the Sioux. How to be strong, how to be brave, those kinds of things. Bravery was just about the most important thing to them. They saw things in black and white: if you weren't brave, you were a coward. It was that simple. They never haggled over fine points or argued about shades of gray – better to die a hero, was their motto, than to live a coward. Because of that, a Sioux warrior preferred to fight an enemy up close, hand to hand, rather than kill him from a distance; it proved that he was brave because he was putting his life in danger. Anyone could just hide behind a rock and kill a Crow or Pawnee by shooting him with an arrow. But to go up and touch him, that was brave. It was a sign of courage, and the first man to touch an enemy was given points – counting coups is what they called it – and this is what it taught the Sioux: not to flinch in the face of danger. And that is what Sitting Bull is teaching me.

Once or twice a week, after school gets out, I go over to the high school and collect a few coups of my own. I dress in jeans and a bulky jacket so they'll think I'm a boy; I wear a black ski mask pulled low on my face, just eyes staring out of narrow slits. I watch the football team, go to the sidelines and brush into those big guys, bump shoulders, knock knees, and they say, Watch where you're going, runt, and sometimes they shove me like I'm on the opposite team. An enemy. I've been doing it for almost seven months, baseball, basketball, and now football, whatever's in season. I'm the phantom Sioux, planning my attacks when the coach is upfield, his back turned, his attention elsewhere; he's never seen me yet. Like last week. Or the week before. It's always the same. I wait until all those bodies are scrunched down near the end zone, wait for the play to begin, wait for someone to be sidelined. The coach has the whistle in his lips, ready to blow away their fouls, and then I see him, this time it's the nose tackle, lumbering across the field, big as a giant, each footstep – I swear this is true – shaking the earth. Number 63. I've clashed with him before. He takes off his helmet and there's a head, blond, Nordic, attached to shoulders, no neck. His gut juts forward and white pads hang out of his green jersey, and I'm thinking, This is a sofa coming unstuffed. He stalks the sidelines, stopping to stretch his hamstrings, then kneels down to tie a shoelace, unaware that an attack is coming. I rush out from behind the bleachers. Smack. *Get the fuck off this field! says 63 as I crash into his shoulder pad, and he raises one of his arms, the underside so creamy white that it hardly looks dangerous, making me think I'm going to get off easy this time, but then he backhands me and I go sprawling across the grass, onto the dirt, cutting my lip on a rock. I retreat behind the bleachers just as the coach sees 63 screaming into the empty air, flinging his arms as if he were a signal man waving to planes. The coach never sees me. Quit screwing around, he yells at 63, you're supposed to be watching the goddamn play, which just gets 63 madder because he knows I'm there, peeking out from behind the bleachers. I taste blood on my lip, but it's okay because every time I touch the enemy, I get stronger, braver. I learn to take my injuries without comment, welcoming them; my bruises become badges; my blood, symbols. I brush the dirt off my jeans, wipe the blood off my lip, and count another coup.*

Even before we moved to Montana, I was familiar with Sioux country, though at the time I didn't know it. My parents are big on the outdoors, and we always do the camping-national-parks-thing for vacations. We've been all over the country doing two weeks in a pitched tent. Yosemite, King's Canyon, Bryce, Badlands, you name it. And just the four of us, Mom, Dad, me, and Billy, because Nora is older and has a job and doesn't come along anymore. On our last trip, over a year ago, we went to Flaming Gorge in Wyoming, Shoshone territory I now know. You kids are going to love this, Mom had said as we drove there, the scenery is majestic. Purple mountains at sunrise, she said, candy-colored mountains; mountains that will take your breath away.

The first day there, we got up early in the a.m., the air so cool we could see it as we talked, all of us bundled in hooded sweatshirts and long pants just so we could see those famous mountains. Mom grabbed me and we started jumping up and down to get warm, both of us laughing and looking silly in our new pink warm-up suits – this was before I started dressing like a guy – and Dad looked at Billy, both of them dressed sensibly in jeans, and he smiled, quirking his eyebrows in our direction and rolling his eyes as if to say, Women, *and then he put his hand on Billy's shoulder and they looked up at the mountains, pretending that the cold air didn't bother them a bit.*

And Mom was right – shades of pink and purple and orange rose in front of us. Sherbet-colored mountains, they were, mountains that I just had to get to the top of, so we hit the trail, me running ahead, whacking bushes with a stick, smelling the flowery scent that exploded and filled the air each time I gave them a swat. I heard Billy huffing behind me, and I turned to see him stumbling up the mountain, air coming out of his mouth in short frosty bursts as he struggled to keep up with me, clapping his hands together to keep warm, his cheeks splotchy from the morning air. He was short and scrawny, a whole head shorter than me, with a face full of freckles and dark hair that fell in bunches over his forehead so you could never see his eyes. You kids, watch where you're going, *Dad yelled after us. I ran ahead of Billy, trying to lose him. He was a year younger than me, and was always tagging along when I wanted to be alone. A year ago he got sick, and now he can't run very fast, and he's smaller than the other boys his age, a lot smaller, and I get tired of Mom and Dad always hovering over him and not me, worrying that he might get even sicker.* Wait! *he called.* Wait for me, Franny! *but I just threw my stick in the air and ran faster.*

When we lived in Davis, I had a paper route. This is what I do now, in Montana: steal bikes. Stealing a valuable horse from an enemy was another way the Sioux proved their bravery, another way for them to collect coups. If I wanted, I could do it in the middle of the night, Mom and Dad not missing me at all while I sneak into a neighbor's open garage, the people inside asleep in their beds, cozy, not worried about crime or a phantom Sioux, while I'm prowling around, catlike, without a sound, searching for a ten-speed, careful not to bang into the garbage can or knock over boxes or drop my flashlight, then take the bike and wheel it away, as easy as one, two, three. Just like that. But that wouldn't be a real test of courage;

it would be too easy. Instead, I collect my coups at school, in broad daylight. I feign an excuse to leave the classroom – like chewing on the skin of my finger until it bleeds, and then raising my hand and saying, I cut my finger. Can I see the nurse? – and I make a detour to the bike racks before I get my finger bandaged. I've already cased the bikes before the bell rang, so I know which one I'm going to take, which one doesn't have a lock, which one is the most valuable, and I look to the right of me, look to the left of me, coast's clear, so I grab the bike. I ride it down to the gully and throw it into the river, and then run back to the nurse, get my Band-Aid, say, Yes ma'am, I'll be more careful from now on, check my watch, and return to class, wiping sweat off my forehead as I sink into my chair, ready to give the teacher an excuse if necessary, Sorry it took so long, but the nurse was busy, I had to stop at the bathroom, etc., but it never is, necessary that is, because, hey, I'm a straight-A student, an example to be followed, maybe a little eccentric with the bald head and everything, but that's to be expected. After all, I am from California.

Each time a bike goes missing, it becomes more dangerous, and each time I steal a bike, I come closer to Sitting Bull. I intend to fill that river with bikes. I never keep them like the Sioux kept the horses, but I figure the effect is the same. I entered the enemy's camp, I survived, I have proof lying on the bottom of the river.

Sometimes I think about summer and if we'll ever go camping again. I hope we do, but if we don't, that's okay, too. I always liked those trips, even though Billy was a nuisance. Our trip to Flaming Gorge was typical – I go off, and he has to follow. I could hear his voice coming through the trees, a whiny voice that was trying to slow me down. Wait for me, Franny! he kept yelling. Wait for me! The path wound up into the mountains, getting narrower as it got higher. The trees thinned out, and the air smelled of dry leaves and dust. When I reached the edge of a cliff, loose rocks crumbled under my feet, and I could hear them as they fell into the canyon far below. I kept going up, following the trail, and I pushed my sleeves up to my elbows, wondering when the air had lost its chill. Then

I heard Billy scream, more like a surprised shriek, and the muffled sound of falling rocks. He had probably stumbled, I thought, and I could picture him sitting in the middle of the path, sulking, his jeans scuffed at the knees, his pea-green sweatshirt plastered with dirt. Or maybe he got scared because he was alone and imagined bears were closing in on him. I hesitated, debating the pros and cons of going back. I wanted to get to the top of the mountain, but if I didn't go back, Mom and Dad would nag at me later. Can't you be more considerate? they would say. Be nice to him for a change – it won't kill you to play with your little brother once in a while. Well, I know how that goes.

I went back to find Billy, taking my time, angry that he always spoiled my fun. If he couldn't keep up with me, he should just stay behind with Mom and Dad. I heard him sobbing and saying something I couldn't understand, and as I turned the bend, right before the cliff, I saw him sliding down where the path had given way. And the first thing I thought was this: he must have been looking at the confetti-colored mountains instead of where he was going. I started to yell at him, to tell him to watch where he was going from now on, and then it hit me: he was just about to go over the edge of the cliff. Sometime earlier he must have taken off his sweatshirt because it was tied around his waist, and his arms were scratched from the pebbles and his hands were clawing at the rocks and dirt, trying to find a hold, but he just kept crying and slipping down. I remembered screaming for my dad – Isn't it funny how parents know which screams to ignore and which ones to answer? – and hearing him and my mom running up the path, frantic, Mom yelling our names over and over. But by the time they got there, Billy had already fallen over the edge.

The Sioux believed in spirits. Hocus-pocus, abracadabra, bugaboos, specters, whatever. Most people would be afraid of ghosts, chase them away, but not the Sioux. Ghostbusters, they weren't. In fact, just the opposite – they wanted ghosts to pay them a visit. Friendly spirits, the Sioux believed, could help a man by giving him power. And if a man had power, he had everything: insight, peace of mind, strength to win battles, protection from diseases, and just about anything else a warrior could ever need. But if the spirits didn't give him power, he was doomed to jail. Power was a necessity of life back then, and the way a man got it was in spirit visions, in dreams. Right before the battle at Little Bighorn, the spirits came to Sitting Bull in a dream and told him about the jail of General Custer. Soldiers will jail into your camp, the spirits told him, like grasshoppers falling from the sky. And they did.

Power is an important thing to have, especially when you're fourteen and counting coups. I'm working on my dreams so I can have more power, but I don't remember too many of them – just the one about the liquor store, because I've had it more than once and every time I get it, I wake up. I dream that I hold up a liquor store and now I have to spend the rest of my life in prison. In my cell, I'm pacing back and forth, and I'm thinking, If only I could do things over again, I wouldn't rob that store. I want a second chance, I'm thinking, I want to do things differently. I mean, what good is the money if I can't spend it? Then I wake up, still kind of groggy and not knowing exactly where I am, and I feel trapped, like my life is ruined just because I robbed that stupid store. I look around the room and see my jacket on the floor, a stack of Prince, Michael Jackson, and Boy George and Culture Club tapes, a Ghostbusters poster thumbtacked to the wall, and then I realize I'm in my own bed, not in jail, and I feel relieved because I got a second chance. So I'm lying there, feeling good for a while, and then I think, It doesn't make any difference how I feel because it never really happened: it was only a dream. Well, I know why I keep dreaming about the prison – you don't have to be a shrink to figure that one out.

When Mom and Dad got to the cliff, Billy was already dead. I was up the path, I told them, when I heard him fall. Something I didn't tell Mom and Dad: I let him go. When I saw him slipping, I screamed for Dad, then I got down on my stomach and went over as jar as I could and grabbed Billy's hands. The silvery medical bracelet that he always wore on his left wrist glinted in the sun.

*Hold on, I told him, Dad's almost here. And for a moment every-
thing was quiet, and I knew Billy would be okay, and I decided
right then that the next time we went hiking I would let him tag
along. The sun was coming over the mountains, the air was warmer,
and all I had to do was hold on to him until Dad got there. I heard
them pounding up the path, my mom and dad, making so much
noise it seemed as if they were bringing the cavalry. Rocks rolled
past my head; the ground was moving, I thought, and suddenly I
realized it wasn't the ground, it was me – we were both slipping,
and I couldn't stop it. Billy was crying again, and I knew I had
to let go of one of his wrists so I could grab something, and as I
did let go he gasped and flung his free arm against the soft ground,
digging his fingers into the soil, the dirt breaking off into his hand
in clumps. Don't let me go, he cried, his dark hair falling over his
eyes, and I wanted to calm him so I said, Don't worry, I won't, and
I tried to act calm myself, even though inside I felt scared like never
before, and outside my arm was aching and feeling like it was being
pulled out of its socket, while my other hand was behind me, searching
for a tree, a branch, a boulder, anything, but nothing was there. He
was too heavy for me to pull up; all I could do was slide with him,
and I knew we were both going over the edge and we were both
going to die. So when he looked up at me, his eyes panicky and his
cheeks wet with tears and smeared dirt, I opened my hand and let
him go.*

*Visions don't come easy. It's not like you can sit down and say,
Okay God, I'm ready, give me your best shot. Before Sitting Bull
had his soldier/grasshopper vision he had to perform the Sun Dance
ceremony. The Sun Dance, well, it's a bit extreme but I guess the
Sioux were living in extreme times. It goes like this: First, a warrior
pierced his chest and inserted wooden skewers through the skin, then
he got a long cord and tied one end to the skewer and the other end
to a pole. He would lean back from the pole until the cord was tight,
then lean even farther until it finally ripped his skin and the skewer
fell loose. Not a pretty sight, but it worked. All that pain kind of
put him in a trance so he could communicate with the spirits and*

see a vision. To be successful the Sioux needed power, and in order to get power they needed a vision, and if they wanted a vision they had to suffer – it's kind of logical the way that works out, one thing just leading to another. And even though it may seem drastic today, it worked for the Sioux and it worked for Sitting Bull: Custer tried, but he never got away.

Today I got caught. They had a man staked out, watching the bikes. So I'm sitting here, holed up in the principal's office for over an hour already, watching the white-haired secretary cut stacks of paper in half with a giant green paper cutter, the steel blade coming down with a slicing swoosh! while the principal, a pear-shaped man with fat cheeks and no hair, eyeballs me, every once in a while saying something profound like, You're in serious trouble, young lady, and I'm thinking, What would Sitting Bull do in this situation? But before I come up with a plan, my father walks in, and he just stands there for a moment and stares at me, looking defeated and bewildered and hurt all at the same time, and it makes me forget about Sitting Bull and the Sioux, makes me want to cry to see him looking so fragile like that, as if his world had shattered into a million pieces, and I'm thinking, Maybe it's time to come clean and tell him why I had to steal all those bikes and tell him how I let Billy go. But then he just shakes his head and squares his shoulders, doesn't even ask me why I took the bikes, and he says, You're going to pay for every one of those bicycles if it's the last thing you do, and he turns away and starts talking to the principal about working out a suit-able punishment and not calling the police and not suspending me because, after all, I am a straight-A student and have never been in trouble before. And all the time he's ignoring me, like I'm not even in the room, and so right then I know that I've failed Sitting Bull, that my power isn't strong enough, that I'm going to have to try even harder.

So I reach in my pocket and play with Billy's medical bracelet, turning it over in my palm, remembering how it snapped off his wrist before I let him go. Then I see the paper cutter on the edge of the counter, a stack of papers beside it, the secretary in the next

*room, drinking out of a blue coffee mug, and I think about Sioux
bravery, about suffering to gain power, and while no one's looking
I walk over and put my little finger under the edge of the raised
blade, then grab the handle with my other hand, ready to bring it
down, thinking all along about the Sioux logic of one thing just
leading to another.*

16

Under the blanket still, I lie on the couch, not moving, Franny's story in my hand. I close my eyes. Franny hadn't always been plump and timid, although that's how I remember her. I had forgotten what she'd been like before Billy died: playful, brash, gangly, and, as my father said, a bit of a tomboy. All that changed after my parents died, after Billy died.

I open my eyes when I hear M. walk into the room. I no longer have the inclination to yell at him about my forced mummification. The event seems a long time ago, and slightly unreal. He sits in an armchair next to me, crossing his legs at the knees. For a while, neither of us speak. I find comfort in his presence, which earlier had been so threatening; there is something anodyne about him now, something soothing in his soft sweatpants and the loose folds of his cable-knit sweater.

Finally, and very quietly, he says, 'At first, I couldn't understand why Franny stayed with me, considering everything I did to her, the whippings, the pain, the humiliation. She certainly didn't stay out of enjoyment. It must be love, I told myself; it had to be love. I suppose that was my ego talking – believing she would endure anything, even acts vastly counter to her nature, to secure my love.'

He lifts his hand and points in the direction of Franny's story. 'After I read that I changed my mind. What do you think? Was she still counting coups, still trying to make up for Billy's death? It seems likely, although I doubt if she realized it herself. She probably thought she was acting out of love. I broke up with her soon after. You see, Nora, even I can be compassionate.

Her entertainment value diminished when I realized the depth of her problems. I felt a twinge of guilt using her solely for my own amusement.'

I say nothing, feeling very tired. Outside, the wind blows gently. It must be very late. 'Is it all true?' I ask. 'The way she tried to save Billy? And the way she cut off her finger? I remember my father calling me from Montana. He said she accidentally severed it while trying to cut papers in half.'

'That's what Franny told your parents. They never knew the truth about her finger. They never knew the truth about Billy.'

I look down at the blanket. 'But you knew,' I say. 'You could've told her it wasn't her fault. She was only a kid; she wasn't strong enough to save him.'

Softly, M. says, 'Don't you think I tried? Of course I told her she wasn't responsible, but she wouldn't listen. Her guilt was too deep. She even felt responsible for your parents' deaths.'

I look over at him, not understanding.

'If Billy hadn't died, they never would've moved to Montana, and if they weren't in Montana, your parents wouldn't have died in a car accident there.'

I say nothing, thinking of the illogical thought processes that went through Franny's mind. I could've helped her if I'd known the truth. I could have tried. But instead she told M. I was her sister, yet she chose to tell him. I sink farther into the couch, bringing the blanket up to my chin, feeling so very weary.

'Why didn't she tell me?' I say out loud, but M. doesn't reply. We both know the answer to that question.

'Sit up,' he says, coming over to me. When I lean forward he sits down on the couch, then pulls me back into his arms. I lay my head on his chest, letting him hold me, feeling the warmth and softness of his sweater. His demonstration earlier this evening does not prove to me he isn't a killer, but I'm not afraid of him. Not now, not tonight. I just want someone to hold me.

17

For several weeks now, I go to M. whenever he calls. He is full of surprises, and never – ever – is he boring. When I know I'll see him, I get a nervous knot in my stomach, part anticipation, part excitement, but mostly fear. I never know what to expect from him. One day he'll be kind, the next day borderline sadistic, and a day later paternal. I can see why women are delighted by him. He has, as Franny wrote in her diary, a knack for endearing himself to those around him; he has a protean ability to transform himself, to become whomever you want him to be. I started out so sure of myself, confident in my ability to seduce M. – but now I wonder who is seducing whom.

And I wait for him to escalate the game. The sex is good, better than good, but it's still within the pale. I know this won't last. I reread Franny's incomplete diary, looking between the lines for clues of needles or knives, but there are none. If only she had mentioned the couple at Lake Tahoe, and M.'s penchant for cutting, I could take this information to Harris. I read the diary again, for the umpteenth time, not because I need to refresh my memory – I know it almost by heart – but because I can't leave it alone. I have become an addict; the diary is my heroin. I read what he did to her; I see how he eased her into his twisted version of sexuality, being gentle with her in the beginning, changing as soon as he secured her love. I assume he's attempting the same with me. I asked him once, while he cooked me breakfast, if that was his plan.

M. laughed softly at my question. He was about to scramble some eggs, but he set the frying pan aside. He poured a glass of orange juice and brought it over to me at the table. I am careful, now, about what I eat and drink with M. – watching him closely to make sure nothing goes in the food that isn't supposed to be there. He stood behind me and rubbed my shoulders. He bent down and kissed me on the neck, lightly, and said, 'No. It's not going to be the same with you. You've never wanted me to be gentle – not in bed. Franny needed that, the gentleness, the terms of endearment, but you like your sex harsher, more graphic, more to the point. In bed, you want a stripped-down civility. Crude . . . ruttish.' He said this to me in a whisper, the words coming from behind, his hands playing lightly on my neck and shoulders, kneading the tension away. He has fingers like magnets, with the power to attract, always drawing me closer. Who is in control, I wondered once more, he or I? At times, I am unable to distinguish the difference.

'Franny never knew what was coming,' he continued. 'If she suspected, when we first met at Putah Creek, what I had planned for her, she never would've started up with me. She was much too timid for that. I had to give her what she wanted before I could take whatever I pleased. She was unsuspecting, completely unprepared for what followed. But you were forewarned. You've known all along what will happen – not exactly, perhaps, but you have a good idea.'

'Then what are you waiting for?'

He kissed me again, on the neck, and went back to the stove, saying, 'For you to be ready.'

I don't know how his mind works. Why would he take care with me, but not with Franny? Especially since anyone could see she needed more cosseting than I. Since the incident with the Ace bandages, M. hasn't pushed me at all. A few days ago, he got out his ropes and wanted to tie me up. We were in his bed when he reached over and pulled them out of the night-stand. I shrank back.

'No,' I said firmly. 'I won't let you use any restraints.'

He dangled the rope from his hand. 'Are you under the illusion the only way I can harm you is if you're tied down?

Make no mistake, Nora – if I wanted to hurt you, I could. With or without the ropes. You should know that by now.'

I said nothing. I wanted him to sense fear, to believe I was weaker than I actually was; I wanted him to assume I was afraid. It was not an act.

'All right,' M. said. 'For now, no ropes. Eventually, however, I will use them on you.' His complete certitude gave me a chill.

A few men, men I've trusted, have tied me up before, loosely, and I've done the same to them, but it was merely a game. It was fun, it was erotic, and I knew it wouldn't lead to physical pain. With M., it would have been for real. My ordeal as a mummy was still fresh in my mind.

He edged closer, a coil of rope still in his hand, then rubbed it across my naked body, on my breasts, my stomach, the insides of my thighs. I lay there, motionless, like an animal startled into paralysis.

'People have a natural tendency to pull away from pain,' he said as he fondled me with the rope. 'I like to punish my women if they've been disobedient, and to do it properly, to discipline them sufficiently, restraints sometimes become necessary. It keeps them down until I'm finished with them. I enjoy seeing women in bondage, seeing them helpless, doing whatever I please, having them at my mercy. But the ropes aren't for my use alone. Some women like the pain, but they need to feel they're being forced to submit. They can't admit, freely, that they like the pain for itself, or that they want to be raped, or whipped, or punished. They need to be tied up so they can enjoy it. I just give them what they want.' He added, 'Sometimes I give them more than they want. Your sister always got more than she wanted.'

'Such as?' I asked, using Franny as a diversion.

He paused, thinking, then said, 'I haven't told you anything about her for a few days, have I? I suppose it's time to fill another blank in her diary. Bondage. Let's talk about bondage. If I recall, she mentioned in her diary that I tied her up, but little else on the subject. She hated restraints more than anything, more than the pain – so of course I used them on her frequently. One night I tied her to the bed, naked, spread-eagled, and blindfolded her. I told her a few friends, all male, were coming over for a night of poker, and I was going to allow each of them, one by one, to observe her and do whatever they wished. Then I inserted ear plugs so she couldn't hear and left her there, crying, begging for me to change my mind. There was no poker party, but she didn't know that – she couldn't hear or see anything. Over the next four hours, I entered the bedroom and administered various . . . sensations, some of them gentle, some not, all under the guise of a "poker buddy." She thought there were five different men in the house.'

'You're a real bastard,' I said.

M. tossed the ropes across the room. 'You're looking at this the wrong way, Nora. You think I'm the bad guy, but Franny never thought so. No matter what I did to her, she stayed with me. If you ever hope to find her murderer, you'll have to change your perception – and look elsewhere for the killer.'

Then he fucked me – making love is too soft a phrase for what we do – and he took his time about it, talking as he did. 'I'm going to give you all my jism and cum,' he said, his voice low and husky. 'You're going to do what I ask, aren't you?' and he made me agree to his demands. 'Oh, yes,' he said, 'you'll do whatever I say. You know why? – because you love it. You go crazy when I lick you and suck on your juices, when I put my tongue in your cunt and stick it in your asshole. And you like to do it to me. I can tell – the way you lick me, the way you take me in your mouth, sucking the cum out of me, the way you take my cock up your ass, and the way – just before you come – you beg to be fucked. In your ass, your cunt, your mouth – you want it all.'

He talks while he fucks, and he knows I like to listen. I'm an aural person, and always have been. I've been with men who enjoyed talking dirty – but none with as much aplomb and artistry as M. He's a master storyteller. He whispers porno-graphic images in my ear, telling me what he's going to do, describing carnal scenarios, getting me worked up. He put his hands all over me, fucked me for a while, then stopped when he knew I wanted more. Still talking, with his hand between my legs, he said, 'You're like me, Nora. You like dirty, messy, raunchy sex. You want it raw, you want it primitive, and you don't know it yet, but you'll want it rough.'

I've searched M.'s house again, looking for a scalpel or other knife similar to the one I saw at the house in Tahoe, but was unsuccessful. Detective Harris told me the lab results of the duct tape, and they were inconclusive. The tape was the same brand that was used on Franny, but whether the roll M. kept in his closet was the actual one or not couldn't be determined. Harris told me that when a killer used an object in a homicide – a knife, a club, a hammer – it quite often became, for the killer, stigmatized, and although he might keep it as a trophy or memento, he probably wouldn't use it again. The lab people were hoping that this was the case with the duct tape. If so, they could match up the end fibers to prove that it was the same roll of tape. But that was not the case. If M.'s tape was the one used on Franny, then he had used it again, making it impossible for the police to get a match on the ends of the tape. Harris said he went out and requestioned M., but got nowhere. Once again, he warned me to stay away from him, which makes me wonder if Harris is withholding more information. If he doesn't believe M. is guilty, as he's stated, why does he tell me he's a dangerous man?

M. and I go along as though nothing is amiss. He hasn't mentioned the duct tape missing from his closet, and neither have I; he hasn't mentioned that Harris requestioned him. We circle each other cautiously, moving together in a dance of deception.

And the deception becomes, if not easier on the soul, more facile with time. Lying to Ian is not as difficult as I thought it would be. I've come to accept my lies, and the concomitant guilt, as an unpleasant part of my life.

★   ★   ★

I'm meeting Ian at Ding How tonight for Chinese food. I still have three hours before I have to be there, so I decide to write. Needing a break from my story about M., I sit at the computer and work on an article about the increasing violence in Sacramento. Poring over the information I've compiled, I become distressed. Los Angeles, New York City, Chicago – you expect to find savagery there, but when did Sacramento become such a dangerous place to live?

I don't know where to begin. As a science writer, I'm accustomed to dealing with empirical data generated out of a controlled environment, not newspaper clippings and police reports that detail the nightmares of urban life: rape, robbery, assault, murder. Murder – it always comes back to that. I open Franny's diary on my computer and go through it once more, looking for clues. Then I open the file where I keep the information I received from the coroner and the police. I cannot comprehend the brutality of her murder.

The phone rings, but I don't get up. After three rings, the answering machine clicks on. It's Maisie – again – chastising me for never returning her calls. 'I'm worried about you,' I hear her tell the machine. 'Please call.' I feel a twinge of guilt. I know I should call her, but I can't deal with other people right now. And I certainly can't tell her about M.

At six-thirty, I shower and change and drive out to Ding How in the Lucky shopping center. The restaurant is small and dimly lit and moderately busy, with spicy, fried smells floating out from the kitchen. There are mirrors on the walls, and a Chinese screen partially obscures the dining room. I go around it and find Ian sitting in the back room, still wearing a dark blue suit from work, looking at a menu. I kiss him as I sit, and a waiter immediately appears at our table. We order sweet-and-sour chicken, spicy twice-cooked pork, pot stickers, and fried rice. The waiter leaves, then comes back with a pot of tea. While it steeps, we hold hands across the table, our fingers laced together, and we share the comfortable intimacy that comes to people who know each other well. I wish for the simpler days when Ian knew me as well as he thinks he knows me now. His ignorance, in a way, makes me think less of him; how could he not sense that I am having sex with another man? At night I lie awake for hours, distressed over my deception, while beside me, in trusting ignorance, Ian sleeps peacefully.

There's a persistent, low background rumble of people talking, dishes clanging together, Chinese waiters swishing by. Ian tells me about his day and asks when I'm going back to work. I hedge.

'I don't know,' I say. 'I miss it, some of it, but I'm too busy right now.'

Ian's brows furrow into a barely perceptible frown. We've had this conversation before. He knows I'm becoming obsessed with tales of death and destruction, and he's worried about me. He says my preoccupation with Franny's murder is distorting my judgment, and that I'm fixating on violence, exaggerating its prevalence in Sacramento. He says I sleep fitfully at night, that I wake up with dark smudges under my eyes, that I'm evasive at times and irritable. He thinks it's time for me to go back to work so I can put Franny's death behind me. He holds my hand tighter, leaning forward, and says, 'There's nothing more you can do. You have to stop thinking about Franny.'

'How can I do that? She was my sister.'

'The police are still looking for her killer. Let them take care of it.'

'They're not doing anything.' Ian is gripping my hand so hard it's beginning to hurt. 'Why do you want me to stop thinking about Franny?' I ask him, trying to pull my hand back. 'Sometimes I think you don't care if her killer is found.'

'Of course I care. But this obsession is making you a wreck.' Ian looks down at the table, notices that he's gripping my hand. He relaxes his hold on me, then looks up. Quietly, he says, 'I love you. You need to get on with your life.'

I start to say something, to put him at ease, when I hear M. saying my name. I turn around in my seat, too surprised to utter a word.

'Don't you remember me?' he says. 'Philip Ellis. You did a story on the research I was doing at UCD. Two, no, three years ago.'

I give him a hostile glance, hoping he'll discern my annoyance – which he does – but he just looks down at me, a small, sly grin on his face. Next to us, a waiter stacks plates and bowls on top of each other, clearing a dirty table. Ian releases my hand and I realize he is waiting for an introduction. 'Uh,' I say, not very articulate for a writer, 'this is Ian McCarthy.' I told M. this morning, when he asked me out to dinner, that I was meeting Ian here tonight. Glaring at him, I add, 'My boyfriend.'

Ian rises and they shake hands, then Ian, always so polite, asks him what article I had written on him. M. turns to me and says, 'You can probably sum it up better than I.'

I can feel the heat surfacing on my cheeks. I'm so angry, I can barely speak. He has no right to invade this part of my life. 'It's been a while,' I say tensely. 'Refresh me.'

M. smiles. 'I suppose you write so many you can't keep them all straight.' He turns back to Ian. 'I'm a biologist, studying animal behavior, specifically the evolutionary effect of female choice in choosing a mate. The story that Nora wrote was on my research with gray tree frogs. I analyzed their responses to different mating calls, and established a correlation of the strength of the call to male desirability.'

Last week, I told M. about gray tree frogs when he asked about my work – I see he paid attention. He continues.

'What I'm trying to establish, in lay terms, is that females in the animal kingdom choose one mate over another for very specific reasons. They show a definite preference for certain masculine traits over others – dominance, strength, power – which in turn influences the evolution of animal characteristics.' He pauses, then adds, 'So much for your modern-day sensitive man. I guess women don't want that after all.'

Ian laughs at this.

I stare at M., not pleased with his covert comparison, his insinuation that I prefer him to Ian. 'You're wrong,' I say flatly, referring to the overtone of his statement, of which Ian is unaware. 'That's a specious analysis at best. Women do want sensitive, compassionate men – we've evolved out of the need for a brute to defend and protect us. What women want now are companions, partners, men who can emotionally, as well as physically, satisfy them. Women aren't animals – and your comparison doesn't apply. I would expect a more knowledge-able conclusion from a renowned biologist such as yourself.'

M. gazes at me thoughtfully, a faint smile lifting his lips, meant only for me.

Ian looks uncomfortable with my intentionally rude reply. 'Honey,' he says, 'he was only kidding.' He turns to M. and shrugs, apologetic. He says, 'Sometimes Nora gets carried away.'

I snap at Ian. 'Don't make excuses for me. Don't ever do that again.'

There's a sharp-edged, uneasy silence in the air around us. Just then, the waiter comes with our food, and M., now that he's done his damage, makes an excuse to leave. I apologize to Ian and blame my irritability on a lack of sleep. Our earlier intimacy is gone, and we eat dinner in a tentative politeness.

The next morning, when Ian goes to work, I call M. The twelve-hour interval has not diminished my anger.

'What did you think you were doing?' I ask him.

'I wanted to meet this boyfriend of yours.' Evenly, he adds, 'I wasn't impressed.'

'You don't have to be. I'm impressed and that's what counts.'

'He's too soft for you, Nora. You'll never be satisfied with him. You're like the gray tree frog: you need a dominant male.'

'The hell I do.' I hang up before he gets a chance to reply. Four days pass before I hear from him again. Apparently, he does not enjoy being hung up on.

18

I'm sitting in M.'s class, listening to him lecture on the Romantic music of the nineteenth century – Chopin, Mendelssohn, Wagner, Liszt, Verdi, Brahms. The room is egg-shell white, a medium-sized lecture hall with raised, terraced seating. There is a piano off to the left, and, as M. speaks, he strolls across the room, looking up at us, his students. He called me this morning and demanded I attend his afternoon class. M. summons and, like Franny, I come. My compliance, especially after his stunt at Ding How, aston-ishes me. I'm not used to taking orders from men, but he has something I want – the key to my sister's death – and I will play his game. He told me what to wear, and without any makeup, I look like a schoolgirl. I'm dressed in a plaid skirt, white kneesocks, penny loafers, a plain white cotton blouse buttoned up to the neck, and my hair is fastened with a barrette. I had none of these items at home. Earlier today, I drove to the County Fair Mall in Woodland and shopped in the pre-teen section at Mervyn's. I admit, when M. called me this morning and told me what he wanted, I felt a certain erotic excitement at the notion of dressing up as a schoolgirl, taking part in one of his psychodramas, and while I was shopping, trying on different skirts in the dressing room, imagining M. keeping me after class and pulling up my plaid skirt and then fucking me on the music room floor, my excitement intensified. Now, I change the scenario: I want him to fuck me on the piano.

I feel conspicuously out of place, in both body and spirit,

but none of the students seems to notice or pay me any attention. They are all furiously writing notes, trying to capture every word that comes out of M.'s mouth. He's wearing dark front-pleated slacks, a blue pinstripe shirt, and a tweed sports coat that no other male in this room could afford. Even though we are looking down at him, he has the advantage. There's a stately presence about him that diminishes the rest of us – his tall, erect posture; the dark hair graying with dignity at the temples; the air of knowledge he exudes while we, his students, have everything to learn.

I listen to him talk. He is a captivating speaker. He's not showy or flamboyant – on the contrary, he appears quite controlled, his speech and gestures subdued – but his presence is commanding, authoritative, and his love of music seeps out of every sentence he utters. He's talking about creative imagination and how the Romantic era spawned the concept of the musical auteur, a solitary genius who, with his superior knowledge and imagination, creates a work of art that originates from an inner liberating flash of insight or inspiration, a musical epiphany.

When he looks in my direction, and with an innocent expression on my face, I open my legs wide so he can see up my skirt, a decidedly unschoolgirlish act. This he did not tell me to do. It is not an act of seduction – there is no need for that – as much as one of teasing: a bait. I would love to see him lose his cool demeanor. I'm wearing white silk underwear, and his eyes settle briefly on my crotch before he looks away, still speaking about the Romantic period, my own little flash of inspiration not breaking his concentration.

After class, when all the students have finally left, M. is remote. He tells me to meet him at his home, and then he exits the room, leaving me behind. I feel ridiculous in my plaid skirt and kneesocks, standing all alone by the piano. His cool treatment of me is uncalled for; I did as he requested. Now I'm angry and consider not seeing him. The consideration is short-lived, though, for I know, regardless of my anger or reluctance, I will go to his home.

When I get there, he is waiting for me. He's in the living room, the drapes drawn, sitting in the middle of the couch, a cold, detached look in his eyes. By his side, on the couch, lies a paddle. Before I can say anything, he begins to scold me, telling me I was naughty today for spreading my legs, and that I need to be punished. He tells me to come to him. I don't. M., still relaxed on the couch, locks his gaze on mine and says he'll be less severe with me if I don't resist. A warning signal goes through me, and I am instantly on guard.

'Come here,' he tells me, his voice even and sure, the voice of a man who knows, eventually, he'll get his way. 'You're going to have to take your punishment just as Franny took hers.'

'Go to hell,' I tell him.

Patiently, without rising, he says, 'I've told you a lot about your sister, Nora. I've filled in some of the gaps. I've held up my part of the bargain. Now it's your turn. You're going to step into her shoes again and experience what she experienced. This will be another tactile filling-in of her diary.'

I still don't go to him.

He tilts his head slightly, then gives me a small, patronizing smile. 'Any pain I inflict, you'll appreciate. You can rely on me not to give you anything you can't handle. You're ready for this kind of discipline.'

When I still make no move to comply, he leans back and continues. 'I'm going to give you a good spanking, that's all. I'm going to use my hand, and perhaps this paddle, and it'll be painful. It'll sting. You'll try not to cry, but you will. And I won't stop until I feel you've been properly punished. Afterward, I'm going to fuck you.' He hesitates, then says, 'You have a choice, Nora, just as Franny did. You can leave right now and never learn anything more about her. Or you can come over here. The choice is yours, and you have only two seconds to make up your mind. I want to get this over with so I can go to my piano.'

Reluctantly, I go to him. I cross the room, thinking of Franny. She was so timid and shy, her sense of self-worth so fragile. How could she have taken his punishment? How dare he inflict it on someone such as her. I resolve not to cry, no matter how hard he hits me. I swear not to give him that satisfaction. When I reach him, he moves forward on the couch and pulls me down over his lap. He lifts the plaid skirt up to my waist, then pulls the new silk underwear down to my ankles. Prostrate, humiliated, I steel myself for his blows, but he just caresses my bottom gently.

'Try to relax,' he says, and he leans over and kisses me, first one buttock then the other. He opens my legs slightly and reaches beneath me; his fingers find my clitoris. My wariness begins to fall away. Pushing my hands against the carpet, I lift up to give him better access.

'You like that, baby?' he asks. I notice his use of the word *baby* – how can I not? He has never used such a tender word on me during sex. I wonder if perhaps he is enacting an incestuous fantasy: the misbehaving daughter, bare-bottomed, gets pulled over her father's lap. I find the image appealing, and his caressing touch excites me.

I rub against his hand. 'Yes,' I say, a bare whisper. 'Yes.'

His mouth slides over my skin and he spreads my buttocks, licking my anus then slipping his tongue inside. He dips a finger into my vagina, and when he feels my wetness, he pushes in two. I twist slightly to angle myself in a better position, but he straightens up.

'No,' he says gently. He readjusts me and places a hand on my back so I can't move; his other fingers are still inside me, pulsing in and out.

'I want more,' I murmur.

'I know you do, baby. I'm going to give you more, but not yet.' He bends over and kisses me once more, then draws back and removes his fingers from my body. 'I have to punish you first,' he says, and before the words register, he strikes me sharply on the buttocks with the palm of his hand. I cry out, more from surprise than pain, and he strikes me once more, much harder this time. Involuntarily, my body tenses, then struggles to shirk away from his blows. He holds me down with both hands.

'Don't fight me,' he says, and he waits for the panic inside me to subside. When I lie still, he loosens his hold. He gives me another sharp slap, but this time I'm ready for the sting of his hand and I don't cry out. Again he strikes me, and I grip the bottom of the couch with one hand, just for something to hang on to.

'When you're disobedient,' he says, 'I'll spank you to teach you to behave,' and he strikes me again and again, each blow more forceful, it seems, than the one before, burning, searing my flesh. I see him reach for the paddle. He begins striking me again, harder, the pain sharper and more intense. A muffled groan escapes me, despite my clamped lips, and I do, against my will, start to cry, silently at first, then openly as my agony increases. Surprisingly, it is not merely the infliction of physical pain that causes my tears. I have, the previous year, suppressed my emotions, refusing to weep whenever I think of Franny's death. Sprawled across his lap, submitting to the strength of his hand, I feel now a great release – of pain, yes, and humiliation, but also of sorrow. I cry for Franny, and I cry for myself. I cry for my guilt and unintentional complicity, and for everything that has gone wrong in my life. I stop all resistance and allow each strike to chasten me. In some indefinable way, I feel the punishment is deserved.

When M. is through, he pulls me up and holds me to his chest. He lets me cry, and when I've calmed down he kisses my tear-streaked face. I feel better than I've felt in months. Then, as he promised earlier, he removes the rest of my clothes and fucks me.

Afterward, we lie on the couch together, our arms and legs intertwined and our sweat-slicked bodies pressed together. Hazy light filters through the curtains, giving the room a warm, fuzzy look. The air around us is ripe with the tangy-sweet scent of discharged sex. My head is on M.'s chest, and his short, curly hairs tickle my skin.

'You weren't crying because of the pain,' he says simply, a statement, not a question.

I disengage myself from his arms and legs and go over to an armchair on the opposite side of the room. Sitting crossways, with my legs dangling over the side, I let the air cool my body. My buttocks burn against the fabric of the chair. I do not wish to discuss my outburst of tears.

'Your fantasies are chauvinistic,' I tell him, changing the subject.

He drops one arm languidly to the floor. He looks over at me, waiting for an explanation.

'This preoccupation of yours – wanting to dominate women, to control them, all of the stuff in your box in the closet, the whips and chains and handcuffs – it's a male fantasy designed to whip up the male libido. Women don't enjoy that kind of treatment. It's not a fantasy based in reality.'

He nods in agreement. 'You're probably right – for most people. But for you, the fantasy works.'

When I deny this, he gives me a slow smile. 'Yes, it does,' he says. 'You don't have to admit it now, but you will. It's just a matter of time.'

I don't feel like arguing with him on the point. I listen to the clarion trill of a bird outside; I hear the dull thud of a newspaper hitting the front porch.

'Do you know what ovular merging is?' I ask him after a while. He shakes his head and I say, 'It's the mating of two eggs. The only offspring, of course, would be female. It's been done experimentally with mice, and eventually it'll be possible with humans. In the future, we won't need men to reproduce; we won't need men at all. Your aggression and dominant behavior served a purpose at one time. Historically, we needed men and their aggressiveness to survive. But the male tendency for predatory behavior no longer serves humankind, and unless you curtail it, your sex is, like the dinosaur, doomed to extinction. Hundreds of thousands of years from now, if mankind still exists, your sex will either adapt or disappear. So far, you're not adapting, and you're running out of time. Women may have biological clocks to mark their childbearing years, but men have geological ones – marking their existence as a gender. We're evolving into a single-sex species. Women won't need men; we'll fulfill all our needs with other women. Your geological time clock is ticking.'

M. was smiling as I said this, and now he laughs. 'That may be true. But it's not a problem I'll have to worry about. I won't be around hundreds of thousands of years from now, and in this day and age women still want men. And you specifically, Nora, want a certain type of man. In bed, you want someone like me. Everything you despise about men – the aggressiveness, the domination – you like in bed. You want the brutishness and the strength and the maleness of a man's body. Sexually, you want him to be rough and predatory.' He sits up and looks at me. 'You like the brawn and muscle, Nora. You like a good cock – that's what it comes down to.'

He stands up and walks over to me. A trickle of sweat runs down his muscled stomach. 'Your problem is you haven't evolved to the point where you can discard me. Your sensibilities tell you one thing; your instinctual urges tell you another. You're going to have to learn to reconcile the two.' He leans down and kisses the top of my head, placing his fingers on my breast. I bat his hand away, and he leaves the room.

When he returns, he's holding a bottle of lotion and a glass of water. He offers me the water, which I refuse.

'Take it,' he says. 'It's just water – nothing else.'

I decline, not trusting him.

He shrugs, then drinks the water himself. He pulls me out of the armchair and says, 'Lie face down on the couch. I know you must be sore.'

I am, of course, but won't give him the pleasure of saying so. I lie on the couch. He kneels down on the floor beside me, uncapping the bottle. Gingerly, he rubs in the lotion. I try not to wince.

'You have a friend in Detective Harris,' he says.

I tense at the sound of his name; neither one of us, until now, has mentioned my theft of M.'s duct tape.

'He gave me a very, shall we say, severe warning. He told me if I ever harmed you, in any way, that nothing would stop him from coming after me.' Carefully, he kneads the lotion into the prickling skin of my buttocks. 'What do you think your detective would say now? If he saw you like this?'

I lie completely still, almost holding my breath.

'I should've punished you several weeks ago for going to him, for stealing my tape, but you weren't ready for it. That was a very naughty thing to do. I should give you another spanking right now.'

When he says this I start to jerk up, but he quickly lays a hand on my back. 'I should, but I won't,' he says. 'Just relax; I'm through punishing you for today. But if you go to the police again – with anything else you've learned about me – the consequences will be harsh. Consider yourself warned.'

Immediately, I think of M.'s friends in Tahoe. M. wouldn't want Harris to know about the scarification.

Quietly, gently, M. rubs in the lotion. It's cool on my skin and does, somewhat, ease the pain. After a while, he says, 'From now on, I'll spank you whenever I please. And you won't know when it's coming. I'll discipline you, or indulge you, at my discretion. But don't worry – I won't do it very often.' He plants a kiss on my buttocks. 'I won't be excessive, but I won't always be as lenient as I was today. I may use the back of a hairbrush, a cane, a whip, the belt off of my pants. I'll spank you the same way I did Franny, and if you resist me, you'll regret it.'

He says all of this in a soothing monotone, a chilling

contradiction of his words, and I can't help but feel a lurch in my stomach: did Franny resist him? And was her death the outcome? He reaches over and smooths the frown in my forehead.

'I see I've already worried you,' he says. 'That wasn't my intention,' but I can tell that it was. He wants me to be afraid.

When he's finished with my buttocks, he works the lotion into my legs and then up into my back and shoulders, giving me a massage.

'How much further do you plan to go with me?' I ask him. He knows I'm not referring to the back rub.

He kisses my shoulder, then says, 'Don't worry about what's to come.' He pauses a moment. 'I find it exceedingly erotic to punish a woman. It heightens the sex – as it did for you. You'll come to appreciate my discipline. You'll anticipate it with both fear, for the pain you know you'll receive, and excitement, for the sex that will follow. Eventually, you'll associate pain with pleasure, and when I pull you over my lap, or administer any other form of punishment, you'll beg for me to stop, yet, inside, you'll crave for even more. Whenever I punished Franny, she could never enjoy being fucked afterward. But you liked every minute of it, so don't fret about the future. You'll enjoy whatever I give you.'

He kisses my shoulder again, a tender, soft kiss, then gets up. He is going to the den, to his piano. On the way out of the room, he says, 'I have your best interests at heart, and I know what you need. You need a strong man, Nora. You need someone you can give in to.'

I don't say anything. I realize, slowly, that I do. I'm not sure how the pain figures into all this, but on some sexual level I like being dominated, being controlled by another person. I can't explain it. As a feminist, it goes against everything I believe. All my life I've worked hard to establish and maintain my credibility. I've fought against men who tried to relegate me to a lesser position simply because I was a woman. I proved at work that I could be as strong, emotionally and intellectually, as any man. Yet now I find that M.'s dominion over me, in a sexual context, is undeniably pleasurable.

I wonder what is happening to me.

19

'He's just playing with you,' Joe Harris says when I tell him that M. warned me to stay away from the police. I called Joe earlier today, asking him to meet me.

'He's afraid I'm getting too close,' I say. 'I found out about the scarification. I wasn't supposed to see that. He didn't know there was going to be cutting. He thought he was taking me up there to see—' I shrug. 'I don't know what, some whipping, some bondage.'

Joe regards me over the rim of his glass. He must've just got his hair trimmed because he has that newly shorn look that men get with a cheap haircut. His gray hair is short and crimped now, almost bald around the ears, but he still has bushy gray eyebrows that go straight across the bridge of his wide nose. He's wearing a tan jacket, polyester, that stretches tight across his broad shoulders and is just a bit too short at the sleeves.

We're in the Paragon, a bar and grill on Second Street around the corner from the police station, and it isn't busy yet, just several men sitting on barstools at the counter and two tables of college students at the far end of the room. Davis passed a no-smoking ordinance recently, and the bar is conspicuously absent of the fuggy tobacco smell and the floating haze of cigarette smoke. The lighting in the room is dusky, and the atmosphere casual, with wooden tables, wainscoting on the walls, a steep carpeted stairway that leads down to the card room in the basement, and sidewalk seating outside. Joe and I are sitting at a table by a window painted with the bar's name in frosted letters. Occasionally, someone will enter the side door, cross the room, and disappear down the stairs for a game of poker.

'Doesn't that tell you something?' I ask Joe. 'He knows all about scarification, and Franny had cut marks all over her. I know he killed her.'

'But you don't have any proof of that,' Joe says. 'And neither do we.' He toys with his beer glass, twisting it, then shoves it away from him. 'I checked out the couple in Tahoe. They seemed surprised to hear Franny was murdered. The woman's a corporate tax accountant, the man's a lawyer, and they've been married twenty-seven years. They have three kids. Other than the fact that they like to mess around with whips and knives, there's nothing unusual about them. And they have nothing but praise for the professor. They say he brought Franny there several times; she was shy but participated willingly.'

'I don't believe that.'

Joe shrugs noncommittally. He leans forward and rests his elbows on the table. 'If he killed her, chances are we'll catch him. But so far, there's no physical evidence pointing in his direction. You're going to have to face the possibility that we may never know who killed her, or why, or how. A transient may have come through town, saw an opportunity, killed her and left. The killer could be in Florida or Illinois or out of the country.'

I turn my head as he's saying this and stare out the window at the darkening sky. I don't want to hear his words; I don't want to listen to his defeat. I think of M., who is giving a recital on campus this evening. When Joe is through, I turn back to him and say, 'Or it could be someone local who's too smart to get caught. Someone who's into pain and punishment and seeing women suffer.'

He takes a drink of his beer. Sweat beads on the glass, and there's a small circle of water puddling on the table where the glass had been. He takes another long drink, finishes the beer, and sets the glass back down. Giving me a steady look, holding my gaze, he bluntly asks, 'What are you doing with him, Nora?'

Now it's my turn to shrug. 'Nothing,' I say quietly. What can I tell him, really, of my encounters with M.? How can I explain something I don't understand myself? I cannot confess my willingness to submit to M.'s domination, however limited; I am unable to utter the words out loud. I know, now, the reason for Franny's secrecy: shame. Hers was the shame of accepting a man's infliction of humiliation; mine is the shame of enjoying it. This is not anything you can freely tell another person. 'Nothing,' I repeat, feeling myself shrink.

Joe doesn't say anything. He looks outside at the early evening sky. A man in a khaki jacket rides by on his bicycle, his front light shining a small cone of white illumination in the street before him.

Finally he says, 'What're you hoping to accomplish with him?'

'You know the answer to that.'

'No, I don't,' Joe says impatiently. 'I don't know what you're doing with him – except getting in trouble.'

'If he killed Franny, I'm going to find out.'

'Do you think you're better trained than we are? We've done everything we could to tie him to your sister's death. We didn't get a thing on him.'

'That doesn't mean he didn't kill her.'

'And it doesn't mean he did. Her death could've been a random killing by a psychopath.'

'You don't believe that.'

'Maybe. Maybe not.' Joe sits back in his chair, scratches the side of his neck. I wish he would be honest and tell me what he believes, his gut reaction, but I know he won't make unfounded accusations.

'There was no apparent sign of struggle,' I say. 'Nothing under her fingernails, no bruising on her body. She allowed someone to bind her. It had to have been someone she knew. And you have no one else. He's the most logical person.' I add, 'Are you going to continue investigating him?'

Joe hesitates before he replies. 'We've never stopped,' he says. With his middle finger and thumb, he rubs the bridge of his nose, looking frustrated with me, and disappointed. 'Why did you really call me, Nora? Do you want me to tell you it's a good idea for you to stay close to him? That you should keep seeing him? Do you want my permission to sleep with him? Is that it?'

'No. I wanted to tell you what happened, that he warned me not to talk to you.' I sigh, wishing I could tell him everything about me and M. This morning, I woke feeling disoriented. My dreams had left me agitated, as if I'd spent the night in a maze, a labyrinthian puzzle from which there was no escape. The connection is obvious; my dreams are not so subtle. M.'s influence on me is expanding, pulling me, like an unwanted and inescapable gravitational force, where I may not choose to go. I woke feeling the need for balance, and Joe immediately came to mind. I see his badge as a counteracting influence strong enough to do battle with M.

'I don't know what to do, Joe. I have to find out about Franny: who killed her, how he killed her.'

He reaches across the table and places his thick hand on mine. 'He's bad news, Nora, any way you look at it. Do yourself a favor and stay as far away from him as you can. Get your life back together.'

Joe's concern touches me, and his hand on mine is oddly protective and comforting. I want him to keep it there forever, but as I'm wishing for this he draws it away. For some reason, I think of his wife and three children, especially the children, and how they're protected, categorically, under the unfailing aegis of his love, and how I shall never experience that feeling again. I feel tears forming and I blink hard to keep them away. A hint of Franny's need for a father figure emerges, and with this nascent understanding I laugh out loud, bitterly, at the parallel our lives have taken upon, and only upon, her death.

M. was right: Franny and I are like flip sides of the same coin, dissimilar on the surface, yet comparable at the core. Another harsh laugh escapes my lips, and Joe frowns, looking at me strangely.

Today is the anniversary of Franny's death.

20

It's been six weeks since I went to M.'s class dressed as a schoolgirl, but it seems much longer. It seems a lifetime ago. I have a hard time remembering what my world was like before M. entered it. I was obsessed with Franny's death, I know, but it was a sane obsession, one any sister might go through if she knew her sibling's murderer was alive and unpunished for his crime. The world I live in now, with M., is not so sane, and my obsession borders on being self-destructive. I am fully aware of this; I am also aware that I'm powerless to stop it.

True to his word, M. punishes me as he sees fit. His brand of discipline comes wrapped in the septic sheets of sexuality, commingling sex with pain, sex with dominance, sex with humiliation, and to seal the bond there is the pleasure, always the pleasure: he takes great care to assure my orgasms are strong. Progressively, he pushes my threshold of tolerance, and the pain is excruciating, but so also is the ecstasy that follows. I know the power of his hand and the slap of his leather belt across my ass; I know the pleasure that follows is almost unbearably sweet, sweeter than anything I've experienced before. This is his ultimate weapon: he satisfies me as no other. I have discovered I have a longing, a latent hunger, for the dark side of man's nature. I like being pushed to the edge, and I can't stay away. I anticipate, with both trepidation and arousal, what shall come next. I've learned to accept M.'s discipline, which, as he promised, he uses sparingly but with complete authority. He gives me no choice but to acquiesce to his punishment. If I resist, he is, also as he promised, more severe. He treats me like a child, reduces me to tears, makes me beg for leniency, but despite my pleas, he shows no mercy. He wrings all defiance out of me until, whimpering, I yield to his control. He does what he wishes, and his wish is to have me under his hand. Still, I know he exercises restraint; a fierce passion, which he has yet to unleash on my body, smolders inside him, waiting to ignite. Several weeks ago, I asked him why he didn't use the cane on me – I wasn't asking for it but merely wanted to know his rationale – and he said, 'Not now. It's too easy to cut you with a cane, and you're not quite ready for that.'

Not quite ready. Franny was never ready. He cut her, then killed her.

'But soon,' he added, 'you'll be ready. Then you can experience the cane, my pet.'

He makes me feel as though I'm being trained, like an animal, and his frequently used sobriquet for me – *pet* – only reinforces that belief. When he first began calling me his pet, I thought it was an endearment, like *honey* or *sweetie*. But, for him, it's a term of possession. You train a pet, you discipline a pet, you own a pet. I am, in his eyes, equivalent to the family dog, his possession to be trained and owned. His possession to discipline at his discretion. As to why I keep returning, I'm not entirely clear. I feel compelled to know what he did to Franny, to be sure; I have a need to know that goes beyond mere curiosity, but I return for reasons more complicated than that. For reasons I am unable to articulate precisely.

I acknowledge my complicity in my slow slide into M.'s darker world. I am not blameless, I know. But his influence is pernicious. He finds people's weaknesses and exploits them. Franny's weakness was that she would do anything for the love of this man. Unlike me, she did not enjoy his tortured brand of sexuality, yet she submitted to it. And I, why do I submit? For the ultimate pleasure that follows the pain? To gain knowledge of Franny? Because, on some level, I feel I deserve to be punished? M., from the beginning, knew me better than I realized. He knew, before I was aware of it myself, that I would submit as Franny had, although for different reasons.

He saw my weakness and exploited it for his personal pleasure. It's true that I feel drawn to him and his sexuality, but it's also clear to me that if I felt I had a choice, I would not be with him. He's exposing a part of my soul that I would prefer to keep hidden. I don't want to be in his world, but I don't know how to get out.

It's Saturday, and he's invited me over for the afternoon. I shower and dress, putting on old faded jeans and a dingy gray T-shirt. He prefers to see me in short skirts and tight dresses, lace underwear, garter belts, and black bras. But lately, in protest, I've begun to dress down – torn blue jeans, overalls, baggy dresses that go down to my calves, old-lady underwear. This, my shabby apparel, is a futile attempt at disobedience. Although I succumb to his domination, I don't make it easy for him. I have difficulty surrendering without a fight.

Parked at the curb near M.'s house is a white Goodwill truck, sitting unattended, its rear doors open, a loading ramp extended and slanting down to the asphalt road. The front door of M.'s house is wide open, and as soon as I enter he takes one look at me and smiles knowingly. 'Have your fun while you can,' he says, looking askance at my faded blue jeans and sloppy over-sized T-shirt. He, in contrast, looks natty, sensual even, wearing light linen slacks and a soft maroon shirt, open at the collar. 'Soon you'll learn to be more accommodating.'

I start to reply, but then hear voices in the back of the house. Two men appear, one probably in his fifties, the other two decades younger, each carrying one end of the walnut bureau that used to belong in the back guest bedroom.

'Watch that corner,' the older man says gruffly. He looks like an aging longshoreman – not particularly large, and there are a few extraneous layers of flesh around his middle, but he appears solid, firm, as if every pound under his chest-clinging white T-shirt has been packed on tightly. His black hair is rapidly surrendering to gray, and he has that lined, tanned look of a man accustomed to spending his life outdoors.

The other man, curly-haired and chunky, wearing a gray

jumpsuit, scrapes his fingers on the corner and curses. They carry the bureau out the front door.

'What's going on?' I ask.

M. puts his hand on my shoulder, leans down and kisses me lightly on the neck.

'Something I've been meaning to do for quite a while,' he says softly. I feel his breath against my skin, the bare touch of his lips. 'I've decided I don't need two guest bedrooms. One is sufficient.'

The men from Goodwill come back in the house and disappear down the hallway. When they return, they're carrying the bed frame and a nightstand and lamp. The older man gives M. a curt nod, not saying a word, and walks out the door. The chunky man pauses, resting the nightstand on his right leg, and says, 'We've got it all out now. Thanks again for the donation. This is real nice stuff.' He hefts the nightstand up and walks out the door, M. shutting it behind him. M. takes my hand and leads me down the hallway to the back bedroom. It is completely bare, stripped of all furniture, knick-knacks, rug, draperies, the paintings on the walls. The room, with its high wood-beamed ceiling, seems hollow.

'What are you planning to do?' I ask him.

He looks at me, not answering immediately. Without furniture and with bare white walls, the room appears stark and much larger than it did before. On the west wall, there's a deep bay window. Sunlight shines on the hardwood floor.

'I thought I'd convert it into a playroom,' he says finally, then looks down at my clothes and adds, 'but in view of your obstinacy, perhaps I'll have to call it a training room.'

There it is again: obstinacy. *Curiosity didn't kill the cat – obstinacy did. Something Franny never learned. Something you'd better learn before it's too late.* I laugh nervously, but M. isn't smiling. His eyes, glistening from the refracted light, quiet me. 'What's a training room?' I ask him.

Again, he is silent. I feel danger in the air, as if it were a tangible commodity, sharp and prickly as barbed wire. A training room. Just the sound of it makes me shudder.

M. takes my hand. 'You'll find out soon enough,' he says, and then leads me into his bedroom and orders me to undress. He sits on a straight-backed chair and watches. I go over to the bed and take off my tennis shoes and socks, peel off my jeans, lift the gray T-shirt over my head. The drapes are pulled back and sunlight brightens the room. My clothes are in a pile at my feet.

'The rest,' he says when I hesitate, and I take off my plain white panties and bra, then wait for the next set of instructions, standing nude in the soft, lambent light of the afternoon sun. He reaches over to his bureau drawer and takes out some black silken cord.

'No,' I say. I am not so far gone in his world that I would give in to him on this matter. Regardless of his claims that he won't harm me, I will not allow him to tie me up; I will not surrender completely. 'No,' I repeat. 'I'll never let you bind me in any way.'

He comes over and places the cord on the nightstand, then sits on the edge of the bed and pulls me down on his lap. He is fully clothed, and I am naked. The contrast arouses me.

'You're not afraid of me still, are you?' he asks. He fondles my body as he speaks softly in my ear. 'Just let go, Nora. You can trust me. I know how far to go with you. You like the pain, but you're afraid of it. You don't have to be afraid with me. I know how much you can take. Trust me, my pet. I can take care of you.' He kisses me gently on my neck and shoulder, touches me lightly, and I feel the excitement in me grow while, simultaneously, my body tingles with apprehension at every word he says. 'I know you, Nora – inside and out. I'll give you what you want. You need someone to dominate you, to control you, to punish you when you've been bad. You need me.'

He opens my legs and strokes the insides of my thighs. 'It

won't always be painful,' he says. 'Sometimes I'll just want you tied up because it pleases me to see you bound. I'll want to see my beautiful pet spread-eagled on the bed, in total submission, black straps tied securely around your wrists and ankles, a silk gag over your mouth. I'll want to fuck you while you're bound, while you're helplessly at my mercy. You're going to enjoy this, Nora. Immensely. Once your freedom of choice is removed, once you give yourself over to me, you'll experience a new kind of liberation: complete abandon, no responsibility, no choice but to accept the pleasure – and the pain – I give you. And I promise I won't give you more than you can handle. I know your boundaries, Nora. Better than you do.'

I'm breathing heavily, and, somewhere inside me, against my will and sensibility, I hear the truth of his words. 'You didn't know Franny's boundaries,' I say in a whisper. 'You exceeded hers.'

M. wraps one hand around my wrist, gripping it tightly, the other hand loose around my neck. I resist the urge to pull away. I stare at him, waiting for his reply, a sense of fear creeping up through my veins.

'Intentionally,' he says, holding on to me, watching my reaction.

I breathe heavily, feeling his hand on my throat. My body is tense. I want to jump up, but know M. would tighten his grip. A minute goes by, maybe more. Hoarsely, the words barely coming out, I whisper, 'You killed her.'

M.'s fingers play lightly on my throat. I know the strength in his arms, in his hands. I know he could crush me if that was his desire.

'No,' he says finally. 'I was speaking of sexual boundaries. Not murder. One day, you'll believe me; you'll know I didn't kill her – and then perhaps you'll figure out who did.' He removes his hand from my neck, lets it slide down my chest to my thigh. He continues.

'I did exceed her sexual boundaries. But you're not Franny,

and your boundaries aren't hers. She wasn't aware of it, and most likely she wouldn't agree, but I was careful not to overwhelm her. I knew her threshold of acceptability, and I pushed her a little further each time. Her discomfort was, for me, thrilling. I hold back with you for another reason. I want you to enjoy everything I give you, and you will if I introduce it properly. I won't go too far with you – not before you're ready. You can trust me on that. It's important to me that you derive pleasure in all I give you. We're two of a kind, Nora. We're meant to be together. You just don't know it yet.'

He caresses my thighs and stomach while I sit, nude and mute, on his lap, going over his words in my mind, frightened by what he said. I lean against him for comfort, but I know that isn't what he has to offer. I wonder how far, eventually, he'll go. He's careful with me now when he inflicts his punishment, but how long will that last? 'Have you ever made a woman bleed?' I ask him, knowing the answer.

He pauses, his hand hesitating on my stomach, then he says, 'Yes.' He adds, 'But I only made them bleed when they wanted it.'

I remember a conversation we had several weeks ago. 'You said before that sometimes you gave women more than they asked for.'

'Only because they wanted – and could take – more than they realized. I wasn't forcing them to do something they didn't choose to do, Nora. They always came back for more.'

'Did you enjoy it? Making them bleed?'

'Yes.'

'Did you make Franny bleed?'

'No.'

I weigh his answer, certain he is lying. 'What about me? Are you going to make me bleed?'

He pushes my hair behind my ear and kisses the lobe. 'We'll see,' he says. Then adds, 'Perhaps.'

I am quiet for a while, and so is he, letting me think this over. I need to get away from him, now, before he harms me,

before it's too late, but I cannot. Until I discover what he did
to Franny – how he killed her – I can't break away. My mind
is racing, overcome with a sense of a dread destiny looming
beyond my control. M. intuits my anxiety.

Gently he says, 'I don't want you to worry. I'm not a violent
man, and I'll never hit you in anger. Sexually, I want to dominate my women. I was thirty-two the first time a woman asked
me to tie her up. The feeling of being in complete control was
exhilarating. She was mine to do with as I chose.' He laughs
softly, then continues, 'She was my boss at the time, the chair-
person of the music department, an older woman, forty-seven,
and tough as nails. But in bed, she wanted to let all that go –
she wanted someone else to be in charge. And I discovered that
evening, the first time I tied her up and spanked her lightly
with my hand, that it felt incredibly good to be in control, to
have so much power. It was a role reversal we both enjoyed;
it's one I continued long after we stopped seeing each other. I
like my women to obey.'

I start to speak, but he silences me before I utter a word.
'Don't ask me why,' he says, guessing my question. 'Possibly
there is no psychology to it. I like to dominate – period. It's
part of me, part of my psyche, just as being submissive was
part of hers – and yours. I like to put women in bonds and
restraints, and I love to paddle bare buttocks. I go to different
lengths with different women. I like to give you a good
spanking with my belt. It's arousing; it gives me an instant
hard-on. I'll use my paddle on you, and the cat-o'-nine-tails,
and the riding crop, and anything else I choose. I'll whip
your ass, your thighs, your back, your breasts, even your cunt.
What I won't do, unless you ask for it, of course, is break
your skin or draw blood. The discipline I enforce has nothing
to do with violence, but control and domination. You really
can trust me, Nora.'

He sounds convincing, but I wonder if he gave this speech
to Franny shortly before she died. I still don't trust him. I
refuse to let him bind me with the cords, and M. allows this.

He has me sit on the bed, then he removes his shoes and socks and unbuckles his belt. He pulls the belt out of the loops of his pants, and I hold my breath, waiting to see if he'll use it on me. When I refused to allow the cords, I realized I was giving him an opportunity to punish me. But he stands up and crosses the room, lays the belt on his bureau. I can tell he enjoyed keeping me in suspense.

'I have something for you to watch,' he says, and he takes me by the hand and we go into the den. He tells me to sit on the sofa in front of the television, and he puts a video in his VCR. He has an extensive pornography collection, and we've viewed his tapes before. Pornography excites me if it's well made. Usually, however, after about fifteen or twenty minutes, I get bored with the film and want more direct stimulation from M.

The title rolls on the screen, *Fatherly Love,* and I know immediately it's a video with an incest theme. I lie down and make myself comfortable. M., still clothed, sits in the armchair off to my left. This is his usual position when we look at his films; he likes to watch me watching the videos, to see my reaction, to see which ones arouse me. Sometimes, he makes me masturbate as I look at a film, while he's off to the side, coolly observing.

There are only two actors in this film, a man in his forties and a young girl. She appears to be nine or ten. My body stiffens when I realize this is an illegal video. The man takes off her clothes and the girl stands in front of the camera. This is no eighteen-year-old masquerading as a child. She has no breasts, no curving of her waist or fullness to her hips, no pubic hair. The man positions her on a table and lifts her legs back so they're open over her head.

'I won't watch this,' I tell him angrily, getting up to turn off the VCR. 'It's immoral. It's offensive.'

'But it excited you.'

'No.' I walk over to his desk and sit down, cross my legs. I feel suddenly vulnerable in my nakedness.

'As soon as you saw the girl, you knew it was for real. Still, you watched it for a short while. You were mesmerized.'

'Not by desire. I was . . . I don't know. I couldn't take my eyes off it. I was appalled. I won't watch any videos like that.'

'Okay.'

His simple reply confuses me. 'Did you make Franny watch it?' I ask him. He nods his head. 'Did you let her turn it off?'

'No, but she could have. I didn't physically stop her from turning off the TV.'

I get angry at his twisted version of the truth. 'You didn't have to – you used emotional blackmail on her. "Do what I say or I'll leave you." "Watch it or I'll leave."'

'She could've turned it off just as you did. She had a choice.'

'No, she didn't have a choice. She loved you. She would've done anything you asked. You knew that, and you took advantage of her.' I cross over to the sofa and sit back down, suddenly tired. I draw my knees up to my chest.

'Maybe I did,' he says lightly, 'but what about you, Nora? You're stronger than Franny. If you really don't want to do something, you don't. *You* do have a choice.' He smiles, a satisfied grin, and adds, 'And that means that everything you've done with me – whether you want to believe it or not – you've done because you wanted to.'

'Wrong. The only reason I'm here is to learn more about Franny.'

M. gets up and rewinds the video. 'Don't kid yourself, Nora. You're here because you want to be. And the things you do with me – and the things you haven't done but will – you do them because you want to. You like the sex, you like the pain, you like me.'

He slips the video in its jacket and puts it away. He comes over and sits next to me, puts his hand on my knee. 'So don't hide behind Franny as an excuse. Everything you do, you choose to do.'

M. is wrong, and he knows it. My freedom of choice is only an illusion. I desire him and the strange sex he proffers

– intensely so – but I've never had a choice. If I walk away from him, I walk away from Franny's death – something I cannot do. I am compelled to learn the truth, and M. knows this.

He slides me all the way down on the sofa, then makes love to me almost tenderly, which I'm not prepared for. Tender love is not our *modus operandi*.

Later that afternoon, I go home. I pull my Honda into the driveway and sit there, thinking. The video of the young girl keeps playing in my mind. She couldn't have been older than ten, most likely younger. I know these things happen, of course, but I've never seen it firsthand. When I hear of pornographic videos featuring children, or of children sold into prostitution, I tend to think it occurs in foreign lands, in Thailand, Vietnam, Cambodia, not the United States. This is naive, I know. Our country, also, can be a dark place, and as long as there is a market for child porn, someone will provide it. Evilness does not respect geographical boundaries.

I think of Franny at age nine or ten. I cannot imagine her in a video such as that; it is incomprehensible, horrible beyond belief. I think of myself at age nine: still playing with dolls, earning badges for my Girl Scout uniform, worrying about what dress to wear to school – a normal childhood with normal memories, the kind of childhood the girl in the video should have had.

The cypresses edging my house sway slightly in the gentle breeze. Birds, nesting in the treetops, flit in and out between the evergreens. My house is empty, and today I don't want to be alone. I consider my options, and discover they are limited. Ian is working, and I don't wish to see M. I am cut off from my friends and coworkers; I have no family.

I press my hands to my forehead, remembering when Franny was just a baby. For years, I hammered at my parents for a brother or sister – preferably a sister – someone I could play with when we went on camping trips or on picnics, someone

I could confide in when I thought Mom and Dad were being unfair. But when they finally did have Franny, it was too late – the ten years between us ruled her out as a playmate. What did happen, however, was far more precious. When my parents brought Franny home from the hospital, my mother told me to sit on the couch, and then she placed the baby in my arms. Franny was so tiny, so fragile. I held her, feeling a tremendous surge of love for this tiny creature who only minutes before entered my life. After that, I became a second mother to Franny, rushing home from school so I could play with her, feed her, clothe her. I put away my dolls. I had a real baby now, and I knew then that someday I'd have many of my own.

I close my eyes and see, as if it were a movie in my mind, Mom sitting at the kitchen table, nursing Billy, while I'm giving Franny a bath in the porcelain sink. I want that time back again. I want to plop Franny in the kitchen sink, filled with tepid water and bubble bath, and watch her giggle and try to smash the bubbles with her short fat fingers; I want to submerge the yellow rubber duck under the bubbles, beneath the water, as if it were a submarine, and hold on to it while Franny splashes around, searching for it, and then, when she isn't looking, I release the duck, and – surprise! – it breaks through the surface, bubble-covered, bobbing on top of the water, and Franny squeals in delight, grabbing for the duck, trying to drown it herself, while Mom looks on, smiling, with Billy at her breast. Then Dad comes home, bursting through the kitchen door with a briefcase under his arm, and tosses the newspaper on the table, adjusting his glasses. His flurry of motion stops us all, as if time has momentarily been suspended, then Franny squeals and flaps her arms, her mouth turned up in a smile so huge you'd think she hadn't seen him for days. Dad laughs, that deep chortle of his, and sets down the briefcase, gives Mom a kiss and rubs the top of Billy's head. Then he comes over to me and says, 'How're my other girls?' and gives me a hug and tickles Franny under her chin.

I want that time back. I want to lift Franny out of the water, being oh-so-careful not to drop her, her body pink and warm and slippery, her chubby legs kicking the air, and lay her on the towel-covered counter, wrap her with her favorite Mickey Mouse-printed terry-cloth towel, and rub her all over until she is dry and tingly; I want to sprinkle baby powder into her skin again, and kiss her tummy, her skin velvety and smelling of the pleasant, lightly scented talc, as Franny reaches for my hair, grabbing fistfuls and yanking impatiently; I want to massage talc into her tiny feet while she smiles and squirms on the towel, and then blow air on the bottoms of her feet and kiss her baby toes, each of them, and watch as she yawns and her eyelids lower; I want to put Franny in her warm fleece one-piece sleeper with the lacy white collar and hold her, almost asleep now, to my chest and smell her sweet breath, her miniature lips slightly parted; and I want to rub my cheek against Franny's hair and kiss her head, just a gentle kiss, just one more time, while she sleeps soundly in my arms.

I open my eyes. I think of Franny at five, her kindergarten picture, smiling shyly, brown curly hair in pigtails, two plastic butterfly barrettes, one hand cupped under her chin. The photographer tried, unsuccessfully, to get Franny to lower her hand. I was fifteen then, and being a second mother had lost its allure. Franny was five, Billy four, and their sense of newness had worn off. I loved them, of course, but they were a constant irritation – following me around the house, nattering endlessly, sneaking into my room and tearing pictures of animals out of my favorite magazines, using my lipstick to paint each other's faces. I was more interested in boys those days, and resented giving up an occasional weekend night to baby-sit so Mom and Dad could go out to a movie, for which I naturally blamed Franny and Billy. And by the time I was seventeen, I was going through my own teenage crises, much too distracted to give heed to younger siblings, and then at eighteen I was off to college. I visited occasionally, but I was busy with school, exams, a part-time job at the local newspaper, trying to build a future for myself, a new life, and my family – Billy, Franny, my parents

– was part of my old life, important, yes, but relegated to a secondary position. From eighteen to twenty-four – when Franny came to live with me – I have few definite memories of her: on trips home for birthday parties, on Christmases, at Billy's funeral where she hovered in the background, trancelike, not speaking to anyone. Vague memories, at best. The process of neglect had already begun. She needed me, but I didn't notice.

I go inside the house, saddened that all my good memories of Franny occurred in the first few years of her life. Ian is coming over this evening, so I start dinner: baked fish, salad, and rolls. When he arrives, he walks up behind me and puts his arms around my waist, kissing me softly on the back of my neck. The air around him is fragrant and sweet-smelling, and I know that he has stopped, as he often does, at the flower stand on F Street to buy me a bouquet of blue and white lupines, foxgloves, or perhaps some yellow monkey flowers.

While we eat dinner, Ian tells me of his day. He stopped at his condo earlier and changed out of his suit into jeans and a red-and-gray-checked shirt, and he looks like a lumberjack, solid, big-boned, Bunyanesque in the way his large hands shrink the knife and fork he holds. Yet his voice is soft, gentle even, and as he tells me about the story he is covering at the capitol, I lean across the table and, every now and then, touch his sleeve while he talks, comforted by the soothing tone of his voice and the soft feel of his shirt, knowing that he would understand I didn't mean to neglect Franny.

Later that night, Ian and I get ready for bed. We undress without ceremony, accustomed to each other's nakedness, and we're in bathrobes as we brush our teeth, floss, use the toilet. I turn back the covers on the bed, then take off my bathrobe. I see my reflection in the mirror on the closet door, my groin hairless. Soon after M. dressed me as a schoolgirl, he shaved my pubic hair. That night, when Ian saw it, he reacted suspiciously.

'Why did you shave?' he asked sharply, looking at my groin. His face was clouded over, his forehead wrinkled.

I hesitated, then said, 'For you.'

He paced across the room, frowning, not saying anything for a while. Then he blurted out, 'Are you seeing another man?'

'What?'

'You heard me. Are you seeing someone else?'

I stood there, not answering, wondering if he knew.

'Did you think I wouldn't notice your absences, Nora? Half the time I want to come over, you tell me you're busy. I call here late at night, and you're not home.'

I felt the guilt passing through me. 'Sometimes I don't answer the phone,' I said lamely. 'If I'm tired, or I don't feel like talking, I let the answering machine pick it up.' Tentatively, I put my arms around him, feeling the tension in his body, the resentment. He backed away.

'That's not an answer to my question.' His voice is hard, bitter, filled with suspicion.

'You're the only man I love,' I said, meaning it. 'The only man.' But not the only one I'm fucking, I thought, knowing myself for what I really was: a liar.

Ian was quiet. Finally, he said, 'Are you sure?'

I nodded.

Slowly, he relaxed. 'I'm sorry, Nora. I don't know why I get like this sometimes. I try not to – it just happens.' He was silent for a while, then he added, 'That's not true. I do know why I'm like this. It was Cheryl.'

I waited for him to continue. His face had a look of torment I've never before seen.

Slowly, he said, 'She brought something out in me that I didn't know existed.'

'That happened with me too, when Franny died. I didn't think I could—'

'No,' Ian said, interrupting me. 'I'm not talking about Cheryl's murder. I'm talking about . . . the way we were together. Our relationship was torturous.' He hesitated, then added, 'She used to lie to me; she used to see other men. Not frequently, but enough to make me crazy. I thought she would change, but she never did. It got so . . . ugly. I didn't know I was capable of such a passionate anger – and it terrified me. I can't go through that again.' He held me close. Softly, he said, 'Don't ever do that to me, Nora. Don't.'

I felt my guilt more acutely then, a thick mass of remorse.

Later that evening, after I convinced Ian I shaved expressly for him, he became wildly excited. He said none of his girl-friends had done that for him before. He couldn't keep his hands off me, and for days afterward he would lift my dress, or pull down my jeans, just because he wanted another look. Now, however, he's used to seeing me without pubic hair, and once, when he saw what a nuisance it was to shave, he said to let it grow back. I told him I liked having no pubic hair; I told him it turned me on. What I didn't tell him was that M. insisted upon it.

22

I start to ring M.'s doorbell, but hesitate when I hear the faint sound of his piano. I try the doorknob. It isn't locked, so I walk in, hearing the music louder now, and shut the door. Rays from the afternoon sun slant down from the skylight, brightening the foyer, and in the corner a potted weeping fig flourishes, its leaves shiny and willowlike. I listen to the music but do not recognize the piece M. is playing – some thing light, lyrical, romantic.

I peek inside the den, but he doesn't look up. His back is straight, his hair slightly mussed, and he looks as if he's a hundred miles away, totally absorbed. His hair droops over his eyes, and I want to step forward and brush it back. But I don't dare. He looks untouchable at the moment, enraptured, lost in a different world. This sight arouses me, and I want to interrupt him anyway. I want him to fuck me on his precious piano, but then I remember my frowsy appearance – dingy gray sweatpants torn at the knee; a long blue workshirt from one of my old boyfriends, the collar and sleeves frayed; hair that hasn't been washed for three days. I change my mind. M.'s aura is too intimidating; he's much too sexy for me.

The melody quickens, his long, elegant fingers at a frenzy all over the keyboard. His brow furrows.

'Damn!' he mutters, and stops playing, runs his fingers through his dark hair, then begins again, still not seeing me. He must've hit a wrong key, although I did not notice it. His head nods, keeping time.

I leave, not disturbing him, and walk down the hallway to the guest bedroom. Opening the door, I see nothing. It is as black as an underground cave. I feel along the wall for the light switch, turn it on, but nothing happens. Apparently, there are still no lamps in the room and no overhead light. I go into the kitchen to look for a flashlight. Opening a utility drawer, I find Scotch tape, scratch pads, pens, a pair of scissors, and operating manuals for his microwave oven and stove. I close the drawer, then walk over to the broom closet in the corner. Besides brooms and mops leaning against the wall, and a trash can sitting on the floor, I see a red fire extinguisher on the top shelf, and next to that a flashlight. I grab it, then go back through the house, stopping at the den entrance. M. is still playing, oblivious of my presence.

Back in the guest bedroom, I turn on the flashlight. A cone of bright light shines on the wall. I move it to the next wall, and then the next. The room is painted entirely black now, with heavy black curtains that block out the afternoon light. I walk over to the curtains, draw them back, and see that the window is covered with blackout screens. A black oval rug, extending to within a foot of the walls, covers the floor, the hardwood only showing on the perimeter.

A training room, that's what M. called it. And he said I'd find out soon enough what it was for. Feeling queasy, I turn off the flashlight and back out of the room, closing the door behind me. I return the flashlight to the kitchen and just stand there, listening to the music. It's different now, funereal, haunting, heavy cords and dramatic pounding. It reminds me of a trip I took along the Big Sur coast in mid-winter, the seascape gray and bleak, fog shrouding the Santa Lucia mountains, the sense of man's inconsequence illumined in the relentlessly crashing waves. I feel my inconsequence now, and leave M.'s house before he notices my presence.

Several days later, while M. is taking a shower, I get the flashlight and see more of the room. No longer can it be called a guest bedroom, for an overnight guest would never stay here. In one corner, hanging from a set of chains, there is some kind of a black leather sling or harness, with leg straps and foot stirrups. And in the middle of the room, a hoist – with chrome steel pulleys, nylon rollers, and rope – dangles from the wooden beam on the ceiling. I run the light along the rest of the ceiling and see metal hooks secured in various locations. Earlier, M. told me that the room is still not complete.

23

Yesterday, hearing M. play that bleak music, I understood how hermetic my life has become. I've slipped into a world of dark isolation, at the center of which stands M. I had a career. I had friends. But little by little, I've lost everything. It's the middle of June, and I haven't seen Maisie since February – the month I began seeing M. She was my closest friend before Franny died, and I've shut her out as well.

On Saturday, I call Maisie, then, at her urging, I drive to her home in midtown Sacramento. Recently, she bought an old mansard-topped Victorian-Gothic home and converted it into a boarding house. For months, I've promised I'd come over and see it. I slow down and turn the corner, checking the address. I pull up to the curb in front of a huge, dilapidated three-story home. The street is shady and charming, canopied with tall graceful elms and stout-trunked sycamores, but the house is in a state of decline. Maisie said she was renovating the home, but I wasn't expecting such a mess: the paint is chipped and peeling, and the porch sags in the center like an old swaybacked horse that's been ridden too many times; shutters droop off their hinges, the windows smudged and nearly opaque; and in the driveway a dented trash can lies carelessly on its side.

I enter the house. In front of me is a flight of old stairs, creaky I'm sure. A bare bulb, unlit, hangs from the ceiling in the dingy hallway, which has been paneled with cheap wood that is warped and buckling in places. I turn to my right and look into a damask-hued living room – which should probably be called a parlor in an old house like this – filled with stale light. The shades are half-drawn, the floor lamps muted with pink embroidered covers. A table along the wall is covered with heavy linen.

'You're here!' I hear Maisie say loudly, and turn around. She's a large woman in her late thirties, bespectacled, with pointy eyebrows and thin, thin lips. She's wearing a white dress with big bold roses. I'd forgotten that Maisie always wore dresses decorated with huge floral prints that made me want to scream. I'd also forgotten about how, in order to compensate for her scanty lips, she would exaggerate her lipstick, using bright reds and painting the lip line fuller than it really was. As a result, whenever she grinned her smile seemed to rove all over her face in a very sloppy way.

'I'm so glad to see you finally,' Maisie says, rushing up to give me a big hug.

'Me too.'

She holds me at arm's length, peering at me over her enormous lavender-tinged wing-shaped glasses. 'You look like hell,' she states matter-of-factly.

I shrug. There's not too much I can say to that.

'Come on,' she says, taking me by the arm. 'Let me give you the grand tour.'

The grand tour turns out to be not so very grand. The banister needs to be fixed, the walls painted, all the plumbing fixtures replaced, the back door repaired. I try to think of something positive to say, and finally comment on the ceiling. 'I like the curlicues painted on the coving,' I say. Fortunately, Maisie's chattering makes up for my lack of enthusiasm.

She takes me into the nursery – the only room halfway decent, painted yellow with a ceiling trim of red and blue clowns – and checks on her two-year-old boy, who sleeps soundly in a white wooden crib, lying on his stomach, thumb in mouth. I reach into the crib and rub his back gently. He's wearing a blue T-shirt and a diaper printed with dinosaurs. His arms and legs are chubby, his hair curly red, and he has a ski-jump nose that turns up at the end. A rash of light freckles bridges his nose.

'You'll want one soon,' Maisie whispers. The boy's lips pucker around his thumb and he makes a soft smacking sound. Ever since Maisie had a baby, she's tried to convince me to have one also, saying that single motherhood isn't so very difficult.

'I don't think so,' I say, and I brush the hair off his forehead and touch his cheek. He has that soft, plump skin that only babies have. When Franny and Billy were young, loving them so much, I knew I would be a mother someday. I'm not, obviously. I watched while I was in my mid-twenties and then thirties as nearly all my friends, one by one, got married and had children. But I had a career – and wasn't that even better? Men seek divorces; children grow up and leave. All you have left, in the end, is your career. Anyway, that's what I told myself and everyone who asked, and it almost sounded convincing.

We leave the nursery, and Maisie shows me her boarders' rooms. The boarders don't seem to mind our intrusion when she knocks and asks permission to see their quarters. She takes me through each room, delighted with her old house.

'Oh, I know it needs a lot of work,' she says, leading me back into the front parlor. 'But think what it'll be worth a couple of years from now, when I get it fixed up.'

I smile. 'I think it's great,' I say, meaning every word. The house is a mess, but I'm envious of Maisie's passion, her determination to build something of value out of ruin. Since Franny died, I have little passion for anything except exposing her murderer. I sit on the sofa, a garishly red piece of furniture with tufted velvet fabric. Maisie stands over me, suddenly quiet. I hear an occasional thud or scrape coming from an upstairs bedroom. I fold my hands in my lap, frowning at them.

'Maisie,' I begin slowly, then hesitate. I begin again. 'I'm sorry,' I say.

'What for?'

'For not returning your phone calls. For disappearing.'

Maisie waves her hand as if she were waving away my apology. 'Don't worry about that,' she says, sitting down next to me. 'But when are you coming back to work?'

'Soon,' I say. 'Soon.'

Maisie raises her pointed eyebrows at me. 'You've been saying that for months. Don't you think it's time to come back?'

'No. Not yet. I'm still . . .' I pause and shake my head. I can't tell her about M., about Franny's involvement with him and now mine. 'I need more time,' I say. 'I'm still struggling to make sense of all this.'

'All what, Nora? There is no sense to how Franny died. But she did, over a year ago, and now it's time for you to get on with your life. You need to get some help. Look at you. You look like you haven't slept for weeks. No makeup, and your hair's a mess. And look what you're wearing: torn jeans and a ratty T-shirt. You never used to dress like this. You look like you've been to hell.'

I gaze down at my T-shirt. There's a milk stain where I spilled my cereal this morning. 'There're lots of ways to go to hell,' I say quietly, thinking of the black room in M.'s house, the leather sling and the steel hoist. 'It's getting back that's the hard part.'

24

'What happened to your afternoon classes?' I ask M., wondering why I'm here, feeling grumpy from too little sleep. He called me from campus earlier today and said to meet him at his house. The kitchen seems too bright and shiny, the afternoon light beaming through the window, reflecting off the appliances, the chrome on the stove and refrigerator glaring – even M.'s cheerfulness grates on me. He's leaning against the counter, and he looks like an ad out of a male fashion magazine, every hair in place, his clothes wrinkle-free, fastidious beyond reproach.

'I canceled them. I wanted the afternoon free.'

I push up the sleeves on my blouse, which is rumpled from being rucked up in the dryer all night long. 'What for?'

'I have something special planned for today.'

I wait for him to continue, but he doesn't. 'So – are you going to tell me?' I ask, getting annoyed. He only smiles, but it looks more like a sneer to me.

'Come with me,' he says, and he walks out of the kitchen. I follow him down the hallway and into the back bedroom, the training room. The room is dark, with lit candles everywhere – some of them thick and squat, others tall and thin, some in candlesticks, others on flat disks. They flicker around the room, and they must be scented, because I smell the faint, spicy-sweet odor of nutmeg.

I look around the room. The leather sling in the corner I've seen before. Likewise the hoist and the hooks in the ceiling. But now there is a bed shoved up against the far wall, and a padded bench of some sort is placed in the middle of the room.

A heavy set of shackles dangle from one wall – far enough apart for outstretched hands – and thick leg irons are bolted to the floor. And displayed on the south wall, hanging from hooks, is M.'s collection of whips, belts, and paddles. In the middle of the display, mounted on two hooks, is the steel cutlass M.'s father used in World War II.

I jerk when I feel M.'s hand on my neck. 'I want to leave,' I say.

'Not yet. I'm going to fuck you first.'

'In your room,' I say.

He holds my arm. 'No – in here.'

I look up at him and see the determination in his eyes. We are going to fuck in this room. He unbuttons my blouse and slides it off my shoulders. Then he takes off my jeans and underwear. I notice the television and VCR, and next to them a tall chest of drawers. In the corner, a camcorder is set up on a tripod. I glance back to the leg irons bolted on the floor.

'That's all I want to do,' I say. 'Just fuck.'

M. sees me looking at the leg irons and he smiles. 'You can trust me, Nora. You know that.'

'Just fuck,' I repeat.

'Okay,' M. says, and he takes me to the bed. I lie down, feeling the soft sheets beneath me. I watch the candles burn. Flame shadows flick in fluid patterns off the black walls. The candles would be romantic in a different setting; now they just look eerie, menacing in a medieval way. I feel the danger in this room.

M. sits on the bed. He's wearing a dark blue shirt, and it's a good color on him. It makes him look sexy. He leans over and kisses me, long and sensual, then runs his hand along my body. I smell the faint scent of his cologne, spicy, woodsy, and I kiss him back, touching his hair, feeling its softness, pulling him closer. He removes my arms, placing them above my head.

'Keep them there,' he says. 'Don't touch me.' He leans down to kiss me again. I feel the urgency in his tongue, in his chest rubbing against mine, and I want him desperately. His hands move all over my body, first my thighs, then up to my breasts, then along my arms.

He whispers, 'I've been thinking about the discussion we had last week – when you said you'd never let me tie you up or bind you in any way.' He pauses for a moment, then adds, 'I've decided not to indulge you any longer.'

I look up at him, feeling apprehensive. 'That decision isn't yours to make,' I say.

'But it is my decision, Nora. You're missing the basic principle of submission. It's quite simple: you do whatever I want, whenever I want it. I don't know why you're having trouble understanding this concept.'

I feel something cold and hard snap around my left wrist. Then, quickly, before I can react, M. holds my other arm and snaps something around it.

I twist my head around to see what is binding my arms, then panic at what I see: handcuffs around my wrists, and short chains welded to the cuffs and bolted into the wall. I feel my heart pounding, then tell myself to calm down. Fear only makes everything worse.

'Let me go,' I say.

M. ignores my request. He kisses me lightly. 'You brought this on yourself,' he says into my ear. 'If you'd trusted me I could've tied you up, had a little fun, then released you.'

'Take these off me,' I say, but he only looks at me coldly.

'Do you understand?' he says. 'Do you realize you brought this on yourself? If you were more compliant, I wouldn't have to take such extreme measures. I warned you not to be so obstinate. Now it's too late. I'm going to teach you a lesson.'

A drop of sweat slides off my forehead – sweat from fear, not from the warmth of the room. M. gets up. He folds my clothes neatly and places them on a table; then he leaves, closing the door behind him.

I pull on the chains, but they are securely attached to the wall. I yank again, and feel the cuffs chafe at my wrists. Beside me is a table with a key on it – but out of my reach. I twist from the waist, throw my leg over, and try to reach the key with my toes. The table is too far away. I try again, stretching every muscle, the cuffs burning into my wrists, but it is hopeless. There is no way I can escape.

I call out, but M. doesn't answer. I watch the burning candles. It was dangerous for him to leave me here alone, the candles unattended. An unwanted image surfaces in my mind: the room catching fire while I'm chained to the bed, helpless.

Suddenly, the door flings open. I jerk, drawing in my breath. All I see, for moments, is the darkness of the hallway.

Then M. enters. The first thing I notice is the black hood. It's an executioner's hood, the kind you see in movies – molded tightly to his head, large holes for his eyes and eyebrows, the hood edging his jaw, then cutting up to the bridge of his nose, completely freeing his mouth and nose. Next I notice the tight jeans – M. never wears jeans – and his bare chest. A black studded armband circles his left upper arm, and he's wearing fingerless black gloves. Clipped on his belt is a knife sheath, with only the handle of the knife visible.

He slams the door shut, walks over to the bed, stares down at me. The body belongs to M., but I don't recognize the eyes behind the hood, eyes so expressionless, so devoid of human feeling, that they could inhabit an automaton. He climbs on the bed, straddling my chest. The weight of his body, the denim against my skin, the knife sheath poking me in the ribs – it all makes me claustrophobic. I breathe heavily, my outstretched arms straining against the cuffs and chains. M. looks up at the handcuffs. He places one gloved hand on my right arm; his bare fingertips, slightly cool, contrast with the warm leather of the glove.

'Let me go,' I say.

His head jerks down, as if he's surprised I have a voice. Dark eyes, now furious with emotion, stare at me behind that horrid hood. He slaps my face, sharply, and I scream.

'Did I tell you to speak?' he yells. 'Did I?!' And he slaps me again.

'Stop it!' I say, but my words only make him angrier. I feel the sting of his hand once more, sharp, burning, and my eyes water.

He leans down, his face inches from mine. 'Say another word,' he hisses, gripping my neck, 'and it'll be your last.'

I blink, and a hot tear of pain runs down my cheek. Lying there, I say nothing, afraid he will slap me again, praying that is the worst thing that will happen.

M. releases my neck, then climbs off me. He reaches over to the table for a candle. It is long, thin, in a brass candlestick. He walks to the foot of the bed, carrying the burning candle.

'Give me your foot,' he says, reaching down with one hand, cupping it so I can place my heel in his palm.

I shake my head, reflexively drawing my feet up closer to my body.

M. is silent for a moment. 'We can do this two ways,' he says finally, his voice controlled. 'Either you put your foot in my hand voluntarily, or I'll tie your legs down. The choice is yours.'

I squeeze my eyes shut, trying to blink back tears. This is a horrible mistake, I think. I shouldn't be here. This isn't what is supposed to happen. I open my eyes and lower my legs. M. reaches down again and I put my right foot in his hand. My leg is shaking, but I can't stop it. M. lowers the candle, then stops and looks up. His eyes gleam in the candlelight, two shiny orbs piercing the black hood.

'Shhh,' he says, before I say anything. 'Remember, you're not allowed to speak.'

He holds the flame close to my skin, and I clench my jaw so I won't call out. I shut my eyes. M. grips my ankle, holding it firmly. I feel heat along my toes, then on the ball of my foot, but no pain. I wait for him to burn me.

It doesn't come. When I open my eyes, he releases my foot and says, 'That was very good. I know you wanted to speak, but didn't. I see you can be trained, after all.' He turns around and switches on the television, then he walks over to the camcorder and turns it on. My image appears on the screen, faint in the dim candlelight. M. scowls.

He walks to the side of the bed, the candle still in his hand. 'I'll permit you to speak now,' he says, and he tips the candle over.

Hot wax drips on my stomach. I flinch and scream out, from shock more so than pain.

M. gives me a disdainful glance. 'You don't know what pain is,' he says, and he lowers the candle a few inches, tips it over again. This time, my scream is warranted. The wax sears my flesh like a hot iron.

'Please,' I say, 'no more,' but M. ignores me. He dribbles the wax around my stomach, around each nipple, on the insides of my thighs. He gauges the distance of the candle to the sounds of my cries, raising and lowering the candle to vary the intensity of pain. He holds it high and the wax cools slightly before touching my skin; he holds it close and the wax scalds like boiling water. I beg for him to stop.

'Stop?' he says, holding the candle inches from my skin. 'You want me to stop?'

I watch the flame, not able to take my eyes off it. 'Yes,' I murmur. 'Please.'

'You don't like this?' I hear the mocking tone in his voice.

I shake my head. M. raises the candle, away from my skin, and I sigh with relief.

'Then perhaps I should give you something else,' he says. He sets the candle on the table and gazes at my body, at the hardened wax on my torso and thighs, appraising me. Then he walks over to the chest of drawers, pulls out the middle drawer, comes back to the foot of the bed with rope in his hands.

'Perhaps a little punishment,' he says, 'to help you with your discipline problem.' He straightens out the rope. There are two long pieces, one end of each attached to a leather cuff through a metal D ring.

Again, reflexively, I draw in my legs. M. reaches down to stop me. I whimper at the touch of his hand, barely resisting, knowing, with my arms chained, it will do no good to fight back. He puts a leather cuff on one ankle, then the other.

He stands on the mattress, raising my legs over my head, doubling me over, then ties the end of each rope to an eye hook in the wall, my legs spread apart, my buttocks off the bed. The insides of the ankle cuffs are lined with something soft, fleece possibly, and don't chafe my skin, but this position is awkward. M. gets off the bed, surveys his work, then walks over to the chest of drawers again and comes back with a long red scarf. He twists it in his arms, pulling it taut, then reaches between my legs and wraps the scarf around my neck. I start to panic, thinking he is going to choke me, but then he lifts it to the back of my head and wraps it around my mouth. He forces it between my teeth, then ties it off in the back.

'I can't have you making too much noise,' he says. Then adds, 'And you will be making noise.'

I watch him as he walks over to the south wall and stands in front of his whips. He chooses a long narrow cane, about three feet long, something he's never used on me before, then returns to the bed.

'Bamboo,' he says, flexing the cane, standing over me. 'This will be different from any beating I've given you in the past,' he continues. 'Consider the spankings and whippings you've experienced previously as sexual foreplay.' He runs his fingers along the length of the cane, touching it lightly. 'This will not excite you. This is punishment,' and he draws back the cane and slashes it across my ass. My legs jerk against the rope, a sharp pain shudders through my body. I moan, and tears instantly come to my eyes and stream down my face.

'I'm not putting up with any more foolishness,' he says. 'Do you understand? I never want to hear you complain when I bring out my rope. I'll bind you whenever I choose.' He walks over to the table next to the television and brings back my clothes. He holds them up.

'I'm sick of seeing you in jeans and dirty blouses,' he says, dropping them in a heap on the rug. 'From now on you'll dress appropriately.'

He slashes the cane down again, on the backs of my thighs. Another jolt of pain, white hot, goes through my body as I scream into the gag. I strain against the ropes and chains.

'Do you understand?' he asks, and I nod through my tears and moans, still feeling the pain on the backs of my legs. What he said, however, is not lost to me. From *now on you'll dress appropriately.* From now on. He does not mean to kill me here. He will not be my executioner. Not here. Not yet.

'Good,' he says, 'but I'm not quite through. Five more strokes with the cane.'

I shake my head vigorously.

'Yes, my pet,' he says, rubbing my calf with his hand. 'I want you to remember this the next time you think of disobeying,' and he brings the cane down five more times, each one harder than the last, each stroke sending a shock wave of pain vibrating through my body.

When he's finished, he unties my legs and lowers them, then unknots the scarf and takes it out of my mouth, but leaves my arms chained to the wall. He sits down on the side of the bed. Tears are still running down my face, my body sweat-covered and maculated with candle wax. It takes me minutes to stop crying.

When I am quiet, he asks, 'Are you going to behave from now on?'

Meekly, I say, 'Yes.'

'That's a good girl,' he says, brushing my cheek lightly. 'You're going to be my good girl from now on, aren't you?'

I nod.

'I thought so.' He looks at me carefully, as if he's deciding what course of action to take next, his face sinister in the black executioner's hood. He unsnaps the knife sheath on his belt. Slowly, he draws out the knife, then rests his hand on his knee. The blade is shiny and curved on the bottom, with a sharp hook on the top. From an encounter with a previous boyfriend,

I recognize the type of blade – it is a hunting knife, for skinning animals. M. taps it gently against his leg.

'It didn't have to be like this,' he says. 'You brought it on yourself.'

I'm breathing hard, watching the knife as he taps it on his jeans. I think of Franny, of the cuttings on her stomach and breasts. The sound of my heart pounds in my ears. I want to say something but am unable to open my mouth. He said from now on, I keep thinking. He said from now on. This won't be the end.

He lifts the knife and puts the tip of it against my breast. When I feel the sharp blade, I let out a small moan.

'You still don't know who you're dealing with, do you? I could be a maniac with a knife.' He presses it against me harder. 'Or even a psycho killer,' he adds.

I smell the fear in my sweat. Tears, again, come to my eyes.

'Spread your legs,' he orders.

I close my eyes. I can't do what he says. I heard his command, but my legs are paralyzed, unable to move, palsied with fear and regret.

'Do it,' he repeats, and I open my eyes and look at him. He stares down at me, his face hard, implacable, unreadable. Suddenly, I know: he will kill me today. He is unrecognizable behind that mask, a different person, gone over the edge. This is what Franny saw on her last day. This is what happened before he carved up her torso. I feel my tears.

'Do it,' he says once more. 'Now.'

I shake my head. M. presses the knife harder against the flesh of my breast. Somehow, my legs part. It is as if they were spread with someone else's hand – not from my own volition.

'Wider,' he says. 'Wider.'

My body is clammy, damp from sweat. I lick my lips. My legs open wider until they are spread-eagled on the bed. I feel vulnerable as never before. Watching the tip of the knife pressed against my breast, I think of Franny.

In a flash, the knife is between my legs. I gasp, feeling the cold tip of the blade on the lips of my vagina. I stare at the hand between my legs, whimpering.

'Don't move,' M. cautions me. With his free hand he cups my chin and forces me to look at him and not at the knife. 'Don't move,' he says again, his face close to mine, his breath hot.

Then he gets down between my legs. I shut my eyes, squeeze them tightly, mumble a prayer to a higher power. I feel the knife scraping against the inside of my left thigh. I tense when I feel the blade, waiting for M. to thrust it inside me, expecting the pain.

The scraping continues; first on one area of my thigh, then another. I look down and see that he is scraping the hardened wax off my leg. He finishes the left, then begins on the right thigh, flicking off all the wax. He works up to my stomach, not leaving so much as a scratch, then, with his fingers, he peels the wax off my nipples and breasts. Chips of wax speckle the bed. When he is through, he puts his finger inside my vagina, twists it around.

'Your pussy's wet,' he says, drawing out his finger, licking it off. 'Amazing what a little fear will do.'

I lie still.

M. gets up and unsnaps the sheath from his belt, replaces the knife, sets it on a table. He takes off his jeans and underwear, but leaves on the black hood, the studded armband, the fingerless gloves. He walks toward me, his penis erect, then reaches for the key on the table and unlocks my wrists.

I am free. It happened so suddenly, I am momentarily stunned. I lower my arms, rubbing them, working out the stiffness and aches. I cannot put my feelings into words. I continue rubbing my arms, stalling for time, trying to make sense of what happened. Feeling tears come again, I blink them back.

'Goddamn you,' I say, and try to sit up.

He pushes me back down, pinions my arms with his. 'Did I frighten you?' he asks, taunting me. I struggle to get up, but he is too strong. My arms are still sore and weak.

'Don't fight me, Nora,' he says, then he laughs. 'It only gets me more excited.' He tries to kiss me, but I move my head to the side. He stands up.

'Shall I put the cuffs back on?'

I lie still, infuriated, and glare at him. He looms over me, his erection hard, jutting out with a feral intensity, the black hood still on his head, making him look foreign yet familiar at the same time.

After that, we fucked. I don't know why – I'm still angry for what he did. I think I must be sick or perverted. We lie in the small bed, not embracing, but our bodies touching. M. takes off the hood and drops it on the floor.

'I had lunch in Sacramento today,' he says. 'At Paragary's. Before you came over.'

I wonder why he is telling me this. 'It was dangerous to leave me in here alone with the candles burning,' I say.

He changes the subject. 'These are nice,' he says, touching the red splotches on my stomach. Round burn marks mottle my skin. There aren't many of them – most of the time M. held the candle high enough so the wax cooled slightly before touching my skin, burning but not searing the flesh – but those marks he did leave are ugly and painful.

'I like to see my marks on you,' he says, tracing them with his finger. 'Turn over – I want to see my handiwork on your ass.'

I roll over on my stomach, watching M. as he smiles appreciatively. 'Did you break the skin?' I ask, feeling sure that he did.

'Not even a little,' he says.

'It feels like you did.'

'No – but you have some nice red welts here. I could've been much harder on you.'

'I didn't like it.'

'You weren't supposed to. This was a whipping for punishment, not for pleasure – you better learn the difference.' He leans over and kisses my ass. 'I do enjoy branding you,' he says. Then adds, 'But the wounds will heal in several days, maybe a week. They're not permanent scars. Didn't I tell you I'd never really harm you? You should've remembered my promise. If you had, you wouldn't have been so frightened. You would've known it was only a game.'

I roll over, frowning. I don't think M. is capable of keeping a promise, and I certainly don't trust him with my life. 'It wasn't a game,' I say. 'You really hurt me.'

M. says, 'You still don't know the meaning of the word – but you will. Soon.'

I cross my arms. Some of the candles have burned out, and the room is much darker. The sword on the wall glints in the remaining candlelight. 'Why did you bring your father's sword in here?' I ask.

M. smiles. 'I thought you'd like that. It's just for atmosphere, to help create the proper mood of fear. Part of the game.'

'And what about the hoist? And the padded bench? What are those for?'

'You'll find out soon enough.' He turns on his side and puts his hand on my breast. 'I do believe you're enjoying this.'

'Enjoying what?'

'The whole scene – the danger, the fright.'

I shake my head. 'You went too far.'

'Your pussy told me differently.'

I climb out of the bed and get my clothes.

M. says, 'You always like it when I'm a little rough with you, when I pull your hair, when I push you around. You like a modicum of fear with your sex. Face it, Nora, you're a danger seeker.'

I deny this is so.

'Yes, you are. I could feel the adrenaline pulsing through your body. I could feel it in your wet pussy.'

I put on my clothes.

M. continues. 'You've discovered you like living on the edge. You think I killed Franny, and you're terrified I might kill you. It horrifies you, frightens you, and turns you on like never before.'

'You don't know what you're talking about,' I say, and open the door to leave.

'Nora,' M. says, his voice harsh.

I turn around, impatient. 'What?' I ask.

'I don't expect to see those clothes again.'

I turn to leave.

'Nora.'

'What now?' I say, pausing in the doorway.

'There's a present for you on the kitchen table.'

I leave him, without saying another word. I go into the kitchen and see several pages of paper lying on the table. The top page is titled 'Water Rat.'

25

WATER RAT
by Frances Tibbs

The girl is distant with herself, her body, her mind. She has a sister, Nora, and when the sister found out what she'd done, she threatened her with punishment. No television for a week, Nora said sharply, as if that could make her stop. But when she looked at the girl, her anger seemed to fade. Nora sat her down for a heart-to-heart, her eyes soft blue and pleading. She held the girl's hand tightly, as if she was afraid of losing her, and with a trembling voice she warned her of the dangers, made her promise not to do it again, her eyes so full of love that the girl, just fifteen, with pale skin and light brown eyebrows, lowered her head and nodded, even though she knew it was a promise she couldn't keep.

What the girl did was walk serenely into the ocean on a chilly, wintry day. Mr Clancy, their postman, had taken the girl and his own daughter out to the coast for a day trip. The girl didn't want to go, but Nora – who had to work that day – said she stayed inside too much, all by herself, never playing with other kids. So the girl went with Mr Clancy and Jeanine, his daughter. Mr Clancy was a tall man, the tallest the girl had ever seen, and she didn't know how he'd get into the tiny Toyota he arrived in, but he did – folding himself up as if his body were made of hinges. Jeanine, in one of the girl's classes at school, rode in the back with her, talking about a boy the girl didn't know and didn't care to know.

They were walking on the beach, bundled in coats – too cold for swimming, Mr Clancy said – when the girl waded in up to her neck, not minding the bitter cold water soaking her clothes and seeping into her skin, not heeding the frantic calls of tall Mr Clancy as he beckoned her ashore. And then it seemed everyone knew of her march into the sea. Around the neighborhood the story went, Mr Clancy dropping off the news as if it were a letter to be delivered.

She just wants to be left alone, but now at school the kids call her Water Rat. They think she loves the ocean, loves it so much she has to play in it on a winter day. Water Rat – she hates the name. They don't know what they're talking about. They don't know the ocean scares her more than almost anything. Even Nora, who should know because she lives with the girl and sees her every day and she's the only one left who really cares – even Nora doesn't know why she walked into the sea.

Now the girl is in her room, sitting on the bed, Nora beside her.

'You have such pretty hair,' Nora says, brushing the girl's hair with her favorite pearl-handled brush, the brush that used to belong to their mother. 'You should let it grow out.'

The girl doesn't think her hair is pretty – not like Nora's. Nora's hair is shiny black and perfectly straight, very chic, the girl thinks, unlike her own, which is dull and brown and barely reaches the top of her shoulders. It used to be much shorter, bristly, not more than an inch long, but she stopped chopping it off the day her parents died.

'I hate leaving you here alone,' Nora says. It's Saturday morning, and she has to work today – like most Saturdays. And Sundays.

'It's okay,' the girl says. 'Besides, I won't be alone. I'll go to the library.'

The girl closes her eyes and feels the brush going through her hair, slowly, gently, over and over again. It reminds her of the time, more than two years ago, before Billy died, when her hair was long and curly, almost down to her waist, and her mother would brush it every night. But after her brother died, the hair brushing stopped and the girl saw no reason to keep her hair long, so she cut it off, inch by inch, until it was all gone.

'I used to do this when you were little,' Nora says, and she continues pulling the brush through her hair. 'It was so silky and smooth – I loved to brush it.' She adds, 'I still do. It's been a long time since I've done this.' They are quiet.

Nora stops and wraps her arms around the girl, leaning close.

Her perfume scents the air, light and flowery. 'Tonight we'll do something special,' she says, hugging her, their heads pressed together. 'We'll go out to dinner, maybe see a movie.'

'All right,' the girl says, but she knows something will come up at work and they won't do anything special at all. The girl isn't bitter, she thinks it must be hard for Nora – who works so many hours at a job that's very demanding, and yet still tries to find time for her. And Nora will try, the girl knows, she'll try; but still she'll be here tonight by herself, alone with her memories.

Nora squeezes the girl's shoulders. 'I know I'm not around very much,' she says. 'I wish it could be different, but I have to work.'

'It's okay,' the girl says, and decides not to go to the library.

Nora gets up and starts to walk out the door. She hesitates, one hand on the door frame. She's wearing a black suit and red blouse, ready for work. 'I'm really proud of you,' she says. 'This year has been so difficult, but you've done really well. You get straight A's in school, you help me around here with the cooking and cleaning. Sometimes you act so adult, I forget you're just a kid.' She smiles and walks out the door.

The girl listens for Nora to leave the apartment. Then, when she hears the door slam, she gets up. She takes off her clothes and puts on a bathing suit, then looks in the mirror. She doesn't feel like she belongs to her body anymore. She's outside of it, somewhere, and whenever she looks in a mirror she sees a strange person staring back at her, someone foreign and unrecognizable. She used to be skinny, but now these extra layers of flesh keep appearing on her stomach and thighs. Her bathing suit is red, with diagonal rainbow stripes, and it fits snugly on her round body. Her legs are chubby, the flesh pale. This isn't a body she's comfortable with, this isn't a body she knows.

She dresses, putting her clothes over the red bathing suit, then leaves the apartment. The cool air hits her immediately, and she zips up her blue jacket. It's fall, and brown leaves litter the sidewalks and gutters. She walks quickly down the street, hearing a neighbor kid who lives next door calling her, telling her to wait. But she can't wait. She has to get to the ocean. She walks several blocks to the *freeway entrance, then sticks out her thumb for a ride. It takes a long time to get to the ocean. She always has to start early in the morning so she'll have time to get back before Nora notices she's gone.*

It takes her four hours to reach the coast this time, and she has to switch rides seven times – once with a lady in a van, a family in a station wagon, a beat-up car of teenagers, and four men in trucks, three of them saying she shouldn't be hitchhiking, a young girl like her could get hurt. The last ride, the old man in a truck hauling sod, lets her off in a little town on the coast – she doesn't know the name – on a narrow asphalt road.

She walks briskly, crossing the road to take a shortcut through a bumpy field, knowing she doesn't have much time before she'll have to turn around and go back home. Outgrowths of meadow grass give way to sandy stretches; above, water birds glide inland, then curve in a gentle arc westward, back to the sea. She skips between a row of run-down concrete houses and heads toward the ocean, toward a cove beneath the rocky promontory where no one can see her. She's learned to be careful: her rendezvous with the ocean are private affairs. She rations them out, holding off as long as she can, and never, ever, does she enter the water if other people are in sight.

As she gets closer to the ocean, her pace quickens, her heart beats faster. The sounds of the sea call to her, pulling her nearer, moving her as the moon moves the tides. She walks faster. Soon she's on the promontory, gazing down at the ocean. A salty breeze tangles her short brown hair. She flinches as she watches the waves coming to life, building up momentum as they roll in, then crashing on the shore in a fury of bubbling froth. Up and down they go, like roller-coaster rides, steep and scary and spine-tingling. Her heart thumping, she follows a snakelike path in the rocks that leads down to the beach.

When she reaches the sand, she shrugs out of her blue jacket, then slips off her shoes and socks. The air is cool, the sky a dreary gun-metal gray; no one else is on the beach. Damp and gritty, the sand is spotted with pods of burnished seaweed, and the air has the dank, brackish smell that always comes right before a storm. She quickly strips off her jeans and gray sweatshirt. Only in her red bathing suit now, she feels exposed and naked on the shore, vulnerable. Wind whips her hair across her face, and goose bumps pimple her skin.

She digs her toes in the sand. In school she learned this: you can't always see physical changes. Year after year, waves wash over rocks, and eventually, even though no one sees it happening, the rocks are beaten down to pebbles, then to sand. She sighs, and grinds her heels into the sand. Wide-eyed, she stares out, far, far ahead, where the ocean is flat and gray, calm. The sea frightens her, the immensity of it, yet she yearns for its calmness. She wants to be out there, out where she can float undisturbed. But the girl also wants its power, its ability to turn rock into sand, to turn something big and solid and overwhelming into nothing at all.

She steps into the ocean, gasping at its iciness, the water raw and cutting on her skin. Still she walks on, farther, willing herself to ignore the cold. A breaker showers her with salty water; seaweed winds around her legs. When the next breaker comes, she dives under it and lets it crash over her body. She comes up shivering, her wet hair dripping down almost to her shoulders. Another breaker comes and takes her under, pulls her farther out to sea. This time when she surfaces she can't touch the ocean's floor. She treads the water, waiting for the next wave. This is a game she started playing several months ago: to see how far she'll push herself; to see if the ocean can scare everything out of her, every memory, good and bad. She wants a wave so big and scary that she'll be sucked into a black hole of fear, remembering nothing. But each time she comes out here it seems harder and harder to reach that black hole, each time she has to push herself to go even further.

Overhead, a seagull shrieks. A small wave pushes her down, covers her head. She feels the water between each toe and finger, forcing itself into every pore and crevice in her body. The water surrounds her, smothering her like Billy's memory. Seaweed feathers her face, and she sees Billy's fingers digging and scraping in the soft ground. His last words come tumbling back, the scared voice, crying, begging her not to let him go. She hears it still, in her dreams. It ebbs and flows, his dream voice, not so gentle, like high-tide violent waves. And like water on the rocks, he's wearing her down, pulling her apart, piece by gritty piece. She surges upward, roughly breaking the surface, then treads in a circle, waiting. On the shore, there is a row of drab houses, some of them listing, and some with awkward gaps in between, like a set of crooked discolored teeth. As she drifts out, the houses get smaller and smaller.

She looks over her shoulder and sees a huge wave building up. It rolls toward her, thunderously, then suddenly it's towering above her head. The wave seems momentarily suspended, like a threat hovering in the air. She feels a knot of fear growing in her stomach just before the wave plummets down. It knocks her under with a terrible, crushing force. She feels herself going down, falling, falling, then tumbling backward, head over heels, as the ocean sucks her out to sea. This is what she wants. She wants everything to be scared out of her, all her thoughts, all the images, sucked into the bottom of the ocean.

Water rushes around her, jerking and twisting her body, pulling her down. Her chest tightens and all at once she panics, forgetting everything, even Billy, everything but the need to survive. Her leg scrapes the ocean's bottom and she frantically digs her fingers into the sand, but still she's uprooted, then dragged along, toppling over and over as the undertow pulls her along. She tries to swim upward, her arms outstretched, reaching and straining for the surface, but a whirlpool of water keeps pushing her down. Her lungs begin to ache and she flails her arms and legs, thrashing about helplessly. She reaches out to grab something, anything, but nothing is there. It seems to her she's been reaching all her life. Her eyes sting of saltwater and her body feels bruised. Just as she thinks her lungs will burst, her head breaks through the surface. She gulps the air, panting, her chest heaving. Then she cries out, feeling nothing but fear and pain and still more fear. Her tears fall into the ocean, unnoticed. Water laps around her, slapping at her face, silencing the sounds of her sobs, silencing her pain. Still crying and frightened, she slowly begins to swim toward the beach, somehow feeling better than she'd felt before, with everything almost, but not quite forgotten.

26

It's six o'clock when I get home. I take a shower, hoping the warm water will wash away all thoughts of M. and his training room and Franny's trips to the ocean. It doesn't work. In the mirror, I see red splotches on my torso from the hot wax, long welts on my ass from the cane, light chafe marks on my wrists. Much worse than the welts and burn marks, I feel my neglect of Franny. How could I have not known her pain?

I dress in long pants and a long-sleeved blouse, then light up the barbecue in the backyard. I'm not really hungry, but I already invited Ian over for dinner. I hear the phone ring and rush in to answer it.

'Hello,' I say, and wait for a reply. 'Hello,' I repeat, when no one answers. 'Is anyone there?' Still, all I get is silence. I hear breathing but no one speaks. Then the breathing becomes louder, more deliberate.

'Christ,' I mutter into the phone. 'Haven't you little boys got better things to do?' and I hang up, annoyed. I remember when I was a kid, and when my friends and I amused ourselves with prank calls for hours, doubling over with laughter imagining the irritation on the other end of the line. I turn on my answering machine so if they call back they'll get a recording.

I go back outside to check the barbecue, then return to the kitchen. Earlier, I'd marinated a pan of chicken breasts and wings, and now I take it out of the refrigerator. On the countertop, a miniature egret in basswood spreads its wings, preparing to fly. It is Ian's latest wood carving, and I love the feel of it, the tension in the outstretched wings suggesting movement. It reminds me of the many times I've seen egrets in the Sacramento area – along the marshes, on the river edges, in the delta.

I'm removing the plastic wrap from the pan of chicken when Ian walks in the door – or maybe I should say rushes in. He has such a springy, loping gait, bouncing just a little on the balls of his feet, that he appears to be swooping into the room, taking it over with the forward motion of his body. I gave him his own key several weeks ago, but not because my feelings for him have, overnight, intensified. I am like a drowning woman scrambling for a lifeline: as M. draws me closer to him, I instinctively reach out to Ian, pulling him nearer for my own safety. He comes up behind me and gives me a big hug, his wrestler's arms thick and strong.

'You smell good,' he says, kissing my neck. He probably smells the shampoo or conditioner from when I washed my hair. I relax against his body, absorbing the warmth of his embrace, accepting the love he offers freely. He has a trunk of a body, solid enough to give support. He just came from the *Bee* and he's wearing a blue suit, rumpled in the back and at the knees, and his tie is pulled loose and lies crooked on his chest. He starts to pull away, but I hold on to his arms around my waist.

'Not so fast,' I tell him. 'It feels good just to have you hold me.'

Ian obliges, wrapping his arms around me tighter. Sometimes, I feel that if he holds me long enough and tight enough, he'll make me forget all about M. I wish Franny had had someone to hold her, as I have Ian.

'We're having chicken tonight?' he asks, looking over my shoulder, loosening his hold.

I let him release me. 'Yes,' I say. 'And you're just in time. If you barbecue, I'll make the salad.'

'Sure,' Ian says, and he slips out of his suit coat, hangs it over a dining room chair, and takes off his tie. He runs his hand through his blond hair, but it immediately falls back into his eyes. He grabs the pan of chicken and a soda from the refrigerator, then goes outside. While I'm cutting up tomatoes and lettuce, I hear him whistling. It makes me smile. He's such an easy person to be with, so good-natured and almost always pleasant. Other than his occasional bouts of jealousy, there is no dark or mysterious side to him, no hidden psychological games he wants to play. The whistling stops and I hear him talking to the neighbors over the fence, laughing about something. Then his melody resumes, a cheerful tune I don't recognize.

After a while, he comes back into the kitchen, gets out the brown dishes, then sets the table while I finish the salad. He tells me what he was working on today, a story on an assemblyman who introduced a bill that would allow the people to decide if California should be split into three states. I listen to him, but his world seems so far removed from mine. I find it difficult to generate interest in state politics when my own problems seem so immediate – and I certainly can't discuss those problems with him. Instead, when he pauses, I tell him about my project on the violence in Sacramento, what I've done earlier this morning.

'I can't seem to get a handle on it,' I tell him. 'There was a man who stabbed his wife, beat her with a rock, then ran over her twice with her own car. And another couple, an older woman and a man, were shot, execution-style, during a bar robbery – for no reason; they gave him all the money in the cash register. And a three-year-old girl was killed when two shoplifters, fleeing from the Pay Less on Fruitridge Road, crashed into the car she was riding in. I just . . . I don't know, Ian. I never had this problem before. I have all the information I need, all the facts, but I can't put it together. I can't get a story out of it.'

I don't tell Ian about the desperation and futility that overwhelms me when I'm working on the story. As I sift through the facts – acts of violence against anonymous people – I think of Franny. I apply each statistic to her. Once, I could read these types of articles and remain unaffected; now I take each offense personally, and it's crippling my ability to write. I don't tell Ian about the powerlessness that overcomes me when I sit at my computer. I don't tell him that I see the world through blood-stained lenses. Instead, I put dressing on the salad and divide it into two bowls. I put the bowls on the table.

Ian, who listened quietly while I was speaking, starts to say something but changes his mind. His blue eyes look at me with concern. He goes outside to check on the chicken, and when he comes back in, he tells me it needs a few more minutes. As I uncork a bottle of wine, he puts his hands on my shoulders.

'Honey,' he says gently, and I'm immediately wary, 'maybe you shouldn't work on this story. You need to get away from these morbid thoughts, not concentrate on them. You're not keeping things in perspective. The crime rate in Sacramento hasn't changed much over the last couple of years, and it's not any worse than any other city its size – it just appears so because you're paying more attention to it since your sister was killed.'

I hand Ian the bottle of wine and two glasses. 'Put them on the table,' I say, and I walk out of the room. I know I should listen to him and do as he says, but I can't. I wish he was more forceful, more adamant, in his request. If he insisted I stop writing the article, if he demanded it, perhaps I would listen. Imperiousness is the only form of authority I seem to follow these days, and Ian – my sweet Ian – has not a single peremptory bone in his body.

During dinner, he is cautious. We keep the conversation light to avoid an argument. I tell him I saw Maisie last Saturday, and that makes him happy – for some time now he's been harping on me to go out more, to visit my old friends. We get through the chicken and salad and are eating thawed berries with whipped cream for dessert when Ian looks over at me and says, 'Oh – I forgot to tell you. I ran into Philip Ellis today.'

'Who?' I say, not recognizing the name.

'You know – the man at Ding How, the biologist, the one

you wrote about who was doing research on frogs. Female choice, or something like that. He was walking by the *Bee* just as I was leaving. We talked for a few minutes, then went out to lunch at Paragary's. He's an interesting man; we had an enjoyable time. Next week, we're going out to the golf course and hit a few balls around. I told him I hadn't played since college.'

I get a sinking feeling in the pit of my stomach. I eat the berries, but don't taste their sweetness. This afternoon, M. mentioned Paragary's, but not that he had lunch with Ian. And their chance meeting, I'm sure, was not fortuitous. I listen as Ian tells me of their lunch. I wonder, with a sense of foreboding, what M. is planning to do.

Later that evening, I undress in the bathroom. I put on a long-sleeved nightgown so Ian will not see my marks. The earlier tension has worked itself out with the passage of time, and once again we feel comfortable in the other's presence. I decide to show him Franny's stories, 'Water Rat' and 'Franny's Last Stand,' omitting that I got them from M. I tell Ian I found them in Franny's computer. Ian reads each story, silently, his eyes watery from withheld tears. Afterward he holds me, saying nothing, knowing words will not help. I feel very close to Ian, and I wonder why I hadn't shown him the first story earlier.

During the night, I lie in his arms, thinking of Franny, thinking of M. and the training room. When Ian holds me I feel as though I've been given a reprieve, several hours of respite to carry me through my next ordeal with M. I'm on safe, familiar ground with Ian. I know what to expect, and can relax in the surety of his saneness. M. takes everything out of me, drains me of all energy like a battery overused. I need Ian for a recharge. He gives me strength so I can take another dose of M.'s seductive madness, so I can travel on the dark side of his soul.

27

I'm wearing a flowered cotton skirt, a white sleeveless blouse, and sandals – all in deference to M. – not very sexy, but nothing he could criticize me for, either.

'Why are you doing this?' I ask him, referring to his newfound and, I suspect, beguiling friendship with Ian. We are having a late lunch at Baker's Square, my favorite coffee shop in town. No one is sitting at the tables next to us, although several waitresses, almost finished with the lunch shift, are rushing through their side work – refilling salt and pepper shakers, clearing and setting tables, wiping down the emerald-green booths – so they can go home. I'm just having coffee and soup, but M. ordered a stir-fried chicken and vegetable platter.

'For my amusement,' he replies, as I knew he would. It is one of his favorite responses. He changes the subject. 'I'm giving a recital at the Crocker gallery this Sunday. I'd like you to be there.'

I don't reply, still angry that he contacted Ian.

M. takes several bites of his lunch, then says, 'Oh, don't look so glum. I won't tell him about us – your secret is safe with me.'

'Nothing is safe with you,' I say. The soup is vegetable, and it tastes homemade. I know there is nothing I can do to prevent M. from seeing Ian, so I decide to salvage what I can. 'Do you plan to continue meeting him?' I ask. When he nods, I say, 'Then give me something in return.'

'What?' he asks.

'You said you stopped seeing Franny three weeks before she died – tell me about that.'

M. finishes chewing what is in his mouth, then he sets down his fork and looks me in the eye. I see his pulse in the vein at his temple.

'Why?' he says. 'Why should I tell you anything?'

I am taken aback by his answer. 'For your amusement,' I say. 'The same reason as always.'

M. picks up his fork and resumes eating. After a while, he says, 'Not today. The subject is boring me. Let's talk about you.'

Slowly, he chews his food, thinking. He wipes his mouth with a napkin. 'I want you to answer my original question, the one I asked the first time we jogged together.' He smiles and says, 'Don't look so bewildered – you know the question I'm talking about. I want to know why you're distant with men.'

I sit back in the booth. 'Now, that would really bore you,' I say.

'I'll chance it,' M. replies, finishing his plate of stir-fried. 'Tell me why you're so casual with the men in your life.'

I take a drink of water. For years, I didn't think there was anything unusual about my treatment of men. I was busy with college and work; I didn't have time to get involved. Only lately, within the last several years, have I begun to question my behavior. When I put the glass down, I say, 'There really is nothing much to report. It's rather banal, actually, the reason, and of no importance to anyone except me.' I take another drink of water. He waits quietly for me to continue.

Shrugging, I say, 'If you're looking for childhood trauma, you won't find it. Nothing horrible or scarring ever happened to me. It was nothing, really, just a familiar, boring story. I got pregnant in my last year of high school, and the guy dumped me. The experience made me cautious with men.' Playing with my soup spoon, I say, 'Period. End of story. It happens to thousands of women all the time. You deal with it and go on.'

M. sits back, looking at me skeptically. 'Except that isn't the end of the story. Expand.'

The soup is still hot, and I blow on it before I eat it. I open a package of saltines, nibble on one and crumble the other in my soup. 'This was eighteen years ago,' I say finally, 'attitudes were different then. It seemed like a bigger deal. The boy – the father of the baby – basically told me that it was my problem, not his, and not to count on him for anything. I expected that: he was a jerk. What I didn't expect was the reaction from my friends. I had a lot of friends in high school. We partied all the time. And each of them reacted the same way as the guy had: it was my problem.'

I set down my spoon and look out the window. Billowing white clouds chug across the sky. On the windowpane, a lone fly buzzes in semicircles, the glass an invisible barrier to its progress. I turn back to M., who is still waiting for me to continue.

'Well, it was my problem. I don't know what I expected from them. Moral support, maybe.' I play with the napkin on my lap, remembering. 'You know what my best friend said? Verbatim, "What will I tell my mother? When she finds out you're pregnant, she'll think I sleep around with boys, too."' I sigh. 'I don't know; I guess I wanted a little sympathy from my best friend. Of course, in retrospect, I understand I was expecting too much from them, from any of them. They were only seventeen; they had their own problems. But I couldn't see that at the time. I just knew that I was facing the biggest problem in my life, and no one was there to help me. I needed someone. I felt alone, abandoned.' I smile, trying to make light of something that had, at one time, affected me profoundly. 'I know that sounds melodramatic,' I say, 'but that's how I felt at the time. And I couldn't tell my parents; I didn't want to disappoint them. I was panicked. Finally, the reality of the situation dawned on me: I was all by myself in this. I would have to handle it. I couldn't count on anyone else for support.

'Anyway, I got an abortion. That took care of the problem. But afterward, after the abortion, all my friends returned. They wanted to resume where we left off. They wanted me to start partying with them, as if nothing had happened.' I watch the fly on the window, still attempting an escape, then flick it away with my fingers. 'But something did happen. I couldn't go back to the way things were before. I finished high school, but differently than I began it. One by one, I systematically eliminated all my friends. I don't think they were even aware of what I was doing. When they called, I said I was busy. After a while, they stopped calling. Which was the way I wanted it, or so I thought at the time.'

I shrug again, and add, 'Anyway, that started a pattern. When I met new people at college, new friends, I was cautious. Not just with men, but with women also. In my mind, I thought I couldn't count on anyone but myself. I didn't want to get close to people. They would just end up disappointing me, hurting me. I had boyfriends, but I kept them at a distance. I was busy at work, work I enjoyed, and I didn't want a guy to get in the way. Recently, I started to wonder if my life would have been different if I'd never got pregnant, if I would've formed closer relationships. By then, however, the pattern was too ingrained. But Ian is different. Franny's death made me vulnerable, and suddenly he was there. He made me understand I could trust him, and count on him.'

I glance out the window, then back at M. 'It was a long time ago,' I say, thinking that if things had gone differently I would've had a son or daughter who would now be eighteen, older than I was at the time of the abortion. It seems incomprehensible: a child, *my* child, a son or daughter, just about to start college. And maybe after that, a grandchild. I twist the napkin in my lap, then spread it out flat. I think about telling M. the rest of the story. But I don't.

His gaze is penetrating, seeing more than I want him to see. He says, 'You're leaving something out.'

'Yes,' I say, 'but I don't want to talk about it right now.'

M. leans forward and places his hand gently on mine – a touching gesture that surprises me. 'All right,' he says. 'But someday I want to hear the rest of the story.'

He leans back and says, 'There's something else I want you to tell me. I want the details of Franny's murder. The—'

'Shouldn't you be giving those to me?' I say coolly. I slide my hand out from under his.

I see a flicker of annoyance in M.'s dark eyes, a tightening of his precise jaw, which he quickly loosens. He continues, as if I hadn't interrupted.

'The newspapers left out the details, and the police, as you can imagine, were reluctant to share their information with me.'

A waitress stops at the table and refills my coffee cup. When she leaves, M. says, 'Give me this and I'll tell you of my last contact with your sister. It's important, Nora. I may be able to help you find Franny's killer.'

I push my soup bowl away. I don't know what game he is playing, or why the act of innocence. He knows very well the circumstances of her death.

We are quiet when the waitress clears our empty plates. She asks if we'd like pie for dessert, and when neither of us answers, she walks away, embarrassed by the silence.

M. says, 'You have nothing to lose by telling me. If I killed Franny, the information is worthless – I already know how she died. But if I didn't kill her, I may be able to help you. I need to know how she died.'

I think this over. 'And you'll tell me about your last contact with Franny? Right before she died?'

'Yes.'

I hesitate, not sure what to do. The fact that he wants this information makes me reluctant to give it. 'Okay,' I say, deciding not to give him very much. 'What they printed in the newspapers was true – they don't know how she died. The cause of death on the certificate reads "undetermined."'

'And the rest?' M. is leaning forward, listening raptly.

I shrug. 'I don't know the rest. When they found her, she was naked and bound. That's all the police told me.' I don't tell him that I know she was bound with duct tape. And that she had cut marks all over her chest and stomach. Not deep lacerations, but superficial marks. Designs. Patterns. Like a work of art that must've taken quite a while to complete. One of the marks was a circle slashed with a line – the universal symbol of no, the mathematical symbol of the empty set, as if the killer were negating her existence. I don't tell him that she'd been gagged so the neighbors wouldn't hear her screams. 'The autopsy didn't reveal anything,' I say. 'They don't know what killed her.'

He leans back in the booth. He is silent. So am I.

Finally, and I have difficulty keeping the sarcasm out of my voice, I say, 'So how does this information help you find Franny's killer?'

M. shakes his head. 'I don't know yet,' he says. 'But I have an idea.'

I say, 'Now it's your turn. I want to hear of your last contact with my sister.'

He flags down the waitress for more coffee. After she fills his cup, he begins talking. I listen intently; I will have to write this all down when I get home.

PART THREE
Franny

28

Franny administered heparin, an anticoagulant, to a fifty-nine-year-old dialysis patient, Mr Cole, then crossed over to the nurses' station to check his lab results. She wanted to keep a close eye on him. He had low blood pressure, extremely low, and last week his graft had clotted off before treatment. She had to send him to the hospital so a doctor could open it up, and they gave him dialysis there, keeping him overnight.

The clinic was fully staffed today, so she was working the floor: passing out medications, interpreting lab results, doing the rounds when the doctor showed up, making sure his orders were carried out. This week had gone fairly well, with no problems other than Mr Cole. All the patients came in three times a week, for two to four hours of dialysis, and they knew the routine. Most of them now were either reading, sleeping, or watching a program on the ceiling-mounted televisions above their recliners. The room seemed brighter today, the pastel walls more cheerful – probably because it was springtime. The blue sky had taken on a new glow, a wonderfully glossy sheen, as if it had been freshly burnished, and trees were sprouting budding leaves that unfurled, tenderly, in a delicate, fragile hue of green. Outside the shaded windows, Franny could see a blue scrub jay flying from the top of one tree to another. She'd always enjoyed spring, her favorite season, the time of renewal and fresh beginnings, but this year the joy of the season escaped her.

She went back to the employees' lounge, got a cup of coffee and two candy bars from the vending machine, then sat down. She had a headache and wasn't feeling well today. Tearing off the candy wrappers, she thought about last night. Michael had bound her again. She didn't understand why he did this. And she didn't understand how someone so gentle could be so rough. He'd held her in his arms, tenderly brushing the hair off her face, listening quietly as she begged him not to hurt her, and then, when she was through, he calmly explained that he would bind her whenever he desired, that he would punish her whenever he desired, and he expected her to acquiesce to his wishes. Kissing her softly, he took off her clothes and stroked her body, lovingly, while she had lain on the bed, crying into a pillow. She'd known then, for the first time really, that it would always be like this, that she couldn't change him and he'd always have a need – for reasons she didn't yet understand – to see her humbled and cowering before him. And she also knew that she was willing to accept his brutality as the price for his eventual love. Perhaps it was a test, his brutality, something she must endure; and deep in her mind, desultory fragments of long-ago thoughts, the flotsam and jetsam of an earlier time, drifted by: suffering to gain power, using pain to relieve pain, the Sioux logic of one thing just leading to another.

He made her kneel in front of the bed then, her chest and face pressed into the mattress, and tied each hand to a bedpost, cinching the bindings so tight she'd got burn marks on her wrists when she'd later tried to pull away. He whipped her with a cane, which was more painful than either the belt or the paddle or the riding crop. She had red welts on her buttocks, ugly marks, like scores on a piece of meat, long, thin, searing brands of his misdirected affection. Michael had apologized later. He said he didn't mean to leave such severe welts but had gotten carried away, and he promised he wouldn't punish her again, at least not physically, until the wounds had healed. But the rest, the nonphysical, was just as bad – worse, even. She couldn't bring herself to record in her diary what he did to her; she was too embarrassed. Every day she thought about breaking off with him, but she knew she never would. Especially now, since Mrs Deever had died. Now she needed him more than ever. Franny finished the two candy bars and got up to buy another.

Two weeks ago, Mrs Deever had come to the clinic looking horrible. She was lethargic, her blood pressure low, and her stomach distended. Franny called the doctor, who told her to send Mrs Deever to Kaiser Hospital. A week later, in the hospital, she died. Franny had expected this to happen – it didn't come as a surprise – but it upset her all the same. She became a nurse to save people, people like Billy, and it hurt whenever a patient died. But Mrs Deever – it was like losing a parent all over again. Those old feelings she'd tried to hide, the loneliness, the abandonment, the insecurity, they all resurfaced, reminding her of her fragile connections to the ones she loved. She was overcome with grief, a grief that extended far deeper than her sorrow for Mrs Deever. Her first impulse was to keep all her feelings to herself, as she had for so many years, but she knew she'd reached a breaking point. She was slipping away, and if she didn't ask for help now, she felt she'd slip away forever, beyond anyone's help. She'd called Nora, but Nora wasn't home and she never returned her call. And Michael, well, he was sympathetic about Mrs Deever, but he didn't really care. She could tell by the way he acted. He didn't know Mrs Deever, so she didn't blame him for not caring about her, but she thought he would've been more sensitive to her own feelings. His unresponsiveness, and Nora's, made her back off. She felt she was standing alone, slowly slipping off into a distant dimension locked inside her mind. Michael was supposed to have saved her from this.

She thought he would've loved her by now, but each week he seemed more and more remote. She did everything he asked of her, but she still couldn't seem to please him. In her heart, she knew their relationship was destructive, but she also knew she'd never leave him. Even if things didn't get any better between them, she would settle for what they had. She remembered what her life was like before she met Michael, and she could never go back to that. She'd been vulnerable, her limited experiences with men painful, and she'd built up a wall, impenetrable, to protect herself from getting hurt. She'd got used to the loneliness. But Michael had torn down that wall, and if he left her now she'd be even more vulnerable than before. She knew, now, what it was like to love, to belong to someone – and she couldn't go back to the way her life had been. Michael was all she had left. She would take his punishment, and the unspeakable things he did to her, the acts much worse than his harshest beatings. As long as he would love her, or try to love her, she would do whatever he asked.

She remembered when they first met. She remembered how she'd wanted to step out of her life and into his. Franny had wanted Michael to teach her the meaning of life; she'd wanted to be his student. She'd felt as though she were going on a journey, a quest, and Michael, her teacher, her mentor, would liberate her, and love her, and protect her – or so she'd thought. It was to be a wonderful journey. They were to have a wonderful life. She didn't think it would turn out like this. How could she possibly have known it would turn out like this?

29

When Franny arrived at Michael's house, she was wary. She'd got caught up in traffic in Sacramento and was ten minutes late. She didn't know anymore what would set him off. She tried her best not to displease him, but lately, no matter what she did, he could always find fault. She parked her black Cadillac next to the curb and locked the door. Walking around the car, she noticed it needed a coat of wax, and she should buff it with a chamois.

When Michael answered the door, she expected him to be annoyed, but instead he invited her in and led her into the living room. He sat on the couch next to her, leaving a polite distance between them. Neatly dressed, he was wearing a white loose-knit sweater, the sleeves pushed up to his elbows, and charcoal-gray slacks.

'I have something to tell you, Franny,' he began, a concerned tone in his voice, which made her instantly alert. 'This isn't working out.'

Nervously, Franny clasped her hands together in her lap. 'What isn't working out?' she asked, but she knew what he meant.

He gave her a slow, sad smile. 'You know what I'm talking about,' he said softly. He took her hand and held it for a minute, a look of compassion in his eyes. Franny couldn't remember the last time he had been so gentle – months ago, perhaps, after they'd first met.

'We're very different,' he said. 'It's time for you to move on to someone else. You don't belong with me.'

Franny got a panicky feeling inside her. 'But I do belong with you,' she said.

Michael just gazed at her, not saying a word. Undisguised pity covered his face, the face she'd grown to love – dark, handsome, square-jawed. But now the face was different, harsher, the wrinkles more prominent, the furrow in his forehead deeper, and his jaw was set tightly – it was as if his decision had hardened not only his feelings, but also his face. She wanted to lean over and kiss him, his eyes, his cheeks, his furrowing forehead, kiss him so much he'd soften his face and take back his words. But that wouldn't work with him. He'd push her away.

'I do belong with you,' she repeated, but Michael just stared at her, impatiently it seemed, his lips slightly pursing as if he'd swallowed something distasteful.

'I know we're different,' she added. 'But I've changed since we met. And I can change even more.' She knew her voice sounded desperate. She was desperate.

He reached up and brushed her cheek, lightly, with the back of his hand. 'Don't,' he said quietly. 'I won't change my mind and nothing you say will make any difference. Our time is over.'

'It doesn't have to be.'

'It's over for me, Franny.' He said it with such a cold finality that she knew nothing she said would make him change his mind.

She tried to keep the emotion out of her voice. 'Why?' she asked.

Michael shrugged. 'Why does anything happen? Sometimes it just does.'

Franny could feel the tears start. Her throat felt constricted and dry. She thought of everything she had done for him, and now he was telling her it had all been for nothing.

'Tell my why,' she said. 'I want the truth. Didn't you ever love me? Or even care for me?'

'Franny, let's not do this.'

'Tell me. I want the truth.'

He sighed and leaned back in the sofa. 'You don't want the truth, Franny. You want me to say that I made a big mistake, that I love you now and always have loved you. You want me to beg your forgiveness.'

She swiped at her face with the palms of her hands, wiping off the tears. 'No,' she said. 'Just tell me the truth. Tell me what I meant to you.'

'Don't—'

'Tell me!'

Michael was silent for a while, then he said, 'I'm fond of you, but that's all. We have nothing in common. The truth is – and I know you won't want to hear this, and it's not a very noble sentiment – but the truth is I brought you into my life for my own amusement.'

'You don't mean that.' Franny chewed on her lower lip. 'You don't mean that,' she repeated.

'You should be glad to get out of this, Franny. You hated every minute of it. You hated what I made you do. You should thank me for ending this.'

'Thank you?' she said, and she started to laugh, then choked on a sob. 'Thank you? How can you say that?'

'I can say it because it's the truth. I'm doing you a favor. You don't need someone like me in your life. I make you miserable, you know that. You're on edge every time you come over here.'

He leaned forward and took her hand again, stroked it gently. She barely noticed. She felt as though she were dreaming, her body numb, without sensation.

'It would just get worse, Franny. I promise you. I would make it even worse for you.'

She shook her head, trying to come out of her dream world. His words seemed so far away. 'You can't do this,' she said. 'I need you. I did things for you, whatever you asked. You can't . . . you can't just . . .'

Michael waited for her to finish, but when he saw she couldn't, he said, 'You don't need me, Franny. If there's one thing you don't need, it's me.'

★   ★   ★

Franny had been sitting in her apartment for seven days now. She called in sick at work, although she knew she'd have to go back eventually. In her bathrobe, she sat in the armchair by the phone, waiting for it to ring. In seven days, she'd only got four calls: two from work, one from the newspaper asking if her delivery was satisfactory, one from a woman selling magazine subscriptions. Her isolation was complete. Mrs Deever was gone, Michael was gone, Nora might as well be gone: Franny had phoned her again, several times, but she still hadn't returned her calls. If only she could talk to Nora, then maybe she could get through this. But Nora didn't want to talk, not to her. She had her own friends, her own life, and whenever they were together – at their monthly dinner date – Franny could feel Nora's restlessness, her desire to leave as soon as she arrived. Franny could not rely on Nora for help. She was alone again, and realized it would always be this way. She could feel herself slipping inward, and she allowed it to happen: she released herself, just as she had – so long ago – released Billy and let him slip away.

PART FOUR

Nora

30

Franny's diary ended there. She never made another entry, although she lived two weeks longer. She went back to work, and her coworkers later told the police that even though she acted distant, none of them had suspected anything was wrong; she had always been shy and a little remote. She just kept to herself even more, performing her duties routinely, avoiding any personal contact with the others. She was courteous to the patients, and efficient, but a detachment had set in, as if she was just going through the motions. She had, as she had feared, slipped into her own world.

Her last entries were perfunctory, a mere recording of the facts, but they substantiated M.'s retelling of the events. Even after he broke off with her, he said she called him, persistently, until she went back to work. He knew of her state of mind. What he provided – and what her last entries lacked – was the emotion, the insight, the feelings behind the facts. Tersely, Franny wrote: 'I called Nora again, but she wasn't home.' Reading that line, how could I have guessed she was reaching out for me, hoping to be saved? My guilt, my complicity in her death, multiplies. I failed her more than I ever imagined.

I did, finally, return her calls, and we made a tentative dinner date at the Radisson. I had meant to call Franny earlier, but this was an especially busy time for me at the newspaper. I was in the middle of two stories, I was traveling to Berkeley and Los Angeles to gather research information, and I was dating several men. At the last minute, I had to cancel the dinner date we'd scheduled – an interview came up with a scientist who was working in a new field of research, polymer photophysics, trying to use light to get polymers to do useful work – and Franny was murdered before I could see her again. She never had the chance to tell me about Mrs Deever, or about M., or about any of the things he made her do. I suppose I never gave her the opportunity. I did love her – she wasn't just a casual acquaintance to me as M. had once said – but he was right: I did treat her as if she was. I wonder now what went through her mind as her murderer bound her with duct tape and began his slow torture. Did she think of me? Did she die thinking no one really cared? If I could be given another chance, Franny, I would make sure you knew I cared.

Parallels. I see parallels everywhere. How could I have been so blind? When she had no one, Franny slipped inward, inside herself; and I, trusting no one, have been there all my adult life. We are alike, so very much alike. And I could have saved her. It was in my power. All I have left is retribution. I shall make sure M. pays for what he did. I shall finish my journey with him, follow the same path that Franny took, and bring it to an end.

Joe Harris and I are in the Paragon again, having another beer. This has become somewhat of a ritual for us. Tuesday nights, when he gets off work, we meet here for a drink before he goes home. I need this ritual more than he. I look to Joe for balance. My life has become limited, a small sphere that, like a dying star, is collapsing in on itself. I see only three people now: Joe, Ian, and M., my own private triad of conflicting morality. Joe and Ian represent everything I admire in men; M., everything I despise. I feel I'm in the middle of a power play, the age-old conflict, good versus evil, wherein the contenders are wrangling for my soul. Like a celestial body, I lean to the mass exerting the greatest pull. I gravitate to M., not because I want to, but because the attraction is strongest. When I was younger – in my teens and early twenties – I was always drawn to the bad boys. I had an affinity for the outlaw mentality, for the excessive, for the outre. I thought I had outgrown my attraction to bad boys and their dangerous games, but it seems I haven't.

Outside, the wind is blowing, a hot muffled breeze that played havoc with my hair as I walked into the bar. Joe loosens his shirt collar and leans back in the chair. The chair squeaks under his weight. He's tired today, and the fan of wrinkles around his eyes seems deeper. He takes a long drink from his glass, looks around the bar.

'He's getting worried,' I say. 'The other day he asked me about the details of Franny's murder. He wanted to know how much the police knew.'

Joe doesn't say anything.

'All I told him was what the newspapers had printed.' His round face is impassive.

'Well?' I say, waiting for him to comment. 'Doesn't that tell you something?'

He shrugs, takes a drink. Finally, he says, 'You're focusing on him so much, you're overlooking other possibilities.'

'What does that mean?' I ask, suddenly alert.

'He's still a suspect, but we're also looking at someone else.'

'Who? Tell me.'

Joe shakes his head. 'No. It's preliminary. And I've told you all along to stay out of this investigation.'

'I have a right to know.'

Again, he shakes his head. 'All you're doing is getting in the way, Nora. And getting in trouble.'

Abruptly, Joe reaches over and takes my hand, holds it firmly in his. I wonder what he's doing, but then he shoves up the sleeve of my blouse. I have ligature marks on the outside of my wrist where M.'s handcuff chafed against my skin. Joe closes his eyes and sighs, then releases my hand.

I push down my sleeve and start to take a sip of beer. Midway, I set the glass back on the table and look at the floor, my hand still around the glass. I'm too ashamed to speak.

'I thought you said you could take care of yourself,' he says.

I lift my shoulders in a small shrug, still staring at the floor. Nervously, without looking, I twist my beer glass in the circle of water on the table.

'Is that what you call taking care of yourself?'

I cannot raise my eyes to look at him. I am embarrassed that he knows I allow M. to bind me. My demise, over the last few weeks, has been complete. M. puts me in shackles, he tethers me to his bed, to the kitchen table, to whatever he chooses. He ties my hands and legs. I feel the crack of his whip on my ass. He brands me with it, as he did with Franny, but he makes no apologies. Afterward, he kisses me tenderly, he unties me and holds me in his arms, he tells me I am loved, then he tells me he will do it again.

And I always return. I need the information – and his brand of sex – which only he can give me.

Joe walks me out to my car. It's a typical July evening in Davis: hot, dry, a feeling of lassitude in the air. As I insert the key in the door, he puts his hand on my shoulder. I turn to face him.

'You need to see someone,' he says.

I look at him, not understanding.

'A therapist,' he adds. 'Someone who can help you.'

I start to deny that I need help, but it is so obvious that I'm in trouble, even to me, that the words won't come out of my mouth. Joe puts his hand on my shoulder again, and I lean my head to the side so I can feel his fingers on my cheek. I close my eyes. When I open them again, Joe is looking at me sadly. I step forward and cling to him, burying my head in his ample chest. He holds me, awkwardly at first, then pats my back and comforts me as if I were a little girl.

I break away and open the car door. 'I'm okay,' I say. 'Really, I am,' and I get in my car and leave.

On the way home, I stop at Taco Bell and pick up a Burrito Supreme for dinner. I rarely cook anymore, not even to throw something from the freezer into the microwave. I either skip meals, or stop at a fast-food restaurant. I am becoming, like Franny, a fast-food junkie. The only decent meals I eat are the ones M. cooks for me.

When I arrive home I get the mail out of the mailbox, set the garbage can on the curb for tomorrow's trash pickup, then go inside the house. I turn on the TV and eat my burrito on the couch in the living room, watching the six o'clock news. The burrito is lukewarm, the news uninteresting, a drab retelling of this afternoon's events. When I'm finished eating, I check my phone machine. There's only one message, from Ian, saying he's going out to dinner and will see me later this evening. I wonder what to do until he gets here. I've never had as much free time as I do now. I was always so busy working, and going out with my girlfriends, and dating different men, that I very rarely spent an evening by myself. From the other room, voices are coming from the television, making me feel less alone. This is what it must've been like for Franny, I think, night after night. No wonder she turned to Mrs Deever and M. I see the mail on the counter and go through it. Several magazines, lots of junk mail, which I instantly toss, the phone bill and MasterCard bill, a letter from a friend in Los Angeles, another letter with no return address, postmarked here in Davis.

I open the last envelope and pull out a photograph. Nothing else is inside. Holding up the photo, I see that it is of me, taken several days ago. I'm unlocking the door to my Honda in front of Nugget Market, a bag of groceries in one arm, my purse strap slung over my shoulder. I check the envelope again, but it is empty. Why would anyone take a picture of me? And why send it anonymously?

The phone rings, and I jump, startled, dropping the photograph to the floor. I pick up the phone.

'Hello,' I say. No one answers. I hear deep breathing. Sharply, I say, 'Don't you kids have anything better to do?' but no one replies. I listen. The breathing is deep and regular. Cradling the phone on my shoulder, I bend down and pick up the photo, looking at it again. What is its significance? The breathing continues. In the picture, I have an odd expression on my face as I'm unlocking the car. What was I thinking at the time? I have no idea, probably something about M.

M. The breathing is louder now, but still regular, rhythmic almost. Could it be M. on the line? Another scare tactic, like the photo?

The photo, the phone call. Something nags at me in the back of my mind, but I can't put it together. I look at the photo, at the picture of myself, while the person on the other end of the line breathes deeply into my ear. Suddenly, I'm gripped by a cold fear. I slam down the phone.

Two hours later, I hear Ian at the front door, his key jiggling in the lock. He comes inside the house and calls my name. Feeling uneasy, I don't respond. I think of Cheryl Mansfield.

He walks into the living room and sets down the gym bag and racquet he's carrying. Every Tuesday he plays racquetball at the athletic club, and he's still wearing black shorts and a white T-shirt. He looks tired, his face slack and his blond hair drooping in his eyes, like a little boy who has played hard all day and comes home exhausted. I smile, thinking how outlandish it was to even consider him capable of wrongdoing. He comes over and kisses me on the cheek, his lips soft and warm.

'Did he beat you again?' I ask.

Ian lets out a long groan and falls onto the couch. 'I don't know how he does it,' he says. 'The guy's good.'

He is referring to M., whom he knows as Philip Ellis. Ian, much to my chagrin, is getting closer to him. They play racquetball together once a week, when I'm with Joe at the Paragon. I think M. does this purposefully, to punish me for talking to Joe. When I told M. I was going to continue seeing Joe, whether he liked it or not, he called Ian that very night, in my presence, and invited him to play racquetball on Tuesday. They've been playing ever since.

'He asked me over to his house for dinner tonight. That's why I was late. You got my message, didn't you?'

A jolt of anxiety lodges in my throat. I pick up the remote control and turn off the TV. 'You went to his house for dinner?' I say.

Ian is leaning back on the couch, eyes closed, relaxed. Drowsily, he says, 'He lives just a few blocks down the street. Down Montgomery and off to the right, where the older homes are. Nice house.'

'I think you should stay away from him. He's kind of weird.' I hear the prickly edge to my voice.

Ian opens his eyes and gives me a strange look. 'No, he isn't. And you refuse to meet us anywhere, so how would you know what he's like? Weird or otherwise?'

I shrug. 'He just seems odd to me. Don't forget, I spent a lot of time interviewing him. He's dubious. You can't trust the man.'

Ian straightens up on the couch. 'That's not true, Nora. I don't know why you don't like him, but he's my friend. It's nice to have a male friend I can talk to.'

'You have lots of friends.'

'Yes, and with most of them we talk about work, or sports, or what's going on in the world, just about anything except our true feelings. Philip isn't afraid to talk about sensitive issues. I like having a man I can talk to. We have a lot in common.'

This makes me wary. Other than me, Ian and M. have nothing in common. 'What do you talk about?' I ask.

Ian hesitates. He scratches his leg, stalling for time. Finally he looks at me and says, 'Everything. Sports, work, of course. But other things, too. We talk about the problems we're having. We talk about women. We talk about you.'

'Me?' I say. Instantly, an alarm goes off. 'You talk about me?'

'Nora,' Ian begins, then he stops and shakes his head. He looks across the room at the bookshelves, thinking. He begins again, his voice troubled. 'Sometimes I feel like I'm going nuts, Nora. You don't talk to me. We're having problems, and you won't discuss them. I need to talk to someone. I talk to Philip.'

I'm sitting on the edge of the couch, my breathing shallow. I am incredulous. I am angry. 'You tell him about me? You tell him about the problems we have?' These sentences come out as accusations, not as questions. 'How could you? You didn't even ask my permission.'

Quietly, and with sarcasm, he says, 'I didn't realize I needed it.'

My voice rises. 'You violated a trust. What goes on between us is private.'

'Not much is going on between us, is there? That's part of the problem.'

Ian is referring to the fact that we rarely have sex anymore. All the passion I had for him, which at one time had been immense, is gone. After my sessions with M., I have nothing left to give Ian except guilt. And there is also the problem of concealment. It takes time for the welts on my buttocks to heal. When they are red and visible, I undress in the dark; I won't let Ian see or touch me. This confuses him, and my refusal to discuss it confuses him even more. He must think I'm becoming frigid, and if so he would be correct. My sexual frigidity, toward him, is almost total.

Ian says, 'You don't want to make love anymore. You don't respond to me at all.'

'And you told him that?' I feel my face burn with anger. 'Jesus! You told him that?'

He sighs. 'Who am I supposed to talk to, Nora?'

'No one!' I say, practically shouting. I get up and walk out of the room. I go into the kitchen and Ian follows.

'This is perfect,' he says, angry now himself. 'Just walk away. That's your answer lately to everything.'

'Leave me alone. Just go away and leave me alone.'

He stands in front of me, and I see his aggravation in the tight set of his jaw. 'No.'

'No? *No?!* In case you've forgotten, this is my house. And I don't want you in it.'

'Don't do this, Nora. Don't.' His words are a warning, cautioning me not to go too far. His face is flushed with anger.

I hesitate. We stare at each other. Ian takes a deep breath, calms himself down, then comes over and places his hands on my shoulders. 'Don't,' he says quietly. 'You don't mean that. You're angry.'

He is right: I am angry. And I don't want him to leave. I don't want it to end like this. Ian isn't perfect. At times he can be irrationally jealous, and I don't like him confiding in M., but in my heart I know he's a good man. I lean my forehead against his chest and feel the anger drain out of my body. I have come very close to losing him, I feel. I have come close to shattering something fragile of which I have desperate need. I am grateful for Ian's maturity, grateful he's giving me another chance.

'I'm sorry,' I say. He puts his arms around me and we are silent, holding each other.

After a while, he says, 'I love you, Nora. When I talk to Philip, it's only because I need someone to confide in. I can't go on like this much longer. Things have to get better between us. If you talked to me, if you told me what was going on, I wouldn't be spilling my guts out to Philip. Eventually, you'll have to talk to me. I won't let this go on.'

I nod. I realize, also, that it can't go on. Fairly soon, one way or another, it will have to be resolved.

Later that night, Ian and I lie next to each other in bed, covered only with a white cotton sheet, a painful silence between us. 'I'm going to get a drink of water,' he finally tells me. 'Are you thirsty?'

I say no, and he gets out of bed. He puts on his underwear and leaves the room. I hear him in the kitchen, the click of the light switch, the cabinet door opening, the water running.

Rolling over, I hug the sheet to my body. We tried to make love, but it didn't work, not very well; for me, not at all. When Ian kisses me, I feel nothing. No, that's not true. There is the guilt. But I don't feel desire for him anymore. When we got into bed this evening, Ian slid next to me and kissed me slowly, then ran his hand along the length of my body, the curve of my breasts, the flat terrain of my stomach, the warm flesh of my inner thighs. I lay there, allowing him to touch me, feeling as though I was tolerating him. I wanted to tell him to stop, but I'd put him off for three weeks already, using one excuse or another – I had a headache, I was on my period and had cramps, I was tired. It had been so long since I allowed him to touch me, I felt I couldn't say no. It was not a pleasant experience. I tried to generate some enthusiasm, but it just wasn't in me. I felt like the proverbial wife who is told she must occasionally give in to her husband's lusty demands. Ian knew I wasn't interested, and he tried his best to arouse me, he did everything that would normally awaken every hormone-driven impulse, but this time nothing inside me stirred. I lay there, not moving, my hands at my sides. Finally, he gave up trying; he just got on top of me and fucked me, angrily, forcing his way inside me, although I didn't resist. Not at all. I just lay there, letting him continue, wondering why his rough treatment did not excite me as did M.'s, wondering when he would be through. Even in anger, Ian did not have a commanding presence.

I get out of bed and slip on a long blue T-shirt, then go into the kitchen. Ian is sitting at the table, and he looks up when I come in.

'I'm sorry,' he says simply.

Sighing, I sit down across from him. 'What for? It was my fault.'

Looking down, he shakes his head. He pulls on his bottom lip, then reaches across the table and takes my hand, holds it in his. He doesn't say anything, just strokes the back of my hand. This is difficult for him. He is such a gentle person, I know he feels as though he raped me, but it wasn't like that at all. I hear a car round the corner and drive down the street.

Finally, he says, 'I'm sorry. I knew you didn't want to make love, but I did it anyway and I shouldn't have.' The words come out slowly, haltingly, and I can hear the ache in his voice. 'I just don't know what to do, Nora. I get so frustrated. You won't tell me what's going on. You won't let me help you.' He pauses, then says, 'I don't want that to happen again. I don't like seeing myself behave that way.' There is another pause. 'Maybe it would be better if we didn't see each other.'

I hear Ian speaking, I feel him touching my hand, yet he seems so far away. He is receding in my life. Not his physical presence, that is still here, but I no longer feel a connection to him. My guilt is pushing him away. I am consumed with remorse: for neglecting Franny, for responding sexually to M., for being unfaithful to Ian. My life is filled with guilt, and it's controlling every action I take. I have two men and two lives, both so different yet as bound together as a mirror image is to the object it beholds. M. is my fantasy life; Ian, reality. But the distinction is blurring. I look from the mirror to the object and have difficulty separating the two. M. is becoming my reality. Ian is still here, but in my thoughts he is fading. I don't want this to be so. I'm living a dual life, and the one I want to prevail, my life with Ian, is dissipating. M. is taking me over.

I kneel on the floor beside Ian. I rest my head on his knee. 'Don't leave me,' I say, my voice barely audible. He leans down so he can hear me.

'I need you,' I tell him. 'It won't always be like this. Give me time.'

But, to myself, I do not think time will be the answer. M.'s hold on me is tightening, his grasp becoming firmer with the passage of time. I can't seem to pull away. I go along with him as Franny had, waiting for the outcome.

We go back to bed, and both of us sleep fitfully. At three a.m. I wake up, sensing a change has taken place. In the darkness, I listen. It is the wind. I can hear it moaning, phantom-like, as it presses against the windows, straining to be let in. Tree branches brush against the side of the house, and a metal trash can tips over, making a scraping sound as the wind rolls it back and forth. I snuggle closer to Ian's sleeping body, put my arm across his chest, and hold on.

31

The days get longer, the summer hotter. I have received more photos in the mail, one of me as I was leaving the athletic club, my gym bag in hand, another as I entered the doctor's office for my yearly physical. I've shown Joe the photos. He checked them for fingerprints, but other than mine, there were none. He says they could be a prank, but still he warns me to stay away from M. It is an eerie feeling to know someone is watching and following me around town. M. denies all knowledge of the pictures. I've tried to ferret him out with his camera, but with no success. The August heat affects my vigilance, slowing me down.

Summer is my least favorite season; I think of it as something that has to be endured and waited out, like a friend's bad mood. I don't mind it so much when the temperature reaches the eighties, and even the nineties are endurable, but when it gets into the hundreds, I suffer. The air conditioner purls all day long, and when I go outside the heat seems to close in on me, smothering me. I should be inured to Sacramento and Davis summers, having experienced thirty-five of them, but I'm not. Driving down a lonely road, on the hottest days, I'll see heat waves floating off the pavement, and the black asphalt, in a melting mirage, will seethe and roll before me. Outside my car, the heat penetrates my skin as if I were being irradiated.

I'm having trouble sleeping, and in my dreams I'm overcome with a smothering, drowning feeling. In the mornings I lie in bed, half asleep, half awake. Part of me wants to surrender to the bliss of unconsciousness: *Go back to sleep,* something will urge me. *Don't get up. Why bother?* And I feel myself floating downward in a pool of water, weightless as a falling leaf. But then, just before I hit bottom, I get a nagging feeling – I have to get up, there are things to do, aren't there? – and the struggle will begin. I have to fight my way up to the surface, fight against that warm, cozy, wet feeling that prods me to relax, to acquiesce. *Just let go, why don't you?* I wake up, exhausted from the struggle. Sometimes I rise to the surface gulping air and my chest will ache, as if I'd been holding my breath under water for too long a time. When this happens, I go outside and take a deep breath of the fresh morning air, and walk around in my bathrobe, barefoot, on the cut grass that is wet with dew. Little shards of grass clippings will stick between my toes and prickle the bottoms of my feet. I'll walk around the lawn, and the panicky, smothering feeling will slowly drift off me, just waft away like steam out of a teapot, thinning and diffusing itself into nothingness. The sun wouldn't have risen yet, and everything – the trees, flowers, the grass, even – blends together in a faded early morning gray that I find soothing. I'll sit on the front porch and watch the sun come up. The yard brightens, filling in the shadows with the colors of day. The lawn has a precise edge to it, and the shrubs are well trimmed. Order prevails. There is no sense of smothering out here.

M. has got up early and is out jogging. I get up, then dress and drive home. Franny's black Cadillac is still at the curb, filthy with dust, the words *Wash me* written anonymously in the dirt clouding the back window. I pick up the *Bee* from the driveway, then go over to the mailbox for yesterday's mail. The box is located around the corner, in front of my neighbor's yard in the other half of the duplex.

Flipping through the mail quickly, I recognize at once the plain envelope, no return address, postmarked in Davis. I open the envelope while I'm walking across the lawn, wondering where the photographer will have captured me on film this time. In front of my house? At the drug store? But inside the envelope, there is not a photo but a sheet of white paper with the words 'You have two weeks to call off your search – if not, you'll be next' glued to it. I stop, stare at the words. A stab of anxiety tightens my chest. The letters, clipped out of a magazine, are pasted in the center of the paper very neatly. Nothing else is in the envelope. I go inside the house.

The phone is ringing, but I don't respond. My answering machine – always activated since I began receiving prank calls – clicks on, and I listen as a woman at the Sacramento Blood Center asks me if I'd like to donate blood. She leaves a phone number and hangs up.

You'll be next. The meaning is obvious. I call Joe Harris and read him the note.

'What now?' I ask him.

'We'll dust it for fingerprints, but I doubt if we'll find any. I'll add it to the MSR.'

An MSR is a miscellaneous service report – for those times when the police can't find a specific crime – just so they can have it down on record. Joe filed an MSR when I received my first photo.

'That's it?' I ask. 'You know it's from him.'

'No, I don't know that. It could be from someone else.'

The last time I met Joe at the Paragon, he told me they were investigating another person for Franny's murder. I am quiet for a while, then say, 'Who?'

Joe sighs. 'Don't ask me to give you that kind of information. You shouldn't be involved in this at all. If you're worried about the note, take the standard precautions. Vary your routine, don't walk in the dark, put an alarm system in your home, get a dog.'

I hang up.

32

I am in M.'s cool, air-conditioned house, alone. I walk from room to room, and despite my ambivalence toward the man, I feel a low-level charge pass through my limbs, an undercurrent of illicit excitement. His house: never before has an inanimate object held such erotic promise for me. I think of what we have done here, and what we will do, and my anticipation waxes. I grow wet thinking about it. Sexually, I want M. as I've wanted no other man.

Lust. It surges inside me, and it is neither pure nor simple, but born out of desperation and pain and sorrow and guilt – yes, there it is again, the guilt – and it makes me reach out to M., to willingly turn myself over to him. In the sadomasochistic ecstasy of pleasure and pain, in the shadow of M.'s dominion, my guilt is eased. And under his sway new hungers awaken in me. It is like opening your eyes one day and discovering a new range to your vision – you must see everything, you must experience each new optical sensation, your sense of sight becomes heightened, and your craving for more stimuli is insatiable. I am walking a fine line with my lust. I know of its danger, but I long for nothing else. I am willing to risk everything for this chastening passion – Ian, my self-respect, my life. I realize this sacrificial attitude is not an admirable trait. I know the folly of my actions, but I cannot help myself. I have passed from one world to another.

I go into the den and take off my shoes and lie on the sofa. I close my eyes and think of what we have done here, in this den, on this sofa. My arousal is great. I want to masturbate and think about doing so, but M. will be home soon and I don't want to take the edge off my desire. Outside, I hear crows squawking and a neighbor boy calling for his dog. *Duke! Duke! Come here, boy!*

A few minutes later, M. comes inside the house. My car is out front so he knows I am here, waiting. I hear him walk through the house, the kitchen, the living room, silently looking for me. He enters the den, sees me lying on the sofa, then sets some books and papers on his desk. He glances over at his piano and frowns. I am impinging on his territory, his precious time with the baby grand, his true mistress. He has warned me against this – and I know he will whip me later for my transgression. He says nothing, but in the way he looks me over, letting his gaze travel across my body, I know that, this time, I have won – I can see the arousal in his eyes. I wonder what he will do, how he will fuck me today. The choice is his; the choice is always his. Perhaps, that is why my excitement for him never wanes. There is always surprise, and the element of danger, and the knowledge that I must surrender to him, to his desires, to his preferences.

He is still by the desk, waiting, looking cool and crisp in a white linen suit and a charcoal dress shirt. My excitement turns to apprehension, and I know that this is what M. wants. I sit up, expectant, too wary to utter a word. I wonder if he will whip me today for my transgression, or save the punishment for a future occasion. Maybe today he will bind me in restraints.

He's leaning against the desk, not moving, and I realize now, fully, what his attraction is. When I first met him, I thought he was a nice-looking man, but I didn't agree with Franny's assessment. She wrote that there was a sensuality about him she didn't understand, powerful yet remote. I dismissed her opinion as jejune, the naive writings of a young woman too easily impressed. But gradually, over the months, I've seen my own response change, grow in intensity with each encounter. M.'s attraction is hypnotic, more psychological than physical, and therefore much more powerful, riveting, dangerous. Franny was afraid of his sensuality – and so am I – but I long for it all the same. Until I met M., I hadn't known the attraction of a dominant man, hadn't known the other side of sex, the darker side, where sexual warfare is as rough as it is sweet.

'Take off your clothes,' he says finally, and he folds his arms across his chest. 'I want to see you naked before me.'

No longer do I dress in jeans and T-shirts for M. I am wearing a short summer dress. It's eggshell white and loose-fitting, made of some crinkly fabric. I get up and take this off. Underneath, I have on a beige silk chemise and I slip this over my head. I unhook my bra and step out of my panties. Naked, with my hands at my sides, I wait for his next set of instructions, for the touch of his hand. I feel the cumbrous ache of desire.

'Now sit on the very edge of the sofa and lean back.'

I comply, with no thoughts of disobedience.

'Slide all the way down and bend your legs to your chest. Put your hands on your knees and spread them. Hold them open for me.'

I do as he asks and wait for him, knees apart. My breathing becomes heavy. My exposure, and submission, excites me.

Leisurely, he comes to me. 'Yes,' he says. 'This is how I like to see you.' He kneels down in front of me. He puts his hand between my legs, the skin of my groin and vulva freshly depilated, smooth and silky soft without pubic hair, and he begins stroking me gently, as if he were petting a small animal. I put my hands around his neck to draw his head down to mine, to kiss his lips, but he removes my hands and places them back on my knees. 'Keep them here,' he orders, and he pets me again.

I try very hard to contain myself, but I feel the heat in my loins and I need more than M. is giving me. 'Touch my breasts,' I say, wanting more stimulation. 'Kiss my lips.'

Grabbing a fistful of my hair, he yanks my head to the side. He looks at me, cocks an eyebrow, and says coldly, 'I don't want your mouth or ass or tits. And I don't want you to speak. I only want your cunt. Do you understand?'

I try to nod, but he has a firm grip on my hair, preventing any movement.

When he's satisfied I will obey, he releases my head. He puts his hands on the insides of my thighs and opens my legs even farther; he lowers his head and puts his mouth on my crotch. At the touch of his lips, I let escape a soft moan. This is what I need. I watch him as he feeds, sucking and licking me, rubbing his tongue on my clitoris, then I close my eyes to block out the visual sensations and enjoy the feel of him on a pure, tactile level. I come quickly and strongly, and as soon as I do he unzips his pants and whips out his penis, already hard, and shoves it inside me. He fucks me roughly, slamming into me, his eyes fiery with a rage I don't understand, and he says, 'Can Ian fuck you like this? Can he? *Can he?!*'

He demands I answer him, and, angrily, I say, 'Yes, he's good in bed. He's great – the best I've ever had.'

He stops fucking me momentarily and throws back his head and laughs. 'You're lying,' he says, then resumes his thrusting, pounding hard into me. 'Does he give it to you like this?' he hisses.

I hear the jealousy in his voice. My breathing is labored from his assault. 'No,' I tell him, panting. 'He's gentle.'

'And boring.' He grips my ass and pulls me up to him, impaling me on his cock. I feel it in the back of my vagina, filling me completely. He begins shoving into me faster. 'This is the way you like it, isn't it? I know you, Nora. You're just like me.'

'I'm not like you!'

'Oh, but you are, my dear, sweet pet. You are,' and with a final, brutal thrust he comes inside me. He lies on me for a few seconds, then gets up and walks away, zipping his pants. He goes over to an armchair and sits, crossing his legs.

I slide up on the couch, feeling slightly bruised and empty. He knows I hate it when he pulls out of me so quickly. I reach for my clothes.

'Not yet,' he says. 'Stay like that for a while.'

I curl up on the couch, tucking my legs beneath me. Disdainfully, M. looks me over, then says, 'How could you be attracted to someone like him? He's weak. He snivels. You should hear some of the things he tells me.'

'Then don't see him.'

He smiles slyly. 'But it brings me such pleasure.'

Over the past few weeks, he has developed an intense hatred of Ian. He's envious of him because I still want him in my life and won't let him go. He derides Ian in front of me all the time now. He'll tell me how he's befriending him – meeting him for lunch occasionally, playing racquetball once a week, even driving up to Lake Tahoe to spend the day gambling – then he'll ridicule him. His scorn for Ian is great, and I think it's because of Ian's innocence, his inherent goodness and inability to be corrupted. Ian believes they are close friends, almost best friends, and this worries me.

'Stay away from him,' I tell M., but I know he won't listen. He never has.

'Why? I won't give away our little secret. And I do enjoy all the information he gives me about you.'

'You're jealous.'

M. comes over to the sofa and sits next to me. The fabric of his white linen suit brushes against my skin. In his presence, I feel overwhelmed, small and helpless, childlike. He puts one arm around me, and with his other hand he plays with my breast. My nipple gets hard, and so does the one he isn't touching. He pinches the nipple gently between his fingers, and I feel the heat come again between my legs.

He says, 'Ian will never know you the way I do. He'll never possess you as I do.'

I lean nearer to M. I put my mouth up to his, and this time he kisses me. He pulls me closer to him, pulls my left leg over his lap, and continues to play with my breasts. He takes his mouth off me and says, 'I want to tell you something.'

'What?' I ask absently, not really paying attention. I don't want him to stop kissing me.

'Listen,' he says. 'I want to tell you something else about Franny,' and he presses my head to his chest. He plays with my nipples while he talks, squeezing them gently at first, then harder so there is a sweet, steady pain. As the pressure increases, my fingers tighten on his arm. But I am compliant; I want him again. He's aware of this, and he applies even more pressure to my nipple, and I cannot help but moan in pain . . . or is it pleasure? I know not which.

'Do you know much about dogs?' he asks. He doesn't wait for my reply. 'If the bitch isn't ready to be mounted, the male will urinate in the surrounding area to warn other dogs that this is his territory, and that the female is his bitch. I told Franny that I wanted to do the same to her, stake her out as my territory, my property. I took her into the bathroom and told her to take off her clothes and get in the bathtub.'

I start to lift my head to say something, but M. presses it to him.

'Shhh,' he says. 'Just listen.' He puts his hand back on my breast, rubs the nipple between his thumb and index finger. 'She did what I asked, of course; she always did what I asked. I gave her no choice. She took off her clothes and lay in the tub. I urinated on her. I pissed on her belly, on her cunt, on her breasts. I told her to close her eyes and I pissed on her face. Then I straddled her chest. I told her I had just a little urine left and to open her mouth. I told her she didn't have to swallow it, that she could just let it drip out, but that I was going to piss in her mouth.'

I shake my head. 'I know you're making this up. There are some things she wouldn't be able to do. That is one of them.'

M. gets up and goes to the desk; he stands there, leaning against it casually. He continues. 'Afterward, I turned on the water and let her rinse out her mouth. I filled up the tub with warm water and washed her so she was clean again, talking to her gently the entire time I lathered the soap on her body. I thanked her for letting me urinate on her. I always thanked her when she pleased me. I wanted her to feel that she had a choice, and that she was doing it of her own accord. I never had to force her to do anything; I very rarely even had to raise my voice with her. As I let the water out of the tub, I told her I wouldn't want to urinate on her very often, but occasionally I would need to. Then I dried her off and took her into the bedroom. I told her she could finish me off now. I placed my hands on the bureau and bent over and had her lick my anus – something else she hated to do – and then fuck me with her tongue as she reached through my legs and stroked my cock. When I was ready to come, I turned around and put it in her mouth.'

I am on the sofa, smiling uneasily. 'Nice story,' I say. 'But I don't believe it.'

He shrugs, then tells me to stand up. After I am standing, he tells me to come with him, that we are going to the bathroom. When I don't move, he calmly explains that I am his property, his bitch, and that he will possess me in a way Ian never will. He tells me that, yes, he is jealous, and he will make me pay for keeping Ian in my life. He demands that I go into the bathroom with him.

I stand still. My nerves are jangled, confused, raw. I begin to realize I don't know what I'm doing. I begin to realize I've entered a bog, a quagmire from which extrication will be difficult. I thought confronting M. would be a simple, straightforward matter. He's the bad guy, I'm the good guy; ergo, I'd prevail. But it's not turning out to be so clear-cut. I feel as if he's pulling me in – no, not pulling – sucking me in, his hold on me seemingly frail yet in actuality tenacious, like being mired in quicksand with only one place to go . . . down, all the way down.

M. waits. He senses my apprehension and says, 'Think of this as taking one more step that will bring you closer to understanding your sister.'

I am unable to move. I hear the boy again, distantly, plaintively. *Duke! Where are you, boy? Heeeeeere, Duke! Come here! Duuuuuuke!* With the sound of the boy's desolate cry comes the understanding that I will not wander from the path Franny traversed. I follow her footsteps closely, duplicating her experiences with each revelation that M. chooses to share.

Finally, I say, 'Not on my face. Or in my mouth.'

He comes over to me and says, 'All right.' He kisses me on my forehead and adds, 'For now,' and he takes my hand and leads me into the bathroom. I feel like a dog on a leash, blindly obedient. I had thought my demise with M. was complete, but I see now I have further to go, that there are lower levels to which I can sink.

As I step into the bathtub, I get a heady feeling that is not unlike the effects of too much alcohol – a slight disorientation; a disgust with myself for allowing this loss of control; and, in spite of the disgust, a numb, boozy warmth that makes everything okay. I slide down into the tub and wonder if this too will be something I'll enjoy.

Later that afternoon, we lie naked together on his bed. 'I got a note in the mail yesterday,' I say, 'warning me to stop looking for Franny's killer. I suppose you'll deny sending it, just as you did the photos.'

M. leans up on an elbow, frowning, looking me in the face. 'Tell me what it said. Exactly.'

After I tell him, he says, 'I think you should show the note and the pictures to your detective. It's probably nothing, just someone playing a sick joke, but it's beginning to worry me.'

He doesn't know that Joe Harris already took the note and pictures. He hasn't got the lab results back from the note yet.

M. is still frowning. His concern seems so genuine, but disbelief must register on my face because he adds, 'Nora, I didn't take those pictures, and I didn't send the note. I swear it.'

I say, 'Did you think they would intimidate me? That I would fall apart and stop searching for Franny's murderer?'

M. shakes his head. 'I want you to find out who killed Franny – if for no other reason than to know it wasn't me. But you're looking in the wrong direction. I had nothing to do with her death.'

He will never admit to sending them, so I drop the subject. I roll over onto my side, and M. curls up next to me.

In my ear, he whispers, 'You know of course you'll be punished. I've warned you not to interfere with my practice time.'

I feel a rush of anticipation, even though I know he won't punish me today. I say, 'I love listening to you play. You're very talented. Why are you teaching and not playing full-time? Why didn't you become . . .' I hesitate, not sure of the word.

'A virtuoso?' he says. 'Talent is not always rewarded.' He pauses, then adds, 'I'm very good, but not good enough. I never was and I never will be. I recognize my limitations, and I've learned to accept them. My desire far exceeds my talent; it's that simple.'

He says this matter-of-factly, without bitterness. He is quiet for a moment, then leans over and kisses my bare shoulder, a very gentle kiss. 'I want you to finish your story,' he says softly, changing the subject. 'You said there was more.'

He is speaking of the abortion. I lie on my back and look up at the ceiling. He places his hand on my stomach, moving his fingers gently on the surface of my skin, waiting patiently for me to find the words.

'I'll probably disappoint you,' I say. 'There isn't a lot to tell.' He strokes my skin lightly, not saying anything. His touch is not sexual, but meant to soothe.

When I don't speak, he says, 'This isn't about disappointing or pleasing me. I care for you. I want to know more about you.'

I sigh, wondering how much to tell him, wondering how much to hold back. 'After the abortion, I was celibate for five years – except nobody knew it. I talked about my boyfriends, but they were phantoms, created so I wouldn't have to answer any questions. When I was twenty-three, I decided that my celibacy wasn't normal. So, just like that, I slept with someone. But he didn't mean anything to me at all. Then I started sleeping with a lot of men, and none of them mattered to me, either. It was only sex, nothing more. And it suited my lifestyle. I had just begun working at the Bee, and I was incredibly busy; casual affairs were all I could handle.'

I stop talking. After a while, I say, 'It's funny how one little event can change the course of everything. You wouldn't think the reverberations would be so far-reaching. A decision you made as a teenager shouldn't be allowed to carry so much influence; it shouldn't be allowed to change your life forever. Choices should be weighted, like questions on an exam. You're eighteen years old and made a poor choice? – okay, that decision will only affect you for four years. But twenty-eight? – well, you're ten years older and should've known better; the same decision will cost you ten years. Forty-eight? – now you blew it; the rest of your life is changed.' I think of Franny and how the course of her life had been altered the day Billy died. Again, I see parallels in our lives. She felt responsible for a death she was powerless to prevent; I, for one I caused; and each of us was changed by the event forever.

I sigh, then say, 'Getting the abortion solved my problem. I didn't think about it much at the time, not about the abortion itself. I was too panicked; I didn't allow myself to think about it. But after several years went by, I couldn't keep it out of my mind. It started coming back to me, like a bad meal I wish I'd never eaten.'

The air conditioner clicks on and fills the house with a hollow, susurrous murmur. The room is suddenly cool, and I pull a blanket over my body. M. reaches under the cover to touch me.

'This wasn't an embryo,' I say. 'I was three and a half months pregnant, almost four. It was a fetus the size of my hand, about six inches long, with arms and legs and fingernails; eyes, nose, mouth; sex organs; a brain, a heart, a nervous system. It was a human being, a living being, a baby, and I, with little thought, took its life.'

I shake my head slowly, thinking. 'I'm pro-choice,' I say. 'I believe women have the right to control their bodies. Abortion should be legal; it should be a woman's choice. But still . . . taking a life . . . it changed me forever; it diminished me. Not immediately, it took years for the consequences to manifest, but it caught up with me. One day I realized my act was irrevocable, eternal. It marred my soul.'

I let out a small, nervous laugh. 'I'm not a religious person,' I say. 'But if I was, I guess this would keep me out of heaven. One act, one moment of indiscretion, and I'm on God's black-list.'

M. does not laugh at my poor attempt at levity. He moves closer and holds me tighter. I want to finish the story – there's only one part left, possibly the most important part – but I can't. As if he could sense my reluctance, he says, 'There's more?'

'Yes.'

'Tell me the rest.'

'No.' He does not press me to continue. He kisses my neck, lightly, then lays his head on my chest.

Very softly, he says, 'You meant nothing to me when we first met, and your adamant belief that I killed Franny amused me. I even enjoyed the role you put me in – is he or isn't he the killer? It was a game for me, making you believe I killed Franny. But all that has changed. I've come to care for you, deeply. I didn't realize in the beginning that I would fall in love with you.'

I am silent as I listen to his declaration of love. His words, and the obvious meaning in his voice, the clear tenderness, take me by surprise. I don't know what to say. My own feelings are not so clear. We lie together quietly, limbs linked, skin pressing together as if in union.

After a while, M. says, 'I'm going to tell you something important.'

I hear the gravity in his tone and pay attention. 'About Franny?' I ask.

'Yes.'

'What?' I ask, feeling the tempo of my heartbeat increase.

M. breaks away from me. Propping himself up on one elbow, he looks down at me, his other hand still under the blanket, playing his fingers lightly on my midriff.

'Ian knew Franny. He fucked her.'

'What?' I say, sitting up.

He doesn't answer. He knows I heard each word he said.

'You're lying.'

'He was so tormented by guilt that he confessed to his new best friend – "Philip Ellis."'

'I don't believe you.'

'You don't have to. It's in her diary. You've read it; she met him at one of your office parties. She didn't mention Ian by name in the diary – only that he was a reporter for the Bee and that she slept with him the night they met. He regretted it the following morning, took her to the Food for Thought Café, and told her their encounter was a mistake.'

'You're lying,' I say. 'Why should I believe you? You read her diary, and you knew about the man from the *Bee*. It could've been anyone – you're just trying to implicate Ian. He wasn't the one she slept with.'

'I didn't make the connection at first, but then Ian confessed to me.'

'I don't believe you. He would've told me.'

M. pauses, then says, 'Not if he killed her. Think about it – you barely knew him, but he shows up miraculously as soon as Franny is murdered. He works his way into your life.'

I get off the bed and go into the den to get my clothes. I'm angry and incredulous.

M. follows me into the room, and, still naked, he leans against the doorjamb, watching me dress. I put on my underwear, slip my dress over my head, and button it, then buckle my shoes.

'Open your eyes, Nora. You're so convinced I killed Franny, you can't see the truth – or don't want to see it. Ask Ian where he was the day Franny died.'

'I will,' I say, and I walk out of the room, out of his house, slamming the door behind me. Outside, blackbirds poke in the glistening grass, still damp from M.'s sprinklers. It's hot and the sky is gleaming, as if it has just been polished to a high shine. Chrome trimming, from a car parked along the street, throws off the brilliant sunshine in shards of bright light, piercing and harsh, that make me squint and turn away. I rummage in my purse for sunglasses.

Right now, I'm about as angry as I've ever been. I should've known M. would try to deflect suspicion from himself, but to say Ian and Franny were fucking – well, it's preposterous. Exercise has always helped me burn away excess stress or anger, so I decide to go to the athletic club. I stop by my house to pick up a gym bag, and as I'm backing my car out of the driveway, I glance – as I always do – at Franny's Cadiliac. I note once again that it needs to be washed. I take the Mace-Covell Boulevard out to the club, a long road on the edge of the city that bypasses the downtown area. A brisk wind flutters the tall grasses on the side of the road.

At the club, the pool is crowded and I have to share lanes with another person. Standing at the shallow end of the pool, wearing a black Speedo, a bathing cap, and goggles around my neck, I watch the swimmers for a few minutes so I can determine who is the fastest. If I have to share a lane, I want to make sure it's with someone who won't slow me down. Two women are using kickboards, splashing water everywhere as they leisurely travel down their lane, talking back and forth. In three other lanes, all the swimmers are going much too slow, and there are too many people in the far lane.

I walk over to the second lane on the right where a young man in his early twenties, with dark hair and a sunburned back, is swimming laps. When he's near the far end of the pool, I put on my goggles. When he starts back, I dive in. I'm under the water only for seconds, and it's like diving into a different, calmer world, an inner fluid space, womblike, without gravity or life's problems to pull me down. But when I break the surface, the tranquillity breaks also. M. resurfaces in my mind. Arm over arm, my strokes propel me forward, and the other swimmer and I pass in the middle of the pool. I increase my speed, and on the next lap I gain an arm's length distance on my lane partner. But in the lap after that we are even again, passing in the middle. We remain even for the next ten laps. Whenever I increase my speed, so does he. I imagine that he is M., my nemesis, and that we're in a race where only one survivor will cross the finishing line. With this thought, I push myself, going faster, I'm sure, than I ever have before, but the young man matches my speed. I think of M.'s words – *Ian fucked Franny. Ask him where he was the day she died* – and my anger returns, propelling me forward. On the fifteenth lap I am determined to gain distance on him, but on the sixteenth I realize I am alone in this lane. The young man is no longer here. I stop a moment, and through the blur of my goggles I see him walking toward the building, then inside the door. I continue with my laps, feeling cheated of a win. Swimming slower now, I concentrate on my form. Each stroke I take is strong and sure and even. I've found a steady pace, and by the twentieth lap my anger mutates into a black, nagging doubt. What if M. is telling the truth?

33

When I get home, I see Ian's wood carving on the countertop in the kitchen: the basswood egret, its wings spread, barely three inches tall, and with such intricate details etched in the wood, such precision, that you know it's the work of a skilled craftsman. I stand there for minutes, thinking of the intricate patterns etched in Franny's torso, also the work of an artist.

Ian. I have the key to his condo and consider driving to Sacramento to search it. I don't know what I hope to find – photos of Franny, perhaps, or something that belonged to her, jewelry, clothing, a hair clip, anything that would indicate he knew her. But just then I hear the front door open and close. Ian calls out my name, and a second later he enters the kitchen, invading the room with his distinctive, headlong gait, shoulders slightly rounded, head bent in thought, still wearing his clothes from work – gray slacks, a wrinkled white shirt. His presence, the blond huskiness of him, looms. He looks up.

'Nora!' he says, his face brightening into a smile. The full lips part to reveal a set of perfectly formed teeth, straight and white. 'I didn't think you were home. Why didn't you answer?' He's carrying a pile of books in one hand, a briefcase in the other. He advances, sets everything on the table, then comes over to give me a kiss. His lips settle on mine, a brief moment of contact. I feel rigid inside, as if all the warmth I felt for this man had solidified into something brittle and hard, and I must force myself not to pull away from him.

He gives me a puzzled look. 'What's the matter?' he asks, and then I do pull away. I walk around the table, putting it between us.

'You knew Franny,' I accuse him. I watch closely. An expression I'm unable to discern crosses his face. Is it fear, sadness, guilt? I can't tell. But he did know Franny; his expression reveals that. I wait for him to lie. Sighing, he places both hands on the back of a chair, tilts his head down, stares at nothing in particular, then finally looks me in the eye.

Quietly, he says, 'I wanted to tell you. I wasn't planning to keep it a secret. When she died, you were so upset – it didn't seem the right time for a confession. And in the weeks afterward, you seemed so fragile, as if the slightest discomfort would bruise you. I couldn't tell you then, not until you were stronger. Then the weeks turned into months, and the moment for telling you passed. I never meant to hide it from you. I was planning to tell you all along, but one day I woke up and realized it was too late. I don't know how that happened. One week I was waiting for the proper moment; the next week the moment had elapsed. So I began to rationalize my deception: no one knew of Franny and me; it wouldn't do any good to tell you; it would just make things worse. My encounter with Franny began to seem unreal, that maybe I never slept with her at all. Only I knew I did. And I was ashamed of the way I treated her. I didn't know how to tell you.'

I'm still standing behind the table, unable to speak. Ian knew Franny. I heard his words, and I saw the expression on his face, but I still expected him to deny it. I was hoping for a denial. I don't want to believe that M. was telling me the truth. But he was. He was.

'How did you find out?' he asks me.

I laugh, a low, bitter laugh. Ian knows M. only as Philip Ellis, and he still has no idea that I'm fucking him. 'The diary,' I say. 'It's in her diary. She mentioned she met someone at one of the office parties I took her to. Only she didn't say who. All she said was that he was a reporter at the *Bee*. I remember the first time I read her diary, wondering who at the office slept with her. The pudgy man who works part-time in Sports? One of the new guys in Metro? Maybe he was feeding her a line and wasn't even a reporter at all; maybe he worked in Accounting or Subscriptions. I never would've suspected you. Not in a million years.' I shrug. Coldly, I add, 'Lucky guess. Perhaps if I hadn't trusted you so completely, I would've put it together sooner.'

Ian winces at my words, but he doesn't avert his eyes. 'It was only one time, Nora. I swear. I was drinking, and I know that's no excuse, but it was a mistake. It happened only one time. Please believe me.'

I see the sorrow in his eyes, his eyes so painfully blue, and I want to believe him, but I'm not sure that I can. 'Go on,' I say.

He looks down at his hands. He's holding one hand in the other, like a nervous child. Dropping them to his sides, he says, 'She called me five or six times after the party, after I slept with her. She was . . . persistent. I think she felt that if I went out with her, I'd grow to like her. I should have told her the truth right from the beginning – that I wasn't romantically interested in her. But I didn't. I knew how difficult it was for her to make those calls. I knew it was an act of desperation, and telling her the truth – that I just wasn't interested – seemed too cruel. So I let her call, and when she did I'd make excuses why I couldn't see her. It was uncomfortable for both of us, and finally I did give her the maybe-we-could-just-be-friends routine. She stopped calling immediately. I was relieved, of course, but also a touch remorseful. I'd handled the situation badly – from the moment we first met. And that was the last I heard of her, until I read of her death in the paper. Then I felt even worse. I knew I should've been kinder to her and I hadn't. I guess I thought I could make up for it by helping you after she died. Trying to make amends, I suppose. I felt drawn to you. I wanted to be by your side, be of assistance in any way I could. Then' – he spreads his arms in a bewildered, hopeless gesture – 'then I fell in love with you.'

I am silent for a while. Franny pursued Ian. She called him half a dozen times to get his attention. In the diary – from her humiliation, no doubt – she admitted to calling him only once. I can't imagine what it would be like to chase after a man, to call him repeatedly when he clearly wasn't interested. I hurt for her now. I feel her rejection and wish I had been there to console her. Bitterly, I say, 'Let me see if I've got this straight. You didn't tell me you fucked Franny because the magical moment for revealing it had passed? And then you fell in love with me, and of course couldn't tell me once that had happened.'

'I was ashamed, Nora. I wasn't proud of the fact that I slept with her and couldn't return her affections.'

The pain in Ian's face quiets me. I want to believe everything he just told me, but I'm not sure anymore. Not about him, not about M.

'What were you doing on the day she was murdered?' I finally ask.

Cocking his head slightly, Ian says nothing at first, then his face seems to crumple inward when it dawns on him what I am thinking. 'How can you ask me that?' he says, clearly offended. 'You think I had something to do with her death?'

I shrug. When he sees I'm waiting for an answer, he says, 'I saw her only one time, six months before she died. Why would I want to kill her? How can you even suggest it?'

How could I? It does sound ridiculous. He had no motivation, and it had been six months since he'd seen her. I rake my hand through my hair, trying to get a grip on reality. Suspecting Ian of murder is farfetched, bordering on insanity. M. is doing this, I think, planting seeds of doubt to increase my confusion.

Ian comes closer and says, 'You know me, Nora. You *know* me. I couldn't have killed her.'

I realize this is true. In my heart, I know Ian is not a killer. But the seeds are still there, and I have my doubts. Or maybe it's confusion. I don't know what to think anymore.

'You should've told me you knew Franny,' I say. 'What am I supposed to think when you keep something like that from me?'

He picks up my hand and holds it in his. Quietly, he says, 'You're supposed to think that I'm human, that I made a mistake, not that I'm a killer.'

There doesn't seem to be anything else to say. I wish I could put my arms around him, hold him close and let him know that I made an error of judgment, that I know he is incapable of murder. But my body doesn't obey. I don't move forward to embrace him. I don't offer any words of assurance. My hand is limp in his, and I finally pull it away.

'Ian, I want to be alone tonight.'

He starts to protest, then changes his mind. 'Call me when you want to see me again,' he says, resigned, and he kisses me lightly on the cheek, just presses his lips softly to my flesh, and leaves. I go to bed, wondering when I'll see him again.

34

Ann Marie, my neighbor across the street, is in her front yard gardening again. She's a tiny slip of a woman, wearing a floppy straw hat, a faded sundress, and garden gloves so big and cumbersome that they make her appear, by comparison, even tinier and more delicate. I walk over and we chat for a few minutes. It seems as if she's always working in the yard, but I know this is an illusion. She's a math teacher in Sacramento and is gone most of the day. The fact that I always catch her while she's gardening is coincidental, and says more about my isolation than her diligence with yardwork. If I spent more time outside, I would see her in other capacities. As it is, I rarely have contact with any of my neighbors. I've been living here a year now, but I feel no connection to the neighborhood. Ann Marie and I attend the same Jazzercise class at the Davis Athletic Club, and that is how I know her.

She is on her hands and knees, poking at the earth with a trowel.

'What are you planting?' I ask.

'Shasta daisies,' she says, and she uproots a clump of flowers from the ground. 'Actually, I'm not planting them. I'm dividing the crowded daisies so there'll be more flowers next summer – giving them a little growing room.' Her tan legs stick out from under her dress. I watch as she thins out a row of daisies. When she's through, she rests back on her heels and surveys the work. With the back of her arm, she wipes off a trickle of sweat inching down her forehead. She stands and begins a slow tour of the lawn, checking for what, I'm not sure. I follow.

'So what's new?' I ask, and by this she knows I'm referring to our neighbors.

She turns on the sprinklers, and there is a low gurgling sound before the water sprouts up and begins its steady spray. 'Well,' she says, and as she bends down to adjust one of the sprinkler heads, she tells me what is happening in the neighborhood. Most everything I know about my neighbors I've learned from her.

'Several houses down,' she says, 'the people are tearing up their front yard and redoing it.'

I look down the street and see a big mound of dirt. It surprises me I hadn't noticed it before. I envy my neighbors for their normal lives, and would like to add a little normalcy to mine. None of them worries about stalkers and killers, nervously watching their backs; none of them wonders what will happen when two weeks are up.

Just then my landlord, Victor Puzo, dressed in beige shorts and a polo shirt, pedals up to my house on his bicycle. He's a rangy man in his early seventies, dark-skinned and soft-spoken, and he stops by occasionally to make sure the gardener is taking care of the yard. I leave Ann Marie to her sprinklers and go back across the street to say hello to Victor. It comes to my mind, in the middle of the street, that I'm talking to more of my neighbors today than I usually do in an entire month. I am beginning to think of myself as one of those eccentric old women who is talked about behind her back, the neighborhood character. I am the Phantom of the 'Hood. The Invisible Woman.

Victor is studying one of the trees in the front yard. His hands are on his hips and his head is tilted to one side, a thoughtful, pensive expression across his face.

'Hello, Victor,' I say, and he looks over and gives me a friendly smile.

'The city wrote me a letter,' he says. 'They're going to replace both trees in the front yard.'

'Why?' I ask, and he shades the sun from his eyes and shoots me a funny look.

'Because they're dying.'

I look up at the trees, and sure enough, they look unhealthy. It's the end of August now, and they're shedding their leaves. I'm fairly certain this is supposed to happen only in autumn. I remember last year when their dense foliage canopied the front yard, offering a lot of shade. Now the leaves are sparse and the branches stingy-looking. When did this begin, I am thinking. Then I realize I don't really care.

'They've got shallow roots,' he says. 'They don't live long.'

'Is that typical?' I ask, feeling indifferent.

'For this kind of tree, yes.' And he tells me about the tree, that they normally only live ten to fifteen years, then he points out the other trees in the neighborhood, which ones are long-lasting, which ones are shade trees.

'See that,' he says, pointing up the street. 'That tree gives good shade.'

I think of the Madonna song with the sexual play on words for fellatio – she gives good face. The tree gives good shade. I start to laugh, and then stifle it when Victor gives me another odd glance.

'How are Richard and Abby?' I ask out of politeness. Richard is his son, also in the construction business, and he and his wife live several houses down the street from me. He and Victor built the duplex I'm living in, and Richard lived here himself until he built the house down the street.

'Fine,' he says, still staring at the leafless tree. 'Just fine. The baby's due in January.'

'The baby?' I say, and he tells me that Abby is pregnant.

'I didn't know that,' I say. 'She's pregnant? That's unbelievable.' For some reason, Abby's pregnancy amazes me. It seems as if I spoke to her a few weeks ago – and she certainly wasn't pregnant then, her stomach as flat as cardboard – but five or six or seven months must have gone by.

'Well,' I say, still amazed. Then I feel that pang again, that little sad nudge in my heart when someone else has a baby. 'That's wonderful. Do they want a boy or girl?'

'Boy. It'll be a boy. She had the amniocentesis test, and the doctor says she's going to have a boy.'

A boy, I think. That's all the world needs, another boy. South Davis is becoming inundated with boys. The man and woman who live in the other half of my duplex just had a boy last month (their second), and two weeks ago the woman across the street in the blue Tudor also had a boy (her fourth). I hadn't known either of them was even pregnant until after the babies were born, when Ann Marie informed me. She must not know that Richard and Abby are going to have a baby. A boy baby. Where are all the little girls? I'm thinking. And why would anyone want four boys? But I know the answer to that.

I've stopped driving into Sacramento unless it's absolutely necessary. The truth is, I've become doddery from my preoccupation with death and my two-week warning. I live in a small world, confined within the city limits of Davis, and as I drive over the Yolo Causeway I feel I am leaving my sanctuary and entering a foreign state. A sanctuary! I laugh. My life in Davis, my life with M., is anything but protective. M. does not offer me safe shelter. Still, Sacramento seems foreign to me. It represents the life I abandoned, and as I cross the Tower Bridge I feel like the native daughter who returns after a long absence and finds she is a stranger in her own land, uncomfortable and a little anxious. This city, and my former way of life, does not belong to me anymore.

Ian has a condominium in the downtown area, and I drive up the Capitol Mall boulevard and turn right at the golden-domed state capitol. Ian lives only a few blocks south on a shaded, elm-lined street. I park my car at the curb and walk over to his condo, a brown stuccoed building with ivy creeping over the walls. The sidewalk is cracked with age, and for some reason this makes me feel less like a stranger.

I ring Ian's doorbell and wait for him to answer. He gave me a key, but I've never used it. It was a symbolic gesture on his part – we rarely met at his house – but I know he was hoping it would evolve into a further intertwining of our lives. It hasn't turned out the way he planned. Since the day I discovered Ian fucked Franny – and even before then, since the day I first slept with M. – our lives began to separate. We see each other less and less often. There was no big argument, no climactic moment of separation, just a gradual fading away. Three days of absence became four, four days became five, and so on. Something broke apart and now there is an awkwardness between us, a breach that we cannot mend. The key remains a symbol, but of failure now rather than hope. It would seem almost presumptuous of me to use it in this stage of our relationship.

I peer inside the glass panels on the side of the door. I see Ian walking toward me, his gaze to the floor, and he looks distracted. He's wearing his reading glasses, his blond hair is disheveled, and he's clutching a sheaf of jumbled papers. He opens the door and sees me. A flash of surprise and annoyance crosses his face. Instantly, he covers it with a smile. But it is too late. I already saw his displeasure at seeing me.

'Nora,' he says, and he nervously rattles the sheaf of papers against the side of his leg.

'Hi. I was just in the neighborhood.'

'In the neighborhood,' he repeats, and he smiles a little because we both know this is a lie.

He still hasn't invited me in. 'I needed to see you,' I say.

He steps back from the door and lets me enter. I walk through the hallway and back into the living room. His condo is light and airy, with ceiling fans and chalky white walls that he still hasn't decorated. He has a single picture hanging on one wall, a Georgia O'Keeffe print of a cow's skull. As I'm sitting down on the couch, a robust woman in her fifties, silver-haired and stout, walks into the living room carrying a green plastic bucket filled with cleaning supplies – a can of Ajax, sponges, yellow rubber gloves, a toilet brush. I assume this is Pat, the cleaning woman he's previously mentioned.

'I'm finished, Ian,' she says, her voice loud and cheerful, then when she sees me, adds, 'Oh, I'm sorry. I didn't realize you had company.'

Ian introduces me as his girlfriend. We exchange a few pleasantries, then she picks up a check off the table, gathers her cleaning supplies, and leaves, telling Ian she'll be back next week. With her departure comes an awkward silence.

'What are you working on?' I ask him, nodding at the papers in his hand.

'These?' he says, and he holds them up absently. 'Oh, nothing, really. I'm working at home today. They're just . . .' and his voice trails off. He tosses the papers on the coffee table – already cluttered with knives and three small blocks of wood – and sits down across from me. Pointedly, he says, 'Why are you here?'

Ian's face is so troubled I want to reach over and smooth his brow. But I don't. The interstices in our frail relationship will not allow the familiarity inherent in such a gesture: it would be too bold.

I concentrate on his question. Why *am* I here? 'I'm not sure,' I say, sighing. 'Not exactly.' I pause, collecting my thoughts, then start over. 'We don't see each other very often. Hardly at all anymore. I know most of it's my fault.' I shrug and give him a wan smile. 'I guess all of it's my fault. I don't blame you for not wanting to see me. I know I've been a real bitch lately.' I take a deep breath and say, 'But I still love you.'

When Ian doesn't respond, I look down at my lap. Quietly, I say, 'I'll work this out somehow. I just need you to be there for me. I need you to wait for me.' Even I can hear the pathetic pleading in my voice; I look over at Ian. 'I'll straighten this mess out. I will.'

He sat mutely while I said this, but now he looks more troubled than before. I lean forward and take his hand and say, 'I will, Ian. I promise. I just need more time. I can't explain what's going on. But I will fix everything. I'll find a way.'

He pulls his hand away from mine. Gently, he says, 'You

can't fix this, Nora. Whatever we had, it's gone. And you're not the only one to blame. I'm just as much at fault.'

I can't help myself; I reach over again and touch his cheek. It's so soft and smooth and pure. 'Oh, Ian. You're not responsible for any of this. You've always been wonderful with me, I know that. And I never meant to doubt you about Franny's death. You're so—'

'Stop it!' He gets up abruptly and paces the room, his face dark and scowling. He looks agitated and compunctious, and I've never seen him like this before. He comes back and sits down. 'I'm not this wonderful person you make me out to be. I'm just an average man, Nora, and I have weaknesses and flaws like any other man. And right now – right now, Nora – I just can't handle your problems. I can't do it.'

He walks over to the living room window and looks outside. With his back to me, he says quietly, 'I love you, too.' Then, even quieter, he says, 'God, Nora, I still love you. But I need some breathing room. I need time to think.'

I watch Ian's back. It is stiff, rigid; I can almost see the tension in it, and it makes me incredibly sad to know that I am responsible for his discomfort. I wish I knew what to say, but I don't. I'm not even sure why I came over here. As I was begging him to give me another chance, part of me realized he had already become a relic of my past. I love him; he loves me – but that doesn't mean much. It's not enough to keep us together, and it's certainly not enough to keep me away from M.

I leave his home while he's still staring out the window, avoiding me. I get on the freeway and drive back to Davis. He says he needs time to think, but I know what that means. It is the slow dissolution of a relationship, the polite way of saying goodbye. I've used that line myself on several men: I need time to think. Translation: I don't want to see you anymore. Ian is perfectly justified, of course. I've given him plenty of reasons to back off, reasons of which he's not even aware. M. has his wish after all. Ian is out of my life.

With this realization, I feel almost relieved, unburdened. I won't have to answer any more of Ian's questions, or try to explain my behavior. But at the same time I feel I've missed an opportunity, made a terrible mistake. I'm on the edge of the abyss now, and there's no one to stop me.

35

M.'s house is unlocked, so I enter without knocking, hearing music as soon as I turn the knob. He is at the piano in the den, but stops playing when I walk into the room. I go over to the sofa and sit.

'You've got your way,' I tell him.

He turns around on the bench so he's facing me, then crosses his arms. The drapes are drawn, the room dim. The light above the piano shines down on M., highlighting his cheekbones and strong chin. His lips curve sensuously at the corners, and I think he must've been quite handsome as a young man. He says, 'I always get my way.'

I feel angry and resentful, and I'm not in the mood for any of his games. 'Thanks to you, Ian doesn't want to see me anymore.' I add, 'If I never met you, Ian and I would still be together.'

M. says, 'Would you like a drink?'

I glare at him.

He comes over and sits next to me. He puts his hand on my knee, a possessive gesture.

I push his hand away, denying him his possession. I want to punish this man for what he's done. I blame him for making Ian reject me, although, in point of sheer fact, I know I have no one but myself to blame.

M. – teacher, strict disciplinarian, Nestor, algolagnic Pygmalion – he looks at me for a while, a studied, patient look, then says, 'You've never had good relationships with men, Nora. Ian was no different. Even if you and I had never met, you still wouldn't have stayed with him for long. You needed him after

Franny died. That's all he was to you – a crutch, someone to lean on.'

'He was someone I loved. Someone I still love.'

'You don't love him any more than you loved any of the other men in your life. And he could never satisfy you the way I do.'

'That's not true.'

'Yes, it is, and you know it. You may relish the idea of being in love with him, but the reality is that you need someone exactly like me.'

Annoyed with his facile analysis, I shake my head. 'You don't know what you're talking about. Ian was special, and I did love him.'

'You loved the idea, Nora. Ian was so safe. With him you'd get married, have two kids, and live happily ever after. Only it wouldn't have worked out that way. You'd be bored out of your skull. You'd make him miserable and end up hating everything he stood for.'

He drapes his hand across the back of the sofa and crosses his legs. He's wearing a light short-sleeved shirt and brown gabardine trousers. He continues, his voice even and poised and, I think, condescending.

'Relationships are difficult, Nora. And I scare the hell out of you.' He shifts his body on the sofa. 'Your sister was frightened of me, but she never backed away. She was quite fearless, in her own peculiar manner. She hated what I did to her, but she wanted me and she had enough guts to stick it out to the end. You love what I do to you, but you can't admit it out loud. I have to coddle you along to assuage all your fears. And as for Ian and all the other men you've dated – you picked them because they were safe and didn't challenge you one bit. It's time for you to grow up, Nora. It's time for you to start dealing with men.'

'And what about you?' I say hotly. 'You're not any different. You go from woman to woman.'

'There's a big difference,' he says calmly. 'I'm not afraid of women, and I'm not afraid to get involved. If I fuck one woman after another, it's because I choose to – not because I'm afraid to take a chance. You don't live in the present, Nora. I have what you need, but you're too frightened to embrace it. You think if you don't deal with me, someone better will come along.' He leans forward. 'We're perfectly suited, Nora, but you're either living for the future, too afraid to live in the present, or living in the past, working out all your old demons, afraid to go on with your life. You like to think you're worldly, sophisticated, but you're more timid than Franny. Just a timid, little soul.'

I am incensed with anger. I can feel my cheeks color, and I am about to explode.

But I don't. M., once more, is right. I have no idea who I am. I feel that he is holding a mirror up to my life, and the reflection I see is one I don't like.

My realization leaves me in a turmoil. I change the subject.

'Did you kill Franny?' I ask. I'm unable to keep the despair out of my voice. Long ago, I gave up any pretense of being M.'s equal. I am no match for him. All I want now is the truth. 'I need to know. I *have* to know. Even if you did, there's nothing I can do about it. There's no evidence, no proof. It'll be your word against mine. You'll never see the inside of a jail. But I need to know if you killed her, and how and why you killed her. Just tell me the truth. Please . . . tell me.'

M. reaches over and strokes my hand. 'Oh, Nora,' he says softly, almost sadly. 'When are you going to open your eyes? I have no proof, but Ian seems the most likely suspect.'

I shake my head. 'He hadn't seen her for six months before she died. And he had no reason to kill her.'

'Sometimes a reason isn't necessary. Besides, he lied to you, didn't he? He never would've mentioned Franny if I hadn't told you they knew each other. So maybe he lied about other things as well. How do you know he hadn't seen her for six months?'

'He told me.'

'And you believed him?' I hear the cynicism in his voice.
'Yes.'

'I see,' he says. Then adds, 'Do you think you're capable of
being objective about Ian? You dismiss every fact that makes
him appear suspicious. He fucked Franny, he lied to you about
knowing her, immediately after she was killed he latches on to
you, and soon after he realizes you suspect him – after you
asked him his whereabouts on the day Franny was murdered
– he pulls away from you. Don't you think Detective Harris
would be interested in knowing this? Tell the police. Let them
ascertain his innocence.'

'He didn't kill Franny.' I get up and pace the room. 'And if
you're positive he's the killer, why didn't you tell me sooner?
You say you care for me, that you're falling in love – weren't
you afraid he'd kill me as well?'

M. watches me pace. Calmly, he says, 'No. Your life was
never in danger. Ian isn't a killer – not by nature. He doesn't
have it in him. I think it was an accident, a mistake.'

'She was bound with duct tape. Are you telling me that was
an accident? A mistake?'

'I don't have all the answers, Nora. I may not have any of
the answers. I just think that he lost control. He's not a cold-
blooded person. I don't think he meant to kill her.'

I sit on the far end of the sofa. Leaning forward, I place my
elbows on my knees, my head in my hands. His words rever-
berate in my mind: *he lost control*. I remember the night Ian
lost control, when he fucked me out of anger, roughly, without
my consent.

'If you really believed he killed her, why didn't you tell me
sooner? Why didn't you tell the police when they questioned
you?'

'I only made the connection recently – when Ian confessed
to his new friend Philip Ellis that he had slept with Franny.
Nora, if I had told you, would you have believed me? You still
don't want to. And the police? Why would they believe any
accusation of mine, the man they prefer to believe is guilty?'

I don't say anything, at a loss for an answer. What he says makes sense, but I no longer trust my judgment.

He leaves the room, then returns a few minutes later, carrying a small cardboard box. 'I brought this home today,' he says. Then he smiles apologetically. 'I kept it at my office so you wouldn't find it.' He sits next to me and opens the flaps on the box. 'I thought you'd like to have these – some things Franny left behind.'

He reaches in the box and pulls out a blue silk scarf. I don't know if it belonged to her or not, but then he places a pair of jade earrings in my palm. I had given these earrings to Franny on her birthday two years ago. I close my hand, and the earrings become warm in my palm. Sensations: I want to feel sensations, her presence in the earrings, a psychic connection that spans both worlds. *Talk to me, Franny.* But nothing comes. Only silence, without significance. Tears form in my eyes, and I squeeze them tightly so M. will not see me cry. I chide myself for my sentimentality. What did I expect? Some sort of signal?

'Here,' M. says, and I open my eyes. He hands me a pair of tinted glasses.

'Franny didn't wear glasses,' I say, and start to give them back.

'Reading glasses,' he says. 'She got them a week before we split up.' Then he hands me a Jean Auel book, *The Clan of the Cave Bear,* and two nursing magazines. He pulls a brown sweater out of the box and hands that to me, also. Last of all, he reaches in and takes out a miniature wood carving, a snake hatching from an egg. As if it was a foreboding, my skin prickles when I see it. I think of the one Ian carved for me over six months ago, still on my coffee table.

I am confused and cannot stay here with M. today. I put everything back in the box – the blue scarf and jade earrings and tinted glasses and magazines and brown sweater and the Jean Auel book and the wood carving – and get up and leave without saying a word. I know he will make me suffer later for walking out on him, but I don't care.

*   *   *

I go home and call a man named Peter Byatt who works the police beat at the *Bee*. Although I've known him for over ten years, we've never socialized outside of work. He's an older man, competent, who's helped me out on several stories in the past. I wait while the call is transferred to his desk. The phone rings repeatedly before a man answers, his voice flat and bored, saying simply, 'Byatt here.'

'Pete, this is Nora Tibbs.'

There is a moment of silence as my name registers, then recognition. 'Nora! How're you doing? When you coming back to work?'

'Soon,' I say. 'I need a favor.'

He pauses briefly, then says, 'What can I do for you?'

'Do you remember the Mansfield murder?'

'The woman on Channel Three? McCarthy's girlfriend? Sure.'

'Tell me about it. About the guy who killed her.'

I hear a chair squeaking, and I picture him leaning back, using one of the filing-cabinet drawers as a footrest, a position I've seen him in many times. 'Mark Kirn,' he says. 'A real wacko. An ex-boyfriend who wouldn't let her go, kept harassing her. A genuine nut case. She got a restraining order to keep him away, but obviously it didn't work. He kept up the harassment; she filed charges. He finally pleaded no contest to a misdemeanor count of stalking, and was put on probation, two years, I think, maybe three, and ordered to undergo psychiatric counseling. It didn't do much good – he stabbed her in the parking lot at the station, eight, nine times, something like that.'

'How did he harass her?'

'It's been several years,' he says, thinking. He hesitates for a minute, then says, 'He used to call her repeatedly, if I remember correctly, professing his undying love and devotion. She finally had to change her number. And he'd follow her around town, showing up wherever she was covering a story, in general making an ass out of himself. He'd take her picture, hundreds of them, and send them to her. When she ignored him, he started mailing threatening letters. He even broke into her house a few times, or so she claimed. He denied everything. He maintains his innocence up to this day. Says he was framed, claimed it was a different boyfriend who killed her, that it was Ian. The two of them got in a fistfight one time, when Kirn was following them to a restaurant. The police checked it out, but they never seriously suspected Ian. The evidence was pretty conclusive against Kirn. No one actually saw him kill her, but his finger-prints were all over the knife. And there was a witness who ID'ed him at the parking lot just a few minutes after the murder.'

As he was speaking, I felt a vague uneasiness spread through me. Ian never told me the man claimed to be innocent; he never told me they had got in a fight. 'Thanks, Pete,' I say, and I hang up before he asks any questions.

My car is in the garage, but I decide, even in the hot weather, to walk downtown to clear my head. It'll take me about an hour of brisk walking to reach Second Street, and that will give me just enough time to get to the Paragon by five-thirty, when I'm supposed to meet Joe Harris.

Ian. I think of Ian.

I walk through the underpass that goes beneath the train tracks, and then into the downtown area.

Joe is waiting for me when I reach the Paragon. I'm sweaty from my long walk, and go directly into the bathroom to wash my face. I'm still charged up from the vigorous walk across town, feeling a little agitated. I think again of Ian.

I sit down, then suddenly start pouring out everything that's happened the past several days, talking so fast that I realize I'm making no sense.

'Slow down, Nora. Slow down. What're you talking about?'

I stare at Joe, flustered. I don't know. I have no idea what I'm talking about.

'The person who killed Franny,' I finally say. 'It could be anyone. Anyone.' And then I realize the cause of my agitation. I'm about to betray Ian.

'I've been telling you that all along,' Joe says cautiously. He's wearing a green polyester shirt, short-sleeved, and it stretches snugly across his chest. He takes a sip of beer, eyeing me over the rim of his glass. Setting it down, he says, 'So you changed your mind finally? You don't think he killed her?'

It's odd the way neither of us says M.'s name out loud to the other, as if the utterance would validate his existence, make him more human.

'No,' I say, then quickly add, 'Yes. Maybe.' I pause to collect my thoughts. 'I don't know. There's someone else.'

Joe raises his bushy eyebrows but is quiet.

I take a deep breath and say, 'You mentioned you were investigating someone else. It's Ian, isn't it?'

There is a sudden burst of laughter, then a cough as Joe chokes on his beer. He's smirking, as if I told a joke. 'Your boyfriend? Jesus, Nora. You can't be serious.'

Now I'm surprised. I thought for sure that Ian was the other suspect. 'I know it sounds a little crazy, but—'

'More than a little.'

'But hear me out.' And I tell him about Ian's encounter with Franny and how he withheld the information, his sudden interest in me upon her death, his skill with knives, the wood carving he gave her before she died. I take a breath, and then ask him if he remembers the Cheryl Mansfield murder. When he says, 'Vaguely,' I tell him she had been Ian's girlfriend. 'What about the photos and letter I've received?' I say. 'Just like the ones she got. They could be from Ian.'

Joe says nothing, gazing thoughtfully at the table, playing absently with the beer glass.

'He broke up with me as soon as I suspected he was the murderer,' I say.

He still remains quiet.

'And when I asked him where he was the day she was killed, he didn't answer.' Listening to myself, accusing Ian, I shake my head slowly and back off. 'I don't know,' I say. 'Maybe I'm crazy. I don't know what to think anymore.'

'No,' Joe says finally, looking up, his gray eyes deep in thought. 'You're not crazy. It's worth checking into.'

I don't go back to M.'s house tonight. My mind is confused, and I need to be alone. Did I do the right thing by telling Joe my suspicions of Ian? I showed him the wood carving of the snake hatching from an egg. It was whittled from holly, the same wood Ian used in the carving he made last February. It was on my coffee table all this time. When Joe drove me home this evening, he took both wood carvings with him.

I go to bed, exhausted from everything that happened today, and fall asleep almost immediately. My dreams are filled with anxiety, and sometime during the night I wake up. Something is wrong, but I'm not sure what. I sit up, looking around, feeling disoriented. My alarm clock, an electronic one with red digitals, is off, the face black, and there is no light from the streetlamps filtering through the curtains. The electricity in the neighborhood went off – that is what woke me, the silence. No humming refrigerator, no sound of my neighbor's air conditioner, which he leaves on all night. The room is black, no moon tonight. A car must've hit an electrical pole, knocking out the electricity.

I lie back down, and am almost asleep, in that halfway, hypnagogic state between drowsiness and unconsciousness, when the phone rings – a jarring, loud sound in the middle of the night, piercing the blackness of the room. I jerk in response. I grab for it, before it rings again, but I miss. The shrill ring resonates, rude and brazen. Grabbing for the phone again, I accidentally knock it over. I fumble in the darkness, then bring the receiver to my ear. Nothing. Then I hear the breathing. I should've let the answering machine pick up the call, but I didn't think when I heard the jarring ring. I hold the receiver to my ear, listening. I don't say anything. Neither does he. The breathing is deep and regular, just to let me know he's there. Is it Ian or M.? I think it's Ian, but how can I be sure? I sit up, listening, unable to utter a word. I should hang up, but I can't. A morbid curiosity – or maybe it's fear, yes, that's it, fear

298 *Laura Reese*

of the unknown – keeps me on the phone. My two weeks are almost up. As I listen to his rhythmic breathing, my chest tightens. The room is so dark. I think I hear noises in my home, but I know that's only my imagination. The house is settling; a cat is crawling on the roof. It's not Ian in my house. It's not M. But one of them is here, on the phone, at the other end of the line. One of them sent me the note. The breathing continues. I squeeze my eyes shut and listen, my own breathing shallow, filled with nervous apprehensions. I hang up the phone, finally, and stay awake the rest of the night.

Every evening after that, I take the phone off the hook before I go to bed.

36

I no longer see Ian, so I spend most of my evenings at M.'s house. Already, we have established routines. He wakes up before I do, makes coffee, and brings a cup into the bedroom while I'm still sleeping, setting it on the nightstand beside the bed. My life is much simpler without Ian. There's no more lying and no more deception. I no longer have to cover my tracks, and it comes as a great relief. I am sleeping better and the dark smudges under my eyes have disappeared.

I'm sitting up when M. walks into the room, a blue towel wrapped around his waist, his hair still damp from a shower. He walks over to the bed and drinks out of the coffee mug, then hands it to me – he knows I won't touch it otherwise. He slides under the covers.

'I like seeing you in my bed when I wake up in the morning,' he says, and I know he means it. He snuggles against my body, his own still warm from the hot shower. 'And I like having you here in the evening,' he adds. He holds me close, and I lean against him, still drinking my coffee, still trying to wake up, waiting for the caffeine to kick in. I look at the alarm clock on the nightstand, and see that it's barely six. Through the bay window, in the early morning light, we watch blackbirds flitting from the fence to the lawn. Rameau, lying peacefully on the patio, ignores them.

M. rubs my head gently. He says, 'Don't you think it's time you told me the rest of your story? I'd like to hear it.'

I sigh, not sure I feel like talking. I get up, put on one of M.'s bathrobes, then walk over to the bay window. I finger the drapes, the fabric loosely latticed and coarse in my hands. Outside, the sky is getting lighter.

Still looking out the window, I say, 'When I was twenty-one I had a tubal ligation; it's a sterilization for women. I had to go to San Francisco for the operation. I couldn't find a doctor in Davis or Sacramento who would do it. They said I was too young, that I would change my mind when I got older, that I would want children someday. Finally, I found a doctor in San Francisco. He had good intentions, but all the other doctors were right: twenty-one is too young to make that kind of a decision, one that would affect me for the rest of my life. I told a few of my friends about it. I was very glib. "I don't need children to be fulfilled." "Kids are just an ego trip, parents trying to produce little creations of themselves." "I'm a woman, a feminist, not a baby-maker" – as if the two were incompatible. The truth was, I was deathly afraid of getting pregnant again.'

I laugh uneasily, still fingering the drapery fabric. 'It was so unnecessary, the sterilization. I wasn't even having sex – that was during my five-year period of celibacy – plus, I was taking birth control pills. I was one well-protected young lady: no sex, on birth control pills, and still I had the tubal ligation.'

Dropping the fabric abruptly, I walk away from the window, then sit in the blue armchair in the corner of the room, crossing my legs. 'When I was twenty-one, it seemed logical,' I continue. 'I couldn't get pregnant again, I couldn't go through that another time – at any cost. So I had the tubal, not even knowing why, not really. I just wanted to forget about the abortion, about the baby, about everything that happened.' Nervously, I play with the arm of the chair, running my right hand up and down the length of it. 'But the past has a way of catching up with you. You can try to deny it, pretend it didn't happen, but it's there, always there, waiting to resurface. Years later, I kept asking myself, Why did I get sterilized when there was no possibility of conception? I was on pills, I was celibate, there was absolutely no need for a tubal ligation. Then the answer started to come to me: I destroyed a life, so I took away my capacity to ever create life again; I'd never give birth. It was a form of punishment.'

I realize now that I had wanted to finish this story for M. I'd been silent for almost twenty years, and saying the words out loud to another person, while difficult, has been cathartic. I needed to talk about this; I should've done it years ago. Only now do I understand that you can't avoid the past; it churns inside you, making itself known in the oddest and most painful ways, until you recognize and acknowledge its presence. Why did it take me so long to learn this?

Silence covers the room like a velvet pall over a coffin. I think of the children I'll never have; the grandchildren who'll never amuse me as I age; no one, ever, to perpetuate the Tibbs lineage. Is the punishment justified? Finally, and for the first time, I can say no. A long, slow sigh, audible, escapes my lips. Relief. I feel relief, although I'm not sure why. Nothing has changed except my perception. Perhaps that will be enough.

I go back to the bed and lie down. M. puts his arms around me but doesn't say anything, just rubs my back and shoulders tenderly. We are quiet for a while. I begin to feel sleepy again and reach for the coffee mug.

Finally, M. says, 'Why don't you move in?'

Instantly, I am wide awake, as if I'm on my sixth cup of coffee. 'Move in?' I repeat, gripping the mug tighter.

He gets up and begins putting on his clothes. 'Just think about it,' he says. 'You know how I feel about you, and you're here most of the time anyway.' He finishes dressing and bends down to kiss me. 'And unless I'm way off the mark, I believe you're beginning to care for me also.' Before I have a chance to reply, he says, 'I have a breakfast meeting before my first class, and if I don't leave now, I'll be late. We'll talk about it later,' and he walks out the room, leaving me confounded.

I lie in bed for a while, contemplating his proposal, the absurdity of it. It's true, my feelings for him are changing, developing, growing. I've confided in M. as I've never done with anyone else, and the sexual games we play – his domination, my submission – enthrall me. He's exciting, intelligent, and a little bit dangerous – a combination I crave. But . . . from murder suspect to live-in companion? I don't think so.

I put all these thoughts aside. I have more pressing business this morning: to meet the man who supposedly killed Cheryl Mansfield.

Mark Kirn is a death-row inmate at San Quentin. When I received clearance to visit him, the prison officials sent me a visitor information handbook telling me how to dress. I couldn't wear anything blue or dark green, no denim, no sweatpants, nothing with a bare midriff, no short skirts, no cleavage, no strapless, backless, or low-cut dresses. So I'm dressed conservatively as I drive to the Bay Area, a plain white skirt down to my knees and a short-sleeved, peach-colored blouse.

I take the toll bridge into San Rafael, then turn onto the road leading up to the prison. It curves around the San Pablo Bay, and soon I begin to wonder if I'm lost. Quaint Victorian homes, all old and very small, some of them run-down, line both sides of the road. Interspersed between the homes are coastal scrub, some scraggly wildflowers, a small patch of a garden here and there. The land slopes down to a rocky coast, and over the bay I can see the San Francisco skyline. The view is picturesque, like something on a postcard – not a likely spot for a prison.

I keep driving. Around a bend in the road I see a large building made of stone, granite I think, old and with a pale yellowish tinge, surrounded by a high concrete wall: San Quentin.

Following the instructions they sent me, I hike up a hill to a long, narrow building where visitors are processed. Inside, I'm overwhelmed by the sounds of screaming babies. The room is dreary, with concrete floors and wooden benches along unpainted walls, and filled with people – a few men, but mostly women and children. I stand in the back of the line and wait. In front of me, a squat blond-haired woman has a sick child slung over her shoulder as if he were a heavy bag of flour. He's whining, squirming around, his nose dripping steadily. He lifts his hand and wipes his nose, then sticks a plump thumb into his mouth, staring at me with big brown eyes.

The line inches forward. At the other end of the room, at irregular intervals, a door is buzzed open and one person is allowed to exit. Most of the women are carrying transparent plastic bags – cheap cosmetic bags – filled with items they're allowed to bring inside the prison: three keys, photo identification, handkerchief or tissue, comb or brush, twenty dollars with no bill larger than a five. No food, no paper or pencils or pens, no tape recorders.

Finally, after about an hour, it's my turn to be buzzed through the door. I walk in and see a guard behind a counter. He's an older man, in his fifties, white hair and dull eyes, wearing a dark forest-green uniform with patches on the sleeves. His name, E. Cullen, is stitched in black on the right breast pocket. I lay my ID, car key, and twenty dollars on the counter. E. Cullen doesn't say anything. He looks bored and he stares at me blandly, with little interest. He visually inspects my clothes, checks my ID against the approved visitors list, then hands me a yellow pass. I pick up my belongings and go through a metal detector. I think this is the end, but the process has only begun.

I walk out of the building and onto the prison grounds. A very long sidewalk leads up to the prison, a massive structure so old it looks sallow and jaundiced. San Quentin was built in 1852, and it has the appearance of an ancient castle, a fortress, with projecting turrets and crenellated rooftops and, in the stone walls, arched lancet windows. A gun tower in the shape of an obelisk, with armed guards, stands apart from the prison. Beyond that, I see the bay, beautifully blue on this clear afternoon.

The sidewalk seems to go on forever, which I suppose is fitting since I'm crossing from one world to another, from the land of the free to the underworld of the condemned. A few low-level security inmates dressed in blue are pulling weeds on a grassy slope.

Finally, I see another gate, with a guard booth adjacent. More processing – sign-up sheets, another metal detector to pass through, another bored guard dressed in green. I show him my visitor pass and he stamps the back of my hand. The imprint is blurred and I can't read it, an iridescent yellowish-green stamp similar to the ones I've received when out dancing at a club. I turn left and walk along the prison wall. Prisoners are exercising on the inside yard, and they sound like they're in the army, grunting in unison, doing calisthenics. In front of me, there are a row of unmarked doors without handles. I stand in front of the third door. It's electronically controlled, with a large panel of glass – or perhaps Plexiglas – so thick and scratched I can barely see inside. When the guard sees me, the door slides open. I walk into a small antechamber, show him my ID and pass, then step out into a metal cage. The glass door slides shut behind me. The cage is the size of a small elevator, with cast-iron black bars, and for a moment I feel as if I'm the prisoner. I hear a click as the door is electronically unlocked. I push open the gate, and finally I'm in the visiting room.

It's not what I expected. This looks like a student union hall at a racially mixed college. There are vending machines – candy, burgers, chicken, french fries, coffee, sodas – and a microwave oven, and rows of tables and chairs in the middle of the room. Close to seventy or eighty people, visitors and inmates, crowd the room, and the noise is loud and chaotic – crying babies, whining toddlers, men and women talking loudly to make themselves heard.

The glassed-in guard booth is to my right and it takes up almost one side of the room. It's built high, and I have to reach up to slide my ID and visitor pass through the slot in the window. The guard, a sharp-faced man with short bristly hair, also in a forest-green uniform, tells me to sit. All the chairs are blue vinyl with metal trim, and they're linked together with other chairs to form a straight row. I find two empty chairs in the corner and wait.

I glance around the room. All the inmates are wearing light blue workshirts and blue jeans. My attention is drawn to the walls, which are painted with colorful murals. I'm sitting next to a plump Hispanic girl, and she gives me a nudge.

'Those were done by the inmates. Pretty good, huh?' The girl has a young-sounding voice, breathy, with no trace of an accent.

One of the murals is an outdoor scene, Yosemite perhaps, with a huge granite dome and a waterfall. The other mural has more of a mythical quality, depicting a buxom, toga-clad woman sitting in front of a winged horse, Pegasus, the symbol of poetic inspiration. I wonder if the inmate who painted this also knew that Pegasus was later captured by Zeus and treated as a pack animal, to fetch his thunderbolts. Probably not. He was most likely more concerned with the buxom lady. Yosemite and Pegasus. Nature and mythology – the murals seem incongruous in this setting.

'Yes,' I say. 'They're nice.' I look at my watch, then shift around in the hard chair. A couple walks across the room, holding hands, two shiny-faced toddlers trailing after them. Another couple, at a table near the candy machine, kiss and grope each other as if they were on a secluded, romantic picnic in the park. Men in blue are bouncing babies on their laps, laughing with their wives or girlfriends. They look like normal, ordinary men. I have to remind myself that every man in this room has murdered one or more people. This is the death-row visitors' room, and all the men dressed in blue are killers. Two tables down, I see a black woman with corn-rowed hair giving her boyfriend a hand job, her fist deep in his pants, pumping up and down. I lean forward and read the sign on the wall above her head: hands must be visible at all times.

I sit back in the chair. A red-headed woman in black pants walks by, wearing a religious collar under a blue and pink Hawaiian shirt. She must have at least a dozen holes pierced in her ear, filled with silver studs and hoops and shiny, dangling jewelry.

'That's Reverend Betsy,' the girl next to me says. 'She comes to visit the men that don't have regular visitors. She's nice, not like the others.' She points over to a table where an inmate is listening to a man reading from a Bible. I look around and notice there is a lot of Bible reading in the room.

'They come in all the time,' she says. 'The Christian people, doing good service. The inmates like them because they buy them cheeseburgers, but then they have to listen to them talk about Jesus and the Bible.' She shrugs. 'It's okay, I guess. At least they get cheeseburgers.'

Fifteen or twenty minutes have gone by. I watch as inmates, one at a time, enter the room through a metal door. Each time the door slams shut, it makes a loud, clanging noise. They give their names to the guard behind the glass window, then find their visitors.

'There's my husband,' the Hispanic girl says, and she gets up to leave. She walks over to a sweet-faced boy who looks barely older than she. They hug, then go immediately to the vending machines, walking hand in hand like two teenagers in a mall – only this boy isn't a teenager and, despite his appearance, not innocent at all.

The metal door clangs shut again. I watch as an inmate gives his name to the guard behind the glass booth, then asks him a question. The guard points his finger at me. Turning around, the prisoner looks where the guard is pointing, then walks toward me stiffly, looking nervous, as if he doesn't belong here. He's tall and slight, with narrow slits for eyes and thin lips that are clamped tightly shut. This must be Mark Kirn. He's a middle-aged man with a bald spot on the top of his head, and if he was dressed in a suit and tie, he would look like a businessman instead of an inmate.

He sits down next to me, saying, 'Are you Nora Tibbs?' When I nod, he says, 'You said in your letter that maybe you could help me. Can you?' His eyes are azure blue, the same color as his prison shirt, and without any warmth at all.

'I'm not sure,' I say, wishing I could have brought paper with me, or a tape recorder. 'I need to know a few things.'

He glances to the left furtively, then back at me, his eyes cold. 'What kind of things?' he asks, tapping his fingers nervously on his knee.

'About the letters you wrote to Cheryl Mansfield. The phone calls.'

He looks at me, then says, 'Would you buy me a cheese-burger? There're cheeseburgers in the vending machines.'

'Okay,' I say, and fumble with the money in my hand. I hold up a five, but Kirn doesn't take it.

'You have to come with me,' he says. 'We're not allowed to touch money in here.'

We walk over to the vending machines. A woman holding a Bible says, 'Jesus died for your sins,' to a man eating microwaved pizza, his body hunched over a table. I put a five-dollar bill into a change machine, then buy a cheeseburger for a dollar seventy-five, and hand it to Kirn.

'Some coffee, too,' he says, walking over to the microwave, putting his cheeseburger inside, 'and that enchilada. We don't get anything spicy here.'

I change another five and get the rest of his food, feeling like a waitress. Kirn warms it in the microwave, then sits down at an empty table. I sit across from him, watching. He eats the cheeseburger in three bites.

'I didn't kill her,' he says. 'Nobody believes me.' He looks up. 'Except maybe you. Do you believe me?'

I don't know the answer to that question. I read all the news-paper clippings on the Mansfield murder, I talked to the detectives who were working the case. Mark Kirn is the murderer; they were positive of that – and so was the jury who convicted him. I shrug. 'The evidence is fairly incriminating,' I say. 'You were seen in the parking lot minutes after she was murdered. And your fingerprints were all over the knife.'

'I was framed,' he says. 'If I killed her, I wouldn't be stupid enough to leave the knife behind.' He glances to the side, nervously looking around. 'Besides, I loved Cheryl. I wouldn't have hurt her.'

'She had a restraining order against you,' I say. 'You were on probation.'

'I shouldn't have gone by the TV station, I know that. But I wanted to see her. That's all. I didn't kill her.'

'Tell me about the stalking. You called her, you took her picture and sent them to her, you broke into her house.'

'The police couldn't prove that,' he says. 'I never broke into her house. It was her word against mine. There weren't any fingerprints.'

'What about the rest?'

He gulps down the last of the coffee. 'Yes, I did the other things. But that doesn't mean I killed her.' He hesitates, then adds, 'We saw each other for two years. We were going to be married. When she broke up with me, I was angry. I did some things I shouldn't have done. I admit that. But I didn't kill her.'

He sits up straight and looks at me in earnest. 'Listen, you have to help me. You're the only one who can.' He leans forward and places his hand on mine. Even though he is begging for my assistance, seemingly sincere, there's a cold, aloof air about him, as if nothing – at least nothing in this world – could really touch him. I draw back my hand.

'Tell me about the letters,' I say.

Kirn folds his arms across his chest. 'Okay,' he says, 'so there were letters. So what?'

'What did you write?'

'I told her how much I loved her.'

'You threatened to kill her.'

Kirn uncrosses his arms. He shifts in the seat. 'I just wanted to get her attention. She was ignoring me. I didn't mean anything by it.' He leans forward again.

'I was angry,' he says. 'The letters, the calls – they don't mean anything. She went to the police and filed charges against me. I was given a misdemeanor and put on probation. I even had to visit a psychiatrist. After that, I stayed away from her. No calls, no letters, nothing. Then one night I decided to go to the TV station and apologize. But after I got there, I changed my mind. I thought she might report me, that she might think I was there to harass her. So I went home. The next thing I know, police are at my house, saying I killed her. Except it wasn't me. Someone else killed her. Someone who knew I was bothering her. There's a man named Ian McCarthy. Check him out if you want to find her murderer. It was probably him. He's a violent man. A jealous man. He beat me up once, in front of Scott's Seafood, just because Cheryl and I were talking.' He leans back into the chair and adds, 'He knew he could kill her and frame it on me.'

I remember the night Ian told me Cheryl was seeing other men behind his back, how it had made him crazy. But crazy enough to kill her? I scrutinize Kirn, wondering how much to believe. I'm not sure what I hoped to gain by visiting him – an insight to his innocence or guilt, I suppose, confirmation that I was correct to hand Ian over to the police. I sit back in my chair, watching him, a man who looks out of place in San Quentin. It could have been Ian.

A guard comes out on the floor with a Polaroid camera. People get up and start walking over to the Yosemite mural.

'What's going on?' I ask.

Kirn says, 'Visiting time is almost up. The guard will take your picture, if you'd like one. I have a ducat for the picture.'

I look at him, not understanding. Isn't a ducat a gold coin?

'It's a ticket,' he explains. 'You can't get the picture for free. You have to buy a ducat.'

I watch as the guard snaps pictures of inmates with their girlfriends, wives, parents, children, with Yosemite in the background. I think what a strange place this is for death-row murderers. Kirn pulls a ticket out of his pocket.

'Let's get our picture taken,' he says. 'I'd like a picture of us together.'

I look at him, his cold blue eyes, and get a queasy feeling in my stomach.

37

I wake up slowly this morning. I didn't fall asleep last night until well after three. It was one of those fitful, sleepless nights where my mind never shuts off and I check the clock every half hour to see what time it is. When I finally did sleep, disjointed images floated through my mind – glaciated cliffs, waterfalls, white winged horses, Yosemite Valley. El Capitan's dome merges into the face of Mark Kirn, his eyes sky blue and glacier cold. Then Pegasus rises, stomping his hoof on Helicon, home of the Muses, and I marvel at the mountain spring that flows from the kick of his hoof, only to discover that it isn't water flowing but blood, and I am under the hoof of Pegasus now, and he's stomping on me and my toga-clad body. Exhausting dreams.

I wake up tired, as if I'd been working all night long. I stretch, yawn, and roll over. Although I want to snuggle deeper under the blanket, I put on a bathrobe and get up. In the kitchen, I see a white envelope in the center of the counter. I frown, not remembering I'd left anything there before going to bed. I wasn't paying bills last night; I wasn't writing letters. Then my body stiffens. I tear open the envelope, my hand shaking. It's similar to the one I received in the mail, the message written from letters torn out of magazines.

'I warned you – your time is up.'

The letter trembles in my unsteady hand. This is from Ian; it has to be Ian. He's the only one who has a key to my house. And he was here last night while I lay sleeping. I bring my arms up and clasp my shoulders, a protective move, hugging myself. He could've killed me if he wanted to.

Suddenly, I freeze. There was a noise in the house. A sharp snap, or maybe it was a click. I'm still hugging myself, and my fingernails dig into my arms. Was it just the house settling, or was the noise something else? Is Ian still here? My ears strain. My breathing stops. I hear nothing.

Next to the front door, on a table, I keep a canister of Mace. I pick it up, then look inside the living room. I check behind all the furniture to make sure Ian isn't here, hiding. Then I walk, tentatively, to the hallway. I stop before I get there. In my bones, I feel the panic and fear accompanying the idea that an intruder may be present, here, now, violating the safety of my home. I hesitate, irresolute. Finally, I continue to tiptoe down the hallway. I check the office. Slowly, I slide the closet door open. No one. Then I crane my head around the bathroom door. There is no one here, either. Still armed with my can of Mace, my heart pounding, I go into the bedroom, check under the bed and in the closets. No one is here. Ian is not in my house. Relaxing, I check the front door. It is locked. I check the garage door and back door, then all the windows. I'll have to change the locks on the doors. I should've done it earlier, when I found out that Ian had fucked Franny.

I return to the kitchen and read the note again. *Your time is up.* Joe Harris must see this note.

38

'Isn't there anything you can do?' I ask Joe Harris. I'm in the police station, sitting at his desk. 'This is the same thing that happened to Cheryl Mansfield,' I say. 'He broke into her house, too. Why aren't you doing anything?'

There's a can of Coke on his desk, and he picks it up to take a drink. Even in the air-conditioned office the air is warm, barely circulating. Joe's face is flushed, his shirt sleeves rolled halfway up his arms. When he sets down the can, he says, 'Give me the note.'

I get it out of my purse. 'Don't you think it's strange I'm being harassed the same way she was, and both of us had the same boyfriend? Don't you think it's strange Ian knew Franny and Cheryl, and they both wound up dead?'

The phone at his desk rings and he picks it up. While he's talking, I glance around the room. It seems unusually quiet today, but I suppose it's because of the weather. The summer heat in Davis is mean, today's temperature rising to 109, enervating even the sturdiest of people. A woman in uniform walks by, dropping a manila folder on Joe's desk. He hangs up the phone and stands. 'I've gotta get going,' he says, and walks out of the office and down a corridor.

I follow him, irked at my summary dismissal. 'So there's nothing else you're going to do?' I say.

Outside, the heat hits us as if we'd opened an oven door. Joe gets in his car and starts the engine. 'It would be a good idea for you to stay with a friend for a while,' he says. 'Just until we find out who's harassing you. Can you do that for me?'

I nod. 'What about Ian?' I say. 'What're you going to do about him?'

He puts the car in reverse, says, 'Stay out of this, Nora,' and drives down F Street.

I cross the street to my car. The sky is clear blue, the sun scorching – you would never guess it's September. A street vendor in plaid shorts and a tank top, selling flowers, sits on an overturned bucket beneath a white umbrella. She sips water from a plastic bottle, her hair hanging limply, her shoulders slouched. I get in my car and drive across town, wondering who I'll stay with. Probably Maisie.

When I get home, I check the mailbox: another envelope without a return address. I close my eyes. My chest feels knotted up, tight and tense. I know what's in the envelope. A hot breeze washes over me, whipping my black hair across my eyes. I take the letter inside the house and open it. 'I'm coming for you,' it says, written in the same manner as the others, on a white sheet of paper with the letters clipped from a magazine. I notice I am chewing my thumbnail, then I notice how quiet the house seems, the silence unsettling. I check the front door to make sure it's locked. Then I check the other doors and all the windows. I go back to the kitchen table and pick up the letter, read it once more, then read it again. *I'm coming for you.*

The air conditioner clicks on softly, but the noise sounds ominous to my sensitive ears. I go to the bedroom and get a suitcase from the closet. I throw in a few dresses, some shorts and tops, underwear. I get my toothbrush, toothpaste, look around for the new package of dental floss I'd just bought. I get angry as I pack, being driven out of my own home. Ian should be the one who's inconvenienced, not me. I fling a nightgown into the suitcase, infuriated that someone can wield so much negative power over another. *I'm coming for you.* How dare he intimidate me! I want to do something, to take some action myself, fight back any way that I can. I don't want to move in with Maisie, just roll over and give in.

I walk into the kitchen and see my car keys lying on the counter where I'd tossed them. On the key chain, I carry my three-inch canister of Mace, my car and house keys, and the key to Ian's condo. I still haven't returned his key. An idea surfaces – for something I should've done before.

On the pretense of a friendly chat, I call the *Bee* and speak to Maisie. She thinks I'm crazy – suspecting Ian of murder – but she's glad to hear from me and proceeds to gossip for a while. I feign interest. Finally, after I make an offhand inquiry, she tells me Ian is on assignment in San Francisco for the day. I hang up, drive to Longs Drug Store to buy a package of latex disposable gloves, then get on the freeway and drive to Sacramento.

I'm coming for you. The words resound in my mind like plangent echoes bouncing in a canyon. I park down the street from Ian's condo, under the shade of a sycamore. In the distance, I hear a car honking, the whine of an ambulance, the smooth whispering of a light-rail train running along its track. *I'm coming for you.*

I open the package of disposable gloves. My fingerprints, undoubtedly, are in Ian's condo from my last visit, but if I find any evidence that he killed Franny, I don't want any fingerprints on it other than his own. I stuff two gloves in my pocket, then get out of the car.

Crossing the street, I notice a handyman on top of a ladder, cleaning out gutters on the east side of the condo. A gray sedan pulls into the common parking area. A garage door, activated by remote control, slides open and the sedan disappears inside, the door shutting behind it. I insert the key into Ian's front door, half expecting it not to work. But it slides in easily, and when I turn the key the door unlocks. I push it open and wait, leaning forward slightly, listening for any noises, making sure Ian isn't home. I remove the key from the lock. I feel like a felon, breaking and entering, and my heart beats fast. I try to calm myself. Technically, I haven't broken in, and can I really be a felon if I have a key?

'Got a problem?'

I straighten with a jerk, dropping my set of keys. Turning quickly, I see the handyman, carrying his ladder horizontally under one arm. He's a rawboned man, his face sallow and gaunt.

'Something the matter?' he says. He has a thick, black mustache that droops dolorously over the edges of his lips, hiding his mouth completely. The words seem to come out of nowhere.

I laugh nervously, stooping to pick up my keys. 'No,' I reply. 'I'm just stalling. It's such a nice day, I hate to go inside.'

'I know what you mean,' he says, the mustache going up and down with the sound of his words, 'but it's a tad hot for my tastes. Wouldn't mind working inside on days like this.'

'Yes,' I say. 'Well . . .' The man stands there, not moving, and I wonder if I appear suspicious. 'I have to do some work myself,' I say. 'I thought I'd work at home today. It's quieter here than at the office.'

He shifts the ladder from one arm to the other.

'I can get more done here,' I add, then slip inside the condo. Through the glass panels adjacent to the door, I watch as he walks down the sidewalk and sets up his ladder on the side of the building. I turn around, lean against the door, and sigh with relief. I look at my watch, two-fifteen, and decide to begin.

Walking down the hallway, I notice how cool the condo is. The living room, with walls as white as calcimine, would seem antiseptic if it weren't for the clutter of wood and knives and miniature carvings in disarray on the coffee table. I go immediately to the bedroom, slip on my gloves, and begin a perfunctory search of the dresser drawers. I really don't expect to find anything in such an obvious place, but I check none-theless. I am correct – just socks, underwear, folded T-shirts and sweaters and jeans. As I'm rummaging through the last drawer, I am reminded of how, only five months ago, I'd searched M.'s house, thinking him the murderer and Ian my savior. The irony is not lost on me.

I search the closet, shoving aside his clothes, checking the top shelves, looking into the corners. Still, I find nothing. In the bathroom, I open all the cabinet doors, then look underneath the sink. Nothing. I walk back into the bedroom. I thought this room would be the most logical place to hide something – not the kitchen or living room. Disappointed, I gaze around the room, studying it. I've checked all the drawers, the nightstands, the closet. I look at the bed. No, I think, it would never be there; much too obvious. Still, I go over and get on my hands and knees, pull up the bedspread, look under the bed.

A nervous flutter thrums inside me. There, way in the back, out of reach, is a cardboard shoebox. I lie on my stomach and crawl forward until I reach the box with my hand. I pull it out and take off the lid. The first objects I notice are the duct tape, a partially used roll, and Billy's old medical bracelet. I stare at the tape and bracelet, unable, momentarily, to move. Relief, fear, anguish – all these emotions, in a matter of seconds, touch my heart. I pick up the bracelet and turn it over. The words DIALYSIS PATIENT are etched on the back. Franny kept this with her always. She would never give it away, especially not to someone with whom she supposedly only had a one-night stand.

I set it on the carpet and look again in the box. There is a small straight-edged knife with a wooden handle. The one used to carve Franny's torso? A haunting unease passes through me, embedding itself in my palm as I hold the knife. I set it aside hastily. I remove the duct tape and find a stack of photographs, six of them. Four are of Franny – obscene pictures, close-ups of her naked body in various lurid positions. Did he take these the night she was killed? Her face is not visible in three of the photos, and I would not be positive it was Franny if it wasn't for the finger missing off her hand. In the fourth photograph, static tears distress her face, and her mouth is skewed in pain.

The last two photos are of me – picking up the newspaper

off the driveway early in the morning, still in my bathrobe and slippers, and another as I'm driving down Pole Line Road in my Honda. I stare at the pictures of Franny again, and my spirit plunges downward, lost in her infinite pain.

Click. Click.

A fuzzy warning goes off in my mind. Suddenly, I freeze.

I heard a noise from the other room; a click, I think, from the front door as it was unlocked. I am motionless, praying it was my imagination. But, no – I hear noises again, the sound of the doorknob turning, the door swinging open, and then banging shut.

Quickly, I replace the photos and duct tape and knife and Billy's medical bracelet. I shove the box under the bed, hearing footsteps in the front hallway. I get up, peel off the gloves, shove them in my pants pocket. More noises sound from the living room – shoes shuffling, a soft thud, each noise more ominous than the one before. The only place I can hide is in the closet. Or should I tell Ian I just came by to drop off his key? The radio goes on, music blares. I open the closet door, slowly so he won't hear it, and am halfway in when a startled scream stops me. I turn and see Pat, the cleaning woman.

'Sweet Jesus!' she says. 'You scared me half to death.' She sets a green bucket on the floor by her feet. 'I didn't think anyone was here. Nora, isn't it?'

'Yes,' I say, thankful that her nervousness camouflages mine. She seems larger than I remember, chunkier, her arms thick and pale. 'I'm sorry. I didn't mean to startle you. I should've called out when I heard you come in.'

She gets a dust cloth out of the bucket and wipes off the dresser. 'Ian didn't tell me you'd be here today,' she says.

I close the closet door, stalling for time, thinking of an excuse. 'He didn't know I was coming over,' I say, hoping he hadn't mentioned that we'd split up. 'I picked up his laundry. I just wanted to drop it off.'

Pat finishes dusting the dresser and walks over to the night-stand. Apparently, she finds the explanation for my presence plausible. 'I guess I better leave,' I say. 'I have to go back to work.'

She flashes me a brief, preoccupied smile, no doubt relieved I won't be getting in her way while she cleans Ian's condo. 'Bye,' she says, and I walk out of the room.

All afternoon I call Joe, but he isn't at the police station. That evening I try him at home, but neither he nor his wife answer the phone. I'm supposed to see M. this evening, but I want to speak to Joe first, to tell him what I found in Ian's condo. Perhaps now, finally, Franny's murderer will be apprehended. When Joe still isn't home by nine o'clock, I give up. I'll have to wait until tomorrow to call him. I grab my keys and decide to walk the several blocks to M.'s house. The night air is cool, refreshing after today's heat, and I'm glad I didn't drive. Stars glitter up above, and the sky is magnificent, as black and shiny as obsidian. I walk west on Montgomery, thinking of Franny and the photos in Ian's condo. I'm relieved, immensely, that it's finally over, that her killer won't go free.

A twig snaps. I turn around but see no one. Immediately, I think of Ian, wondering if Pat told him I was in his bedroom today. I pull my keys out of my pocket, then take the safety cap off the canister of Mace. I walk faster, looking over my shoulder. No one is there. I feel spooked, the darkness suddenly threatening, and decide to jog, the can of Mace firmly in my hand. I think I hear shuffling behind me, then the sound of loose gravel on asphalt, and I break out in a full-speed run. *I'm coming for you.* When I reach the older section of Willowbank, I turn onto Meadowbrook Drive. There are no streetlamps here, and I run faster, my chest aching, then turn left on Almond. When I get to M.'s house, I am panting and sweaty, tendrils of hair sticking to the sides of my face and the back of my neck. I bend over, catching my breath, not taking my eyes off the street. M. sees me from the front window and comes outside.

'What's the matter?' he asks, walking toward me.

I point up the street, still panting. 'Someone followed me,' I say, choking out the words. 'Chased me.'

He looks up the street but doesn't see anyone. 'Are you sure?' he asks.

I nod, still breathing heavily, then put the safety cap back on the Mace. M. wraps his arms around me, holding me. A few minutes later, a young boy, maybe seventeen or eighteen, saunters by, wearing headphones as he listens to a Walkman.

'There's your stalker,' M. says, laughing. 'You see? Just a teenager. You're letting your imagination get away from you. He's only a boy.'

I shake my head. 'No,' I say. 'There was someone else. I'm sure. It was Ian. I know it was him,' and I tell M. what happened today, and what I found under Ian's bed.

M. releases me and backs away, frowning, his face dark in the shadows from the porch light. 'God, Nora. That was a dangerous thing to do. Why didn't you call me? I would've gone over with you. Better yet, why couldn't you let the police handle it?' I hear the anger in his voice, see it in his face.

'I had to find out,' I say. 'I had to be sure.' Abruptly, he walks into the house, still angry. I follow. 'You're sounding like Joe,' I accuse him. 'Telling me to stay out of it.'

'Maybe you should listen to him.' He is silent for a minute, shakes his head, then touches my hand lightly. 'Nora, sometimes you can be so exasperating. What if Ian had walked in on you?'

'He didn't.'

'No, but he could have. And he might have hurt you.' He puts his arms around me, holds me close. 'Don't you know how much you mean to me?'

The warmth of his body presses against mine. I feel him shudder, just a slight tremble, and I'm instantly chastised, touched by the depth of his feeling. I didn't know he cared so much; a month ago, I would've thought him incapable of such an intensity of emotion.

'I'm sorry,' I say. 'I guess it was foolish to go over there alone. I wasn't thinking. After I got another letter, I just wanted to take some action so I wouldn't feel like such a victim.'

M. takes me into the living room and we sit on the couch. For minutes, he just holds me, hugging me tenderly. I feel the soughing of his breath, feathery and warm, against my neck. Finally, very quietly, he says, 'You've affected me, Nora, as no one else has. I'm not even sure I know why; I just know that you have. I love you, and I want to tell you everything about me, everything about my life. I want to share myself with you, and that's a new feeling for me.'

He speaks the words into my neck, our bodies still crushed tightly together. I cannot see his face, but I hear the soft beating in his chest, reaching out to me. He cups my chin in his hand, lifts my head, and says, 'You're changing me, Nora.' He smiles sweetly – an expression I've rarely seen from him – and adds, 'I think it's a good change.'

I lay my head back on his chest, snuggling closer. We breathe together, the rise and fall of my chest coinciding with his. After a while, he whispers sadly, 'You never say my name. Never.'

I am silent for several minutes, thinking, feeling very confused. What does this mean? He is asking me to share his life, unthinkable a few months ago. But now I feel something softening inside me, a warm sensation at the center of my heart. I thought Ian was the man for whom I was destined, but could it have been M. all along? Can my feelings for him be more than sexual? It is possible, I think, and very softly I say, 'Michael.'

'I like the sound of that,' he says, and I smile, feeling suddenly aroused at the prospect of our union – not of the love but of the sex, his continual domination and control. I kneel before him, the first time I've done this without his command, and say, 'I want . . .' But I hesitate, not finishing the thought, bowing my head.

'Say it,' he says, and he holds my head between his hands, forcing me to look him in the eye. 'Tell me what you want. Say it.'

I know what I want, what I need, but am reluctant to say it

out loud. I try to look away, but he holds my head firmly. 'I want you to spank me,' I say, barely a whisper.

He releases me, strokes my cheek.

'I want you to whip me,' I tell him, louder this time, more urgent. 'Please,' I add, and I take off my clothes and lie, willingly, across his lap, waiting for the sweet release that comforts me, for the erotic adjunct that comes with the pain.

39

The police have not yet arrested Ian, but it is forthcoming. They searched his condo and found the shoebox under his bed. His fingerprints were on everything – the duct tape, the photos, Billy's bracelet, the knife, the box itself. Ian admits the knife belongs to him – one of his wood-carving knives, which he claims has been missing for several weeks – but everything else he swears he's never seen. The investigation continues anew, Ian now the prime suspect.

He has left many phone calls on my answering machine, urging me to return his calls, asking for my help. I don't phone him back. I have nothing to say to Ian, and I certainly won't help him in any way. My sense of betrayal is acute. I feel foolish for trusting him for so long. Like most people, I thought myself a good judge of character. Put two men side by side, and I could certainly descry a murderer amongst the two. Not so. No longer do I trust my sense of perception. Ian had me fooled completely. Even now, with all the evidence pointed clearly at him, even now I have trouble imagining him poised over Franny's bound body, a knife in hand. So much for gut instinct.

I'm backing my Honda out of the garage, looking in the rear-view mirror, when Ian's blue Bronco suddenly careens in the driveway. I slam on the brakes, barely avoiding a collision, and put the car in park, leaving the ignition on. In the mirror, I see Ian jump out of his car, stalk purposefully toward mine. He's burly, and would look like a gangster in his gray pinstripe suit if it weren't for his youngish face and flaxen hair. Normally smooth-skinned and pleasant, his face now is scrunched up in a scowl, dark and ugly. I press the button that locks all the doors just as he reaches my car.

'Goddammit, Nora!' he says when he hears the click of the lock. He pulls the handle, but the door doesn't open.

'Why are you doing this?' He leans down, his angry face and broad shoulders filling the window. The tip of his nose touches the glass, flattens to the diameter of a dime. 'Why?!' he shouts, and I pull back, away from the window, but the seat belt and bucket seat halt my progress. He slaps the top of my car with the palm of his hand, making a loud tinny noise, then walks a few feet away, shaking his head. He stops and looks around, hands planted firmly on hips, his chest heaving from breathing hard, trying to contain his anger.

A neighbor's dog barks at a passing car, and a small boy, maybe four or five, wearing dungarees and jabbering to himself, shambles past Franny's Cadillac, trailing a stick on the ground. A woman's voice calls out from up the street, and he freezes in midstep with his head cocked, like a cartoon character whose film reel has stalled. Then, as abruptly as he'd stopped, he resumes motion, weaving up the sidewalk toward the voice.

Ian returns, calmer now, and looks down at me. He says, 'You're afraid of me, Nora? You have to hide in the car?'

I stare at the steering wheel, unable to meet his gaze, unable to answer his questions.

'I don't understand,' he says. 'Why are you doing this to me?' There is a note of desperation in his voice, faint but unmistakable. I grip the bottom of the steering wheel, head bowed.

'The police questioned me today – again. They came by the office while I was working.' He places both palms on the glass, reminding me of a small boy leaving fingerprints. 'They asked if I'd be willing to give them samples of my hair and carpet fibers from my house. I had to hire a lawyer, Nora. A lawyer.' His head drops. 'How could you tell them I killed Franny? How could you even think it?'

Sighing, he turns around and leans against the car, his back to me, and folds his arms. A light breeze ripples through his hair.

Talking to the wind, he says, 'Why are you doing this, Nora? I loved you – I still love you. When I said I needed time to be alone for a while, time to think things through, that's all I wanted – time. Just a little time. I wasn't splitting up with you; I would've said so if that was the case. I think of you every day, wondering if I did the right thing by distancing myself from you, knowing in my heart that I didn't. I decided to call you and explain what really happened, why I needed to be alone for a while, but then the police started questioning me about Franny.' He hesitates, looks at the ground, then says quietly, 'I suppose I can understand your being angry if you thought I broke off with you – but to tell the police I was stalking you, sending threatening letters, and making anonymous calls, and that I killed your sister? That goes way beyond vindictive. I had nothing to do with it, Nora. Not with any of it. I swear.'

He stops talking, and I hear the quiet vibration of the car's engine. The plea in his voice was obvious, undisguised. *I still love you.* Does he think he can change my mind with a declaration of love? His affection – sincere or not – doesn't change the fact that his fingerprints were on each item in the shoebox. Inwardly, I shudder. This is what stalkers do – kill with their love.

'I'm not sure what upsets me the most,' he says. 'The police barging in on me while I'm working, or finding all that stuff under my bed, or knowing you believe I stalked you and killed your sister.' Another pause. 'I didn't do it, Nora. You know me better than that.' He turns his head so he can see me and lowers his voice. 'You know better.' I barely hear his words.

Through the windshield, the sun glistens and throws glints of light off the glass. The sky is bright blue, cheerful, and I wish Ian would leave. I don't want to be burdened with his problems – or anyone else's. He will be arrested soon, and a jury will determine his innocence or guilt, not I. All I want is to be left alone.

'I was hiking the day she died,' he continues. He's still addressing the wind, his back pressed against the car. 'With a friend in Desolation Wilderness. The only problem is, my friend doesn't remember exactly which day we were there. It was too long ago; he just can't be sure of the date.'

How convenient, I think. Another suspect with no alibi.

The sound of a roaring motor shatters through the air. A gardener is cutting down a tree next door, and he looks like a scrawny lumberjack in his yellow hard hat, steel-toed boots, and plastic goggles. His hands, one wrapped around the throttle control handle and the other around the front handlebar, vibrate under the roar of the saw. Specks of sawdust fly out from the chain. The loud, ratcheting buzz penetrates the air, choking out the sounds of skirring birds, barking dogs, passing traffic. The yard seems to shrink in this earsplitting, pressing noise; it doesn't leave room for anything else.

Ian sighs. Minutes go by before he speaks again. When the gardener turns off the chain saw, he says, 'It wasn't me, Nora. You should know that. Listen to your heart.'

Without giving me another glance, he walks slowly back to his Bronco. Sunlight streams down between the tree branches and casts a silvery sheen on the hood of my car. Even with the windows rolled up, I can hear the treetops softly rustling, murmuring, as the breeze blows through their leaves. In my rearview mirror, I watch Ian drive away, which leaves only one other object reflected in my mirror: the black fin-tailed Cadillac, a constant reminder of how I failed to understand my sister.

Once, when I was driving around Sacramento on an errand, I spotted Franny in her Cadillac, going in the opposite direction on her way to the dialysis clinic. I hollered and waved, trying to get her attention; just as I was about to honk the horn, something made me stop. She looked so serene, oblivious of me and everyone else, a contented smile spread across her face, that I didn't want to disturb her. Transfixed, I watched her as she sailed past, looking like there was nothing else in the world she would rather be doing than riding around in her shiny black Cadillac. I felt like an interloper, intruding on someone else's private moment. I wanted to avert my head, look the other way, but I couldn't. I turned my car around and followed her surreptitiously. It was like a whale, her Cadillac, and seemed not so much to cruise as to float down the road, ponderously, weighted down and bloated, taking up the entire lane. I hadn't remembered the car being so large; it seemed as if it had grown over the years, like a living body, expanding with time. Even from a distance of two car lengths, I could hear the Cadillac announcing its presence in a low, steady rumble. Passing cars got out of Franny's way. They hugged the shoulder of the road, swerving around the car as if it might be a huge, predatory fish, and when she pulled into the clinic, she parked in the very back, on the white line, and took up two parking spaces. With a shudder and a deep moan, the engine stopped. Franny got out of the car like a dignitary exiting a limousine: first the head, a look around, a smile to no one in particular, then the body. She stood up, slung her purse over her shoulder, and then, with hands on hips, nodded at the car approvingly, a look of pure delight on her face. I spied on her from across the street, wondering what she saw in the car that gave her such joy. She looked as if she had discovered something priceless, something intangible, like the secret of happiness. What was it? I wanted to know. What was the secret?

But then I went on my way, soon forgetting all about her, wrapped up in my own concerns. Later that day, when I recalled the incident, I was amused – at myself for following her, and at Franny for allowing a car to define and validate her presence. I couldn't understand that type of thinking at all. I asked her once why she was so enamored with the Cadillac, but she only smiled cryptically and said, 'It leaves me room to grow.'

40

Autumn arrives on a chilly, windswept day. Ian has been arrested for the murder of my sister. Although neither his hair strands, fingerprints, nor carpet fibers matched those found in Franny's apartment, the duct tape did. A chemical analysis proved, without a doubt, that the end fibers matched those of the tape over Franny's mouth. Ian still maintains his innocence, and will not reveal how he murdered her. The cause of her death remains unknown. I may never learn how or why he killed Franny, and I wonder if this is where her story will end. Perhaps there was no reason. People kill without conscience – it's reported in the newspapers every day. Mark Kirn is still in San Quentin for the murder of Cheryl Mansfield, but I doubt his guilt. Ian could've killed her as well. I don't know the answers, and I probably never will. I can accept that now . . . I think.

Since the day Ian was arrested, the phone calls and threatening letters and photos have stopped. A languid mantle of serenity has settled on my life, and M. and I get along quite well. We have a unique arrangement: he orders and I obey. I guess this is what he meant when he said I'd have to learn to deal with men. It is a satisfactory alliance. What little control I had left, I have relinquished, and I have no responsibility now but to do as he asks. This is fine with me. My protracted search for Franny's killer has left me drained. I feel emotionally bruised, betrayed by the one man I thought I could trust completely. How could I be so wrong about Ian? Now my only desire is to retire into the cocoon of M.'s authority. I'm content to be on autopilot with him as my helmsman, plotting my course. My subjugation, for the most part, is confined to the sexual arena, although the boundaries of this arena do blur and cross over to the other areas of our lives. At times, I feel like a nonperson, someone with little weight or substance – like a child or a slave, with no obligation but to obey and please my parent, my master. As time goes by, it is a role I assume with less and less difficulty. Let someone take care of me for a change. My peace of mind – the first I've had since Franny died – is achieved by the loss of personal power, but it is a loss with which I can live.

I, however, am not the sole person to give up my power. In his love for me, M. also has relinquished some of his control. At first, I thought this was a ruse, another attempt to deceive me. The way he treated Franny was despicable, and I did not believe him capable of change, capable of love. But his manner suggests otherwise. Many nights we talk well past midnight. And in these nocturnal interlocutions, hidden from the light of day, he opens up to me, shares his feelings, tells me his weaknesses, his frailties, his vulnerabilities – everything that makes him human – exposing the quiddities of his soul. I am the safekeeper of this knowledge. He trusts me to guard it well, and perhaps that makes him more vulnerable than I. At the very least, we are equals.

A mean sky, as black as anthracite, covers the city. Clouds churn and a stiff wind forces the rain down in slanting sheets, flooding the downtown gutter on Second Street. Bits of urban duff – shredded paper, tinfoil gum wrappers, cigarette butts – and scratchings of twigs roil in the muddy water like toy boats tossed about on choppy seas. The water and debris rush along the curb, then become trapped in the vortex above the sewer grate where they whirl, briefly, before the drain sucks it all down. It's going to be a wet Halloween.

This evening M. is making dinner for me. He enjoys cooking, and he's much better at it than I. He gives me a glass of red wine and I perch on a barstool to watch him. He's wearing a burgundy shirt the same color as the wine, open at the collar, and his forehead glistens in the warm kitchen. He reminds me of one of those gourmet cooks on television, his movements rapid but precise, a hand towel flung over one shoulder, his shirt sleeves rolled up to his elbows. A glass pan of lasagna is cooling on the stove top, its cheeses bubbling and golden brown. He is finishing a salad, and I smell the garlic and butter from the sourdough bread under the broiler. He swirls around the kitchen, tossing the salad with Italian dressing, snatching the bread out of the oven before it burns, arranging it on a platter. His black slacks are creased down the middle, not wrinkled at all. I think of moving in with M.; the idea does not seem as absurd as it once did.

'We're set,' he says, and he tosses the hand towel on the counter. He disappears for a minute – says he wants to turn off the porch light so we won't be disturbed by trick-or-treaters – then returns. He uses a hot pad to pick up the lasagna and carries it and the garlic bread into the dining room. I follow him, with the salad and bottle of wine. I've already set the table, and we sit down to eat. He's at the head of the table and I'm next to him, on his right. As he dishes up the lasagna, he tells me about one of his students, a pianist.

'He has this incredible desire to perform,' M. says. He tastes the lasagna, then offers me the platter of garlic bread. 'He's so driven, yet his playing is mediocre at best. He'll never be a great musician.'

'How old is he, Michael?' I ask. Michael. It seems strange to call him by his first name. The word sticks in my mouth like chewy caramel clinging to my teeth.

'Twenty-one.'

'Give him time. If he's got the drive, he'll improve.' I pause to eat what's on my fork. 'This is great,' I say, referring to the lasagna.

'Thanks,' he says, then a tiny frown furrows his dark eyebrows. 'His technique will improve with time, but he'll never be a great pianist. He lacks the creative impulse that separates the good from the great. He understands the music, intellectually, but he doesn't *feel* it.'

I smile at him and say, 'Well, he's got a good teacher.'

M. dismisses my comment with an impatient wave of his hand. 'It's not something you can learn,' he says. 'You either have it or you don't. All the technique in the world, all the instruction, won't help him. He'll improve to some degree, maybe even a lot, given his drive, but he'll never be a great musician. Hard work isn't enough.'

'Thomas Edison wouldn't have agreed with you. He thought genius was due to hard work more than creative impulses. "One percent inspiration, ninety-nine percent perspiration." If your student works at his music long enough, and hard enough, he'll probably succeed.'

'Don't quote aphorisms to me, Nora. They're utterly banal and almost always oversimplified – which means they bring scant understanding to individualized situations. My student lacks true genius, and perspiration will never fill that void. He'd be better off if he recognized his limitations. He'd be happier as a top-rate lawyer or accountant than as a second-rate musician who would always know he'd never be good enough. And it'll only get worse for him: wanting something desperately, knowing it will always be denied him, and the ultimate wound – seeing others less worthy than he, less diligent, blessed with, and taking for granted, the talent and genius he lacks. He's in for a life of disappointment.'

I hear a trace of sympathy in his voice. I wonder if he's speaking of himself also. Several times, in the middle of the night, I've woken up to the sounds of his piano. Once I snuck into the den and found him bent over the keyboard, a painful look of agony on his face as he played a beautiful, sad composition. It was a dirge, I believe. A shock of his fine, dark hair tumbled down over his forehead; his long, elegant fingers moved fluidly over the keys – and I thought I had never seen such an exquisite sight. It was so intensely personal, so private, so passionate, that I backed out of the room, feeling very much like an interloper. After that, whenever I heard his midnight melodies I remained in bed. M. is very well known, but even

I – who understand little of the music world – know he's not one of the great contemporary musicians. I thought he was content being a professor, but now, as he speaks of his student's lack of genius, I begin to wonder.

I also begin to wonder about the psychology of his sadomasochism, and if his desire to dominate has a direct correlation to his inability to truly excel as a musician. He once told me he accepted his limitations as a pianist, and perhaps his sadomasochism is part of an elaborate Jungian balancing act – his lack of control over his innate talent, his lack of genius, forces him to demand complete control over me. I, of course, am not exempt from this analysis. My balancing act moves in the opposite direction. I've always had a great deal of control – calling the shots in my personal relationships, excelling in my professional career – and perhaps that allows me to willingly surrender to M. and to the bliss of noncontrol.

'Will you tell your student this?' I ask. 'That he lacks genius?'

M. smiles slowly, sadly, and his voice softens. 'No,' he says. 'Destroying dreams is not my job. I'm there to teach him all I can. He'll have to come to that recognition himself' He pauses, then adds, 'I suppose if he came out and asked me directly, I would owe him the truth. But he won't ask – they never do.'

I go into the kitchen to look for Parmesan cheese. The doorbell rings and, unthinking, I answer it. Two small boys, thin and blue-lipped, wearing yellow raincoats over their costumes, give me a weary 'Trick-or-treat' and hold out two damp pillowcases they're using as bags. M. doesn't have any candy, so I look in my purse for coins, then drop quarters in each boy's bag. They trudge down the walkway in their rain boots, leaving muddy imprints on the porch. Down the driveway, in the street, their parents are huddled under an umbrella, reminding me of all those Halloweens when I'd been a small child myself – before Franny was born – going from door to door collecting sweets while my father crouched down, watched over me from the curb, his presence nothing but a dark, shadowy mass with a red-tipped glow from his burning cigarette.

I return to the dining room and eat my lasagna, thinking again of M. and his late-night rendezvous with the piano. He looks over at me and smiles, slyly this time.

'Take off your blouse and bra,' he tells me. 'I want to look at you while I eat.'

As soon as he says this, I feel a flutter in my stomach and a tingle in my groin. That's all he has to say – 'Take off your blouse' – to get me aroused. I hesitate, my fork in midair. For some people, the thought of sex has a galvanizing effect, spurring them to action. For me, the reverse holds true. I become transfixed with anticipation; a paralysis of sorts, albeit lasting only seconds, sets in. And in the silence of those seconds, my heart beats faster and my breathing becomes deep and heavy.

M. locks his eyes on mine, and I surrender, willingly, under his gaze. I put down my fork and pull my blouse out from my skirt. The blouse is white with a high-necked collar, and it has tiny pearl buttons all down the front. I begin to undo them, one by one. My fingers feel suddenly awkward, and it takes me longer than it normally would. The buttonholes seem unusually small, my fingers large and clumsy. I push each pearl button through the small opening. M. still watches me, eating his dinner. When I finish with the last button, I slip the blouse off my shoulders and let it fall to the floor. Thinking of Franny – how she must have sat in this chair, doing the same for M. – I reach around and unhook my bra and let it slide to the floor also.

He nods his approval. 'Good,' he says, 'you can finish eating now.'

I pick up my fork and begin again on the lasagna. M. has ordered me to do this for him many times before – sometimes he'll just want my breasts exposed, sometimes he'll want to see me only from the waist down – yet it never fails to excite me. His command over me is thrilling; my forced exposure arouses me completely. I want him to fuck me, but I know he won't, not yet, not until he's ready, and this delay makes me desire him even more.

He reaches over and brushes each nipple lightly, making them erect. I arch my back just a little, pushing my breasts out to him.

'Nice,' he says, and goes back to his dinner.

I want to tell him to squeeze and fondle them, but I know he won't. He never does as I ask, only as he pleases. I eat also, my nipples stiff and ready for his touch.

The doorbell rings and, with a smirk, M. says, 'Did you want to answer it?'

I shake my head. We hear shuffling feet, whispers, then the sounds of retreat.

'Would you like me to tell you another story about Franny?' he asks. He reaches for the wine bottle and refills both our glasses.

'Yes,' I say, wondering what he will tell me now. I know we won't have sex for a while, so I begin to relax.

He leans back in his chair, finished with his dinner. 'Soon after I took Franny to the hog barn, I told her of my other interests in animals. In fact, it was after dinner, much as we're speaking now, her breasts exposed to me as yours are.' He lifts his wineglass and takes a sip. 'Of course, hers were much larger. Yours are very nice, but I admit I am a breast man. They can't be large enough for me.'

I blush – something I don't do very often – because my breasts are rather small and, in front of M., knowing he prefers big-breasted women, I feel self-conscious about their size.

He reaches over and rubs his wineglass across my nipples, getting them hard again, getting me excited. 'Oh, you have nothing to be embarrassed about,' he says. 'Yours are very nice, even if they're small. And you love to display them for me, don't you? Franny was always uncomfortable doing this, but not you. I'll bet your pussy's wet right now, isn't it? My sweet pet needs a good fucking. Would you like me to take care of you, baby?'

I'm flushed and feel as though I can't talk. I want him so much, but I hate it when he makes me say it. Sometimes, he purposely arouses me, gets me on the edge of an orgasm, then won't continue until I beg him to fuck me. He likes to see me this way, begging, promising him I'll do anything if he'll just finish. I demean myself by complying, but I fall for it every time. My passion for him has no limits, and before him my presence is diminished. If he wants me to beg, I shall do so. He reduces me so easily. 'Yes,' I whisper hoarsely, 'I want you to take care of me.'

He leans back in his chair and smiles. 'I know you do, Nora. But you're going to have to wait. I want to tell you my story first.' He takes another sip of wine, and once again I feel I have been manipulated.

'After dinner, I took Franny into the den and removed the rest of her clothes.' He gives me a wink and says, 'You know how I love to see my women naked.' Again, I try to imagine Franny prancing around his house, naked. The image doesn't come. I have difficulty seeing her as a sexual being, and even more difficulty seeing her as M.'s sexual being, as an object to satisfy his cravings. When I imagine her, she's always dressed primly in a nurse's uniform and white thick-soled shoes. I realize this is not an accurate image of her – if nothing else, M. has taught me this – but it is the image with which I am comfortable.

'I had her sit on the couch and I told her how much I enjoyed her in the hog barn with the little piglets sucking on her breasts. I also told her that I was pleased she got along so well with my dog. Franny liked Rameau very much. She'd feed him and go out in the backyard and play with him. And at nights, sometimes she and I would take Rameau for a long walk around the neighborhood. I explained to her that I was an animal lover, and that I wanted to see her with an animal. She was confused; she had no idea what I was talking about. I told her I wanted to watch her get fucked by an animal. Poor Franny. She was so agitated. She knew I would make her do it, and she didn't know what to say. She just sat there, biting her lip, shaking her head, her poor naked body shivering on the couch. I told her she was going to have to do this for me. She started to cry – she did a lot of that – and I held her close to me and comforted her, but I was still firm with her and explained that it was something I needed to see. I told her she was going to have to do it, but I would let her choose what kind of animal she wanted, either a pig or dog. She just shook her head, held on to me tightly, as if her distress, her tears, would change my mind. Well, the opposite always happened. Her fear always brought out the worst in me. "Choose," I told her. She said no, she couldn't. "Let me tell you the difference," I said. "That will help you decide. If you want a dog, we'll put you down on all fours and let Rameau mount you from behind. He ejaculates almost immediately, soon after he begins thrusting inside you – all dogs do – but as soon as he shoots his cum into you, the base of his cock will swell up into a big knot so he's stuck inside your cunt. He'll lift his leg over you and turn around one hundred and eighty degrees so you're ass to ass, still joined together with his cock in your cunt until the knot goes down. With Rameau, the swelling takes about a half hour to subside, so I could watch you while you were joined like this, take a few pictures, leisurely jerk off.

'"Now, a pig is much different," I told her. "A pig's cock is a long, stiff coil, like a corkscrew, and when he comes it'll take him about ten minutes to shoot it all into you. He ejaculates almost two cups of pig cum. You'd like that," I said to her, "a nice long cock, and he'd be shooting and shooting inside you, filling your cunt with a pint of sperm." This frightened poor Franny. Actually, I've never seen a pig with a woman. I'm not sure about the logistics of it, how I would get the boar to mount her, but I wanted to take her down to the pig barn and give it a try. "If you don't choose, I'll choose for you," I said, but still she shook her head and cried. "All right," I said. "I'll choose. I want to see you with—" And she cried out, "A dog! Not a pig! A dog! A dog!" Poor Franny. She panicked. She was desperate; she didn't want either, but a dog, for her, was by far the lesser of the degrading. I held her until she stopped crying, then I made her get down on the den floor, on all fours, and I brought Rameau into the room.' M. lifts his shoulders in a shrug. 'You can imagine the rest,' he says.

I am mesmerized by his story. I do not believe it, though, not a word. It's like some of his other stories about Franny – they're too outlandish to be true. Not with Franny.

'You're lying,' I tell him. 'She wouldn't do that, not even for you. You shouldn't make your stories so bizarre – that just renders them unbelievable.'

He makes a little clucking noise with his tongue. 'You're a difficult audience,' he says, then he smiles nicely. 'But enough of this. Storytime is through.' He takes me by the hand and leads me into the den. Kneeling down in front of me, he unlaces my shoes. He slips them off my feet and kisses the insides of both ankles. Then he unzips my skirt and lets it fall to the floor. Hooking his fingers under the elastic of the waistband, he slides my panties down, smoothly, and I lift up one foot at a time to step out of them. He puts his face in my hairless crotch and kisses my vaginal lips, almost reverently. I part my legs for him, slightly, and feel the tip of his tongue on my clitoris. My hands clutch his dark hair, holding him to me, but, gently, he breaks away.

'Come,' he says, 'sit on the couch for a minute.' He seats me there, then goes to the sliding glass door, opens it, and whistles. Rameau comes bounding into the room. He's a big dog, almost three feet tall, probably close to 150 pounds, and he's beautiful. Most of the Great Danes I've seen have golden, brownish fur, but Rameau's coat is short and black and shiny. He comes up to me and nuzzles his nose and square jaw on the side of my leg. I pet him, and he rests his massive head on my thigh.

M. comes back to me on the couch. 'Don't get any ideas,' I say. 'I'm not going to fuck Rameau.' The doorbell rings again, but both of us ignore it.

He sits down and reaches over to scratch the dog behind his ear. 'I know,' he tells me. 'Rameau is going to fuck you.

First, you'll get on the floor and let him fuck you from behind. Then, after that, after he relaxes and is ready to fuck you again, you'll sit on the couch, leaning back with your legs spread, and he'll mount you while you're facing him. I want you to watch while Rameau fucks you, I want you to know you're being fucked by a dog, and that you're doing it for me.'

I cross my legs and shake my head. 'Forget it,' I say.

But M. just smiles. He says, 'Rameau is well trained, and he hasn't had human pussy for a long time, not since Franny. I'll have him lick you really well before I allow him to mount you.'

41

When I wake up this morning, M. has already left for work. I lie in bed, thinking of last night. It astounds me that I protested so little, that my objections were so shallow. Having sex with the dog was different than I thought it would be. As M. said, dogs ejaculate almost immediately. Once Rameau entered me and began thrusting, he came really fast, within seconds, twenty at the most. Still, it was fascinating to feel his warm tongue on my sex, to have him penetrate me, to feel his short fur between my legs, rubbing against my body. Before M. let Rameau mount me, he used his fingers on me, playing with my clitoris and nipples while the dog lapped at me with his tongue. The taboo nature of the act aroused me immensely, and when Rameau put his paws on my back he as prepared to mount, then leaned forward and clutched me around the waist with his legs, I did not protest. M. guided the dog's penis inside me, while he still fingered my clit, and I came the same time Rameau did. And I came strongly, getting a perverse pleasure out of doing something so bizarre, so far beyond the pale. It's difficult to describe my response. The dog's penis was smaller than a man's, and the actual fucking was over almost before it began, but the sensation was unimaginably erotic – no, not erotic, pornographic. The instant I felt the tip of Rameau's penis between my legs, probing for an entrance, my body quaked with such carnal, ruttish lust that I momentarily lost cognizance of the den and my presence in it. I was transported, but to where I do not know – someplace primitive and dissolute and purely sexual. The sex was depraved, and it was enjoyable beyond belief. The dog fucked me twice last night, from behind and while I was facing him, and then M. had his turn with me. 'You'll learn to take him in your mouth,' he said as he fucked me. 'No,' I told him. 'I don't want to do that,' but M. just grasped my hips firmly and pumped inside me harder and said, 'Yes. You will.'

I get out of bed and take a shower. I took one before I fell asleep last night, but feel I need another. I wash my hair again, then rub myself dry with a towel. Putting on one of M.'s bathrobes, I walk into the bedroom. From the window, I see Rameau lying on the grass. I wonder if the dog is going to become part of our regular lovemaking, or if M. will want to see me with the dog only occasionally. I am a dogfucker. I don't know what to make of this. Now, with a clarity of mind illumined by early morning light, I can see the degradation of the act – for that's what it is, to M. He wants to see me with an animal, a beast, to prove his mastery over me.

A dogfucker, that's what I am. As soon as Rameau started licking me, I enjoyed every minute of it. I am a normal person, I am thinking. How can I be a dogfucker?

Rameau sees me standing in front of the window, and his tail beats against the grass. I go into the kitchen and make a fresh pot of coffee, then wait for it to brew. On the kitchen table, there is a video with a note taped to the top of it. 'For your viewing pleasure – I kept this as a memento,' it says in M.'s handwriting.

With my coffee mug in hand, I take the video into the den and slip it into the VCR. Sipping my coffee, I turn on the television and sit down to watch the tape. It is black at first, with no picture or sound, then suddenly the image appears: Franny, naked, crying, on all fours. Rameau is behind her, his head down between her legs, licking her genitals. The camera goes around her so I can see her and the dog from all sides. 'Please, Michael,' Franny sobs, looking into the camera, 'don't make me do this.' But M. doesn't reply. The camera circles around her again. Rameau brings his head up and climbs on her back, clenching her waist with his paws, and begins thrusting. Franny screams out and starts to shift her body. I hear M. – who is behind the camera, not visible to me, but a lurking presence all the same – yell at her sharply, 'Don't move!' She stays there, silent now but still sobbing, tears running down her face, her mouth in a bewildered, painful *O*, a grim rictus of her humiliation and despair.

I turn off the video. I don't want to see any more. I can't watch the rest. Her experience with Rameau was the opposite of mine. Although reluctant at first, I was a willing participant. M. aroused me, made me want the dog, and I was ready for him when he mounted. But with Franny, M. was sadistic, brutal. He enjoyed her humiliation. My pleasure last night, after watching the tape, seems less erotic. It seems, in fact, tainted. There is a fine line, I am learning, between eroticism and degradation. With my sister, he crossed the line. And I know now that everything he told me about Franny was true. The hog barn, the urination, the dog fucking, and everything else – it was all true. I thought he was just tormenting me, getting a twisted pleasure out of making me squirm, but it was all true. Parallels. More parallels. I'm following Franny's footsteps even closer than I had imagined.

I rewind the video and take it out of the VCR. Franny, if she were alive, wouldn't want anyone to see this. I get a pair of scissors, then go out to the garage and find a hammer. My intention is to break the video case, then cut the tape into small pieces and throw it in the trash can. I bring the hammer up, ready to smash the video, then stop. This is the only video I have of Franny and, however awful it may be, I can't bring myself to destroy it.

I go back to the den and put the video inside the VCR. I turn it on, and this time I force myself to watch it, all the way through. I feel that I owe this to Franny, that I have to experience the pain and humiliation with her so she won't be alone, a vicarious sharing of her degradation. The video is truly despicable, and even though I watch, I find myself concentrating on other objects in the film – the brown carpet, Billy's medical bracelet around her wrist, the white skin of her body – rather than focusing on the painful sight of Rameau licking and fucking.

When it is over, I sit back on the sofa, feeling drained. The images keep running through my mind. Franny on the floor, on all fours, naked, then Rameau climbing on her. I rub my temples. An image, half formed, cloudy, nags at my mind. Something is wrong, but I don't know what. Something beyond Franny's humiliation. She is on the floor, she is naked, the dog licks her genitals. Franny's head is bowed, tears cover her face, her breasts sag, her skin is so white, her buttocks . . . What did I see on her buttocks? Some kind of mark. A welt from his whip? No. Something else, more like a birthmark.

I get up and rewind the video. I stop it just before Rameau climbs on her back, then I watch. I see it on her right buttock, some kind of mark, a scar, I think. It's barely visible, like a wound that has almost, but not quite, healed. The viewer's eye ordinarily would be drawn automatically to Rameau, and if I hadn't been looking elsewhere, I never would have noticed it. I press the rewind button and watch the video again. I still can't make it out. I watch it once more, then press the pause button. The picture freezes. On her right buttock, down low and on the side, there is a circle with a line drawn through it, the universal symbol for no. It is faint, just the barest trace of a mark, but I see it.

I stand back. I know what this means. When Franny was found, her torso was covered with cut marks – circles, squares, lines. Because of the body's decomposition, the coroner could not identify most of the designs. But one of the marks she could make out was a circle with a line drawn through it.

M. killed Franny. The wound on her buttock, so faint he didn't notice it, had almost healed when he took the video. And it healed completely by the time he killed her because the coroner didn't find any cut marks on her buttocks. But it's here, in the video, the identical design he later cut into her stomach, proof that M. killed Franny. Proof enough, yes, but only for me, not for the police. M. is not in the video, only Franny and Rameau. He will deny the video belongs to him. I feel myself shudder, not with a chill but with red-hot fury. All those pent-up emotions from the previous year – all the anger, the guilt – burn inside me like a raging fire of vengeance. I won't let him get away. Not again. Not this time.

I rewind the video, calm down, and collect my thoughts, thinking of what I must do. I walk out of the den, then down the long hallway toward the master bedroom. Until now, M.'s house was fraught with sexual meaning. The living room, the den, the furniture – all of it conjured up past memories that readied me for future encounters. It was phallic and carnal his house, our own private seraglio of licentious pleasure. But now, as I go through the rooms, I sense a different image before me: one of pain and suffering. I am haunted by the video of Franny. She walks here still, down this hallway, her footsteps tentative, her silent cries echoing in my mind. I will never see this house as I had before.

I enter M.'s bedroom and start to get dressed. He has collected my clothes from last night – my blouse and bra from the dining room; skirt, shoes, and panties from the den – and he has folded them neatly and placed them on the embrasure of the window. With me, he is considerate and orderly, and during the last few weeks I suppressed my original claim that he was a cruel, evil man. I was so sure, at first, that he was. Then, as time passed and I became better acquainted with him, I thought perhaps I had been mistaken. My needs clouded my judgment. I wanted to understand Franny, to know what she was really like, and M. introduced me to her. Because of him, I know my sister better than I'd ever known her when she was alive.

But somewhere along the way, I lost my objectivity. I stopped believing he was a cruel man simply because I didn't want it to be so. I was wrong. What kind of man – other than a brutal one – would force a woman to fuck a dog, and then take pleasure in her tears?

All day, I wait for M., getting ready for his return. I go through his house and put everything that belongs to me – the clothes I've left in his closet, my shampoo and toothbrush and deodorant, the Larry McMurtry novel I began but never finished – in a brown shopping bag. I am amazed at my control, at my calm. Now that I know what I have to do, I am resolute.

I open the door to the backyard. Rameau is lying on the grass, and his ears perk up when he hears the door slide open. It's a gray, sunless morning, and the air is cold and damp. I feel my hair frizzing up, and I button my sweater, shivering. Rameau keeps his gaze glued to me, his eyes big and brown, his tail wagging against the grass, but he doesn't get up. We stare at each other. I know very little about dogs, and I wonder if he remembers our encounter last night. I step out the door, and Rameau instantly springs up and lopes over to me. He is sleek and powerful, and his black head comes up to the top of my leg. He stands motionless while I scratch him behind the ears, and when I stop he drops his head and nuzzles my thigh. I fill his water bowl and watch him take a few laps, then I go inside and close the door. I get the shopping bag and take it into the living room, hiding it behind a chair so M. will not know I am planning to leave. I walk over to the front window, the sky bleak and overcast. Outside, a cat noses in a flower bed, looks up suddenly, startled by a noise I can't hear, then streaks across the lawn, disappearing behind a neighbor's car.

When I saw the video of Franny, the design on her right buttock, when I knew M. was the one who killed her – something inside me snapped. My life, and the small part of the universe I inhabit, I see more clearly now; perhaps the clearest since my sister was murdered. How could I have even considered staying with M.? I gave up too much for him, and I must learn – all over again – how to take care of myself. I'm the only one who can do that.

He made a mistake showing me the video of Franny. It was

an error of monumental import. How could he have been so stupid? Even if I hadn't noticed the mark, why would he show me the video? Why would he want me to view his mental torture of Franny? It can only conclude he doesn't understand, or refuses to acknowledge, that his behavior – his immorality, his lack of restraint – with my sister was wrong. If he hadn't shown me the video, I might've stayed with him. I could have stayed. Oh, yes, it was in my realm of possibilities. He seduced me easily, led me into temptation as he had Franny, but – unlike her – I enjoyed his seduction. Immensely. He took me on a sexual odyssey of uncommon pleasure, and if I hadn't seen the video, I might have stayed forever. This is what frightens me. I could've lived under his control. I could've been slave to his master.

But I did see the video, and now everything has changed. Even if he hadn't killed my sister, how could I stay with him now? After viewing his torment of Franny? His appalling lack of restraint is evil. He goes too far. M. killed Franny, and I will avenge her death. He will pay for what he did.

I start my preparations. He will not return until three-thirty, so I have plenty of time. I go into his bathroom and open the medicine cabinet. I take out his sleeping pills and put them in my pocket. Then I go into the back bedroom, the training room, and light several candles. This is M.'s favorite room – and I confess it had been mine also – and he brought me to it frequently. Incongruously, a stack of cardboard boxes are stored temporarily near the bed. They contain papers and files and books that M. brought home from campus but hasn't yet sorted or put away. And in the closet, my clothes hang – my play clothes that M. has purchased. Lace and satin lingerie, bodysuits, teddys, a French maid's outfit, a little girl's pleated skirt and vest, a little girl's baby-dolls, big-girl bustiers and G-strings and thigh-high nylons. I take out the four-piece black vinyl set and put it on: a push-up bra, fingerless gloves that go up to my elbows, garter belt, and a G-string, all in shiny, wet-looking black vinyl. I sit on the bed and slip into black fishnet stockings, then slide my feet into black high heels. I walk into M.'s bathroom and apply my makeup, then gaze in the full-length mirror. My stomach is flat, my thighs firm. I look good. Except for the bright slash of red lipstick on my lips, I'm all in black, from my hair to my heels. This is how M. will remember me: his sex slave in black vinyl.

I return to the training room and light more candles – all of them. They flicker around the room, on every table, on the TV, on the cardboard boxes, on the floor, shining light everywhere, enough light to get a good picture on the camcorder. I put the video of Franny in the VCR, then check to make sure there is a cassette in the camcorder.

I go into the kitchen and pour M. and me a glass of red wine. I wonder how many sleeping pills to put into his glass, and decide on only one. I want him drowsy, not knocked out. I break open the capsule and stir it in the wine, then write a note and place it on the table: 'I'm in the training room, Master, waiting for you.' I pick up the wineglasses and go to the back bedroom. The room glows amber in the candlelight. Everything is ready. I set M.'s glass on the table next to the bed, next to the key for the handcuffs, then recline on the bed and wait, sipping the wine.

At three thirty-five, I hear M. at the front door. The doorknob clicks, the door swings open. He's standing in the foyer, probably with his brown leather briefcase. My car is in the driveway, so he knows I'm here. He pushes the door shut; it makes a soft, scraping sound as it closes. I hear footsteps. He'll go into the den, set down his briefcase, then look at the piano. He'll want to play for an hour or two, as is his custom when he returns from school, but first he will look for me. M. is so predictable. He'll take off his coat, loosen and remove his tie, then go into the kitchen for a drink and see my note. The note will make him frown. He had wanted to play the piano, not me. He'll read the note again – he pictures me in the training room, shackled to the wall, and lust wins out. He'll come to me.

I hear him walking across the house, then down the hall. He stands in the doorway and gazes at me, saying nothing, one eyebrow rising appreciatively at my black bra and G-string outfit. He leans a shoulder casually against the door frame, and with his hand he loosens his tie – I was wrong about the tie, but he's not wearing a coat. His slacks are dark, his shirt a pale mauve color, his tie an Italian silk jacquard. Even fully dressed, one can tell he's hard-muscled and lean, his clothes fitting perfectly over a well-preserved forty-nine-year-old body. He's slender, sensual, and deadly.

'I thought we could play,' I say, and I take a sip of wine. 'I've been bad, and I need to be punished.'

M. rolls up his shirt sleeves, slowly, then enters the room, gazing at my body. His lips turn up at the corners in a sultry curve. He picks up the glass of wine on the table and takes a sip, still staring. He takes another drink, then sits next to me, runs his hand along my leg, the bare flesh of my thigh, the fishnet stocking.

'How bad?' he asks.

'Very,' I say. 'I need to be whipped.' I sit up. 'But first I want to suck your cock.' I slide off the bed. M. grabs my hand.

'Where are you going?' he says.

'Nowhere. I just want to change places with you. I want you to lie down so I can suck your cock.'

'Did I tell you to move?'

'No.'

He sets his wineglass on the table, then pulls me down on his lap, still gripping my wrist. 'Maybe I want to whip you first.'

My heartbeat quickens. I don't say anything. Has he guessed I put something in his drink? No, he wouldn't be able to taste it – I hadn't. Suddenly, it occurs to me that maybe he knew, all along, about the mark on Franny. Maybe he wanted me to see it and know he killed her. Maybe this is a prelude to my own death.

'Okay,' I say, 'I'll get the whip.' I hear the nervous flutter in my voice. M. looks at me strangely – he knows something is wrong. He doesn't release me. I wait, to see what he will do.

Abruptly, he grabs a fistful of my hair and pulls my head back. I gasp. My wineglass falls to the floor. I'm breathing heavily, my head bent back so I'm staring at the ceiling. I know if I resist, he'll pull me back even farther. His hand digs into my hair, twisting it until I groan.

Then he kisses me on the neck. He kisses me again and releases my hair. His other hand is still clamped around my wrist. I feel the slow movement of his lips and wet tongue on my bare shoulders and neck; I smell his sweat, the briny musk-iness of his desire.

'You look really tired,' I mumble. 'I thought maybe you'd like me to suck you for a while, give you a little energy.'

M. looks at me. 'Is that what you thought?' he says, and he releases my wrist.

Tentatively, I get off his lap and down on my knees. I unzip his pants, waiting to see if he is going to stop me. He doesn't. He stands, and I pull off his pants and shoes. He sits down again. I unknot his tie, then unbutton his shirt. I fold all of his clothes neatly, as he would do. He slides back on the bed so his back is against the wall. I hand him his glass of wine.

'Here,' I say, and he takes it. 'I want you to relax,' I tell him, using what I hope is a very sexy voice. 'Just close your eyes, drink the wine, and enjoy this. I'm going to suck you longer and better than you've ever been sucked before.'

I begin licking him slowly. His cock is already tense and hard, a blue vein bulging along the shaft, but my goal is the opposite, to slow him down. M., eyes closed, drinks the wine. I see his shoulders relax, his body settle. His head moves languidly from side to side. Smoothly, without changing tempo, I shift my mouth from his cock to the inside of his thigh, a less volatile part of his anatomy. I keep my mouth there, brushing my lips against him lightly. M. doesn't care that I've relinquished his cock, or he's too far gone to notice. He finishes the wine. I move my mouth to his other thigh, then later up to his stomach, noticing his penis is quite limp. He moans, a deep, relaxing sound. His palm opens, and the empty wineglass rolls out of his hand.

'Lie down,' I say.

M. moans, then says, sleepily, 'What?' His eyes open, barely.

'Lie down,' I repeat, picking up his glass and setting it on the table. 'You'll be more comfortable,' and I help him stretch out on the bed.

'I'm really tired,' he mumbles. 'I just need a few minutes,' and he closes his eyes.

I massage his legs and thighs, gently, then work up to his arms and shoulders. The pressure in my hands is soft, soothing, meant to relax. When I think he's asleep, I lift one arm above his head. He mumbles something, but complies. The handcuffs dangle from the wall. Each cuff is connected to a very thick two-foot chain, which is bolted to the wall. Slowly, I put the handcuff on his wrist, then lock it. The chain is slack, not stretching his arms, and he doesn't feel it. I lift his other arm and do the same.

I stand back and look at him, naked, his cock limp, Franny's killer, and I feel nothing but disgust. I get the belt from his pants and wrap it around his neck. Then I get two pieces of rope from the dresser and tie his legs to the bed frame. I walk over to the VCR and turn it on. Franny is crying, the camera circling her, Rameau licking. M. still sleeps. I turn up the volume.

He jerks awake, a startled expression on his face. Disoriented, he looks at the blaring television, then feels his arms shackled to the wall. He twists his head and shoulders, craning to see, quite alert now, then he notices the belt around his neck. He looks back at me.

'Unlock these,' he says, his voice stern. 'Now.'

He's still playing the role of the disciplinarian. He still thinks he holds sway over me.

I lower the volume. 'Why did you show me this video?'

'You didn't believe I had Franny fuck the dog. I wanted you

to know that I always tell the truth.' His voice is even and without remorse.

'Except you don't tell the truth,' I say. 'You've never told me the truth.'

'Unlock the cuffs,' he says. 'The longer you keep them on me, the harder I'll be on you.'

I ignore him. I hear Franny crying, and I also hear M. yelling at her to stay on the floor. His words infuriate me. I lower the volume even more. 'I agreed to everything we did. Maybe I was reluctant, but I agreed. And that's okay. But Franny didn't agree, not to any of the things you did. You forced them on her. You . . . you went too far. There have to be restraints.'

Smiling slightly, he looks at me with a complacent expression. He is still unaware of the gravity of his mistake, unaware that there is a rift between us that cannot be mended. 'Restraints,' he says mildly. 'That's a bourgeois concept.'

'You can't just do whatever you like.'

'I see no reason why not.'

'Because you hurt people. You hurt Franny. You shouldn't have done those things to her. It was immoral.' My voice trembles with rage.

He spits out a laugh at the word. 'Immoral?' he says disdainfully. 'She was under no obligation to stay with me. She could've left at any time. She chose not to. It was her decision, not mine.'

'She couldn't say no to you.'

'And now you want to blame me for her weakness?'

'Yes,' I say, 'you are responsible.' I hear the strain in my voice, feel the anger blazing beneath my modulated tone as I fight for self-control. I want him dead, and I know, in my present state of mind, I could perform the act easily. 'You were the stronger one,' I say. 'You can't do the things you did without repercussions.'

'Repercussions? What repercussions? I feel no guilt for what I did with her. She was an adult. A consenting adult.'

He still isn't aware that I know he killed Franny. He thinks my anger is about Rameau and all the sexual and sadistic acts he forced upon her. I glower at M. and he stares back at me, coolly.

He says, 'She made her own choices. Maybe they were the wrong ones for her, but she made them. Why should I feel guilt because of that? I enjoyed watching her with Rameau – just as I enjoyed watching you. I know what I want, Nora, and I go after it. It's that simple.'

'Not this time,' I say, shaking my head. 'And not with me. You almost had me fooled. You said you loved me – and I almost believed it. But you don't love me, or anyone else. You're incapable of that.'

He looks at me placidly. I feel the urge to throw something at him, to knock the smug equanimity off his face. 'You must really hate women,' I say. 'You're not even satisfied with control-ling them – you have to humiliate them as well.'

He listens to this with an amused expression. Finally he says, 'Are you going to throw a tantrum, Nora? You know I'll have to punish you for that.'

I shake my head. 'You just don't get it, do you? I'm not playing this game anymore, and you can't punish me if I'm not following the rules.' I walk closer to M. I place my palm on his head. His dark hair is soft and fine, like fleece in my fingers. 'You forget who's in bondage now,' I say. I reach lower, for his neck. 'You forget you're the one with a belt around your neck.'

As I touch the belt, I see, by the change in M.'s expression, that he finally recognizes the seriousness of my intentions. He is silent. I feel his body tense. Finally, he speaks.

'So this is how it's going to end? You and I are through?' he says, and I hear a note of irritation in his voice. He was vain enough to believe I would never leave him, even if he showed me the video of Franny.

'Yes,' I say, and I cross the room to the television. He doesn't know it yet, but my leaving him is the least of his worries. It's time for him to learn that I know he killed Franny.

He quirks his eyebrow in a shrug. 'All right,' he says. 'So you and I are through. Now unlock the cuffs.'

'Watch the video,' I say. Franny looks at the camera, tears rolling down her face. I feel my anger resurfacing.

'Get these off—'

'Watch it!' I scream. My body shudders, and I take a deep breath to get myself under control. I need control now, I need it more than ever.

I play the shot that shows the mark on Franny's buttock. I rewind the video, then play it over.

'You don't see it, do you? You made a mistake, and now it's going to cost you.' I freeze the picture. 'Look at that,' I say, pointing to the mark.

'What?'

'You can barely see it. It almost looks like a birthmark, except Franny didn't have any birthmarks.'

M. is squinting at the TV, trying to make it out.

'It's a circle,' I say. 'With a line slashed through it – exactly like the one the coroner found on Franny's stomach.'

I see a look of panic – just a brief look, lasting only a second – before M. tries to cover it up.

'You can't tell what that is,' he says. 'It could be anything.'

'Only it's not. It's a circle with a line through it. Just like the one you cut on Franny's stomach.'

I turn off the television. I walk over to the camcorder and switch it on, then go back to M. I straddle his chest, feeling his bare skin against my thighs. 'You're going to tell me how you killed Franny,' I say. 'With the video you took of Franny, and the one I'm taking now of your confession, you'll be in jail for the rest of your life – if you're lucky. They just might give you the death penalty.'

M. looks me coolly in the eyes. 'What makes you think I'll tell you anything?'

I pick up the ends of the belt around his neck. 'Because if you don't, I'll kill you.'

He lets out a short, snide laugh.

I pull the belt tight, cutting off his air. He struggles, and it takes all my strength to keep the belt tight. I am not prepared for the force of his efforts to stop me. Before I have time to react, he brings up his left elbow and shoulder, twists his torso, and jabs me in the ribs. A sharp jolt of pain cuts me in the side. It stuns me, and I gasp for breath. The slack in the chain gives M. room enough to maneuver. He slams his elbow into me again. The force of his blow knocks me off his chest and I fall into the table. It topples over, crashing to the floor, spilling his wineglass and the three candles and everything else on the tabletop. The drawer falls open, and a box of condoms, lube, nipple clamps, and metal ben-wa balls spew across the floor. The ben-wa balls, sounding like steel ball bearings, roll across the oval rug and onto the hardwood floor, bouncing into the wall. Two of the candles burned out on the way to the floor, but the third is burning a small hole in the rug. I stomp on it with my high heels, extinguishing the fire. There's a pain in my side, and I see a mark on my shoulder where I knocked into the table. The skin is broken and bloody.

M. smiles, smugly. I pull off the heels and throw them across the room, then go to the foot of the bed. I grab the bed frame and yank hard, pulling the bed out, stretching M.'s arms until there is no slack in the chain that connects the handcuffs to the wall. I'm breathing heavily, the stitch in my side painful. I pull again, and hear him yell.

'Goddammit, Nora! These are cutting into my wrists.'

I go over to him and straddle his chest. 'Now, we're going to try this again,' I say. 'You tell me how you killed Franny, or I'll kill you.' I grab the belt.

M. sneers. 'You won't kill me,' he says.

I grip the belt tighter. 'Try me,' I say.

'If you kill me, you'll go to jail.'

I shake my head. 'Harris knows what you're like. I'd tell him you wanted me to do something really extreme, something on the edge. I'd tell him you wanted to experiment with breath control, that you wanted me to choke you. I objected, of course, but you said you'd beat me if I didn't. So I played your game. Only problem, I choked you too long and too hard. So sorry. You die. It was an accident.' My rib aches from M.'s attack.

'They'd still go after you.'

'Maybe. Maybe not. They couldn't prove murder. Manslaughter, possibly, or reckless endangerment. I'll take that to see you pay for Franny's murder.' I pull the belt so M. can feel it. 'Now, start talking.'

He doesn't say anything. His face is set tight, his jaw clenched. I yank the belt tight. He starts to gasp for air, and his face turns a dark red. Beneath me, his torso bucks slightly, but he's stretched out completely now, and his efforts to fight me are useless. I release my hold.

'Ready to talk?' I say, but I don't give him a chance to reply. I know he won't give in so easily. I choke him again. I see the defiance in his eyes, and I pull tighter. His face turns dark red once more. He stares at me for as long as he can, then his eyes water and roll back. His mouth is open, gaping, soundless. I feel the aches in my upper arms and chest. My breath comes out hard and labored. I hadn't realized choking a man would be so difficult, so strenuous. I keep pulling the belt, wondering if I'm going to stop. It would be a short step, from here to death. Just a little longer, and he'd be dead.

I drop the belt. M. coughs, gasps for air. His lungs make long, wheezing noises as he sucks in the oxygen.

'Are you going to talk now?' I ask, and he nods, gasping, still unable to speak. I get off his chest and stand back. He coughs, clears his throat, then breathes desperately in big gulps, his neck muscles contracting in spasms. He doesn't look so smug now. I give him several minutes to recover, then go over to the camcorder and stop it from recording. I rewind the cassette, and begin again – no need to have that scene on film. I turn around to face M. He's lying still now, and he eyes me with an intense hatred I've never before seen him display.

He says, 'Okay, I'll tell you what happened. But it won't do you any good. You can't see me in the first video, and this one won't help, either. It was made under duress. Besides, videotapes aren't admissible in court.'

I don't say anything. I have no idea if they're admissible or not, but when Joe sees his confession, he'll make sure M. goes to jail. 'Start talking,' I say.

M. hesitates. He purses his lips petulantly, then says, 'Undo my legs first.'

'No.'

'They're beginning to cramp. If you want a confession, undo my legs.'

I think this over. I'm not inclined to bargain with him – and his comfort is of no concern to me – but I'm close, so close, to learning how Franny died, that I consider his request. I feel my impatience as if it were a tormenting itch, demanding relief. I can't wait a minute longer. I need the truth. I look down at M. With his arms shackled, there's no way he can come after me. I untie his legs, standing back in case he decides to kick.

'Okay,' I say. 'Now start talking.'

'I'll talk. But we're going to do it my way. I need to explain a few things before I tell you about Franny.'

'I'm not interested in anything else.'

'Too bad. You're going to hear it.'

I cross my arms. M. senses my impatience, and once again, he is yanking my chain. I feel the manipulation, cold and hard, as surely as if stainless-steel links were connected from my neck to his hand. I want to know how he killed Franny, everything about it. He knows this, but his concatenating hold over me is gone. I'll listen to his explanations, but that won't change the outcome. I'll get his confession. He's going to prison.

'This isn't the ending I had planned for us,' he says. He looks smug, confident, his face a blank wall of indifference, as if we'd never been lovers.

'Start talking,' I say.

His brows knit into a small frown. He appears momentarily distracted, as if he's having trouble deciding where to start.

'First,' M. begins, 'I want to tell you about Ian.'

At the mention of Ian's name, I feel a terrible pang of remorse for what I've put him through. I recognize the immensity of my error. I wait, impatient, to hear what he'll say about Ian.

'Yes,' M. says, his voice taunting. 'I want you to know that Ian – whom you always claimed to be so noble and good; your loyal, caring Ian – he cheated on you.'

I mull this over, then discount it. I would've known if Ian had been sleeping with someone else; I would've sensed it. 'You're lying, and even if he did, he wouldn't tell you.'

He gazes at me, unperturbed. 'Wouldn't he? Weren't he and I confidants? He told me everything else, why wouldn't he tell me this?'

I don't reply.

'Well, you're right,' he says. 'He didn't tell me – he didn't have to. You see, I'm the one with whom he cheated. Your sweet Ian had his first taste of cock.'

'You're lying.'

'Nora, Nora, Nora.' He makes a clucking sound with his tongue, mocking me. 'When will you ever learn? You know I always tell the truth.' He smiles. 'Well, almost always. You can understand why I didn't tell you I killed Franny. But everything else I told you was true.'

I still don't say anything.

'I can see I'll have to convince you. Very well.' He stretches his legs. He looks at me and says, 'Ian occasionally came back here after we played racquetball – for a drink, sometimes for dinner, whatever. I was such a sympathetic ear, and you weren't giving him any attention. He couldn't understand why you were turning away from him. He couldn't understand why you didn't want to make love anymore. Poor Ian. He was in such a state of confusion. The last time he was here – this was several days before he broke up with you – I gave him a scotch and let him pour his heart out to me. Such a touching scene.' M. says this sarcastically, his voice dripping false sympathy. 'I made him another drink and told him you didn't deserve him. He said he wished he could talk to you the way he talked to me.' M. looks up at his handcuffed wrists, then gazes back at me.

'Well, you can guess the rest. One thing led to another. I told him I felt really close to him, that I loved him like a brother. He said he felt the same. A little kiss, a little caress – he was easy. He hesitated when I put my hand on his cock, but he got so hard that it wasn't difficult to convince him to let me suck it. A few drinks loosened him right up, Nora. That, plus he hadn't been fucking you for a while. He was so horny I suppose one could say you led Ian right into my lap. I kept him the entire night. And I kept him boozed up so he would be most compliant. I made him suck me, and I gave it to him in the ass. Your Ian isn't the sweet virgin he once was.'

Still, I say nothing. I know he's telling the truth.

'The poor boy was terribly confused. The next morning he left before I woke. Bad manners, if you want my opinion – he didn't even kiss me goodbye. He called the next day. Told me it was a big mistake. He apologized, said he was sorry it happened and that he couldn't return my affections. What a laugh! The idiot didn't even know he was purposefully seduced.' M. chuckles contemptuously. 'He was anguishing because he thought he had hurt my feelings and led me on.'

Finally I find my voice. I know he is telling the truth, but I'm having a difficult time accepting it. I don't know why. He killed Franny – his cold seduction of Ian shouldn't surprise me at all. 'Why?' I say. 'Why did you do it?'

'I didn't want you to see him anymore. You were continually telling me what a wonderful man he was. Well – there's your honest, noble Ian, Nora. He broke up with you rather than tell you the truth. Just as I knew he would.'

But he didn't break up with me, I think. I assumed he had, but he only wanted time to be alone for a while, time to think about what had happened between him and M. 'There was no reason for that,' I say. 'Ian and I were growing apart because of you. It was only a matter of time before we split up. You didn't have to fuck him. There was no need to.'

I feel tears in my eyes – for Ian, for myself, but mostly for Franny. 'There was no need,' I repeat. 'No need at all,' but I realize need had nothing to do with it. He did it out of spite, meanness. And that's why he's telling me about Ian now. He's a vindictive man, wanting to hurt me as much as possible. I'm not able to undo the damage he's caused Ian, but I will avenge Franny. He thinks I can't hold him accountable for her death, but he is wrong. Dead wrong.

'But there was a need,' he says. 'I had to fuck him.' He tilts his head, gloating at his victory, then says, 'I left out a small detail: I put a sleeping pill in Ian's drink. You see, I had a few things to accomplish that evening. I needed Ian unconscious for a short while, just long enough to put his fingerprints on a few objects and borrow his house key and make a quick trip to Sacramento.' He smiles. 'You are so easy to manipulate, Nora. As easy as Franny. As easy as Ian. You searched his condo, just as I knew you would.'

I feel an ache in my heart. I've caused Ian so much trouble, suspecting him of murder, sharing my suspicions with the police, leading them to evidence that precipitated his arrest. And even after I went to the police, Ian still said he loved me. His loyalty and trust run much deeper than mine. I know I was foolish to let him slip away, and I fear I will regret this always.

M. smiles that arrogant smile of his. I wait for him to continue.

'Are you sure you want to hear the rest?' he finally asks me. 'I can tell you what happened with Franny, but what good will it do you? My confession won't be admissible in court. You'll just get angry, frustrated, unable to do anything with the knowledge I give you.' He raises his head and says, 'Wouldn't ignorance be the better alternative?'

The false concern in his voice is unmistakable. 'No.'

'Good,' he says, laying his head back on the pillow. I see an expression of satisfaction cover his face, as if he wanted to tell me all along, as if he was calling the shots. From the conversation, one would deduce our positions were reversed – me in shackles, he a free man – but I know, given a choice, M. would not be forthcoming with a confession.

'Very good,' he says. 'I was hoping that would be your answer. You see, I want to tell you what happened. I need to tell someone – just as you needed to speak of your abortion and sterilization. You can understand that, can't you? Of course you can. I was your confessor; now you can be mine. By listening, you will do me the favor of relieving my guilt.'

His eyebrows rise. 'Ah,' he says, 'I can see by your expression that you don't believe me capable of guilt. I feel no remorse for my behavior with Franny – that much is true – but I do regret her death. It was an unfortunate incident.'

I cringe at his phrase for Franny's murder: an unfortunate incident. 'If you think you'll find forgiveness in me, you're mistaken,' I say.

'Not *find* forgiveness, Nora. I shall *take* it from you. Admitting your sin is the first step toward absolution. You know that. And who should take my confession but you? A bit ironic, isn't it? I give you the truth you seek, and you, inadvertently, give me peace of mind.' He smirks.

'Remember when I told you Franny refused me nothing? That wasn't true. There were several things she denied me, some of them dangerous. I respected her more for saying no – although I never told her that. In fact, I made her pay dearly for her intransigence. She got quite a whipping for her refusals.

'But after I broke up with her, she said she'd allow me to do anything. I think she had it in her mind that I was the only man who would ever love her. She wouldn't let go of me. Her diary ended two weeks before she died, so you have no idea what she was like after that. She called me every day, sometimes five or six times, making a real nuisance of herself. God, she was tenacious. I tried to be kind, but nothing I said deterred her. She would come over uninvited, at all times of the day, and beg me to give her another chance, plead with me to love her. It was too much. Finally, I thought that if I took her to the edge, if I forced her to do those few things she had refused me, she would come to her senses and see we were incompatible. She would realize I was the wrong man for her.

'I packed a black duffel bag and went over to her apartment. It was the first time I'd been there; she always came to my house. I told her to take off her clothes and lie on the floor. Then I took duct tape out of my bag.'

He gazes thoughtfully at the ceiling. After a few seconds, he continues, his voice lower. 'Duct tape – it's not a material one would ordinarily bind a person with. It's very painful when you rip it off, but I wanted to teach her a lesson. I stretched her arms above her head and bound her wrists, then wound the tape around the leg of the couch. Next I taped her ankles together. I got a scalpel out of the bag and laid it lengthwise on her midriff. I told her I was going to cut her on her stomach. I'd done it once before, on her ass, as you saw from the video. After that, she never let me cut her again. She was frightened of the knife.

'Anyway, I thought placing the scalpel on her body would be enough, just the sight of the knife, but it wasn't. "Do it, Michael," she said. "Then you'll know how much I love you." Beads of sweat were forming on her forehead. She was scared, but wasn't going to back down, not if she thought it would make me love her. I put duct tape over her mouth and began cutting her. First, a diamond shape around her navel. I could hear her moans through the tape. I tore it off and asked her if she'd had enough. She shook her head, told me she'd do anything if I'd stay with her, so I replaced the tape and began cutting again. Different shapes, circles, squares, stars, lines up and down her body, and yes, a circle with a slash through it. Tears covered her face; her screams came out as pathetic muffles. Still, she wouldn't give in. Twice, I removed the tape to see if she wanted me to stop. Both times, she said, I love you. I'll never let you go.' It was infuriating. Who would have thought Franny, timid Franny, would've turned out to be so obstinate? And so desperate.'

M. pauses. I think of what he told me so long ago. *Curiosity didn't kill the cat – obstinacy did. Something Franny never learned.* He turns his head and rubs his forehead on his outstretched arm. His eyes are blank, and I can tell he is thinking of that day, seeing Franny before him. My stomach tightens, and I realize my hands are clenched into fists, my knuckles white. I see Franny also, and it's all I can do to stand here and listen.

'Anyway, there was a lot of blood, but the cuts weren't deep – and she still refused to ask me to stop. Finally, I got a shock box out of my duffel bag; it's a hand crank generator I'd ordered through the mail. She'd seen the box before and heard me talk about it. Electrotorture. I had wanted to use it on Franny months earlier, but she was afraid of electricity, more than the cutting, and never allowed me to. She was very adamant about it. So that day I thought even if the cutting hadn't scared her off, the electricity would. I ripped off the duct tape one more time. She was crying, almost hysterical, tears dripping down her wet cheeks. I waited for her to calm down, then said, "This is how it would be from now on, Franny. I'd do whatever I wished, without your consent. Haven't you had enough? Can't you see I'm not the man for you?" She'd stopped crying, but her chest was still heaving, and I thought she was going to relent. Then she took a deep breath, and I saw it in her eyes – the stubbornness. On some deep, subconscious level, I think she wanted me to hurt her. I think she felt she deserved the pain – probably still trying to make amends for Billy. "I'll do anything," she whispered, her voice hoarse from her silent screams. "Anything. I need you." Her compliance maddened me. I just wanted her out of my life. I put the tape back over her mouth. Then I wired up her nipples, put an electrode on each, and ran a current through her.'

He looks at the ceiling, slowly shaking his head. He continues, his voice even lower. 'I don't know what happened. It shouldn't have killed her. The voltage was low; there weren't any burn marks on her body. I just wanted to frighten her, that's all; just shock her. I wanted to make her realize I wasn't good for her. I wanted her to stop calling me, harassing me five, six, sometimes seven times a day.'

He is silent. So am I. The mystery is solved. Finally. M. killed her, and he did it with electricity. He says it was an accident, and for some reason, I believe he's telling the truth. This information sinks in slowly. I feel as though I'm outside of my body, watching, listening from a distance. I hear his words, but I cannot respond.

He says, 'So that's how she died. Her heart just stopped beating. It happened so fast, in seconds, and I didn't know what to do. I tried CPR, but I'd never done it before and I couldn't revive her. I tore off the duct tape and breathed into her mouth. I pumped on her chest, trying to make her live. I worked on her for so long, half an hour, forty-five minutes, I don't know. It seemed forever. Nothing worked. I suppose I knew she was dead after the first five minutes, but I couldn't stop. I couldn't let her die. I alternated breathing with pumping, breathing with pumping, over and over again.' M. speaks slowly. 'Finally, when I did stop, I just rocked back on my heels and looked at her. I realized the enormity of what I had done. How could she have died? How did this happen? I never meant to kill her. It was an accident.'

He hesitates, then says, 'I've done a lot of reading about electricity since then. The voltage interfered with the electrical impulses of her heart, causing her to go into cardiac arrest. She didn't have heart problems, and the current was low. It was just a freak accident, and never should've happened. But it did . . . it did.'

He laughs nervously. He says, 'Well, I knew how it looked. The police would never believe it was an accident; they would never believe Franny allowed the cutting, the electricity. I put the tape over her mouth once more, for the last time. The knife marks all over her body, the blood, the tape – it looked like premeditated murder, the work of a psycho, a random killing. That's what I wanted the police to believe also, that a psycho had come through town.'

I still feel removed from M. and all he's telling me. His words float across the room, their significance softened in the diffusive, candle-scented air. He almost committed the perfect murder, with an undetectable weapon. 'How did you know the autopsy wouldn't reveal the electricity?' I ask him.

'I didn't. In fact, when the newspaper printed her cause of death as undetermined, I thought the police had pointedly withheld the information. I assumed you and the police knew how she died. I didn't realize it was a mystery.'

He didn't realize. The coroner was baffled, and M. didn't even know he'd created a mystery. 'You were very thorough,' I say, and the unruffled tone of my voice bothers me. All this time I've been obsessed with Franny's murder, and now that I have the answers I'm unable to react. It's as though the news of her accidental death is a letdown, anticlimactic to my mind's imagining of her cold-blooded murder.

'The police found no fingerprints that belonged to you,' I say. 'No hairs, no carpet fibers from your shoes. How did you manage that?'

'It was dumb luck, pure and simple. Just dumb luck. It was raining when I went over, a spring shower.' He laughs again, nervously. 'More like an unseasonable thunderstorm. It was chilly, the rain gutters were overflowing. Before I left my home, I put on rain boots, raincoat, and a hat. The raincoat and boots I'd always kept in my garage so I wouldn't drip water or mud inside the house; since I'd never worn the boots in my house, there weren't any carpet fibers on them. And there were no fingerprints because I wore gloves the entire time. When I got to Franny's, the first thing I did was exchange my wool gloves for rubber ones. Again, just dumb luck – worrying about leaving fingerprints hadn't crossed my mind. Frequently, I'd wear latex gloves when I punished Franny. It was a psychological move, designed to frighten her, to get her to imagine the worst. But that day there was another reason. I knew if she didn't back down, I'd be cutting her. I didn't want to get bloody, so I wore the gloves.

'As for the lack of hair strands – I didn't take off my coat or hat. I thought I was just going to be there for minutes. In and out, fast, just enough time to scare her. But afterward, just to make sure I didn't leave any hair behind, I vacuumed the floor really well. Then I changed the vacuum cleaner bag and put it in my duffel bag. I took one last look around – everything seemed okay – then I looked at Franny. She was wearing Billy's medical bracelet on her wrist. I don't know why, but I unclasped it and put it in my pocket. When I got home, I took off all my clothes. I put everything in a bag – the clothes, scalpel, boots, gloves, shock box, the vacuum cleaner bag, everything except the duct tape and bracelet – and disposed of them. I buried the duct tape and medical bracelet in my backyard. I don't know why I kept them – a reminder, I suppose, of what I'd done. The tape you found in my closet was a different roll. I kept a few other things of hers – the sweater, eyeglasses, the earrings, a few pictures, the video with Rameau – but stored them at my office when I began seeing you. At any rate, there was no evidence, nothing to tie me to Franny's murder. I knew her diary mentioned me, and I considered taking the disks to her computer, but decided against it. Taking the disks would look too suspicious, especially if the police found extra copies of them hidden somewhere else in her apartment. A psycho killer wouldn't stop to remove computer disks. Besides, there was nothing on them to convict me. All they proved is that I like rough sex. And that Franny acquiesced to it.'

Reflectively, he looks off into the distance, in the space beyond the door. Turning back to me, he says, 'If it hadn't rained that day, I would probably be in jail. I wouldn't have worn my wool gloves when I arrived – my fingerprints would've been on the front door. It was the only thunderstorm that spring. The next day, the sky cleared and the sun came out.'

I nod, assimilating this information, still feeling detached. 'What about the wood carving?' I ask him. 'The one you said Ian gave Franny?'

'I bought it in a shop in Sonoma.' He attempts to shrug his shoulders, but his arms are stretched taut and the movement is slight. 'I wanted you to feel comfortable with me, and it was easy to make Ian look guilty. Too easy. I hadn't planned on that. It worked out nicely that he knew Franny. Once you suspected him, I appeared less guilty.'

'And Mark Kirn?'

I see the amusement in M.'s face. 'You really should trust the police, Nora. Of course they had the right man. The evidence against him was conclusive.' He smirks. 'But it was quite enjoyable to watch you run down to San Quentin.'

The room is warm from the burning candles; I feel it closing in on me. 'You made the anonymous phone calls. And sent the letters and photos. You broke into my house at night while I was sleeping.'

M. nods.

'How did you get a key to my house?'

'That was easy – the same way I got Ian's. I made a duplicate back in March, the day I drugged and wrapped you in Ace bandages.'

M. had a key to my house all along. I thought I was secure in my Torrey Street home, but that was only an illusion.

'And you were the one who almost ran me over at the grocery store.'

'No,' he says quickly. 'I didn't do that. It was probably just an accident, or a kid fooling around. I never tried to harm you. Never.' He smiles. 'But it did come in handy.'

Suddenly tired, I push my hair back, then cover my face with my hands. I am horrified at what I have done to Ian.

M. says, 'Nora, I never meant to kill her. It was a freak accident. It should've given her a jolt, a shock, not stop her heart from beating.'

I hear a sigh, not of regret but of impatience – as if now

that he's told me the truth, the incident is behind him and it's time to move on. He continues.

'Well, you can understand why I didn't call the police. They would've arrested me for sure – why should my life be destroyed by an accident?'

The reality of all he has told me finally sinks in. The distance closes; his words take back their edge. I remove my hands from my face. 'You murdered Franny,' I say.

His face is placid, cold and unreadable. Evenly, he says, 'I wouldn't take that moral tone if I were you. A death is a death. Whether it's an accidental death or an abortion, it amounts to the same thing.'

'No,' I say hotly. 'It doesn't amount to the same thing.'

M. continues, not acknowledging my objection. 'You've taken a life; so have I. We're both murderers, Nora. Only mine was unintentional, yours wasn't. So you tell me – who is more at fault? Who has more guilt to bear? I don't know. I feel remorse. I wish I could replay that day, but I can't. It was an accident. And Franny was not without fault. She consented to the electricity; she played a part in her own death.'

I bristle at M.'s words. 'You're very good at twisting the truth,' I tell him. 'You can rationalize all you want, you can say she participated in her own death, but it doesn't change anything.' Like the candles' scent wafting upward, my anger is rising. 'You abused her, you cut her, you killed her – and you'll pay for it.'

He smiles coldly. 'Useless threats, Nora? The police can't touch me, not even with this so-called confession. The only thing this video proves is that her death was an accident. There's nothing you can do.'

I hear the taunt in M.'s voice, the jeering, the scorn. It infuriates me, makes me want to grab the belt and choke the derision out of him.

'There's nothing you can do,' he repeats, the scorn still present.

'I wouldn't count on that,' I say, edging closer to the bed, knowing I'm losing control. 'You'll spend the rest of your life in prison.'

'I won't spend a day.'

My anger is hot, straining against the rein with which I'm holding it under control. 'When the police arrive,' I say, my voice rising, almost shouting, 'when they see you like this, stretched out on the bed, when they see both videos – maybe they'll take their time arresting you.'

I grab the cat-o'-nine-tails from the wall, then return to M. 'Maybe they'll use one of these whips on you first,' I say, holding it up. 'Or the cane. How would you like that? I'll bet you've never felt pain, have you? You just like to inflict it.'

M. gives a curt laugh. 'You look ridiculous,' he says.

I hear his words, so contemptuous. To him, this is just a game – and Franny's death just an unfortunate incident. My arm trembles with a newfound, murderous rage. I bring the whip down, hard, and it lands across his groin and thighs with a loud, stinging slap. A red mark instantly appears. M. groans and brings his legs up, trying to protect his genitals. He glares at me, his eyes dark with fury.

'You don't like that, do you?' I say, taunting him now. I drop the whip and get the bamboo cane. I strike him again, with all my force, leaving a tattoo of a long red welt down the length of his right thigh. He grimaces in pain but doesn't call out. Then something happens inside me, something savage and atavistic. I enjoy the pain on his face. I want to see more. I want him to scream in agony just as Franny had. I hit him again and again, each crack of the cane fueling my anger. M. thrashes on the bed, kicking, but he can't avoid my aim. The cane opens his flesh; thin lines of blood appear. I step forward and bring down the cane once more, realizing, too late, that I'm too close to the bed. M. lashes out with his leg, striking me in the thigh. I jump back, crashing into the cardboard boxes, and several topple over. I glare at M., my heart racing.

He stares at me coldly, his face rigid with indignity and contempt, his body marked with welts and blood. My chest heaves; my body shudders. I do not know who that person was – that person striking out in an uncontrolled fury, with no thought but the destruction of another human being. I shake my head in disgust, with myself and with M., then drop the cane. 'I'm going to call the police,' I say, walking to the door.

'Go ahead,' M. says, breathing hard, his voice pained. 'I'm in handcuffs without my consent. You'll be the one who goes to prison.'

I walk out of the room and down the hallway. I hear M. calling me back, but, ignoring him, I go into the master bedroom. I pick up the phone, then hesitate. M. is still yelling, saying the room is on fire. At first I think this is a ruse so I won't call the police, but I replace the receiver anyway and walk slowly down the hallway. Then, several feet from the room, I smell smoke. I rush inside.

In the corner, next to the bed, the boxes are burning.

'The candles,' M. says when he sees me, trying to act calm now, his body still covered with blood. 'The boxes caught on fire when you knocked them over.' I remember placing several candles on the boxes earlier today when I was setting up the room. The fire is still small, not larger than a campfire.

I glance quickly around the room, looking for a blanket to smother the flames. Once, after M. whipped me, I got a chill and he covered me with a pale green comforter. 'Where do you keep the blanket?' I say, yanking out all the dresser drawers.

'Unlock me, Nora,' M. says. I hear the restrained panic in his voice. 'Forget the blanket. Unlock me!'

The drawers crash to the floor as I pull them out of the dresser. I don't find a blanket, or anything else heavy enough to beat out the flames. I rush over to M., to remove the handcuffs, then stop. The key was on the table next to the bed, and the table is still lying on its side, everything in and on it – including the key to the handcuffs – scattered all over the floor. I don't see the key anywhere.

'Unlock me!'

'I have to find the key.' I drop to my knees and search for

it. 'It was on the table,' I say. I shove aside the box of condoms and wineglass and tubes of lubricant. It's not here. I turn the table over, but I still can't find the key. I look under the bed and see the blanket, folded, in a corner. I search for the key.

'Nora!'

I look up. The fire is much higher, closer to the foot of the bed. I grab the blanket and start beating on the flames. Smoke billows upward. Sparks fly out, igniting the curtain hem; the flames spread quickly over the material and race to the ceiling. The room is sweltering, the fire a hot, consuming blaze, growing larger, more intense, more deadly. The blanket isn't doing any good. I stand back, glance at M., and see his fear-stricken face.

'The fire extinguisher,' I say, and run from the room. I grab it out of the broom closet from the kitchen, then dash back. I freeze in the doorway, overwhelmed by what I see. In the seconds that I was gone, the fire expanded, more than doubling in size. The corner of the room looks like a giant bonfire, golden hot flames shooting upward, the stacks of boxes a fiery blaze. Flames lick the walls. The rug is burning, the ceiling blackened with smoke. M., his face a contorted mask of fear, watches as flames snake toward the foot of the bed, just inches from it.

I pull the ring pin out of the extinguisher and spray near the bed. There's a whooshing burst of white powder. I spray again, smothering the flames closest to the bed. Then I aim the nozzle at the boxes and squeeze the handle. White powder dribbles out of the extinguisher. I squeeze once more. Nothing. I look at the dial on the top. It's in the red zone. The extinguisher is empty.

I throw it down, roll up the rug as much as possible so the entire floor won't be covered with fire, then run from the room. I hear M. screaming after me. He thinks I'm leaving him there to die. I run into the master bedroom and grab the phone. I start to dial 911, then hesitate. I could just leave him there to die. I could. He deserves to die. The world would be a better place without him. For the second time today, I play God to M.'s existence, debating the value of his life. I hear a wrenching scream from the back room, and my choice becomes clear: I am not an executioner.

I dial 911, give the dispatcher all the information he asks for, then slam down the phone. I pull the bedspread off the bed. Running back to the room, I hear M. screaming my name, begging me not to leave him there to burn.

When I reach him, I see the fire has completely covered one side of the room. The heat is oppressive, the air suffocating, heavy and thick with smoke. I throw the bedspread on the flames blazing near the bed, and beat out the fire by M.'s feet. The bedspread catches fire. I try to put the flames out with my hands, then back away, not knowing what to do. M.'s screams ring in my ears. I look around. There's nothing I can use to put the fire out. I could get a bucket of water, but that wouldn't help. I need a hose. The fire fans outward, creeping up to the bed again and moving toward the door.

'Do something!' M. screams. He's twisted halfway off the bed, his legs – bloodied and marked from the cane – over the side, his arms stretched tight, still shackled to the wall. The skin around his wrists is bloody, rubbed raw from the handcuffs. He pulls on the chains, desperately trying to yank the bolts from the wall. It is useless, they're screwed into studs, but he is beyond rational thought.

'My tools!' he says. 'In the garage! The tool box!'

It is too late for that. The window is blocked with fire, and the flames are almost at the door. Within minutes, perhaps only seconds, we'll be trapped in the room, without escape.

I see the sword on the wall. I take it down.

Hoarsely, with a futile resignation, M. says, 'That'll never work. The chain is too thick.'

'I know,' I say, walking nearer to him.

M. coughs, choking from the smoke, looking at me blankly, not understanding why I need the sword, then a new wave of panic crosses his face. He thinks I'm going to kill him.

I stand over M., looking down at him. If I don't do something now, we'll both burn. Thinking of how he made Franny suffer,

I move closer to the wall so I'm directly over his forearms. With both hands on the hilt, I lift the sword over my head.

A look of horror covers M.'s face, the same look Franny must have worn the day she was killed. 'No!' he screams, when he sees that I'm not going to kill him. 'No!'

I bring the sword down, freeing M. from the bed.

42

I think quite often about justice, frontier justice: an eye for an eye, a tooth for a tooth. When I chopped off M.'s hands, did I do it to save or punish him? I don't have the answer to that question. Franny was on my mind as I brought down the sword, but he would've burned in the fire if I hadn't acted immediately. I like to think that I'm not like M., that I'm not his real-life doppelganger: cold, manipulative, cruel. But maybe we're more similar than I care to admit. I have the capacity to be like M., that much I know, but it's a part of myself that I choose to suppress. Twice that afternoon, I could have killed him – and I wanted to, badly – but twice I pulled back. I didn't strangle M., I didn't let him die in the fire.

I saw M. only once after that, in the hospital, his arms, ending in stumps below the elbows, wrapped in white bandages. He accused me of deliberately cutting off his arms to exact revenge. Maybe. But I know, upon reflection, I had no alternative.

The fire engines arrived just minutes after, not in time to help M. but his home was spared. The fire destroyed only the training room. I was taken to the hospital along with M. My hands were burned in the fire – just second-degree burns, some redness and blistering – although I had no knowledge of this until after the fire trucks arrived.

The two videos, the only evidence that M. killed Franny, were destroyed. He will never be prosecuted for her murder. But I believe in karma, and evil people will ultimately suffer, if not in this lifetime than in another. One cannot commit evil acts and walk away untouched. There is an ineffable order to the universe – I must believe this – and although M. will not go to jail, he has suffered a fate that, for him, is truly worse than death. His life with music – the only part of life he truly cherished – is destroyed; he will never play the piano again.

No charges were filed against me. The district attorney concluded the bondage was consensual, the fire accidental, and that I acted in good faith to prevent M.'s death. M. claimed he was drugged and handcuffed without his consent, but it came down to his word against mine. The charred remains of the room, the leg irons and shackles and hoist, indicated that he willingly participated in sadomasochism; also, he was unable to provide the district attorney with a reasonable motive to explain why I drugged him: he could not say it was revenge for killing my sister. I wait to see if his attorney files a civil suit against me.

No one is being prosecuted for Franny's murder, and it's been several weeks since the district attorney's office dropped their case against Ian. I related M.'s confession to Joe Harris – which, predictably, M. denied – but more important, Ian has secured an alibi. He was hiking with a friend in Desolation Wilderness on the day Franny died, and although his friend couldn't recall the exact date of their trip, he belatedly remembered they'd run into a forest ranger that afternoon. Wilderness permits are required every day of the year in Desolation Wilderness, and neither Ian nor his friend had obtained one. Luckily, the ranger remembered them; it was his first day on the job and he leniently gave them a verbal warning rather than issue the obligatory violation notice. In the tumult of the arrest, neither Ian nor his friend recalled the incident; had they not remembered it later, and had the ranger forgotten them, Ian would be in jail today. Even though he's no longer a viable suspect, his reputation is tarnished. I feel personally responsible for the terrible suffering I've caused him, and only wish I could ease his pain.

★   ★   ★

Today, I sit at the computer and begin writing the last section of Franny's story. I began it with the intention of seeking publication. My written account of her story, of which M. knew nothing, was to be my final retaliation, to expose him as Franny's murderer. But it has grown into something much greater, and much more personal, than that: a painful journal, a memoir, of my sister's life and death, a postmortem reconciliation.

I work for six hours, then take a break. Ian is on my mind. I have so many things to tell him. I've tried, numerous times, to contact him, but he has spurned all my efforts. He wants nothing to do with me, which, of course, is understandable. I leave messages on his answering machine, but he doesn't return my calls. I've written him letters, but he doesn't respond. I've even asked Maisie to intervene, but she said he refuses to discuss me.

Later this afternoon, I decide to drive to Sacramento. All day, the sun has been trying to sneak out from behind flat, gray clouds, and now it succeeds in struggling through, throwing down slender slants of light. I go out to the garage. I've paid a neighbor's teenage son to take care of Franny's old Cadillac. It's been washed, waxed, and tuned up, and although I've come out here to sit in the front seat often, I still haven't driven it. I put the key in the ignition and let it warm up, its deep rumbling mercifully drowning out the apprehensions screaming in my mind. The tailpipe puffs out frosty clouds that roil around the car.

I pull out of the garage and drive up Rosario, then turn left on Montgomery. I honk and wave at a neighbor – whose name and identity I haven't a clue – an elderly man bundled in a plaid mackinaw, who is out walking his fluffy-haired poodle. I sail up the street, feeling as if I'm in a barge going upriver. I'm not used to the size of the Cadillac, of its sheer, black, shining immensity. Whenever I went to the garage and sat in the car, I seemed to shrink a few inches. I felt like a small child who had to peer through the steering wheel and whose feet could barely touch the accelerator. This was all in my mind, of course – I have no trouble reaching the floor pedals whatsoever – but I still feel overpowered in the Cadillac.

I catch Interstate 80 and go east, carried along by the late-afternoon traffic. Is it my imagination or do other cars edge away from me? I seem to be taking up more space than I should – but, no, I'm well within the broken white lines dividing the freeway. I crack the window open and let the chilly air seep inside the car. It makes me more alert, puts me on edge, like a cup of hot, strong coffee.

I go over the bridge, around the state capitol, then pull up to Ian's condo, my tires crunching through brown, fallen leaves in the gutter. I turn off the car. It rattles for a long moment before the engine shuts off. I huddle behind the steering wheel, stalling for time. A breeze stirs the branches of the tree under which I'm parked, and a few brown leaves float lightly to the pavement. The tree is nearly bare, its naked branches reaching out in supplication. I get out of the Cadillac.

Ian isn't home, but I use my key – for only the second time – and let myself in. It's been weeks since I've seen him, the last time in September, before he was arrested. I hope it isn't too late.

I wait on the couch, wondering what I'll say. The walls are white, pristine, blank except for the Georgia O'Keeffe print. I close my eyes, and the cow's skull remains an imprint on the back of my eyelids. Where do I begin with Ian? I am not the person I was a year ago, that I must tell him first. M. knows so much more about me – my secrets, my insecurities – yet it is Ian with whom I should have placed my trust. I know it's time to put my life in order, to regain the freedom I so passively relinquished to M.

I open my eyes when I hear the key in the lock. The door swings open and Ian enters. His body – husky, blond, a little clumsy-looking, the opposite of M.'s sleek, almost elegant appearance – fills the doorway. He's wearing the gray pinstripe gangster's suit, the same suit he wore the last time I saw him, before he was arrested. The suit is wrinkled, the coat unbuttoned and hanging on him crookedly. He slams the door shut and takes two steps before he notices me. The surprise registers on his face, then the annoyance.

'I know I shouldn't be here,' I say quickly, rising to my feet. 'I had to see you and I drove over, even though I knew you'd probably be at work.'

He's frowning, his blue eyes wary. 'You should've called.'

'I was afraid you'd tell me not to come. I didn't think you'd want to see me.'

'I don't. Give me my key back.'

He looks tired, his face drawn, his shoulders slouched. He walks over to me, a hand extended for the key. Even his gait, which used to be springy and full of life, is sluggish.

'Give it to me,' he says.

I work the key off my aluminum key ring. I see the hurt in his face, the distrust. 'Let me explain,' I say. 'I'll give the key back, but let me explain. Please.'

'Why should I listen? You've caused me enough trouble. There's nothing you can say that will make me forgive you.' His voice is cynical, hard, the voice of a bitter man. He's lost so much all at once, his untarnished reputation, his girlfriend, his best friend, and his innocence – and I am the cause.

'I don't expect you to forgive me,' I say. 'I just want to tell you what happened. You loved me once. Give me a minute to explain, then I'll leave.'

Ian sighs, rubbing his hand across his face. Looking defeated and very tired, he walks across the room and takes off his coat and tie. He hangs them on the back of a chair, then looks over at me. He remains there, the entire room between us, a distance greater than the length of the room itself.

'I'm moving back to Sacramento,' I say. 'And I'm going to start working again.' I pause. I'm not sure how to continue, Ian has, undoubtedly, drawn his own conclusions. The newspapers were quite thorough in covering the fire, reporting how M. and I 'were engaging in activities involving bondage,' during the course of which a fire was accidentally started, and I 'saved his life' by cutting off his hands. This Ian knows. But how do I explain everything that led up to that day? How do I tell him everything we did together?

I start with something easier. I tell him of M.'s private confession to me, that he was the one who killed Franny. I also tell him how Franny's diary led me to suspect M., and how I worked myself into his life, hoping to expose him. Then I tell Ian we were lovers, which he must have guessed by now. He cringes, just slightly, when I say this, his nose wrinkling in distress, but he doesn't interrupt. I leave out the sexual details – those will come later.

'I made a lot of mistakes,' I say. 'My judgment was clouded.'

He listens from across the room, saying nothing, pulling absently on his lower lip.

'But my biggest mistake,' I continue, 'was not trusting you,' and then I tell Ian of all the years I spent trusting no one. I fill in the blanks of my history. I tell him I have changed, then walk over and wrap my arms around his waist. His body stiffens at my touch, and I can feel him pulling away. I hold him tighter. I rest my head on his shoulder. 'Give me another chance,' I say, feeling that I should be able to stand alone. But I can't. Not now. I need Ian's strength and honesty.

He sighs, and I say it again: 'Please. Give me another chance,' and this time he raises one arm and puts it lightly on the small of my back, a very fragile embrace, and I think that perhaps, after all we've been through, it isn't necessary to stand alone.

Before I End . . .

Sometimes, when I read fiction or go to the movies, I get the idea that life is ordered and clear-cut, that virtue is rewarded and all villainy repelled. Not so in real life. The innocent are punished, the guilty go free. Even though the police have dropped all charges against Ian, some colleagues and friends still eye him suspiciously, wondering if he is, indeed, a killer. And M., although one could argue his loss of hands is punishment enough, still lives in Davis with impunity, his professional reputation intact. Fiction may be tidy, but life, I am learning, is a messy business.

Almost a year has elapsed since I began my pursuit of M. My journey – if one can call it that – is over, and I have resumed my life. Packing boxes, dozens of them, clutter the duplex on Torrey Street; each day I fill several boxes, seal them with tape, and stack them against the wall, ready for the movers at the end of the month. I've found an apartment in Sacramento, and next week I start working full-time again for the *Bee*. It will be difficult – everyone there knows of my involvement with M. – but I've spoken with the editor and he agreed to let me come back.

In my driveway, still, sits Franny's old fin-tailed Cadillac: bright, black, and big. A monstrosity, really. It's a car you have to grow into; it's a car that grows onto you. A person could feel safe in it, secure. With its solid steel and heavy weight, it isn't likely to crumble in an accident. It isn't like those smaller newer cars – toy cars, really – that seem made of tin, falling in on themselves at the slightest collision. When I settle behind the wheel, I feel suddenly, immensely, comfortable in it. And now, whenever I ease the Cadillac on the street, I can admire its grace, understanding, at last, why Franny loved this car: it just feels good. I don't drive it all the time – there are occasions when I prefer my Honda – and perhaps one day I will sell the Cadillac. For now, though, I like having it around.

Ian and I are getting along. I told him the details of my affair with M., as I knew that I must. I considered hiding the truth from him, but it would've been wrong. I don't know if our relationship will survive the truth, but without it, it is doomed to fail. Only with honesty can we survive – Ian taught me that. The corrosive power of lies weakens the underpinnings of a relationship, one lie necessitating another and another, each abrading the foundation of trust until little of true value is left. Ian understands this. He told me everything about him and M., as I knew he would. Deception is not in his nature, which only goes to show that he is a better person than I. And he did not cloud the truth, he did not say M. seduced him, but rather that it was a mutual decision – although one he came to regret the following day. He thought he was risking my love by telling me the truth, and still he told it – while I stood by, cowardly, with my own confession yet to come, keeping my dirty little secret to myself. My betrayal was far greater than his.

I don't know where I'll go from here. I see the folly of my actions with M., but I taste the temptation still. He opened carnal doors from which, once I walked through, there was no turning back. Like Pygmalion with his ivory statue of Aphrodite, M. created me; and like Eliza with Henry Higgins, I can no longer return whence I came. At night, I close my eyes and dream of the man who forced me to obey, of the leather whip that kept me in line, of the bonds that constrained my flesh and the commands that harnessed my soul, of the primordial need – so deep and dark and pagan – that united pleasure with pain. In my dreams I cringe under his demands, but I submit and I want him still. My needs and desires are inexplicable, even to me. M. once told me that I needed to reconcile my intellectual inclinations with my instinctual ones. This I must learn to do, but I'm not sure if Ian will ever understand. He's trying, but it's difficult for him. He cannot comprehend my split desires, to command at work yet obey in bed. Perhaps, one day, he will leave me. It might be for the best. M. awakened in me passions I didn't know existed, and I may not belong with a man such as Ian. He may not belong with a woman such as me.

I reread the first few pages of this story – written, it seems, half a lifetime ago. My tone has softened, I know. Now that I've walked the fine line between eroticism and sadomasochism, I've discovered that, for me, the demarcation blurs: they are the same. But I know the dangers of standing too close to the edge, of giving yourself to a man lacking a moral code, and only the sight of Franny in the video pulled me back. Her humiliation forced me to consider the requisite of restraint, forced me to realize that M. is not the person with whom to surrender control. He is without morals, and that makes him dangerous.

A year ago, I would've said there was a clear line separating the good from the evil. I would've said that evilness belonged in the netherworld, and that evil men existed beyond the peripheries of decency. Now I'm not so sure. I believe there is a dark side that belongs to us all, lying beneath the surface of our humanity, twisted and extreme and savage in some of us, less severe in others, but always present and always at struggle with the civilized soul. I saw it in myself on the day of the fire. I felt the influence of M.

Nietzsche wrote: 'Whoever fights monsters should see to it that in the process he does not become a monster. And when you look long into the abyss, the abyss also looks into you.' Only now, after M. is out of my life and with the perspective of distance, do I see that I succumbed to M.'s darker side. How rash I was when I began my pursuit of him! I thought I could get close to him and not be harmed. My sense of probity and justice would exempt me from his influence, I foolishly thought, but I did not come away from him unscathed. I have the scars, physical and emotional, to prove it.

My journey with M. began as a quest for truth, and although the costs may have been too great, I found the answers for which I searched. Franny's journey was much worse. Unintentionally, she walked into the heart of an evil man from which there was no return. I will regret, always, that I hadn't been there for her, to pull her back when she herself stood, alone and frightened, on the edge of the abyss.

Nora C. Tibbs
Davis, California

Do you wish this wasn't the end?

Join us at www.hodder.co.uk, or follow us on
Twitter @hodderbooks to be a part of our community
of people who love the very best in books and reading.

Whether you want to discover more about a book
or an author, watch trailers and interviews, have the
chance to win early limited editions, or simply browse
our expert readers' selection of the very best books,
we think you'll find what you're looking for.

And if you don't,
that's the place to tell us what's missing.

We love what we do, and we'd love you to be part of it.

www.hodder.co.uk

 @hodderbooks

 HodderBooks

HodderBooks